VENI, VIDI, VERO

VERY VERO * BOOK ONE

GRETCHEN ROSE

VENI, VIDI, VERO
Copyright © 2021 by Gretchen Rose

ISBN: 978-1-953735-21-8

Melange Books, LLC
White Bear Lake, MN 55110
www.melange-books.com

Published in the United States of America.

Cover Design by Caroline Andrus

PRAISE FOR GRETCHEN ROSE

Gretchen Rose blends romance with mystery in a fast-paced tale of characters on the brink of change and surrounded by danger. Her main character, Tara ,must find the courage to meet the challenges of a new life and new love. Ms. Rose's well-rounded portraits of people living in "paradise" will hook you and propel you through to the exciting end."

—SUSAN SQUIRES, *NYT BEST-SELLING AUTHOR OF "THE COMPANION" SERIES, THE "DAVINCI TIME TRAVEL" SERIES, AND THE "MAGIC" SERIES*

"There is an artful fluidity in the voice crafting this romantic drama in a familiar human terrain of foibles, privilege, and downfall... with myriad crossings over the solemn [and tidal] lagoon of being in a peculiar Paradise."

—SEAN SEXTON, INDIAN RIVER COUNTY POET LAUREATE, AUTHOR OF "*MAY DARKNESS RESTORE, AND "BLOOD WRITING, POEMS"*

"... a fun read... Gretchen Rose creates characters that come alive while weaving a compelling story about determination, transformation, and triumph."

—MARTHA LEMASTERS, AUTHOR OF *THE STEP, ONE WOMAN'S JOURNEY TO FINDING HER OWN HAPPINESS AND SUCCESS DURING THE APOLLO SPACE PROGRAM*

This book is dedicated to the love of my life, Mel Laracey. Thank you for always encouraging me to keep writing, and for supplying me with a plethora of zany plot-twists when my imagination flags. And to all my wonderful Vero Beach family, friends, and neighbors. I love you. We are blessed.

"If music be the food of love, play on."

—SHAKESPEARE—TWELFTH NIGHT, ACT 1, SCENE 1

CHAPTER ONE

AS LUCK WOULD HAVE IT

"What numbers?" The slender, young man tamped down his impatience and turned toward the wraith at the breakfast table. She was gaunt with deep bags under her eyes, and her wiry grey hair was a tangle.

"Eric! Haven't you been listening?" Caroline laced her coffee with Jim Beam. "I told you. I seen the numbers, clear as can be. One after the other—puffed up and cloud-like. Really weird. Then the dog barked and woke me, and I figured I'd best write them down." She thrust a scrap of paper toward him. "It's a sign, I tell you. I want you to play the lotto for me using these numbers."

Eric sighed. "Okay, Mom." He took the note from his mother's gnarled hand and glanced at it briefly before stuffing it in his pocket.

Eric Brady was an obedient son. Two days later, he purchased a lottery ticket and played the numbers his mother had requested. While he was at it, he splurged and bought a couple for himself, even threw in a few scratch-offs, but they were duds. After that, he put the entire incident out of his mind.

Until now.

His eyes latched onto a newspaper someone had left on the coffee table in the break room. He flopped into a chair and reached for it. Might as well check out the winning numbers, he thought. When he turned to the inside page and scanned the results, a jolt of adrenaline coursed through his veins.

Suddenly light-headed, Eric dug the ticket stubs out of his wallet and sorted through them. "My God," he breathed. The numbers his mother had insisted he play were the winning combination to a whopping twelve point two-million-dollar jackpot! Eric bolted to his feet, holding the ticket over his head. "Who-hoo!" he cried.

Then, through the wall of glass, he spied Rick Cochran rounding the corner, and Eric's joy quickly morphed to panic. His boss was a jerk. There was something not right about the ex-G.I.

Eric was stuffing the chits into his wallet when Cochran charged in. "What's up, Brady?" the stocky service manager growled.

"Not a thing, Maj." Eric scrambled for a plausible excuse for his outburst. Glancing down at the newspaper, the answer came to him. "The Braves shut out the Dodgers," he said, plastering a soppy grin on his face.

"Is that so? Didn't take you for a big sports fan."

"Oh, yes, sir. Big."

"Well, keep it down, son." Rick favored Eric with what passed as a smile, but it never reached his eyes. "Don't be too long here." Turning on his heel, he strode out the door leaving Eric weak-kneed and shaken.

～

Tara sat at her breakfast table listening to the rain pounding overhead. It rushed in waterfalls from gutters on the eaves, while thunder rumbled faintly in the distance. As she gazed out over her neatly landscaped, sodden yard, the worry, and self-doubt that persistently plagued her retreated.

She was safe.

Tara picked up her phone and scrolled through the headlines on *mobile.nytimes.com*. Try as she might, she couldn't concentrate on the news. Instead, she keyed *astrology.com* into her browser where she found *Today's Birthday* horoscope.

> *The security you thought you had*
> *may turn out to be an illusion.*

Tara's brows knit.

During the year ahead,
you may find it necessary to rely on others and to stop taking your family
members for granted.

"That's a heck of a prediction," she muttered, as she continued on to Sagittarius in hopes of better news. After all, her birthday fell on the cusp, between Scorpio and Sagittarius.

What lies behind is a small matter compared to what lies ahead, but
what's most important is what lies within. In the year to come, pay
attention to your inner needs.

"That's more like it."

Birthday horoscopes were forgotten when her Yorkshire terrier commenced barking madly. Tara swiveled to see what the commotion was about, only to find Josh bounding into the kitchen with Chanel at his heels.

"Hey, little guy." Josh bent to pat the Yorkie's silken head.

"Good morning, honey." Tara gazed at her son, marveling how, seemingly overnight, he'd grown from a child into a man. "Sleep well?"

"Uh-huh." Josh surveyed the contents of the refrigerator. "I hope this weather clears. We're scrimmaging this afternoon."

"Shall I scramble up some eggs?"

"Nah." Josh grabbed a Coke and crossed to the pantry. "I've got to run." The sandy-haired teen dug out two granola bars and swung around to face his mother. "Hey, I almost forgot. Happy birthday, Mom."

"Thanks, sweetie."

Josh gathered up his bag and crossed to the side door.

"Wait." Tara pivoted in her chair, and Josh turned back. "My car's being serviced. Could you pick me up at church at five?"

"Sure, but how're you getting there?"

"Marguerite is taking me."

"Gotcha." Josh hefted his sports duffel. "I must say, old lady…" He arched a brow and struck a rakish pose. "You don't look a day—"

"I know," Tara interrupted, rolling her eyes. "Over forty. Very funny."

She waved him off and headed upstairs, but the jangle of a mobile phone stopped her in her tracks. The distinctive chime told her it was Jack's, and Tara imagined how annoyed he'd be to have left this lifeline behind. The jazz riff ended, only to immediately resume. She dashed back down the stairs and found the phone on the kitchen counter.

"Hello, hello," she said, but she was too late. The call had ended. Exasperated, Tara tossed the cell back onto the countertop.

She'd nearly reached the landing, when another ringtone sounded, signaling an incoming text. "Darn it!" Tara raced back down the stairs and picked up the cell. The message displayed on the screen was from a D. Shaw.

Tonight at 6?

A stab of fear pricked Tara's heart. Jack had been short-tempered and distant these last few months. She'd chalked it up to stress. Could there be another reason? She did a quick search of Jack's messages but found no saved texts from D. Shaw, and her hands stopped shaking. That didn't keep her from jotting down the number on a post-it.

"Just might go on a fishing expedition," Tara muttered. "See if there's a ladyfish on the end of the line."

Within the walls of the old, stone-faced cathedral, shadows collected in corners grimy with the dust of ages. On either side of the sacristy, the darkness was dispelled by tiers of votive candles— golden halos floating above myriad tiny flames. In the side chapels, where the images of saints were displayed, more candles flickered. The exotic smell of burnt incense perfumed the space and the stern faces of angels and martyrs, having been preserved in stained glass, glowed like jewels as they looked down upon the faithful.

Over it all the sweet voices of children wafted. The last chord of the hymn hung on the air before gradually dissolving into memory.

"That was very good." Marguerite nodded toward the students

assembled on the platform before her. Having been deprived of an outdoor recess, her choristers were fidgety and longing for dismissal.

"Daniel!" Marguerite waved her baton in the air. "Keep your hands to yourself and your eyes on the director, young man."

Giggles and snatches of whispered conversation erupted. Marguerite rapped her baton on the music stand, and, with the thumb and index finger of her left hand, drew an imaginary line across pursed lips.

"Children, please. We're nearly finished." Marguerite turned to Tara. "Play the alto line for us once again. Won't you, Ms. Tara? Altos sing out," she instructed. "Everyone else on melody. And a one, and a..."

Tara's fingers moved effortlessly over the keyboard, plunking out the alto line. Furtively, Marguerite motioned to a pair of eighth-grade girls, and the two bolted from their seats and scurried through the door leading to the robing room.

Redirecting her attention to her remaining charges, the elderly choir director touched a finger to her lips, silently exhorting them to keep quiet. "That will do for today," she said, raising her eyebrows in unspoken communication.

Hymnals slammed shut, dust motes danced in the air, and a cacophony of voices erupted. The children stampeded toward the door through which the older girls had vanished. Marguerite and Tara gathered up their personal belongings and followed on the heels of their students.

When Tara crossed the threshold, the children shouted, "Surprise, surprise!"

In the small room beyond, a card table had been set with paper plates and napkins, plastic cups and forks. The featured attraction, however, was a large, white sheet cake embellished with pink icing roses.

Marguerite warbled, "Happy birthday to you," in her tremulous soprano, flapping her arms and encouraging the choristers to join in.

"What a surprise," Tara fibbed. "I never suspected a thing."

"Who has the card?" Marguerite asked.

Daniel waved a large envelope in the air before presenting it.

After making a show of opening the card, Tara read aloud. "For all the joy you share, each and every one of us knows just how much you care." She beamed at the children. "And look. You've all signed it."

"Not me," a masculine voice called from the back of the room. "I didn't sign it, Ms. Tara."

"Josh!" Tara pivoted to face her son. His wavy head of hair glistened with rain, and his sweats were grass- and mud-stained. "Look at you. You're soaked."

Several other voices called out greetings. "Hey, Josh," the children cried.

Suddenly, the air seemed charged with sexual currents. The pubescent girls tittered, casting sidelong glances at the good-looking teen who'd had the audacity to invade their sanctum.

Josh leaned indolently against the door frame, seemingly unaware of the effect he was having on the young ladies. "Aw, don't cry, Mom," he teased. "Cut to the chase and slice the darn cake."

"Joshua, mind your manners," Marguerite scolded. "Have you forgotten you're in church? I'd expect you'd want to set an example."

"Why would I want to reform at this late date?" Josh's eyes twinkled, as he helped himself to a large slice of cake. "You know I was always the troublemaker, Mrs. Brock."

Eric had all he could do to keep from walking off the job and never looking back. Then he'd think of *The Curse of the Lotto*, remembering all the previous winners who'd gone berserk, spent wildly, only to end up flat broke within years of striking it rich. He wasn't about to make that mistake. You never know. He just might need a reference someday. He'd stuck it out, was at the wheel of a white LS Sedan when an irresistible urge to double-check the winning numbers came over him. He scanned the gargantuan lot, but it appeared empty. Eric pulled out his worn, leather wallet and withdrew the lottery tickets.

"You beauty," he breathed, bringing the winner to his lips. A rapping on the passenger window and Eric's head snapped up. It was Cochran.

Where had he come from?

"What the hell are you doing, son?" The service manager rotated a fist, indicating that Eric should roll the window down.

Eric's eyes fastened on Rick's steely blues. He crammed the lotto tickets into his pants' pocket with one hand and powered the window down with the other, which was why he never saw one flimsy receipt separate from the rest and fall between the seat and the center console. "I was just going to drive this car into the bay before punching out."

"You're acting a little strange today. Everything all right?"

Eric's emotions seesawed.

What a ridiculous question!

Everything was totally awesome and only going to get a whole lot better, but all he said was, "Fine, sir. Absolutely."

"Then you wouldn't mind working overtime tonight? We're behind, and I want to get a couple more warranty jobs out the door."

Eric groaned inwardly. He'd been counting the minutes, didn't think he could contain himself a second longer, but he said, "Sure thing. I'll just have to pop home for a minute to check on my mom." He never noticed when another draft of air blew in, wedging the winning chit even farther down and out of sight.

~

"Thanks for the lift," Tara said, as Josh pulled into the garage.

"You bet." Josh put the Jeep in park, letting the engine idle. "I'm going to head back out. Supposed to meet up with some of the guys for a burger. You don't mind, do you?"

"Not at all. I don't feel like cooking."

Chanel waited for her in the mudroom, and he barked a greeting. "Hey, little guy." Tara massaged the little sentinel's furry head. "Let's get you some dinner."

Once the dog had been fed, Tara did a quick check of her messages and voicemails. The first recording was from an eight hundred number, and she deleted it. The second was from Patty Meyer, and Tara chuckled at the sound of her friend's flutie soprano belting out an off-key rendition of *Happy Birthday*.

The third and final message was from Jack: "Hi, babe. I think I left my cell at home. At least I hope so." Tara smiled, but at his next words, her smile vanished. "I'm afraid I'm going to be late again. We're entertaining clients from Korea. Sorry, birthday girl. I'll make it up to you tomorrow. I made reservations at the City Grill, and listen, don't wait up. I'll catch a few winks on the sofa in my office and shower at the gym in the morning. Later, babe."

Tara narrowed her eyes while digesting this news. It wasn't unusual for Jack to entertain clients, but that particular task had fallen to him more often of late. Was he being honest with her or was there another explanation for his absences? Tara's mind veered away from that horror. She sighed and squared her shoulders, resolving not to obsess over this unexpected development. She told herself there was probably nothing to it. It was her birthday, and she'd darn well have her own little celebration, pop up a bag microwave popcorn, uncork a bottle of wine, and treat herself to a generous serving of birthday cake.

It occurred to her that Pat was probably all alone, knocking around in that palatial manse of hers. On impulse, Tara barked into her cell, "Hey, Siri! Call Pat."

In the next instant, her friend's distinctive voice erupted from the speaker. "Happy birthday, girl."

"Hi, Patty."

"Why aren't you out celebrating?"

"It's too wet, and Jack has clients in town. We have reservations tomorrow at City Grill."

"Worth waiting for."

"Yeah, but I was wondering. Is Cliff home?"

"Just what is it you want with my husband?"

Tara snorted. "I don't want him. I've got enough trouble with my own. I just want to know if he's there, dummy."

"Call me up to give me grief, is it? Sticks and stones, girlfriend."

"Is he?"

"No, Sherlock, he's not."

"Good. Then you can come to my birthday. Girls night in.

"Twist my arm," Pat said. "What's to eat?"

"How about I dig out some frozen chicken filets?"

"Whoop-de-do. You're really going all out, huh?"

"Let me sweeten the pot. I've got half a birthday cake from Piggly Wiggly, a solid block of saturated fat and refined sugar."

"You have my attention. Got any booze?"

"Affirmative. All the fixings for my world-famous Cosmos."

"I'll be there in about an hour. Why don't I pick us up some sushi? My treat."

"Now you're talking."

~

They sat at opposite ends of the sofa watching a romantic movie about past lives. As the credits rolled, Pat unfolded herself from the sofa. "Oh, dear." She yawned widely. "It's after eleven. I've got to run."

"Why don't you stay the night?" Tara gathered up their glasses and deposited them in the kitchen sink. "The guest room is all made up."

"Thanks, but I can't. I volunteered for the Junior League Tour of Homes, and I'm to be at my assigned house bright and early."

"Then join me for a walk." Tara grabbed a raincoat from the hall closet. "I need to take Chanel out, and you could do with a bit of metabolizing."

"Translation," Pat snickered. "You want to sober me up."

"I don't like the idea of you driving home this late, especially in this weather."

It had nearly stopped raining, but droplets continued to spill from the oaks lining the street, and overhead, distant stars sparkled without warmth in empty patches of the clearing sky. The rain had brought cooler weather with it, and Tara could feel the approach of winter.

"Thanks for coming tonight. You made my birthday."

"My pleasure." Pat matched Tara's footsteps.

"What did you think about that movie?" Tara drew her coat more snugly about her slender frame.

"It's an interesting concept." Pat gazed up at a half-moon peeking out from scudding clouds.

"Do you buy it?"

"What?" Pat carefully picked her way around a large puddle. "That everyone has a soul mate?"

"Yeah." A car approached, its headlights blinding, and Tara and Pat jumped to the curb to avoid being splashed.

"I don't know. Do you?" The car zoomed by, and they hopped back down to the pavement.

"I'd like to."

"Brr. A cold front's coming through." Pat blew on her hands to warm them. "If that's the case, I'm willing to bet I screwed up bigtime this go around."

"I know what you mean." Tara flicked a bead of water from her forehead. "I love Jack. I really do, but I don't think we're connected in that way. Jack is private by nature."

Pat stopped walking and faced Tara. "Are you sure of that?"

"What?" Tara looked askance at Pat.

"That he's not just holding out on you?"

Perhaps it was the liquor that loosened Tara's tongue, for she found herself confessing her fears. "It's probably nothing," she said, "but I think Jack might be having an affair." As soon as the words were out, she regretted them.

"Not Jack."

"Why not Jack?" Tara's voice rose, shrilly, and Chanel stopped sniffing and turned to eye his mistress. "Look at me. I'm forty, for heaven's sake. Do you know what those girls in the office look like? How they pursue the execs?"

"You get no sympathy from me in that department. You're freakin' gorgeous, and you know it. Take me, on the other hand." Pat placed both palms on her generous hips. "I've gained thirty pounds in ten years. I can't remember the last time I had my hair styled, but I think big hair was fashionable then. No wonder Cliff looks for romance elsewhere."

"So, you gained a few pounds." Tara resumed walking, and Pat followed her lead. "You're fabulous, and Cliff is a fool."

"No argument from me on that last bit."

"I wish I knew for sure."

"Be careful what you wish for."

Tara tugged lightly on the leash. "Come on, Chanel," she said. "Let's go home."

The two women reversed their course and walked abreast, both lost in thought.

Pat sighed. "You know what they say. If you suspect something, it's probably true. But, hey, it isn't the end of the world. It doesn't mean he doesn't love you. Cliff would do anything for me. It just so happens…he strays.

Tara frowned. "I couldn't put up with that. I don't see how you can."

"It's enormously freeing. I have a kind of leverage over Cliff. Maybe, if I were motivated to take spinning classes…" she backhanded the soft skin beneath her jaw. Have a little work done—"

"Pat," Tara interrupted, "you don't really believe that."

"I don't know what I believe."

"If Jack really is fooling around, I won't stand for it. He'll end it, or I'll leave him."

Pat turned to Tara. "I know you don't mean that, but honestly, it might not be such a bad thing."

"You never cared for Jack."

"That's not true. I just don't think he's good for you."

"Look at the life I've got, Patty. I don't have to work. I have a big house with a pool, a three-car garage, and my own Lexus to park in it. He's obviously good for me."

"Things." Pat tossed a hand in the air.

"Things are important. Try being without them sometime."

"Oh, honey. It's that damned insecurity thing, right?" Pat stopped and took Tara's free hand. "Isn't it time you let it go?"

Tara pulled away, stung. "You know me too well."

Pat threw an arm around Tara's shoulder. "Hey," she said. "I was there, remember? I know how hard it was for you when your mother died. Your dad did the best he could."

"Dragging us kids around from neighborhood to neighborhood, school to school." Tara compressed her lips into a thin line, struggling to rein in her emotions.

"I'm sorry. She was a remarkable woman. I loved her, too." Pat pinched her nose and wiped a droplet from her cheek.

"She was always pushing me."

"She dreamed you'd grow up to be a great pianist, set the world on fire." Pat looked away. "When I think of what you've given up for Jack…it really burns me."

"You're one to talk."

Pat turned back. "I'm living the life I want, Tara. Sure, there are some big trade-offs, but life's about compromises. You, on the other hand…" Her voice trailed off.

"What about me?"

"You sacrificed your own ambitions to become the perfect little wife Jack wanted. You traded your dreams for a safety net."

"That's not true!"

"Oh, no? Played any concert halls lately?"

"I accompany the children's choir," Tara said, hotly.

"That's about on par with a brain surgeon changing bedpans. It's a waste. No pun intended."

~

Eric had worked three more hours of drudgery, and it was finally time to call it quits. Shrugging into his leather bomber jacket, he sauntered out into the cool, wet night. He didn't mind the rain. He thought the world never looked so beautiful, could hardly wait to celebrate with his mother. They were rich!

Eric had only covered about twenty yards, was rounding the corner to the back lot where his car was parked, when his luck ran out entirely. The front and sides of the service garage were brightly lit, but back there, only two mercury vapor lamps held the darkness at bay. The rain further obscured his view, so that he could hardly make out the heap that was his 2012 sedan. Still, the sight of it made him happy. In his mind's eye, Eric pictured its replacement, a Maserati GranTurismo, black as pitch and fast as—

There was a deafening noise before the lights went out.

~

Tara listened with half an ear to the news anchor while rummaging through the vanity drawer for her hairbrush. Instead, her fingers found the crumbled post-it. She studied the note, tempted to dial the phone number, but she didn't want her own number displayed on D. Shaw's cellphone. She'd have to call from a payphone, and she didn't know where to find one of those dinosaurs. Then the words *Atlanta Lexus* and *homicide* pierced her fog, and Tara hiked out into the bedroom. Her eyes fastened on the television screen where the newscaster was recounting sketchy details surrounding the murder of a young man at the very dealership where she'd left her car for servicing.

"The victim's name is being withheld until next of kin can be located," the news anchor said. "More on this as the investigation continues."

Tara couldn't wrap her head around this news. A murder at Atlanta Lexus. She powered down the TV remote and climbed into bed. The Yorkie snuffled a doggie snore, and Tara gently repositioned him so that he lay curled next to her thigh. "What do you think, Chanel?" Tara turned off the bedside lamp. "It's been one heck of a birthday, huh?

CHAPTER TWO

FULL DISCLOSURE

She peered out the passenger window as Josh exited the expressway. "Turn right at the light."

"Yeah, I know." Josh flicked on his blinker. "Zoe's house isn't far from here."

"That's right. What do you hear from her?"

"Not much. She's so busy rushing sororities, mixers, parties. We haven't spoken in weeks."

"Oh." Tara frowned. "Well, you know what they say: Absence makes the heart grow fonder."

"Uh-huh." Josh shot her a meaningful look. "They also say out of sight out of mind."

Tara chuckled, but her smile faded when Josh turned into the enormous dealership parking lot where two police cars were conspicuously parked outside the showroom. Josh slid in behind them, cut the engine, and exchanged grim looks with his mother.

Tara levered the door open. "Here goes."

"Do you want me to come in with you?"

"No thanks, honey. I'll be fine." She climbed out of the Jeep and waved him away. "See you tonight."

The automatic glass doors whooshed open, and Tara crossed the threshold only to find herself thrust into a crime scene. Her eyes fell on the yellow tape festooning the side entry, then fastened on the glass walls of the service manager's office where a pair of uniformed deputies were interviewing a stocky gentleman. Feeling the voyeur, Tara quickly turned toward the unusually subdued receptionist. The young woman swiped her credit card, her face gloomy.

"Not your usual day at the office, I guess," Tara said, as the receptionist retrieved her keys.

"It's awful," the woman agreed. "A tragedy." She bit her lip. "He was a fine young man."

"I'm so sorry. I hope they find the person who did it."

"What's this world coming to?"

Tara merely shook her head before hiking to the entrance. In the lot, she retrieved her car and pulled out onto the highway. Up ahead, a Walgreen's pharmacy dominated the intersection, and Tara decided to make a quick stop. As she made her way to the entry, the sight of a payphone tucked into the outside wall of the store brought her up short. She rummaged through her pocketbook for the post-it bearing D. Shaw's number.

"It must be fate," she mumbled. Surely this was the last remaining payphone in greater Atlanta.

While slotting coins into the machine, Tara wondered what she would do if a woman picked up. When, on the fourth ring, no one had answered, a feeling of relief washed over her, but just as she was about to replace the receiver, a female said, "Hello?"

Tara's stomach lurched. It was a charming voice, low-pitched and cultured sounding, with a slight Southern drawl.

"Hello. Who is this?"

Tara held her breath. It seemed an eternity before the line went dead. In that time, the Earth seemed to tilt on its axis. Suddenly, all the little inconsistencies—Jack's distancing, her niggling doubts—could no longer be ignored.

Jack was having an affair with this woman.

Tara was struck by a more horrifying thought. What if he were in love with her?

Tara's hands trembled as she pulled out of the parking lot and into the bustling afternoon traffic. Tires squealed and an angry horn blared. She swerved, narrowly avoiding an oncoming car that appeared, seemingly out of nowhere. Fortunately, the adjacent lane was clear, and Tara recovered without further mishap. At least that's what she thought until the wail of a siren told her otherwise. She glanced in the rearview mirror and, with a sinking heart, saw the police car on her tail. She pulled over and immediately began rifling through the glove box for the proper documents.

"Lady, y'all always drive like that?" The cop leaned in and speared her with a hard look. "Driver's license and registration."

Tara handed over the papers.

"Stay put," the policeman ordered, before striding back to his car.

Time dragged. The light atop the cruiser was still flashing, and traffic slowed to a crawl as rubberneckers ogled her rudely. What was taking so long? Did the kid think she was a criminal? Get a grip, she told herself, while struggling to regain her composure.

At last, the young man returned. "Lady, I can see y'all are upset."

"My husband's having an affair," Tara blurted.

God almighty!

What had possessed her to say such a thing?

The cop was temporarily taken aback. When no protocol seemed to come to mind as how to deal with hormonal shipwrecks, he simply ignored the remark. "I could ticket you for reckless driving." He thrust out his lower lip and affected a stern demeanor. "You don't want that. Do you?"

Tara felt an insane urge to laugh. Although he feigned the tough guy, this baby-faced rookie was little more than a child. How would he handle a real desperado? And what had possessed her to tell him her husband was unfaithful? This was turning into a situation bordering on the ridiculous, and she was acting the raving lunatic. It was a wonder the kid didn't haul her away—throw her in a tank somewhere with the rest of the loonies.

The policeman continued to eye her suspiciously. "Now do you?"

Tara shook her head. *No!* She didn't want that.

"Alrighty, then." He handed her a citation. "This is a warning. Buckle up, you hea'?"

~

When she arrived home, Jack was there, and he seemed every bit his old self. Tara's frazzled nerves knit up in an instant when he wished her a happy birthday, calling her babe. Several hours later, she was thoroughly enjoying her birthday celebration.

She climbed the enormous flight leading to the restaurant, each step hewn from a massive block of marble, marveling at the ostentatious decadence of the building and its opulent interior. Having formerly housed a branch of the Federal Reserve, it had been —in the truest sense—a temple dedicated to the worship of Mammon. This was no dreary, run-of-the-mill government building. Rather, it had been designed on a grand scale, ornamented and embellished with an unrestrained hand. The excesses of the nineties had, however, given way to prudence.

Under pressure, the Feds had vacated the premises, heeding the voices of the masses who demanded accountability for the appropriation of billions of tax dollars. Their loss provided the perfect opportunity for an ambitious restaurateur who replaced desks and vaults with tables and banquettes. Tara loved every inch of it, from the soaring ceilings, the trompe l'oeil, and murals, to the crystal chandeliers and brass accents that, from every vantage point, gleamed like gold.

The imperious host showed them to their table. Impassively, he held Tara's chair, as she took her seat. Then, with a dramatic flourish, he produced menus. His face was as stiff as the starched napkin he attempted to place on her lap. Tara thwarted him, snatching the serviette from him, while, at the same time, catching Jack's eye. This was their longstanding joke, not allowing the host to place the napkin on her lap. Tara smiled tightly and arched a brow. Jack's eyes held hers for a moment before sliding away.

"He certainly takes himself seriously," Tara said, eyeing the host's retreating figure.

"It's all show. He probably has a tattoo as big as a house under that shirt and a moped Harley-wannabe parked out back."

Their waiter arrived and rattled off the evening's specials. Tara ordered a glass of white wine, Jack, a Dewar's on ice.

"What will you have to eat?" Tara asked, when the waiter had vanished.

"Steak Au Poivre, fingerling potatoes, creamed spinach."

"Some things never change." Tara grinned at Jack. She'd come to her senses. Of course, he wasn't having an affair.

"Some do," Jack said, cryptically.

Tara's smile wobbled. "What do you mean by that?"

"Nothing." Jack shook his head as if to clear it. "I can't get over the fact that your car was being serviced at the very dealership where that young man was murdered."

"I know." Tara's face clouded. "It's incomprehensible."

"Ah, let's not dwell on it. This is your special night." Jack withdrew a small, gift-wrapped package from his coat pocket and placed it before her. "Happy birthday,"

Tara tore into the tiny package, her eyes lighting up at the sight of the oversized Mojabi pearl earrings set in gold filigree.

"Oh, Jack," she breathed, "they're beautiful. Thank you."

"Pretty women should have pretty things."

Tara slipped in between the sheets and snuggled up against Jack's rock-hard body. He'd kept himself in shape, playing racquetball and working out at the gym. For the thousandth time, she thought what a lucky girl she was and turned toward her husband, anticipating his welcoming embrace. His response left her cold. He tousled her hair, gave her a quick peck, and then tossed on to his side.

"Sorry, babe. I'm beat."

"Come on, Jack," Tara coaxed. "You can sleep late in the morning."

"I'm just not up for anything, and I mean that literally." Jack found her hand and gave it a gentle squeeze, dismissing her.

Tara inched over and curled her body against his. "Good night," she said. "Thanks for the lovely birthday."

If Jack heard, he didn't let on.

The television was muted, and the dog was asleep on the rug at Caroline's feet. A few incongruously perky, potted plants were scattered about the drab little flat, as were a number of condolence cards—all bearing testimony to her recent loss. It had been six days since her son's murder, and, as was usual at that late hour, Caroline was nodding off on the sofa.

The old, yellow Lab raised his snout, ears flattened. He scrambled to his arthritic paws, fur bristling, and growled.

Caroline stirred. "Stop, Jake," she mumbled.

The dog paced restively, his nails clicking on the hardwood floor. Then, he bolted to the entry and scratched at the door.

"Wha…the matter?" Groggily, Caroline tried to focus.

Before she had time to come to her senses, the door imploded. The Lab lunged at the intruder, only to be delivered a swift kick that propelled him across the room. He yelped and retreated to a far corner.

"…the hell?" Caroline swung her legs over the seat cushion, but she froze when a black form swooped in and loomed over her. "Who are you? What do you want?" Caroline's voice quavered as she collapsed back down on the sofa. She shrank before the menacing giant whose features were concealed by the ski mask covering his face. When she saw that his hands were clad in surgical gloves, her terror mounted.

"Where is it?"

"Please, don't hurt me," she pleaded.

"Tell me where the lottery ticket is, and I won't."

"Ticket? I don't know what you're talk—" A meaty fist smashed into Caroline's jaw, whipping her head sideways.

"Where is it? Tell me, or you'll be joining your precious son."

It took a moment for her to recover from the blow, the man's words to register. When they did, Caroline experienced a moment of lucidity. "You!" she spat. "You killed my boy!"

"Where is it?" the man roared. He fell upon the frail woman, throttling her corded neck with powerful hands.

Caroline opened her mouth, desperate to inhale. She was suffocating, and her heart pounded loudly in her ears. In the next instant, she was released with a brutal shove. The wizened woman scuttled to the far end of the sofa, gasping for breath. "I…I don't know. Eric had it. Said it was a winner, but I never seen it. That's the God's honest truth." Any fight Caroline had in her fled, and she babbled. "Take my watch." She ripped an old Seiko from her boney wrist and thrust it toward her attacker. "I've got some cash in my purse over there. Take it. Anything you want."

Her executioner evinced no interest in those things, and the last thing Caroline saw on this Earth was the muzzle of a steel revolver dissolving in a cloud of red.

CHAPTER THREE

AN UNFORTUNATE TRUTH

"Rest, little fish," Tara murmured as she plated two tuna steaks. She deglazed the pan with a squeeze of fresh lemon juice and a glug of chardonnay. Then, she added capers and chopped parsley. Steam rose from the pan, bathing her face in a piquant bouquet. Now, it was time for her to rest. After pouring a glass of wine from the open bottle, she located her Apple Home Pod, sighing contentedly when Diana Krall's soothing voice filled the air with a languorous melody. She went to stand in the doorway and peered across the hallway into Jack's study. He was stuffing papers into his briefcase, unaware of her eyes upon him.

"Time for dinner."

Jack's head shot up, and Tara crossed the distance between them.

"I told you I wasn't hungry.".

"I've prepared a lovely meal."

Jack placed the briefcase on his desk and rose to his feet. "You shouldn't have," he said, coming to stand before her.

"What do you mean? Why not?"

"I'm leaving."

"Leaving?" Tara gazed at him, uncomprehending. "Where?"

"Come sit down for a moment."

～

Her hands were tightly clasped in her lap, her face mottled from crying. "What are you going to tell Josh?"

Jack sat with his hands on his knees, ready to bolt. "The truth. He's a big boy."

Bile rose in Tara's throat. "That you'll always love me, but you've found someone who makes you feel young again?"

"Something like that, I suppose."

"Some Tootsie Roll you've been diddling who's closer to his age than yours?" Her voice was thick with sarcasm.

Jack recoiled as if he'd been struck. Tara took satisfaction in the fact that her words had stung, but Jack recovered quickly. "I'm sorry, Tara. I know you don't deserve this." He rose to his full height. "I was hoping we could maintain some level of civility—"

"Talk to my lawyer," Tara hissed. "I can assure you he'll be civil."

"I'm going to pack a few things." Jack turned and walked away.

"And very expensive!"

Tara continued to sit, seemingly incapable of motion. How long had Jack been planning this? Obviously, he'd waited until after her birthday to drop his bombshell.

Eventually, Jack reappeared toting a carry-on bag. Briefly, he made eye contact, but then he focused on her hands. "Good-bye, Tara," he said, rather gallantly.

Was that part of his script? Tara's mind was a jumble. She couldn't focus. He was leaving. She blurted out the first thing that came to mind. "What about Thanksgiving?" As soon as the words were out, she yearned to retract them. She was pleading, giving him the upper hand.

Jack just stood there, momentarily dumbfounded until, with eyes full of regret, he let himself out the door.

~

As she trudged over the threshold, Tara's phone rang. She deposited her grocery totes on the kitchen table and rifled through her bag for her cell.

"What are you going to do?" Pat asked.

"I don't know. Have my eyes done? You should see me, big black circles under them." Tara unpacked packages of Freshpet from a shopping bag, hiked to the fridge, and tossed them into the crisper.

"You'll be fine. Trust me."

"Damn it, Pat." Tara stacked canned goods in the pantry. "You're just feeling vindicated."

"He's cold and controlling. Look on the bright side. You're still young."

"Not young enough to keep a husband. Hell, I don't know what I'm going to do about money. Jack handled all of our finances."

"Jack handled *everything*, you included. It's called disclosure, darlin'. Your lawyer will take care of it. You'll be okay in the money department and count your lucky stars you don't have a job."

"Riiight," Tara said. "I'm totally at his mercy."

"Nope. This way, he'll have to support you. You'll get alimony. At least for the time being, until you get back on your feet. Take my advice, open up your own bank account, pronto. Start stashing away anything you can get your hands on."

Having dispensed with the groceries, Tara plunked down on a side chair. "In any event, I can't afford to stay here. Besides, this house is too big for me. My only ties here are the children's choir, Junior League, and you."

"Well, that's compelling. Although there are countless other children's choirs and Junior League chapters, there is, unfortunately, only one lil' ole me."

Tara snickered. "They broke the mold."

"How about I take you someplace for dinner tomorrow night? A nice meal, a good bottle of wine."

"Let me check my calendar." After a brief pause, Tara continued with false gaiety. "What a coincidence. It just so happens I'm free."

"Pick you up at seven."

Tara slid the phone's disconnect and slumped back in her chair. She felt as though she'd been set adrift in a vast ocean where there were no landfalls, no points of reference. The phone rang again, and a small smile tugged at the corners of her mouth.

It must be Pat with one final bit of advice to offer.

"What's up, Patty?"

"Mrs. Purcell?" The gruff voice was unfamiliar and vaguely

threatening. Tara's smile faded. Only then did she note the number on the display. It was a local exchange, but she didn't recognize it.

"I'm sorry. This is she," she said, but the caller had disconnected. "That was weird," Tara murmured, feeling unsettled, but then she put it out of her mind. She had other things to worry about. If it were important—whoever it was—he'd call back.

～

"Jeez, Tara," Earl's gravelly baritone came to her from across the miles. Tara could picture her dad—thin to the point of gauntness, the loose skin of his jowls. "I wasn't surprised when your sister and that fool husband of hers split up," he growled. There was a pause, and Tara knew he was taking a drag from the ubiquitous cigarillo dangling from between his lips. She heard his exhalation before he continued. "I figured that marriage wouldn't last, but I thought you and Jack had something special."

"Me, too, Dad. I never saw this coming. I always thought Jack and I would grow old together." Tara felt a familiar heaviness in the back of her throat.

Earl cursed under his breath. "How's Josh?"

"He's taking it pretty hard. I'm worried about him…being on his own for the first time and adjusting to university life."

"You sure it's not too much for him?"

"I don't know. You know Josh. He's resilient."

Neither spoke for a moment, each lost in thought. Then Earl resumed. "What do you plan to do, honey?

"That's the sixty-four dollar-question, and I don't have the answer."

"Why don't you and Josh come down south for a breather? You could stay with me. Get some sun. It'd do you both good. The ocean's a tonic."

"Gee Dad, let me think about it."

"Sure thing, sweetheart. I'd love to see you."

"I'll call soon."

Tara's mind raced. The Thanksgiving holiday loomed. Unlike past years, she had no intention of cooking the traditional dinner. Pat had invited her and Josh to join the Meyer clan for a holiday feast, but Tara had declined. She was too raw. Nevertheless, she'd felt compelled to mark the occasion, to provide some sense of normalcy, if only for Josh's sake. So, she'd made a reservation for the early seating at the Laurel Oaks Country Club on the twenty-seventh.

Now, the idea of packing up and heading south for a few days had taken hold. A change of scenery would do her good, but there was no way she and Josh could stay at her dad's minuscule, two-bedroom, one-bath apartment. Suddenly, the thought of Pat's luxurious condo in Vero flooded her consciousness. Surely, they could stay there. If Josh were on board, she'd book a flight. That is if she could get one. Thanksgiving was less than a week away.

CHAPTER FOUR

THE SEDUCTION

Foam-crested waves broke in a mesmerizing succession of turquoise folds, and, out past the breakers, a fishing trawler chugged north toward the inlet. Idly, Tara drew her fingers through the sand, sifting for shells and sea glass. Instead, she unearthed a tiny ghost crab. He skittered away, only to be swallowed up in one of the myriad bubble pockets opening on the shore.

"I know how you feel, buddy," she muttered, thinking how, sometimes, all she wanted to do was to run away and hide.

Here, she felt worlds away from her miseries. The sun was working its magic, melting the tension from her body. A week ago, she'd been stuck in a bad dream. Now, a brisk sea breeze was blowing the cobwebs from her mind. In this dramatic setting, Tara's troubles seemed inconsequential. Her old life belonged to someone else. She was being pushed out of her comfort zone into uncharted territory, and, although she didn't like it one little bit, she had the good sense to accept the fact that she was powerless to stop the natural progression of events. Tara sighed and closed her eyes.

An hour later, she awakened to gentle pressure on her shoulder. "Hey, Mom." Josh tossed a few seashells and a small shard of China onto her lap. "Look what I found." He hunkered down beside her.

Tara inspected each perfectly formed shell, examined the blue-and-white porcelain, and then turned to gaze up at her son. Only then did she realize he was not alone. Standing behind him was a sun-bronzed young man clad in brightly patterned swim trunks.

"Hi!" Tara took in the startlingly blue eyes and a face with the chiseled perfection of a Calvin Klein model.

"How do, Mrs. Purcell?"

"Mom, this is Ben," Josh turned to regard the young man. "He's a freshman at UF, home for Thanksgiving."

"Very nice to meet you, Ben. You live here?"

"Yes, ma'am, Florida boy, born and raised."

"How did you two meet?"

"At Wabasso Beach," Josh said.

"It's where the locals hang out," Ben added.

"Ben's having a few friends over tonight. Mind if I join them?"

"Will your parents be there?"

"Mom!" Josh bawled.

"Yes, ma'am. My folks are having a little get-together, and I've invited a few of my friends. We'll probably just play some pool and hang out."

"I suppose that's all right." Tara burrowed through her beach bag for her cell. "Copy me your contact information." She handed Ben her phone.

"Aw, hell!" Josh scoffed. "I'm nineteen. Give me a break."

Tara's eyes cut to Ben's. "I apologize if I seem overly protective."

"No apologies necessary. My mom's exactly the same," Ben said. "I think you two would really hit it off."

～

Naked, but for a terrycloth robe, Tara stood before the sliding glass door in Pat's condo, gazing out at the ocean. After a lazy day spent doing nothing more than sunbathing and reading, she'd treated herself to a long, hot soak in the tub.

The sun had slipped below the horizon, and, in the absence of light, the ocean had lost its sparkle. It was now the color of beaten pewter, and the sky had taken on the same pearly hue, making it difficult to discern the line of demarcation between the two. A squadron of pelicans flew reconnaissance overhead. Tara counted eighteen of them, flying in a ragged V formation. They looked like B-52s, solid and deliberate.

Tara stepped out onto the balcony and craned her head to the north, but there was nothing to see but more condominiums rising up from their concrete pads. In the lengthening shadows, light glimmered from dozens of window openings. Tara clutched the robe more securely about her, shivering as a gust of wind lifted damp strands of hair from the nape of her neck. Retreating into the living room, she bent to switch on a table lamp, and her eye fell upon her cell phone. Without thinking, Tara snatched it up and called the number Ben had keyed in.

"Hello," a pleasant voice intoned over a babble in the background.

"Hi. Is this Ben's mother?" Only then did she realize she didn't know Ben's surname.

"Hold on a minute. I can barely hear you." There was a brief pause, then the voice resumed, but the background noise had subsided. "Sorry about that. It's pandemonium here. Is everything all right?"

Tara detected a note of panic in the woman's voice. "Yes, everything's fine," she said, rushing to reassure her. "I'm Tara, Josh's mom. Ben invited him to your home this evening. I just thought I'd call and introduce myself."

"I see." The woman sounded relieved. "I'm Sarah Hazelton. Your son's here somewhere. Shall I get him?"

"That's not necessary." Tara felt foolish. She sounded like a controlling nut case. "I was just checking in."

"I'm glad you called, Tara." Sarah's voice brightened. "My husband and I are having a few people over for cocktails. Why don't you join us?"

"Thanks, but I couldn't. I just stepped out of the shower and I'm dripping."

Sarah chuckled. "Go dry off and slip into something. I insist. We're just casual. Slacks and a sweater are the order of the day. Come on over and let us buy you a drink."

Tara considered her options. She could scrounge up a meager meal and spend the evening with a movie channel or pull herself together, get out, and meet some new people. Feeling uncharacteristically adventurous, she decided to chance it. "I'd love to."

~

Driving south on A1A, Tara passed one gated enclave after another. She continued on past the St. Theodore's school campus and the Moorings Golf and Yacht Club community, and the landscape began to subtly change. Here, the development was less dense, given over to sprawling, single-family residences constructed on multi-acre parcels. In a short time, she spotted the intricately detailed cast-iron gate Sarah had told her to look for. Suspended between a pair of concrete pillars supporting oversized coach lanterns, it was an imposing entrance.

Tara keyed in the code Sarah had provided, and the gates swung open. The driveway was long and serpentine. Comprised of terracotta pavers flanked by towering queen palms, it ended in a circle where a number of late-model automobiles were parked. As she stepped away from her economy class rental, Tara had the fleeting thought that it was in good company among the Jaguars, Mercedes, BMWs, and the one sleek, black Rolls Royce Ghost with its gleaming chrome grille and modern, rectangular headlights.

The Hazelton residence, a rambling California contemporary, was approached by a series of wide, low steps—a combination of cypress planks and a close-cropped lawn interspersed with a variety of succulents. The walkway was illuminated by ornamental ground lights that coordinated with the lanterns at the entrance, as well as those mounted at either side of the massive, double door entry.

Tara rang the bell, only to wait a full minute before doing so again. When another thirty seconds elapsed, she let herself in. Once inside, she immediately felt dwarfed by the vast ceiling heights and the lofty scale of the interior. A library beckoned at her left, its paneled walls lined with leather-bound books threatening to waylay her. Across the hall, a formal dining room had not one, but two chandeliers suspended from a coffered ceiling. Tara continued down the hallway until she stood before an enormous great room where a dozen or so guests had gathered.

Feeling supremely self-conscious, Tara affixed a smile to her face and entered the room. She gazed about, attempting to catch a sympathetic eye. When no one took any notice of her, she regretted having accepted the invitation. Unlike Jack, she'd never been much good at mixing with strangers. Just as she was about to make her escape, Tara felt the weight of a hand upon her shoulder. She spun around, only to find herself face to face with the mold from which Ben had been cast. Although this fellow's hair was gray, rather than blonde, and thinning at the temples, the resemblance was uncanny. Heavier than his son, his slight paunch attested to a lifetime of country club dining. But he was tan and fit and extremely good-looking. Vivid blue eyes crinkled at the corners creating small white fissures in a face weathered by long hours on the golf course.

"Hello and welcome." He extended a hand. "I'm Cal Hazelton."

"Hello." Tara shook his hand. "I'm Tara, Josh's mom."

"Ah, yes, Ben's new friend." Her host rested a palm lightly on her back, steering her toward a wet bar opposite a sleek and shiny stainless-steel kitchen. "Sarah mentioned that you might be joining us. We're delighted to have you."

Two middle-aged women were working behind the counter. Identically attired in white starched shirts, bow ties, and slim-fitting black trousers, they were arranging hors d' oeuvres on silver trays. Cal nodded toward the women. "Charlene, would you get the lady a drink?" he asked.

Both servers looked up, smiling pleasantly. The prettier of the two, her strawberry blonde tresses pulled back in a clip, said, "Certainly, Mr. Hazelton. What may I get you, ma'am?"

"A glass of white wine, please."

"And another Courvoisier for me," Cal said. Once their drinks were in hand, Cal steered Tara toward a small group seated before the fireplace. "Darling." Cal caught the eye of a slender brunette seated on a leather ottoman. "Here's Tara."

Instantly, the conversation ceased, and all eyes turned toward Cal and the newcomer. The woman gazed up at her husband with large, doe-like eyes in a heart-shaped face. Glossy, light brown hair was gathered at the nape of her neck in a loose twist.

"Tara," Cal said, "my better half, Sarah."

Sarah beamed at the late arrival. "Tara, I'm so glad you decided to join us." She scooted to the edge of the ottoman and patted the empty place beside her. "Come sit next to me."

Tara did as she was told and, much to her consternation, found herself the center of attention.

"Tara and her son, Josh..." Cal said, waving a hand vaguely in the direction of the stairway, "...are here for the Thanksgiving holiday." He turned back to Tara. "I suppose you're wondering what we've done with him?" Tara merely shrugged her shoulders and Cal resumed, "I assume he's downstairs shooting pool with Ben and his buddies."

A stocky, balding fellow hooted derisively. "You hope they're playing pool, Calhoun," he said, with a salacious wink. "I saw several lovely, young things disappear down into the lion's den earlier this evening."

"You're a dirty old man, Ralph," Cal said, dismissively. He turned toward the fireplace and prodded a log with a metal poker. Then, he added another from a stack on the hearth. Once satisfied with this arrangement, he blew gently on the glowing embers, coaxing the fire to new life. "They're good kids."

"Will your husband be joining you?" a plump and well-preserved blonde in pink cashmere asked, as the men resumed their seats.

"No," Tara said, feeling the inevitable flush creep up her face. "My husband and I are...We're separating. I thought it would be good to get away."

"Poor thing," the blonde clucked. "Divorce is simply devastating, isn't it?"

Diamonds sparkled from the woman's ears and fingers, and Tara couldn't help but think that she mustn't have fared too badly.

"You ought to know, Deena," Ralph piped in. "What has it been? Three? Or four trips down the aisle for you?"

"Ralph, do shut up," Deena snapped, but there was no venom in her voice. She leaned into Tara and spoke in a stage whisper. "It's true," she admitted. "I happen to be between husbands just now. Is this your first divorce, dear?"

Tara was momentarily nonplussed by the directness of the question. "And last, I hope." She laughed self-consciously. "Right now, I can't imagine ever getting married again."

"We all think that at one time or another, now. Don't we? Mark my words. You'll get back in the saddle soon enough." Several of the men guffawed, and Sarah raised an eyebrow.

"How aptly put, Deena," Cal quipped.

"Well, she will." Deena pretended to pout as she turned back to Tara. "An attractive woman like you won't stay single for long."

Sarah pursed her lips and wrinkled her brow, seeming to consider her friend's statement. Then she flashed another smile in Tara's direction, immediately putting her at ease. "What is it you do, Tara?"

"A lot of volunteer work. I'm also a musician. I accompany a church choir," Tara explained. "I used to offer private instruction, and I'm thinking of taking it up again."

"How wonderful." Sarah rose from the ottoman and gazed about. "Who will join me for a cappuccino?" Taking Tara's hand, Sarah helped her to her feet. "Cal, drag Tara over to the piano. Get her to play something for us, but no sacred music."

"Oh, I couldn't. I've had wine."

"We're not too particular," Cal persisted.

Eventually, Tara was persuaded to play. Although she judged her performance mediocre at best, her less than discerning audience clapped their hands in delight and called for more. Tara segued into a medley of show tunes and, with a little coaxing, inveigled the others to join her in a sing-along.

The party didn't break up until well past midnight, Ben and his friends having long since vanished. Sarah stood in the doorway looking as fresh as she had when Tara first set eyes on her. She waved merrily to her departing guests, cautioning them to drive safely. "Thanks for taking Deena home, Ralph," she called out. "She'll be mad as a cat in the morning, but she's in no shape to drive."

Ralph grunted a reply as he hoisted the blonde into his Rolls.

"We'll have the boys drop her car off tomorrow," Cal added while escorting Tara to her rental.

"I can't thank you enough," Tara said, slipping behind the wheel. "I hope I didn't wear out my welcome."

"Nonsense." Cal shook his head. "It was our pleasure. Hell," he added, "we didn't even have to pay for the entertainment."

"Bye-bye," Sarah cried. "Don't be a stranger."

The days flew by, and a week passed in an instant. Thanksgiving found Tara and Josh idling away an afternoon with Earl, motoring along the Indian River in his refurbished Criss Craft. They moored at one of the many waterfront restaurants hugging the Palm Beach waterway and enjoyed an untraditional feast of fresh seafood and beer. The rest of the time found Josh in the company of Ben and his pals, while Tara either walked the beach or had her nose in Debbie Macomber's newest bestseller. Toward the end of their sojourn, Tara met Sarah for lunch at the posh Vero Beach Hotel and Club. After their meal, the two spent a pleasant afternoon shopping in the upscale boutiques lining Ocean Drive.

"You must buy them," Sarah insisted, indicating the pair of sandals Tara deliberated over.

"I suppose you're right," Tara agreed. "They're so very Vero."

"You'll be back soon. Everyone comes back to Vero. It's a little slice of Paradise."

"I'm beginning to realize that," Tara agreed. The elegant little town, with its friendly locals, had insinuated itself into her psyche, and she was reluctant to leave.

The metal walls of the Boeing 757 rattled as the aircraft zoomed down the runway, the roar of jet engines drowning out all other sounds. Gray tarmac, indecipherable signage, and utilitarian buildings flashed by in a kaleidoscopic blur of images. Then the aircraft gathered itself, like an ungainly bird, and hoisted its enormous body aloft.

Josh turned away from the window to steal a look at the woman seated beside him. He'd always been proud of his attractive mother, but in the past month, she'd become a specter of her former self. Slender to begin with, she'd gotten thin to the point of gauntness, and bruised hollows ringed her eyes. Today, she looked chic in her navy linen blazer and tapered winter-white slacks. Her hair was styled in a soft coif and brushed away from a face that was suntanned and carefully made-up. If she hadn't gained weight, at least she appeared healthier. The trip, he decided, had done them both a world of good.

Feeling Josh's eyes upon her, Tara glanced up and met his gaze. "That was fun, wasn't it?"

"It was terrific. I really like Ben and his buddies."

"You were busy every minute."

"It was such a great time. In fact, one of Ben's friends…" Josh turned away and peered blindly out the tiny oval window.

"Yes?"

Josh cut his eyes back to Tara's. "It's a she."

"I see. Anything serious?"

"No. I just met her…but I like her. She's different."

"Different can go one of two ways."

"Different in a good way. Believe me."

"Well, that's exciting. It's time to get over Zoe and move on."

"Oh, yeah."

"If she's a friend of Ben's, I'm sure she's lovely. He's a nice young man, and I'm glad to have met his parents. They're wonderful people. In fact," she continued, "our impromptu getaway started me thinking."

"Uh-oh." Josh chuckled.

"I'm serious. What would you say if I told you I'm considering the possibility of relocating to Vero Beach?"

"No kidding?" Josh's eyes lit up, "Sweet."

"Do you really think so?" Tara searched her son's face. She so wanted him to be happy. "I could see Pat when she's down, and you'd still have a home base. You'd be able to keep in touch with your friends. Your dad's not going anywhere, and you'll want to spend time with him."

"It's going to take a little time. I'm not ready for a steady diet of dad's girlfriend, Desiree."

Tara reached for Josh's hand and gave it a squeeze. "I know it's not easy, but these things happen, son. We move on and make the best of it."

"Yeah? Well, it'd be awesome moving on with a pad in Florida."

Tara arched a brow. "Don't get your hopes up just yet, Surfer Joe, but the idea is starting to resonate."

Josh was thrilled at the prospect of relocating to Florida. The idea of hanging at the beach over semester breaks was enticing, but there was an even more compelling reason to return to Vero. Her image suffused his consciousness, huge gray-green eyes in an elfin face that was framed by a mass of flaming red hair, Grace McKenzie.

Josh reflected on the chain of events that had brought them together.

Ben had suggested they join up with a couple of his former classmates and score some girls. It wasn't long before they'd enlisted the exotic-looking Danny, with his mix of Asian and Caucasian blood, and Caleb, tall and lanky with a tattooed bicep and a pierced ear boasting a tiny gold ring. Their first stop had been Ben's house, where they'd filched a couple six-packs from the well-stocked refrigerator.

Next, they'd headed down to the boardwalk at the Golden Sands Public Beach, where they picked up four pretty girls. Three of them had seemed cut from the same mold, tanned and leggy, clad in skimpy bikinis that left little to the imagination. The fourth girl, Grace, stood apart. Her slender body was milky white, and she kept it that way with an ample slick of sunscreen. A wild mane of red hair sizzled against a jet black, one-piece suit that plunged both front and back, molding her curves. The other girls—Lacey, Brook, and Allison—were attractive, no doubt about it, but as far as Josh was concerned, they didn't hold a candle to the spitfire, Grace McKenzie.

The Jeep Sahara, with its canvas top, unsnapped and open to the elements, had been crammed full of young male flesh. Then the girls piled in. It had seemed perfectly natural for Grace to climb in over that tangle of bodies and gamely perch on Josh's lap. The weight of her had been next to nothing.

As the Jeep bumped and rocked down the highway, he'd felt her bones shift beneath the soft skin of her thighs, and when Ben flew over a speed bump, Grace had bounced into the air and might have ejected had Josh not firmly held her down. From then on, he'd kept his arms locked around her tiny waist, glad for his strength, but feeling a bit of an oafish giant beneath the delicate Grace. As they rolled along, her scarlet tresses whipped about his face, at times threatening to blind him. He hadn't minded a bit.

In a little over a quarter of an hour, they'd left the upscale enclave of Vero behind and entered the less populated, unincorporated area between Sebastian and Winter Beach. Another ten minutes passed, and Ben pulled off the highway, parking in the sandy soil along an isolated stretch of A1A.

Scrub palm and wild shrubs lined the shoulder where some resourceful soul had hacked out a path leading to a dune-crossover. They trekked down this narrow corridor single file, the girls with beach bags in tow, the guys bearing towels, a football, and the cooler.

Wresting his eyes from the titillating sway of Grace's derrière, Josh soon became aware of the unique ecosystem they'd entered—a dense hammock comprised of a woven tunnel of fronds and saplings. Hoary trunks of sea oaks curled and twisted, their branches looping themselves in an improbable cursive. A web of vines spun itself in and among the knurled limbs, filling in what few blank spaces there were. Lower to the ground—plush with its carpet of pine needles and decaying leaves—the path was lined with the razor-sharp blades of spiky Spanish bayonet and prickly cactus. Saw palmetto snaked their scaly trunks across the earth like monstrous serpents, fronds splayed out like antenna. Overhead the sky was all but obscured, Australian pines and sea oaks providing a thick canopy that shielded them from the sun.

As they tramped along, the only sounds were the muffled tread of their footsteps and the whir of insects in the brush. Abruptly, the wall of foliage parted, and their ears were filled with the roar of the sea. It spread out before them, a dazzling flounce of blue-green, like a sparkling sequin-spangled ball gown with a white, frothy petticoat at its hem. After the confines of the hammock, the open vista—the arching vault and endless sea—seemed as vast as eternity.

With hoots and shouts, the young people hurtled down the escarpment, recklessly throwing themselves into the sea. They swam out to where the waves broke in thundering, curling crests, and bodysurfed. The girls squealed in protest, as they were scooped up in strong masculine arms and hurled into the crashing waves. They came ashore and desultorily tossed the football, the guys, with their practiced expertise, lording it over the girls, tackling them and pinning them down in the sand at every opportune moment.

When they'd tired of their exertions, they lounged on beach

towels, gossiping and guzzling long necks. Someone produced a bag of weed, and a couple of joints were rolled. When one was passed to her, Grace waved it away. Josh followed her lead, not wanting to make a misstep in her eyes.

He'd managed to position himself next to her, and as the others succumbed to the effects of the marijuana, he furtively eyed Grace, thinking she was the prettiest, most desirable girl he'd ever met. For her part, Grace was acutely aware of his scrutiny, yet she pretended not to notice.

When the sun was directly overhead, Ben stirred. "I'm famished," he announced.

"There's a mini-mart not too far up the road where we could pick up sandwiches and chips," Grace said.

"Great." Ben looked to Caleb and Danny. "Who's got cash?"

"You supplied the beer, to say nothing of the wheels." Josh gained his legs and dug his wallet out of his pocket. "I've got a credit card. I'll spring for lunch."

Grace scrambled to her feet. "I'll show you the way."

Ben belched loudly, and Lacey, who'd been lying at his side, clamped a hand over his mouth. "Eew, gross," she laughed. "How very Vero of you."

Ben snatched her hand away and pulled her to him, stealing a kiss and showing off his superior strength all at the same time. "I'll show you virile." Releasing her, he winked indolently at Josh and tossed him the keys to the Jeep. "You two go on then. Make it a ham and cheese for me."

The others chimed in with their orders, and both Danny and Caleb pressed bills into his hands.

They padded up the footpath, but had only gained a few paces when Grace, who was walking ahead, stumbled on an exposed root. She would have lost her balance if Josh hadn't leaped forward, arms outstretched, and caught her.

Clutched in his arms, the redhead turned to him, giggling sheepishly. "Just call me Grace," she said.

Josh continued to hold her, and Grace's laughter faded away. Wordlessly, she gazed into his eyes, and in the next instant, found herself being crushed in his embrace. Yielding her lips to his, Grace fell headlong into the kiss. Until reason returned, and she drew away.

"Dude," she laughed. "We'd better get lunch, or there'll be mutiny from that bunch back there." Taking his hand, she led him back along the pathway to the Jeep.

From then on, the two were seldom separated. There had not been many occasions for them to be alone, but they'd made the most of those few opportunities, holding hands in the back seat of Ben's jeep, making out on her front stoop with goodnight kisses that went on and on. Now, with each passing minute, as he flew farther away from her, Josh desired nothing more than to return to Vero, and, once again, hold Grace McKenzie in his arms.

～

The estimated flight time from Orlando International Airport to Hartsfield-Jackson was an hour and nine minutes. Bad weather had caused delays so that now the Atlanta airport was thronged with weary holiday travelers. Tara was grateful to be traveling with Josh. Effortlessly, he plucked their bags from off the luggage carousel and quickly crossed the distance to the exit.

Forty minutes later, they pulled into their drive. Josh pressed the button on the rear-view mirror, and the garage door slowly rose up revealing a scene of such unexpected havoc the two could only gape in bewilderment.

"What the—" Josh exclaimed.

Uncomprehending, Tara gawped at the garage interior. What had once been orderly—as orderly as any garage could be—was total chaos. Cabinet doors and drawers yawned open, their contents spilling out. Jack's tools were everywhere, and there were rags, warranty papers, Christmas garlands, and paint cans strewn about helter-skelter. It looked as though a madman had gone on a rampage. In shock, Tara was unable to process. There was no plausible explanation for such devastation. Why would anyone want to tear her garage apart?

They picked their way through the clutter and cautiously opened the door to the laundry room, each of them silently praying that the house would be as they'd left it.

That was not the case.

"My God!" Tara cried, tears welling in her eyes. Tables were overturned and upholstery gutted, so that hundreds of down feathers blanketed the interior like an early snow.

~

You don't have any idea who might have done this?" Officer Ellis, a veritable giant of a man, let his eyes rove over the once-orderly room.

Tara shook her head, bringing the delicate cup to her lips. Her addled brain fastened on the tea, a bit of normalcy in what was otherwise a surrealistic dimension into which she'd been rudely thrust.

"Have y'all done anything out of the ordinary," the younger man asked. "Changed your routine in any way?"

"We went to Florida," Josh said.

"Just took off, spur of the moment," Tara added.

"I see."

"I'm going through a divorce." The deputies exchanged meaningful looks. "My car was being serviced at the Lexus dealership. At the same time the homicide occurred."

Once those words were out, Tara heard a tiny clink in her brain. It was as though a piece of a puzzle had fallen into place. But, try as she might, she couldn't make any sense of it. Jack abhorred disorder. Besides, he could come and go as he pleased. Surely, this was a random act, some desperate addict looking for money or jewelry to bankroll his habit. It made sense, except for one glaring detail: Nothing appeared to be missing.

"Excuse me, officers," Josh said. "My mother's exhausted. I've booked a night at the Marriott. I'm sure you understand."

The young deputy rose to his feet. "Good idea," he said. "We're going to need to dust for prints. I'm afraid the mess is only going to get worse."

Tara groaned.

"We'll need you at headquarters at nine tomorrow morning." Ellis unfolded his ungainly body from a disemboweled lounge chair, presented a card, and a sympathetic smile. "I'm sorry, ma'am. This is a hell of a thing. You've got my personal cell number there. If anything comes up—anything at all—phone me. You hea'?" His southern accent softened the command.

Tara mustered her reserves in an effort to appear gracious. "Gentlemen, you've been most kind," she said, as she escorted them out. "We'll see you tomorrow."

~

"You've made up your mind?" Pat asked. "Nothing I can say to make you stay?"

Tara gazed about her living room. Without furniture and awash in packing boxes, she hardly recognized it. "The break-in cinched it for me. Everything—my life included—was in such disarray. I figured it was the perfect time to start packing."

Pat folded her arms over her chest. "Can't fault that logic, but I'm going to miss my BFF."

"I know, but it's Vero. You'll be down spending time at the condo. We'll stay in touch." With practiced efficiency, Tara sealed a box with packing tape.

"Of course, we will. Say, it's been almost two months. Have the police made any headway? Any leads?"

"No." Tara grimaced. "Between you and me, I don't think this case is going anywhere. The place was trashed, but nothing was stolen. It's strange. I can't wrap my brain around it. I just want to get away and move on with my life."

"I hear you," Pat sighed. "You've had nothing but rotten luck all around. It's definitely time for a fresh start."

"I only hope I'm making the right decision."

"Girl, there's only one way to find out."

CHAPTER FIVE

FIRST IMPRESSIONS

The last several weeks had been a whirlwind, packing up the house, seeing to countless details, making a break from her former, unsatisfactory life. In the turmoil, she hadn't had time to thoroughly process the fact that she was running away from home.

In an unfamiliar room, on a night alive with movement and noise, Tara lay awake mulling over her self-imposed exile. With so many unfamiliar sounds and the rumble of the ocean a half-mile away, was it any wonder she couldn't sleep? She was just beginning to doze off when the beams from a car's headlights illuminated the bedroom. Chanel growled softly, and Tara awoke with a start. In the next instant, soppy strains of a Country western recording spilled out into night air.

"Good Lord, Chanel," Tara muttered. "What have we gotten ourselves into?" Once again, the room was plunged into darkness. Unseeing, Tara stared, at the ceiling, straining to hear. In the next moment, she was rewarded with the sound of first one, then another car door slamming shut followed by raucous male voices, laughing drunkenly.

"Gawd damn it! Get out of my way, idiot."

"Oops!" Another voice guffawed loudly.

Grr. Chanel stood, stiff-legged on the bed, prepared to defend his mistress.

"Oh, look. Someone's moved into old Cameron's house," cried voice number one.

"If I'd known you were coming, I'd have baked a cake," sang his companion.

"Baked a cake, baked a cake." The off-key singing grew fainter until it ceased entirely. By then Tara was wide awake, ears attuned to the wind threading through pine needles and the muffled boom of waves pounding ashore. Chanel growled half-heartedly, then quickly gave it up. With a resigned snort, he nestled down beside Tara.

Pulling the blanket up to her chin, Tara tossed onto her side. "Dear God," she entreated, "help me make it through this night."

Chanel burrowed into the curve of her thigh, and the weight of his body was as soothing as a hot water bottle. When he began to snore, Tara's breathing lengthened. Her last thought, before sleep delivered her to welcome oblivion, was the hope that moving here hadn't been the mistake of a lifetime.

The humidity had lifted, the air light and pure with not a cloud to sully the blue vault overhead. It was the kind of day a Hollywood set designer might have created. Unmoored by the gentle wind, lemon drop petals showered down like confetti from golden rain trees, and blue-blooded plumes of aristocratic royal poinciana cascaded in improbable electric arcs. On this glorious day, Nathan McCourt was uncharacteristically subdued. He climbed out of the Lincoln Town Car, then turned and extended a hand to his daughter.

All the well-heeled denizens of the Treasure Coast elite had turned out for this afternoon's affair. It was the usual cast of characters—the movers and shakers—the society mavens, and the local politicians. Dulcie Woodward stood apart from the crowd, the indisputable star. Any social climber with brains and substance knew to include Dulcie's name at the top of their A-list of invitees. No soiree, wedding, or cotillion was deemed a success lest she graced the affair with her presence. As always, she was impeccably dressed. Her classic, charcoal-colored Armani suit provided a dramatic contrast to the lustrous, silvery chignon she'd fashioned, not a hair out of place. Despite heat that wilted lesser mortals, she appeared cool and elegant, a stately blue heron among a gaggle of rowdy geese.

Nathan's eyes caught and held Dulcie's before veering away. He, alone, knew that beneath her polished veneer, passion smoldered. He recalled their first encounter. It had been at the Kravis Center in Palm Beach, during the intermission of some Lloyd Webber touring production. She and Ernestine had been waiting for their escorts to fetch them drinks from one of several beverage purveyors, all of whom were doing a brisk trade dispensing liquid fortitude for those daunted by the prospect of a second act.

He'd been fresh out of nowhere, armed with only an MBA, his good looks, and a truckload of moxie. Boldly, he'd stepped up to Ernestine and thrust a hand toward her. There was no recognition in her eyes, yet Ernestine had taken his hand. He made introductions, fabricated a prior meeting at a Windsor polo match. It was a flimsy deception, but, graciously, Ernestine had taken him at his word, welcoming him and Elisa into her closely-knit circle of powerful friends.

Years later, Dulcie confessed that she'd seen right through his deception, had known from the get-go that he'd been an opportunist. She was fond of telling him he was blessed with the gift of gab, that he could charm the skin off a rattler—and the naked snake would slither off feeling that, somehow, he'd gotten the better part of the bargain.

Today, however, Nathan felt as though his luck had finally run out. He grasped Jennifer's tiny hand, leading her down the tree-lined path to the clearing ahead. The oddly silent crowd converged behind them as a keyboard-generated melody commenced.

The child skipped beside her father, softly humming along with the song. Then, she stopped abruptly, nearly stumbling as her father continued on. "Where's Mommy?" Jennifer asked. "Isn't she coming, too?"

From somewhere behind them, a muffled sob was heard. Nathan turned toward the girl, hunkered down, and spoke to her in a low voice. Just then, a petite, buxom woman emerged from the crowd. She was clothed in a billowing black caftan, a wide-brimmed hat of the same shade crowning her expertly tinted, copper locks.

Nathan rose to greet her. "Ernestine," he breathed.

The woman took Jennifer's free hand, and the three continued on to a place where a canvas pavilion afforded shade to several rows of folding chairs. The gleaming bronze casket smothered in yellow roses looked like a prop delivered to the wrong set.

As the threesome drew near, the casket lid sprang open and buttercup-colored blooms spilled to the ground. Jennifer's mouth formed a perfect O, as she howled a blood-curdling scream. Nathan looked on in horror, as Ernestine gathered Jennifer in her arms.

Nathan crossed to the coffin, gazed down at Elisa, and bent to kiss her. His wife's eyelids fluttered, and Nathan shrank back. But when Elisa raised her slender arms toward him, he leaned in to embrace her.

Then all was darkness.

Jennifer's screams grew distant. A pinprick of light appeared at the far end of a passageway. The light grew ever larger until it pulsated radiantly.

Nathan jolted awake. He lay there for a moment, reconnecting with reality, then he leaped from the bed. A few short strides took him to the east wall of the master suite where a bank of floor-to-ceiling windows afforded a view of the terrace and ocean beyond. With a flick of his wrist, the veins of a plantation shutter opened to reveal a panorama that never failed to satisfy.

Breathing deeply, Nathan shook off the black mood his recurring nightmare inevitably triggered. His eyes roved over his Eden—the vine-woven esplanade that spilled garish trails of bougainvillea upon the stone terrace, the assortment of terracotta pots harboring nests of spiky pink and cream-colored bromeliads.

Beyond the stucco wall, dawn's first slanted rays created a shimmering diamond surface on the sparkling Atlantic. Directly beneath him, the Olympic-sized pool masqueraded as a natural pond. Mammoth blocks of bleached coral lined its banks, and a cleverly engineered waterfall cascaded down its surface into the reclaimed saltwater basin.

After changing into a tee, shorts, and a pair of well-worn sneakers, Nathan bolted from the room and took the stairs of the elegant staircase in a most inelegant fashion, two at a time. He hiked through the great room, paying no attention to the magnificent coffered ceiling that was shrouded in shadows. Pushing open one of the colossal, mahogany doors, he emerged into the pale light of a new day and his heart expanded.

Just as he did so, Willie pulled onto the oleander-lined driveway. His heavyset housekeeper was squeezed behind the wheel of her Honda Civic, and she raised a palm in greeting. With a perfunctory wave of his hand, Nathan acknowledged her, turned left, and lengthened his stride. This was his favorite time of the day when he emptied his head of all the countless details surrounding his burgeoning business and worrisome family.

~

Scottly Ulysses Preston peered critically at his reflection in the mirror. His eyes looked like blue yolks in half-baked custards. He dabbed Polo into the soft wattle under his chin and cursed softly. "Damn. You're getting a little jowly, old boy."

His innate cheerfulness buoyed to the surface as he gazed about his well-appointed bath, thinking he'd made a success of it. What did it matter if he were going to pot? His passion for beautiful things had provided him a lifestyle beyond his wildest dreams.

Stepping into his neatly-ordered closet, Scottly donned a crisp, cotton dress shirt, trousers in the finest wool, and a raw silk, camel-colored jacket. Then he slipped his bare feet into tasseled loafers and cinched an alligator skin belt around his waist.

His costume was not complete without his jewelry, the heavy gold chain with its citrine pendant and a gold pinkie ring set with an enormous emerald. Scottly knew such ostentation was considered gauche. He simply didn't care.

Where was Kevin? If the lazybones didn't hurry, they'd be late. Scottly was a model of punctuality, and Kevin's perpetual tardiness was a bone of contention between them. Their differences didn't end there. For the hundredth time, he consoled himself with the fact that opposites attract.

The two of them had been together for nearly three of the happiest years of his life. Of course, he had oodles of friends, but it was a family he yearned for, and Kevin had come to represent that.

Scottly waltzed into his efficiently designed galley kitchen and poured a steaming mug of coffee for his indolent partner. Then, wearing an indulgent smile, he sailed into the master bedroom.

"Wake up, gorgeous," he regaled. Standing at the bedside, he waited for Kevin to evince signs of life. As always, Scottly found Kevin's tousled black curls and wiry, olive-skinned frame adorable, but the clock was ticking, and he was fast losing patience. "Rise, shit, and Shinola," he said, through clenched teeth.

"I'm not going," Kevin groaned.

Scottly placed the coffee mug on a side table. With hands on hips, he inched closer. "Oh, yes you are." He bent to shake the bare shoulder poking out from under the coverlet. "You must." Kevin merely tossed to his side. "Kev, he was your friend."

"They're all *your* friends. No one will even notice my absence." Kevin snatched up a pillow and burrowed his head beneath it. "Go away."

Scottly glanced at the bedside clock and lowered himself to the edge of bed. At this pace, they might well make their entrance with the coffin and process down the aisle with the priest and grieving family.

At the thought of that spectacle, he redoubled his efforts. "Listen, Kevin, you were the man's guest. You sat at his table, drank his wine. He laughed at your terrible jokes, for God's sake." Scottly gave Kevin's shoulder another, more vigorous shake. "You're going to his funeral to pay your respects, and that's final."

"Fuck!" In one fluid motion, Kevin threw the coverlet aside and bounded out of bed. "Now that I'm awake, I might as well go." He yawned and stretched, running a hand through his untidy mane. "It's always your schedule, your friends. Ugh!"

Scottly presented the brew as a peace offering. "Take this and into the shower with you. I'll make the bed."

Grumbling, Kevin took the mug and headed for the bath. Scottly eyed the smooth skin of his partner's lean muscled back, his six-pack abs, and tight little ass and shook his head. Yes, he surely *was* a sucker for beautiful things.

As Scottly finished tidying up the room, the whine of a hairdryer could be heard over a device tuned to 92.7 Country on the FM dial. He winced at the twangy vocals and simple four-chord accompaniment blaring from the bath and beat a hasty retreat to the kitchen. After dumping the coffee grounds in the trash, he made his way to the foyer and unlocked the front door.

When he stepped out onto the front porch, the beauty of the morning nearly bowled him over. Scottly inhaled deeply, savoring the sweet fragrance of orange blossom wafting in the air. Low on the eastern horizon, rosy streaks glowed, while overhead a tenuous slice of moon, like a smile resolutely affixed to the morning sky, shone translucently. If he'd had to venture a guess, he would have put the temperature at a mild seventy degrees. Except for the showy trills of a mockingbird, boisterously practicing his scales, all was still.

"Ah, another day in Paradise." Scottly bent to retrieve the Vero Beach Press Journal. When he glanced across the hedge that separated his property from Cameron's, the tranquility of the day's tender beginning was forgotten. A figure appeared, first rising from Cameron's porch, and then coasting down the drive.

Suddenly, he recalled the events of the previous evening. Had he and Kevin actually been singing? He prayed their antics hadn't disturbed this newly arrived stranger.

In the next instant, a high-pitched yipping grabbed his attention. "Good Lord," he muttered, eyes glued to what was, decidedly, a female with a dog in tow. As she drew near, Scottly realized the woman was on rollerblades. Arms akimbo, she swayed precariously in an effort to remain upright.

In his mind's eye, Scottly could see it: the mutt being cut down beneath flying steel wheels or, worse yet, strangled on his own leash and expiring in a tangled heap. All because of this foolish woman and those damned in-line skates. With mounting dread, he watched as she sailed toward the street. Then, out of the corner of his eye, he caught sight of a jogger turning from Frangipani onto Pelican. Intent on his run, the unsuspecting fellow was rushing headlong toward certain disaster. By the time the runner realized his predicament, it was too late.

Scottly cried out a warning, but the woman was out of control and unable to brake. She crashed into the unsuspecting fellow, and the two tumbled to the pavement. The little dog, his barking even more high-pitched and hysterical, had, indeed, become entangled in his leash. With an ominous sense of déjà vu, Scottly dropped his newspaper and rushed to assist.

Hastily, the disgruntled fellow picked himself up from the pavement, refusing Scottly's offer of assistance. After extricating himself from the snarl of leash, dog, and woman, he sprinted off in a huff.

Unlike the dog.

Upon *his* release, the terrified creature fairly leaped into the crook of Scottly's arm.

"Come here, Chanel." the woman made as if to relieve him of his burden, but the mutt bared his fangs and snarled at her. "I guess he doesn't trust me," she said, backing off. "At this point, can't say as I blame him."

Awkwardly, holding the dog in one arm, Scottly extended his free hand toward her. "My dear, are you all right?" The woman gripped his hand and rose unsteadily to her feet. "Take my arm," he said, and she complied.

Scottly escorted her up the drive to Cameron's front porch and lowered her to the stoop. "Any broken bones?"

She sat clumsily and began unfastening her skates. "I'm fine, just thoroughly humiliated." The woman screwed up her face, but her eyes twinkled. "What a klutz I am." She thrust a hand toward him. "Hello. I'm Tara Purcell, your new neighbor."

"Scottly Preston." He took her hand in his. "Very pleased to meet you and welcome."

Having thoroughly taken to his champion, Chanel administered a series of wet kisses to Scottly's neck. "Who, might I ask, is this affectionate creature?" He asked while attempting to ward off the unwelcome onslaught.

"Mr. Preston, meet Chanel."

Gently, Scottly set the dog down next to Tara. "You must come over for cocktails sometime," he said. "But now, I'm afraid, you'll have to excuse me. I'm late, and I simply must fly."

Willie surveyed her domain while the electric juicer extracted nectar from freshly picked fruit. It was all form and function, hopeless and spare as a condemned man's cell. She'd always found the nucleus of this house, with its professional-grade appliances and lacquer-finished cabinets, cold and unappealing. Her own cramped kitchen was cluttered and humble, but she wouldn't trade it for this antiseptic decorator's nightmare. Affixing an everchanging collage comprised of the McCourt children's schoolwork, their photographs, and party invitations to the gargantuan Sub-Zero refrigerator in an effort to warm up the place hadn't helped. She'd hung a potted spider plant over the sink, replacing it periodically when, inevitably, it withered and died, but these small measures did little to dispel the chill.

Willie's musings were interrupted when Jennifer sashayed into the room. One look at the girl's attire, shredded jeans and a skimpy tee that revealed far too much flesh, and she morphed to combat mode. "Girl, you march right back upstairs and get some clothes on."

"I'm wearing clothes," Jennifer hissed. "It's dress-down day, and this outfit is perfectly fine."

At that moment, Harry stumbled into the kitchen. Half-awake and clutching a book, he jostled Jennifer on his way to the table.

"Don't push me," she snarled, daring him to cross her. Harry merely ignored her, and Jennifer turned back to Willie. "You're not my mother, and I don't have to do what you say."

"That's right. I'm not your Mama. Poor woman would turn in her grave if she saw you dressed like this." She set a plate of scrambled eggs and bacon in front of the boy. "Here you go, Harry."

"Thanks, Willie." Harry opened his novel and was soon lost in the latest trials of the protagonist who shared his moniker, the indomitable Harry Potter.

The housekeeper poured the boy a glass of orange juice. "Miss Jennifer best do as I say, or I won't talk to her father about that party this weekend."

"You're so mean." Jennifer narrowed her eyes. "You just want me to look like a baby."

"I want you to look like a young lady. Now hurry or you'll be late. You don't want to spend another Saturday in detention.

"It wasn't detention. I had to make up a test." Jennifer stormed out of the room, muttering under her breath.

Willie sighed. She'd won this battle, but the war was far from over.

~

Head down, Jennifer steamed up the staircase. On the landing, she nearly collided with her father. "Jenn," Nathan exclaimed. "Good morning, sweetheart."

The rebellious girl glanced sidelong at her father. Then, taking in his bloody knee, she stopped up short. "What happened? Ugh!"

Before Nathan could make a reply, she'd flounced past him and pounded up the stairs. Nathan stared after her, flinching when an overhead door slammed shut with a resounding bang.

As he hobbled into the kitchen, he wondered what had set the girl off this time.

"Morning, Mr. McCourt." Willie slid a plate of scrambled eggs and toast before her employer, and her eyes fell on his injured knee. "What have you gone and done?"

Harry lowered his book, eyeing his father's frayed knee.

"You wouldn't believe it if I told you."

"Try me." Willie rummaged through a drawer and returned to the table with antiseptic pads, cotton swabs, and a box of bandages.

"I can do it." Nathan shooed the woman away and blotted the ragged flesh with a paper napkin. Undeterred, Willie tended to his wound, and Nathan succumbed to her ministrations.

"Come on, Dad," Harry implored. "Tell what happened."

"I was just jogging along on Frangipani, where so many of those older homes are being renovated. You know the area I'm talking about?" Both the housekeeper and Harry nodded. "I turned on to Pelican Way, was just rounding the corner, when some damn fool woman on in-line skates, fairly leapt out onto the sidewalk and mowed me down."

Willie's body jerked, stiffened, and then froze in place. "I've seen it," she moaned, her eyes big and white as golf balls and focused on another dimension. "I've seen it, Mr. McCourt. I prophesized you be coming to harm." Willie rocked back and forth, speaking in a sing-song voice. "There's more where that come from, too, so help me, Jesus."

Nathan and Harry exchanged bemused looks while struggling to contain their laughter. Willie was a big prophesier. Over the years, the McCourts had learned that the best course was to just go along with her portents.

"Yes, Lawd. Much more," the housekeeper intoned. "Don't you worry, Mr. McCourt. It's all going to turn out for the best. Praise God."

In the next instant, Willie transformed to her usual self, speaking in a matter-of-fact voice, as though nothing out of the ordinary had occurred. "The sidewalks and streets are crazy with people, and not just kids. Old ladies with gray hair and baldheaded codgers wearing nylon sweatpants and three-hundred-dollar sneakers, acting foolish like teenagers. Um-umm. Punks with their tongues pierced and eyebrow rings, whizzing back and forth on skateboards, and cycle riders all hunched over their fancy bikes, thinking they own the road. And those in-line-skaters. There's a white lady, sixty if she's a day, blades all up and down A1A. I see her every morning. She's dressed all in black. Looks like Cat Woman. Got the figure for it, too."

"I've seen her," Harry babbled, excitedly. "I know who you mean, Willie! She *does* look like Cat Woman, Dad."

"She's a machine." Willie shook her head. "You don't want to get in that woman's way. It's not safe out on the streets anymore."

"We ought to try skateboarding, Dad," Harry said. "Or get a couple of those cool, recumbent bikes."

The air was sucked out of the room when Jennifer strutted in and fixed Harry with a withering glare. "What would you know about cool, you little geek?"

Harry knew better than to answer. He merely pushed his glasses up the bridge of his nose and retreated to his book.

"Jenn, enough." With a troubled face, Nathan attacked his eggs. "Willie, you haven't forgotten that I fly to Houston on Friday. You'll stay the weekend?"

"I'll stay, but you'd best find another nanny soon. I've got my hands full at home."

"I understand," Nathan said. "There's not enough of you to go around."

"Humph!" The housekeeper snorted. "There's enough of me, all right. It's just too bad Miss Jenny chased off that last nanny. She was a real gem."

Nathan arched a brow but gave Jennifer's shoulder an affectionate squeeze before crossing to the side door.

He was nearly through it when Willie called out to him. "Mr. McCourt, don't forget about that piano teacher. It's been three weeks since Harry's had a lesson."

Nathan spun around to face the housekeeper and snapped his fingers.

"Right. Thanks for reminding me." He was out the door, his voice trailing after him. "Can't have our own Van Cliburn slacking off, now. Can we?"

"Jeez," Harry grumbled.

Nathan hiked through the great room and out into the sunshiny morning. As the door closed behind him, a weight seemed to lift from his heart. As always, he was eager to immerse himself in the world of acquiring and selling, profit and loss. It was all so eminently satisfying—so devoid of emotion.

Five hundred miles away, across the state line in Gwinnett County, Rick Cochran was fuming. In his glory days, while serving in Nam, he'd been in prime condition—a lean, mean, fighting machine—all muscle and sinew. Those days were gone. The rock-hard muscles of his youth had turned to blubber. He could have popped that old lady's head off had he wanted. Still, he wasn't as fit as he'd once been, and his reflexes weren't what they used to be, either. Doc had cautioned that the excess weight, in combination with his naturally high blood pressure, was putting entirely too much strain on his heart—like stress had anything to do with the palpitations and cold sweats. If the man only knew, but no one knew.

His secret life remained just that, secret. Rick kneaded his forehead with a hand that had snuffed out more lives than he cared to remember. The Eric business was turning into a nightmare. He'd clearly seen the kid doing a happy dance in the employee lounge, and later, thumbing through lottery tickets in one of the cars being serviced. It hadn't taken a genius to figure out what *that* had been about.

Where the hell was the winner? Not on Eric. He'd searched his pockets, even taken off the kid's shoes and socks, but he'd come up empty-handed. It wasn't in the shop, either. He'd turned the service bays upside down, ostensibly cleaning, looked everywhere. The kid's old lady sure as hell didn't know where it was, and he was damn sure it wasn't at the house on Laurel Oaks.

Rick glanced up at the display of memorabilia behind his desk, the grainy photos of him and his buds. All of them young and movie star-handsome, mugging for the camera as if they hadn't a care in the world. The two purple hearts, in their Lucite cases, one for his testicles, which had put a kibosh on his sex life, the other for a head wound that had nearly ended his life altogether. He wasn't bitter. At least that's what he'd told himself throughout the years. He was proud of his service.

"Soldiers follow orders, warriors know their duty," he muttered, anesthetizing himself to the pain.

He'd internalized that life-defining phrase in 1970, Fort Bragg, North Carolina, where the US Army ingested ordinary boys and spat out exceptional warriors. At the top of his class, he'd been eager to distinguish himself and itching for action. Nothing prepared him for the morass, the hideous moral-less war he'd been deployed to. Surprisingly, U.S. Army Special Forces Richard Cochran had taken to that nightmare like a pig to pooh. He'd thrived, thrilling to the imminent threat of danger, the immediate challenges that kept him on his feet, both literally and figuratively.

Special Forces had imbued him with particular skills—skills honed over the years. For a time, he'd done a stint as a professional assassin, painstakingly planning the hits, all of which had gone off without a hitch. The rewards had been well worth the risks, until one day, when the work simply dried up, his services no longer required. He knew why. He was too old and too slow. He'd considered putting the gun to his own head and just ending it all.

Then, Sally had called, and he'd been totally unprepared for the emotion that flooded over him.

"Hi," she said, and he grunted a reply.

"Is this Richard Cochran?"

"Who wants to know?"

"Are you sitting down?"

"What the hell does that have to do with anything?"

"Because I think you might be my dad."

Rick's first reaction had been to put up a wall of defense. He was an old man and easy prey. He figured this for a scam; some slick con playing him for a fool. There was no way he'd fathered a child, but a part of him wanted to believe the impossible.

When he didn't respond, the caller continued. "You remember Arlene Fletcher?"

Rick searched his memory bank, struggling to recall an Arlene. Try as he might, he couldn't place her. Over the years there'd been women, but they'd all been turned off by his little handicap. Eventually, he'd stopped making advances, but then Rick's brain glommed onto a happy recollection from way back when. In the next instant, his heart nearly leaped out of his chest, for he knew with complete certainty that this woman spoke the truth.

It had all happened light years ago when he'd been a lowly recruit at Fort Bragg with a furlough into town, hanging out at the local pub. That's where he'd met her. Lena, vivacious, and engaging. She'd flirted with him, shamelessly, and he'd responded in kind. He was to ship out the following week, and he was eager to score some loving.

Lena had been a real peach, sweet and genuine, much more than he'd bargained for or reckoned he deserved, for that matter. They'd dined on burgers and fries and knocked back way too many beers. Then they'd slow-danced and gotten shit-faced like the rest of the men in his company. Eventually, he and Lena Bean—as he'd dubbed her—had found their way back to her apartment where they'd fallen upon one another. Now, forty-some years later, he finds he has a daughter. Incredible.

Rick's narrow little world had suddenly expanded. He had family. He'd fathered a child, and he wanted to get to know her while he had a few good years left. "I...I..." His mind had been working overtime, conjuring a dozen different scenarios, yet his mouth refused to function.

"I'm sorry. I know this is a lot to digest over the phone, but I didn't want to risk making the trip to confront you face-to-face, only to find that you weren't receptive."

Rick cleared his throat, struggling for words. "Honey," he finally croaked. "I'm just..."

"Overwhelmed? I get it, Dad. You don't mind if I call you that, do you?"

"Of course not."

"I've been rehearsing. I even have notes. You're winging it. Doing good, I might add."

Tears brimmed in Rick's eyes the moment when his world changed. Emotions he'd tamped down for a lifetime, resurfaced. He would let the love in, and it was surely going to alter things. Too bad, he'd thought, fleetingly, as the walls he'd built had begun to crumble.

"I want to see you," he'd said. "Soon."

"Great! Oh, and Dad...you have a grandson. His name is Connor.

Rick had been tempted to just give up on finding that lottery ticket. He didn't have the stomach for the sort of things he'd been doing anymore, but after the rest of that conversation with Sally, there were new complications in his life. He needed to put his hands on a large sum of cash in order to deal with them. He'd just have to proceed with extreme caution and see it through.

"The third-degree burns he suffered are very slow to heal due to skin tissue and structure being destroyed," she'd said, "usually resulting in extensive scarring."

The boy required surgeries, and Medicaid wouldn't cover them. Rick wanted to leave him and his daughter a legacy—a little stipend to make up for all those years he'd been oblivious to their existence.

～

FULTON COUNTY NEWS
MULTIPLE CAR BURGLARIES REPORTED

Deputies have reported a spike in the number of car burglaries in the greater Atlanta area over the last several months, according to incident reports released Friday by the Gwinnett County Sheriff's Office. While some of the residents said their vehicles had been unsecured, at least five of the cars broken into had been locked up tight, according to their owners. Yet, there were no pry marks on the doors or back hatches, indicating that no force had been used in those break-ins.

The first report was made at 2:48 a.m. Friday in Lawrenceville, where the resident stated that nothing was missing. The rest of the reports were made between 3:30 a.m. Friday and 7:30 a.m. Sunday. Stolen items included an iPad, a car stereo, a digital camera, and a small caliber revolver. Nine of the cars were newer Lexus models recently serviced at Atlanta Lexus. Anyone with information about these crimes should call the Gwinnett County Sheriff's Office.

CHAPTER SIX

FULL OF SURPRISES

The short drive from Nathan's private estate to his suite of offices was a breeze. The automobile practically drove itself as he navigated from A1A to Ocean Drive, a journey taking all of fifteen minutes. Braking for a red light on Beachland, his gaze strayed to the regal edifices of masonry and glass lining the lushly planted boulevard. So many financial institutions, so much Treasure Coast capital and so many enterprising individuals who'd made fortunes growing those assets.

In the early days of the new millennium many investors had taken a bath, having purchased over-priced tech stocks and eventually dumping them for a fraction of their initial accessed worth. He, on the other hand, had steered clear of the tech sector altogether, thinking it entirely too volatile, and his theory had proven sound. The recession presented another opportunity. Sure, they'd all lost millions when the housing bubble burst, but they still had millions. Florida real estate was now so undervalued, he was buying, and suddenly, tech was coming to the Treasure Coast in a big way. He was investing. What a life.

Nathan pulled into his dedicated slot in the covered parking garage behind the most elegant building on Ocean Drive. Eschewing the elevator, he sprinted up the back stairway to the third floor. Why take the lift when he was dressed in his jogging gear? Having only broken a light sweat, Nate arrived at the entrance to his suite of offices. McCourt Enterprises occupied the entire top floor of the building. He hiked to his private dressing room, opened the door to his bath, and was confounded to hear the sound of running water. Puzzled, he rounded the corner only to be greeted by an unexpected, but delightful surprise, a willowy female, buck naked, in his shower. Lissome, with cropped blonde hair, the young woman was achingly beautiful. In the next instant, this vision turned to him, revealing pert breasts and an inviting smile.

She saluted jauntily. "Morning, boss."

How lucky could a man get? Nathan shucked out of his clothes. "Gloria," he cried, practically leaping into the shower. "What the hell are you doing here?"

Unabashed, the woman pivoted and reached for a bar of soap. "What does it look like?" She drew the bar across her breasts, encircling nipples that instantly beaded, and then she traced a path down to her groin. "I tried you on your cell, but there was no answer." She lathered Nathan's chest. "I called your house phone, but your housekeeper said you were already on your way."

Gloria chuckled, eyeing Nathan's swelling member. "I see that appears to be the case." She reached for him, demanding to be kissed.

"And?" Nathan groaned.

"There was something I wanted to see you about."

"Really?" Nathan asked hoarsely. "What?"

Worry niggled at the edge of his consciousness. Gloria was becoming entirely too bold, but his concern was fleeting, and he wrapped his arms around his assistant's compact body. Naked, she was even more beautiful than he'd imagined.

Gloria let the bar of soap slip from her hand, moaning as Nathan crushed her against the granite wall. "This," she breathed.

Twenty minutes later, Nathan was seated at the desk in his office. He buzzed for his secretary and was almost immediately rewarded with the click-click of her pointy-toed heels on the stone floor. She relayed his messages, ticking off his appointments for the day. Once she'd left to fetch his coffee, he opened his laptop, keyed in *www.monstor.com* and searched the classified ads. He located several ads for piano instruction in Vero Beach but found only one that offered private lessons in the comfort of one's own home.

Nathan jotted down the email address associated, and when Julie arrived with his coffee, he handed her the note. "Will you please contact this person and see if you can arrange for an interview with Willie?"

"Consider it done."

With that detail out of the way, Nathan put thoughts of his problematic family out of his mind. Willie could hold down the fort. Nathan muted the large flat screen TV mounted on the wall across from his desk, tuned to StockCharts TV, and picked up the phone, eager to immerse himself in the great game of trading. Making money didn't require any messy emotional involvement. Which was just the way he liked it.

~

Harry slid into the nearest available seat and immediately cracked open a book. Jennifer made a beeline to the back of the bus and planted herself next to her best friend, Hillary Fordham. All the lower school kids on the bus were attired in the requisite uniform— navy blue slacks or jumpers, and white cotton shirts or blouses, depending on gender. The boys, however, were burdened with the additional obligation of a tie cinched about their necks. Most opted for the clip-on model, which could be found discarded just about anywhere on the lower school campus. Harry was not one of those boys.

One evening, after a particularly satisfying day at the office, Nathan had decided that Harry should learn to tie a tie. They had practiced in the time-honored fashion, Nathan standing behind the boy, both of them facing the mirror. This bonding experience had taken all of ten minutes, Harry having mastered the art almost instantly. Nathan had come away congratulating himself for the gratifying father-son interaction. What did he know? Harry had been mortified. Now he had to wear a *real* tie. Just like a tether, it held him down, but Harry already felt so restrained, he guessed it didn't much matter.

Hillary and Jennifer attended the upper school, and upper

schoolgirls weren't required to wear a uniform. They both scorned the dweebs in the lower school, shamelessly sucking up to the seniors. They held their teachers in contempt and probably would have been asked to enroll elsewhere had it not been for the fact that their parents donated generously whenever called upon to do so. Jennifer and Hilly managed to be a source of irritation to just about everyone at St. Theodore's.

Today, they were conspiring how best to out Grace McKenzie and Coach Brendon. Coach was the available bachelor on campus and so hot. All the girls were secretly in lust with him. Hillary was fairly bursting with the latest, delicious tidbit. She swore she'd seen them together after last night's football game locked in an embrace and *making out*

"How'd you happen to see it?"

"I realized I'd left my Patagonia jacket somewhere. My mom will kill me if I lose one more article of clothing. Everyone had left the field. At least that's what I'd thought, then I heard voices coming from the visitor's stands, and I was curious. It was just too rich. They were under the bleachers."

"No! I can't believe it."

"I swear." Hillary grinned. "We got the goods on Saint Grace."

Grace McKenzie had more than one claim to fame at St. Ted's, which is why the two girls hated her so. Not only was she a straight-A student, but as first-soprano with a sweet clear voice, she was often called upon to sing solos in the choir. Jennifer and Hillary had been inducted into the Rockapella Choir but harbored no such aspirations. It was all they could do to keep up, which didn't mean they weren't jealous of the attention Grace received. Additionally, McKenzie was a member of St. Theodore's award-winning debate team, and she excelled at girls' varsity lacrosse, playing the position of forward-center. Thanks in part to her crackerjack defense, the Buccaneers had gone to the state championships in Orlando the last two years running.

In Hillary and Jennifer's opinion, the most pertinent aspect regarding Grace's matriculation at St. Ted's was the fact that she was *there* only because she had been *graced* with a full academic scholarship. In other words, she wasn't one of them.

Barbarian at the gate.

Poor Grace had become their latest target. The two had mutually decided to concentrate their considerable efforts toward the business of destroying her. Besides clothes, boys, and hooking-up, texting at all hours, and raiding their parent's medicine cabinets for pills, it's what they lived for.

CHAPTER SEVEN

HOT AND BOTHERED

Cerita pushed through the framed glass door and into the lab, only to encounter one of her classmates. The pudgy young woman, with lank, dishwater-blonde hair, was seated behind the counter and turned to Cerita, exclaiming, "Hey there. Long time no see."

"Hi, Sidney." Cerita handed the technician her prescription.

"What are we looking for, huh?" Sidney glanced at the list of prescribed tests and whistled softly. "Holy moly," she said, a look of concern crossing her face. "Just about everything, I guess."

"It's a fishing expedition," Cerita explained. "I had a..." She waggled her fingers, "...a *questionable* Pap. Doc Merrill wanted to run some tests, just in case. I had one once before, a positive Pap. Scared me to death. Then, when it was repeated, the darn thing came back negative."

"Happens all the time," Sidney said. "It's probably nothing." She wheeled over a two-tiered cart laden with row upon row of glass vials and motioned Cerita to a chair. "Have a seat, hon."

"It darn well better be." Cerita sat in the plastic chair and rolled up her sleeve. "Can't afford to be sick. Too much to do."

"I hear you." Sidney tightened a slender rubber hose around the soft flesh of Cerita's upper arm. "Now make a fist, and let's see if I can find a big ole vein."

Cerita obliged, and her colleague slid the needle home. She winced as she felt a pinch, and the blood was drawn with minimal discomfort. The technician placed a cotton ball over the puncture, securing it with a bit of gauze and a bandage.

"There you go," Sidney said. "Good as new."

"Sid," she said, regaining her feet and collecting her bag, "you're really getting good at this. You can poke me anytime, girl."

"Blah, blah!" Sidney did her best Dracula imitation. "I vant your blahd!" She grinned, waving Cerita away.

Cerita climbed into her Toyota and pulled out onto 37th Avenue, heading for US Highway 1. Damn, she thought, it was November, for cripes sake, and still so hot. She was feeling a little woozy, which she attributed to the bloodletting, but then she was struck by a horrifying thought. What if she really *were* sick? Cerita flipped down the visor and checked out her reflection in the mirror. After a brief but critical evaluation, she decided that she looked good. Foxy even. She was always tired, but that went with the territory. All the nursing students complained of chronic exhaustion. What with a 30-hour workweek, carrying a full academic load at the college, tending to the kids and Granny—and squeezing in a few hours for her social life—was it any wonder sleep was a luxury?

Today was to be no exception. After biology class, she was scheduled at the hospital until nine. When her shift was over, she and her girlfriend, Tamika, were going to grab a drink somewhere, maybe do a little clubbing. She only hoped Jarod would show. The thought of the EMT's buff body, intense eyes, and easy smile made Cerita feel warm all over again.

She hadn't been looking for another man to complicate her life. She'd had two kids with two different daddies, and neither one of them—the daddies, that is—had stuck. That had been the sum of her experience with men. They'd been there at night for the loving, but when it came time for the daily grind, they vamoosed. It was a common pattern in her family, women without partners. Granny had lost Jasper years ago, and Willie's marriage had been short-lived.

Cerita had come to terms with the fact that she wasn't going to hang on to a man, either. Lord knows, she didn't want any more babies. At least that's what she'd thought until she met Jarod. They had so much in common. They were both ambitious. Not only did Jarod hold down a full-time job as an EMT, he was taking online classes, working toward a law degree, and he was so *fine*. Their first encounter had not lacked for drama. Talk about getting choked up over a guy.

It had been Independence Day, a steamy grand finale to a long four-day weekend, and the ER staff had jokingly cautioned her to be prepared for any eventuality. There would be burns from exploding fireworks, they'd explained, as well as abuse cases, typically at the hands of some inebriated working-class stiff with just one drink and one day off too many. Gunshot wounds were also common. There were always some revelers who chose to demonstrate their freedom by firing pistols into the air. The bullets that inevitably returned to earth occasionally came to rest in a live body. There were sporting mishaps, kids with fishhooks embedded in their scalps, or dogged clam-diggers, their bare feet shredded on razor-sharp shells. Nor would it be a holiday without the usual potato-salad-left-too-long-in-the-sun food poisonings or the steady stream of mangled bodies extracted by the Jaws-of-Life from the crushed and twisted vehicles that I-95 inevitably yielded.

The EMTs and auxiliary personnel responding to the Indian River County police dispatch, arrived at the address of the altercation a few minutes past eleven, and it was to a scene from a nightmare. The flashing red lights of squad cars etched across a slate-colored sky, one that was eerily illuminated by the acid, yellow glow of mercury-vapor lamps. The periodic pop-pop of fireworks in the distance resounded like gunfire, and a small throng of gawkers pressed forward, eager for the sight of blood.

Jarod had become accustomed to the drill, but his hackles rose as he prepared for the worst. He and Clayton, a newly recruited deputy assigned to assist the Public Works Department, hoisted the gurney from the back of the ambulance and trotted toward the scene of the crime. Another fleshy, young deputy stood guard at the plate-glass door. He nodded to the responders, waving them into their purgatory of the moment.

Cuffed, the perpetrator lay sprawled on a floor littered with candy-bars, packages of chewing gum, and breath mints toppled from rows of shelving at the checkout counter. In spite of the heat, the perp, one Avril Thomas, was shaking uncontrollably. Jarod looked around, noted that the deputies' hands were protected in latex gloves. Now that the suspect had been subdued, and there was no fear of gunfire, precautions had to be taken.

As they raced toward the hospital, sirens blaring, another call came in. All units in their vicinity were to respond to a major crack-up on the I. It was turning into a real humdinger of a shift all right.

The van screeched to a stop before the ER trauma curbside entrance. "What the hell?" Clayton exclaimed, as he and Jarod hopped from the ambulance, muscled out the gurney, and wheeled their charge into the emergency room.

"You'll get used to it," Jarod said.

The place was a madhouse. Clay sauntered to the office window to fill out the necessary forms, while Jarod remained behind to watch over his charge. He did a quick check of the man's vitals and examined the makeshift dressing he'd applied to his shoulder. There was nothing more to be done for this unsavory specimen. They'd just have to wait for him to be seen by an attending physician. Jarod leaned against the wall and let his eyes wander about the ER. As was usual, the injured and the suffering bore their pain stoically.

Clayton stood before the check-in counter, openly flirting with an attractive young woman manning the desk. Jarod didn't blame him. She was a looker.

Feeling Jarod's eyes on him, Clayton glanced up and flashed him a rueful grin before returning his attentions to the staffer.

The rush of adrenaline that had sustained him to that point was but a memory, and Jarod realized he was exhausted. He slid down the wall and rested on his haunches. No sooner had he done so, than Avril moaned. Jarod shot up to his full height and peered over the rails of the gurney at the miserable creature. The jerk presented no threat. His eyes were closed, and he appeared to be dozing.

Having completed the necessary forms, Clayton turned away from the registrar and crossed the distance to Jarod. "How is he?"

"It's a superficial wound. He's lost a little blood. That's all."

"Well, isn't that just ducky," Clay quipped. "Our own little, punk bandit's catching some shut-eye."

Jarod yawned. "Seems like the sensible thing to me. I was thinking of crawling up there next to him. That's how tired I am."

"Hey, I've got to go. This place is a zoo. I'm going to hit the men's room, then run down to the cafeteria and get us some coffee. Is that okay with you?"

"Sure." Jarod angled his head toward the recumbent perp. "This joker's not going to bolt and run.

"It don't appear likely," Clayton agreed. "I'm not supposed to leave him. Even with you, my friend." The deputy dangled a set of handcuffs before Jarod. "If I cuff him to you, though, we'll be covered."

Jarod gave him a hard look. "Come on."

"I'm sorry, man," Clayton said, while cuffing Jarod's wrist to that of the criminal. "It'll just be for a minute. I'll be back in a jiff."

Time dragged. Jarod glanced at his watch. He was looking forward to the promised cup of coffee when a door to the treatment area swung open, and a gorgeous black nurse emerged. Weary and befuddled, it took him a moment to realize the hot chick was calling for Avril Thomas and beckoning in his direction. Awkwardly, with his right wrist cuffed to that of his patient's, Jarod jockeyed the gurney toward the treatment area.

"Shit," he cursed, under his breath. Where was Clay? He felt like a damned fool, and he was keenly aware of the nurse who was watching him with ill-concealed humor as he struggled to maneuver the wheeled contraption through the narrow opening.

The triage area was one large room sectioned off into a series of smaller cubicles. Each of those individual spaces backed into the surrounding wall, curtained panels affording a modicum of privacy between them. At the core of this arrangement was a medical station, behind which the ER staff retreated to consult charts, check monitors, and make phone calls.

Once inside the cubicle, Jarod watched as the nurse conducted a series of diagnostic procedures. When asked, Jarod recounted the circumstances of the shooting. He went on to explain why Avril's scrawny wrist was now attached to his own.

"It's hard to tell who's cuffed to whom," she said, and Jarod knew he was being teased.

Continuing her examination, the young woman's body inadvertently pressed against his, and an electric current seemed to pass between them. He admired the long, graceful curve of her neck as she bent and peeled away the dressing he'd applied to the man's shoulder. Her almond-shaped eyes were flecked with gold, and her skin was flawless. He inhaled her fresh scent, at the same time, ruing the fact that his own antiperspirant had long since given up the ghost. Noting the small tag pinned to her blouse, he saw that her name was Cerita, that she was not an RN, as he'd assumed, but a student aide.

With a yank, Avril stirred. He drew his shackled wrist up, throwing the metal chain over Cerita's head in a makeshift noose. She tried to scream, but the only sound that escaped her lips was a strangled gasp. Jarod's response was to resist, to pull in the other direction, a course of action that met with disastrous results. The chain only tightened about the terrified woman's neck.

Realizing his folly, Jarod immediately slackened the tension on the garrote while delivering a clumsy, left-handed blow to Avril's forehead.

The front curtain parted, and Clayton appeared, a Styrofoam cup in each hand. "Well, I'll be——" The deputy dropped the containers, splattering coffee on the floor and against the white cloth-paneled walls. In three swift strides, Clayton crossed to the entangled threesome, weapon drawn. A vein in his neck pulsed as he pressed the barrel of his gun to Avril's temple.

"Go ahead," he spat, eyes narrowed to slits. "Make my day, creep."

With the cold metal of the standard-issue pressing against his brow, Avril grasped the futility of his situation and relented. He relaxed his arm, freeing Cerita, and eyed Clayton sullenly.

Cerita inhaled raggedly and staggered toward the curtained entrance, all the while massaging her throat.

Clay continued to hold his gun on the punk, while retrieving the key to the cuffs from his back pocket. "Jesus!" he exclaimed, tossing the key to Jarod. "Leave you alone for a minute, and all hell breaks loose."

"That son of a bitch hit me," Avril sniveled. "I know my rights."

"Shut up!" Clayton said. "Keep it up, and I swear, you'll find out what police brutality is all about."

Jarod removed the restraint from his wrist and affixed it to a strut on the gurney's frame. "Clayton, you bozo," he said. "This is what you should have done in the first place. Regulations my ass."

A curtain rustled, and both Jarod and the deputy looked up in alarm as a brawny medic charged into the cubicle with Cerita close behind. Jarod's eyes flicked to the muscles bulging from beneath the man's short-sleeved lab coat, and he figured Cerita had chosen her reinforcement well.

"Gentlemen," the man bawled. "What seems to be the problem?"

Clayton snorted, shaking his head at the absurdity of their situation. "I think we've got it under control, doc," he said. "This sucker's been shot, though." He gestured with his gun toward Avril. "If you hadn't appeared just now—"

"He might have been in worse condition," Jarod said.

At that, the deputy and Jarod dissolved in laughter, while Cerita and her cohort regarded the pair with a healthy dose of suspicion.

Swiping at his eyes, Jarod crossed to the plucky, yet visibly shaken young woman. Cerita flinched but held her ground, and, after a cursory nod to the physician, Jarod turned his attention back to her.

"I'm sorry, miss. Are you all right?" Gently, he touched her throat. Again, she did not recoil.

CHAPTER EIGHT

REUNION

Traffic on PGA Boulevard was even more congested than she remembered, but Tara didn't mind. It was probably an illusion, attributable to an overabundance of sunshine, but everything seemed cleaner here—as if bathed by the light.

Carmine's Trattoria, the restaurant her father had suggested, was a pleasant surprise. With its architecturally simulated, old-world facade, the establishment masqueraded as a modest Tuscan villa. After circling the lot and finally claiming a newly vacated slot, she shifted into park and withdrew a lipstick from her bag, applied a slick of gloss to her lips, and then tossed the golden cylinder in the direction of her purse. Her aim was poor, and the lipstick fell between the seat and the console.

"Oh, hell," Tara muttered. She thrust a hand into the crevice, fingers scrabbling blindly for the cosmetic. Instead, they closed around a small slip of paper. Curious, Tara examined her find. It was a lotto ticket.

Strange.

She couldn't remember the last time she'd sprung for one, but she didn't have time to think about that. Tara crammed the lotto card into her bag and resumed rummaging for her lipstick. Eventually, her efforts were rewarded, and she scrambled out of the car, eager to be on her way, only to be confronted with another dilemma. Where was the entrance to the dining room?

The doorway fronting PGA led to a delicatessen, and once inside, it nearly sidetracked her. The huge deli case, with its tantalizing rounds of sharp pecorino, creamy mascarpone, buffalo mozzarella, and a variety of cured meats, tantalized, but she remained steadfast, continuing on in search of the formal restaurant. Exiting, she made a circuit around the building. There, another surprise awaited her. The rear of the shopping plaza bordered on a bustling marina.

Unprepared for the view, Tara paused to gaze out over the harbor, where stately yachts shared moorings with lesser vessels. The sun was low on the western horizon, and the watercraft—catching and reflecting the last slanting rays—gleamed like pearls against the silvery backdrop of sky and water. How she loved this time of day.

The back of the building opened to a loggia where patio furnishings were arranged beneath a large canvas awning. Tables varied in size from tiny bistros for intimate tête-à-têtes to rounds large enough to accommodate parties of ten. The outdoor seating area opened to the dining room. Glass doors separated the two spaces. Eureka. She'd come the back way, yet somehow managed to stumble upon her destination.

Many of the patrons had chosen to sit outside for an aperitif or a glass of wine, to enjoy the mild evening and the spectacular view. A quick look around told her Earl was not among them. Feeling a twinge of panic, Tara castigated herself for not insisting they make a reservation until her gaze fell upon the bar.

Set against the north wall, it was devoid of windows. No view could compete with that of the marina to the east, but an enormous mirror created the illusion of another portal, offering a reflection of the yacht basin. At that inviting oasis, Tara finally caught sight of her father. Seated on a stool at the end of the bar, he'd been leaning over an unoccupied seat, deep in conversation with a middle-aged couple. He looked rather dashing in his de rigueur blue blazer and khaki trousers. Their eyes met, and he waved her over. Tara grinned and hastened toward him.

Tara hugged him and pecked a bristly, hollowed cheek that smelled of Bay Rum and those disgusting cigarillos he so favored. The man was skin and bones. When she drew away from him, she saw he was tanned and gleaming like polished mahogany. The bit of hair remaining on his scalp was sparse and gray, forming a ring about a freckled pate that was shiny as a speckled sea pebble.

Thoughts of skin cancer flicked through her mind, but Tara held her tongue. It would be a futile exercise to caution her father about the damaging effects of UV. He'd spent nearly a lifetime laboring outside, yet Earl was as likely to apply sunscreen as an ornery old bull gator.

"Tara, look at you. It's wonderful to see you again, sweetheart."

He nodded toward the empty stool. Gamely, Tara climbed up, and Earl resumed his seat beside her.

"What'll it be for the little lady?" the bartender asked.

Tara ordered a glass of the house Sauvignon Blanc and swiveled toward her father. "How's life been treating you?"

"Not too bad."

"What are you up to these days?" She scooped up a handful of peanuts from the small crystal bowl the bartender set before her.

"I'm working on a little kitchen redo in one of my apartments, and I got me another boat I'm fixing up." Earl shrugged. "Hate to admit it, but I'm not as strong as I once was. My damn hands shake so bad, I'm afraid to use the skill saw, and there are always a million things that need looking after in the apartments. I'm not complaining."

"Are all the units rented?"

"All but one, and I'm showing it tomorrow."

Tara took a quick inventory of the dining room and, with a sinking heart, realized it was filled to capacity. "Dad, about dinner—"

"Not to worry, sweetie," Earl said. "We have a table outside." He patted the packet of cigarillos in his breast pocket. "I figured my habit wouldn't bother you out in the fresh air."

"Perfect."

"Yeah, I'm a great guy." Earl slid off the barstool. "Unfortunately, the pipes are working overtime these days. Prostate, you know. It's hell getting old."

Earl dug in his coat pocket, pulled out a few bills, and tossed them onto the bar. "I'll meet you out there." He nodded toward the exterior patio where the stunning view of the yacht basin bathed in the fiery glow cast by the setting sun. Following his gaze, Tara spied an unoccupied table set for two.

"Terrific, I'm starving. I haven't had a decent meal in… I don't know how long."

"I was hoping you'd have an appetite," Earl said. "The food here is magnifico."

As she gazed out over the harbor, Tara let her mind wander. It was incomprehensible to find herself at this juncture in her life, starting over and in Florida of all places.

The host interrupted her reverie. "Your table's ready," he said. Tara slipped off her stool and followed him. Sneaking up behind her, and with perfect timing, Earl slid her chair out. "Prego, Senora."

Once they were settled and menus presented, Earl lit a cigarillo. A plume of smoke engulfed him momentarily and then dissipated, but the acrid aroma lingered. As a child, that act had always conjured images of a smoke-breathing dragon. Now, she merely found it irritating.

Tara wrinkled her nose. "After Mom, I would have thought…" Her voice trailed off.

Earl inhaled deeply. "I know," he said, as smoke curled out of his nostrils. "Believe me. I've tried to quit, but I've been smoking since I was twelve. Same time I started driving."

"You drove when you were twelve?" Tara had never heard that particular tidbit. It would have been immensely helpful to know at sixteen, when she'd wheedled for permission to take the family car, that her father had already been driving four years at her age.

"Had to. Drove a truck on the farm, hauling potatoes. All us kids did. Never thought much of it. It was just work."

"You had it pretty rough, didn't you?" Tara was eager to learn more about this taciturn man whose genes she shared.

"Nah. Wasn't abused if that's what you're getting at. Nobody beat us or anything. We were just ignored. Grandpa did the best he could. Your grandma was sick—suffered from depression, I guess. Dad didn't have any…What do you call it? Parenting skills. At least we had food. There was always something to eat on the farm. Maybe our beds weren't made, and we'd go to them dirty and bone tired at night, but we didn't know any better."

"Gosh, I'm sorry."

Earl ground out the cigarillo and picked up his menu. "I think I'm just too old to change. I don't have much of a social life, never sailed away on one of those fancy cruises everybody goes on about. Don't spend afternoons on the golf course or have the pleasure of driving a new Cadillac. I don't encourage any lady friends. Don't want any. My one vice is smoking. I know it's not good for me, but I'm hooked. Maybe it'll kill me like it did your mother. If that's so, then I'm sorry."

He swirled the ice in his glass, and then took a generous swig. "Since I'm spilling my guts here," Earl winked at her. "I admit to a fondness for this particular elixir." He raised his glass. "Tara, my dear, a man's got to have some vice in his life. Otherwise, he might as well be the Dalai Lama." Earl set his glass down and perused the bill of fare.

Tara stared at him, dumbfounded. Never had she been privy to such a revealing discourse from her taciturn father.

Earl lowered the menu and smiled roguishly. "Sweetheart, this is just about all the fun I can muster."

"I know, Dad. I love you, too."

They'd eaten their way through snow crab claw appetizers and parmesan-crusted grouper entrees. Now, they sat in companionable silence. Earl's chair was pushed away from the table, and he was lighting yet another cigarillo.

Tara gazed out over the marina feeling replete and content. The inky water of the bay had taken on a marbled appearance, iridescent swirls of reflected, multi-colored light glimmering on its surface. Carmine Giordano's really knew how to do it, Tara thought. From the impeccable service to the warm ambiance, to the extraordinary food, the dining experience was perfection.

She watched as her father blew smoke rings toward the harbor, remembering how, as a little girl, that particular trick had always seemed magical to her. Although the magic was gone and she abhorred his habit, Tara couldn't help but admire Earl's skill. When he turned to her, she was prepared for the questions that had hung, unvoiced, between them.

"How are you doing?" he asked.

"I'm moving forward," Tara said. "I was numb for a while. I think that's a defense mechanism, you know?" Earl nodded. Tara propped her elbows on the table and cupped her chin in her hands. "I've come to terms with it. It's a different life. Not what I expected, but at least I know I'll be okay. For a while, I wasn't so sure."

"You've been through a lot."

"Yes, and the break-in on top of everything else."

"The police never unearthed any leads?"

Tara shook her head. "I just want to forget about it."

Earl jiggled the dregs of ice in his glass before downing the last of his bourbon. "Heard from Jack?"

"We keep in touch. As soon as the divorce was final, he moved in with Desiree."

"That sonofabitch."

"It's no use being angry. I'm not anymore. Such a classic scenario, it's almost funny. Take one successful, middle-aged businessman, add one blonde bimbo secretary, mix well, and simmer until the goose—that's me, by the way—is cooked. Standard recipe for marital disaster."

"How's Josh taking it?"

"Pretty hard. I worry about him."

"Will he be all right?"

"He's got a lot on his plate—adjusting to university life, living away from home for the first time…"

"So, what's the good news?"

Tara smiled. "He's looking forward to spending spring break in Florida with a few of his pals."

"I'll bet he is." Earl held his empty glass up to a passing waiter, silently requesting a refill. "And what are your plans?"

The stars had come out, a scattering of pinpricks in a black velvet sky, and a soft breeze caressed the palm fronds, seductively.

Tara turned back to her father. "I've been so preoccupied with getting Josh settled on campus and my own move, I really didn't have time to think about it much. Now things seem to be falling into place. My house needs a lot of work, but it's located in a very desirable location, and most all of the houses in the area are either new or have been completely renovated. I picked the property up for a song, and I think it's going to prove a sound investment."

"You chose well. I drove by to see it a couple weeks ago. Nice neighborhood. Just let me know how I can help. I haven't forgotten how to swing a hammer."

"Why don't you come up some time next week? I'll fix us some lunch, and you can get a better look at the place, maybe give me some advice on how best to proceed. Quite frankly, Dad, I find the prospect of renovating overwhelming."

"You're on."

Tara fixed her eyes on the yacht basin. A three-quarter moon pressed against the night sky like a glimmering thumbprint. Lights twinkled from inside vessels moored to pilings. It was hard to believe it was December. She turned back to her father. "One more thing, I'm going to offer private piano lessons again."

"That-a girl."

By the time Tara pulled back out onto PGA Boulevard, she felt her life surging ahead. It was as though, with the turn of a page, a new chapter had begun, and what had seemed a predictable plot had suddenly veered off in a completely unforeseen direction. She felt the faint stirrings of hope and was suddenly eager to get on with it.

CHAPTER NINE

THE REIGNING QUEEN

Dulcie Woodward smacked the gavel down on the podium, and the Riverside Theatre Board Meeting adjourned. A gabble of voices erupted as Dulcie rose from her seat, eyes fixed on Nathan's retreating figure. Several board members sought to sidetrack her, but she was hot on Nate's trail.

"Sorry, have to go," she said, deflecting them. "Call me." Dulcie scrambled to catch up with Nathan, and luck was with her. He'd paused in the lobby to check the messages on his cellphone. Dulcie slithered up to him, seamlessly linking her arm in his. "Darling," she purred. "Walk with me."

Nathan allowed himself to be steered toward the main exit. "To what do I owe this honor?" he asked, arching a brow.

"Nathan," Dulcie breathed, huskily. "I have a proposition."

"Be still my beating heart," Nathan chuckled. "This, after how many years of cat-and-mouse?"

Dulcie ignored his comment. "You must co-chair the Beaux Arts Ball with me."

"Forget it. I don't have the requisite time, energy, or brown-nosing skills to chair an event. God knows I don't have the patience."

"Dearest, the committee will do the work, and I'll do all the brown-nosing."

"You're so good at it." Nathan squeezed her arm.

"All you'll need to do is to be charming and bask in the glory, as usual. It's certainly worked for you in the past."

"Dulcie Woodard, you are a persuasive minx." Nathan planted a kiss on her forehead. "I suppose I'll have to find a date."

"I wouldn't think that too difficult. They must be beating down your doors."

"Of course, I'd ask you, but people are already talking."

"Don't toy with me, Nate," Dulcie chided, secretly wishing he'd do just that. "Just find someone more suitable than that tramp you've taken up with. She's a gold-digger, and you're a fool not to see it."

"That's a bit harsh. What do you have against her?"

Annoyed, Dulcie threw an arm in the air. "I don't trust that skinny-assed trollop and neither should you. She's trouble. You'd realize that if you weren't, in such typical male fashion, thinking with your—"

"Ms. Woodard!" Nathan feigned a look of horror.

"Get yourself a woman in your league. That's all I ask." Dulcie fished in her Versace bag for keys to the Mercedes parked on the curb. "By that, I mean someone more age-appropriate with a *little* class and do agree to co-chair the ball with me. In exchange, I'll see to it that McCourt Enterprises gets lots of lovely, free publicity."

Nathan held the door for her. "Yes, ma'am," he drawled, watching as she seated herself behind the steering wheel and pressed the ignition.

"See to it that you do." The Benz roared to life, tires screeching on pavement.

~

Startled, Nathan leapt back onto the sidewalk. The queen bee was riled. In his mind's eye, he conjured Dulcie's face—one that had been lifted so many times there was no softness to it. The surgeon had done her a disservice. She looked harder than she was. Which set him thinking. Do people really see each other for what they are, he mused.

That truth taken a step further, made him wonder if there was something to Dulcie's assessment of his attractive assistant. In the next moment, he dismissed that thought. Dulcie was simply jealous of Gloria's youth. It was the one thing her money couldn't buy. For all her shortcomings, she'd been good to him. He'd co-chair the ball. Furthermore, he'd arrive at that function with someone other than Gloria on his arm. Nathan recalled this morning's interlude—Gloria's lithe body pressed against his. Their lovemaking had been off the charts, all the more so given its spontaneity, and yet there was something not quite right. How had Gloria managed to gain access to his private bath? He hadn't given her a key.

Nathan, who had always managed to separate business from his personal life, felt the lines blurring. He didn't completely trust Gloria, and he was uncomfortable with the idea of her having unlimited access to his office and personal files. Then, he chided himself for being overly cautious. It all boiled down to his fear of intimacy. He didn't want to let her in, to let anyone in, for that matter. He'd simply grown accustomed to keeping his emotions in check, becoming a master at remaining closed off. How could he allow himself to have feelings for another when he continued to hold a torch for Elisa? There was a hole in his heart that no one else could fill. That's what he'd been telling himself all these years.

Then a radical thought occurred to him. Perhaps it was time to put himself out there and risk heartache again. It had been ten long, empty years since Elisa's passing, and a part of him had died with her. He was ready to live again, damn it. He was not going to feel guilty about Gloria. Wasn't she just about the best thing to happen to him in a long time? Here he was trying to second guess her every move. Well, no more of that.

Screw the queen bee.

CHAPTER TEN

THE CONTRACT

The two men melting in a desolate stretch of swampland west of Lake Okeechobee made an unlikely pair. Melvin Combs was rail-thin, his flannel shirt sweat-stained, boots caked with dried mud. Lucas Dawson was beefy, fine features crowded into the center of a wide face, with a body bursting at the seams of an immaculate and fastidiously pressed gray uniform.

When the drone of an airplane distinguished itself over the incessant whirr of insects, they craned their necks in tandem. Furrowing a deeply tanned brow, Combs squinted into the harsh glare of the afternoon sun. "Thar she is."

Dawson's reflective glasses were full of white clouds and blue sky. "If you don't start wearing shades, you're gonna get cataracts."

Extending his neck like a cormorant, Melvin hawked a wad of chewing tobacco into the bush. "Assuming I live that long."

The stout lawman raised his eyebrows, considering the life expectancy of his partner. "How many years we been doing this?"

"I dunno…a couple. Why?"

"Demand is drying up. People want pills, oxies, roxies, Xanax."

"Hell, there's plenty who still want this crap." The unkempt fellow jerked his head in the direction of the approaching plane. "You want out or sumthin'?"

Lucas cut his eyes to his companion. "Do you?"

"What're you trying to say?"

"I'm saying we've got a nice little thing going here. You don't want that to change. Do you?"

The grubby creature dug a small metal cylinder from his filthy shirt pocket and pried it open. He pinched a wad of tobacco, popped it between the bitter lines of his permanently down-turned mouth, then slowly pivoted to face the cop. "Get to the point, why don't you."

"There's something I want you to do for me." Dawson retrieved a wallet from his back pocket and withdrew a small photograph. "You recognize this creep?" He held the image before his cohort.

Combs eyed the photo. "I've dealt with him on occasion. He's small time, clean-cut, a preppy boy."

"I want him dead."

"Why? What did he do?"

"He killed my nephew. The kid was a little light on his feet. You know what I mean? But a hell of a young man, with a great future ahead of him. This punk..." Dawson held the photo up to the thin man's face. "He was selling him heroin laced with fentanyl. The kid died of an overdose. My sister's a fuckin' basket case."

"You can't pull it off?"

"Too obvious. They'd tie me to it in a heartbeat. You've got to do it."

"Like hell——" The retort died in Melvin's throat when a ham hock of a paw clamped on his shoulder.

"Make it happen. I'm sure you'll find a way." The officer looked hard at the tattered scarecrow. "Then we can just keep on like we've been, till nobody wants the white powder anymore. Catch my drift?"

Combs stared back at him, but all he saw was his own vile reflection in the fat man's silvery shades. He shrugged. "Whatever you say." His words were lost in the roar of the single-engine falling out of the sky. The trim Beechcraft Bonanza leveled out over the narrow runway bisecting the cane field. It bobbled as its wheels bounced on the scorching tarmac, then righted itself and braked.

Dawson clapped the husk of a human being on his narrow back and grinned, but it was all false bonhomie. "Good," he said, ambling toward the plane. "Now, let's go do some bidness."

~

The day seemed overly long and no wonder. After biology class, Cerita had done another stint at the E.R. and was on her feet for the duration. Now that quitting time had rolled around, she'd gotten her second wind, and she was ready for some action.

"Where do you want to go?" Tamika asked as the two climbed into Cerita's Toyota.

"I thought we'd head over the causeway to the barrier island. It's such a beautiful evening. How about Wave at Costa d' Este?"

"Gloria and Emilio Estefan's place?" Tamika shrugged out of her lab coat and tossed it in the back seat.

"Yeah. Great bar, good music." Cerita unclipped her hair and let it fall loosely to her shoulders. "Besides," she said, scrutinizing her reflection in the visor mirror while digging an eyeliner out of her purse. "That's where I told Jarod we'd be."

"You've got it bad for that guy." Tamika rummaged through her bag for a lipstick.

"When you see him, you'll know why. He's a hunk. I only hope he shows."

Tamika balled her fists and rolled them, singing in Gloria fashion. "Come on, shake your body, baby, do the conga."

Ever since their first meeting, Jarod had been front and center in Cerita's mind. When she'd run into him that morning at the hospital, it had seemed only natural to casually mention that she and Tamika planned on stopping for a drink after work. Now, as she gazed out over the Wave's late-night crowd, she hoped he'd taken the bait, and couldn't keep from glancing at the entrance.

She'd nearly finished her drink—had resigned herself to the fact that he wasn't coming—when she felt a tap on her shoulder. Cerita swiveled around, expecting Jarod.

"Hey there." A slightly built, middle-aged white fellow stood before her. "Care to dance?"

Struggling to keep the disappointment from her face, Cerita shook her head. Then, from over the guy's shoulder, she spotted Jarod. He was sauntering toward her, and her breath caught in her throat. The EMT was even better looking than she'd remembered. "There's my date," she explained, flashing Jarod a dazzling smile.

The man melted into the crowd, which was just as well. Cerita had eyes for Jarod only. Walking tall, projecting an aura of self-confidence, he made his way through the crush of people as though he owned the place. Not cocky, mind you, but no apology there, either. His demeanor alone was enough to make her love him. Was it any wonder her early-warning-defense-system had been knocked out? He was the kind of man she'd always dreamed about—sweet, self-effacing, and bright. She knew Willie would approve.

When Jarod casually draped an arm across the back of her barstool, the gesture was not lost on her. He'd staked his claim. She could feel her heart fluttering against her push-up bra. Maybe she should just topple off the barstool into the poor man's unsuspecting arms. Instead, she flirted shamelessly and ordered another rum punch.

Jarod entertained them all, recounting the unusual circumstances of their first meeting. "I was a mess, sweaty, dog-tired, and cuffed to that cretin." He turned to Cerita. "After that jerk tried to strangle this pretty lady, she was so poised and cool." He placed his index finger under her chin and tilted her head up to meet his eyes.

"It was all an act," Cerita laughed off the compliment.

They danced until the band stopped playing. When Jarod's friend, Darrell, left with Tamika on his arm, Jarod suggested they find a booth and order one of The Wave's signature desserts. The two perused the menu of mouth-watering confections, taking turns reading the descriptions to one another. Finally, they decided on the Bombon Cubano, a dense flourless chocolate cake with a liquid ganache center, and two espressos. When the dessert arrived, there were two spoons and, accompanying it, two tiny cups of intensely strong coffee.

While she ate, the significance of the small repast struck her: Jarod was looking out for her, seeing that she had a little something to eat and a jolt of caffeine in her system before climbing behind the wheel. That's how considerate he was. Cerita's malaise vanished, and she felt young and alive again, and magically connected to this wonderful man.

~

The door to her mother's bedroom was ajar, and Cerita peeked inside as she crept past. The blinds were drawn and the room was dark, but she could make out Willie's form. Sprawled upon her back, she was snoring like a basset hound with a deviated septum. Cerita stifled a giggle before gently closing the door. Her poor mother deserved a good rest at the end of the day.

Willie's physical appearance had always bothered Cerita, but now she was more concerned about her mother's health. The excess pounds increased her risk for heart attack, stroke, diabetes, and every deadly virus out there. Cerita made a snap decision. Tomorrow, Mom was going to be introduced to the joys of healthy eating. As a healthcare provider, it was her duty to start Willie on a path to a healthier lifestyle.

Cerita tip-toed across the tiny living area toward her room, had nearly reached the doorway when, from the corner of her eye, she detected movement. Someone was behind her, lurking in the shadows. Suddenly, Cerita's knees grew weak and her heart lodged in her throat. She'd locked the front door. Who was there? Her eyes darted about the room, seeking a weapon. Nothing! In desperation, she waved her arms about, and her hand brushed against one of the family photographs. Encased in glass, it was hanging on the wall above her. The metal frame was insubstantial, but its corners were sharp. She dislodged the portrait, holding it before her like a shield.

Great, she thought. How much damage can I possibly inflict by beating someone with a picture of Granny on her wedding day?

Wielding the makeshift weapon before her, Cerita turned toward the living room. It was difficult to make out objects in the gloom, but the furnishings were so familiar, she immediately sensed something out of place. Then, she spied a strange shape in the far corner.

"Who's there?" Cerita croaked, her voice tight with fear. Holding the picture frame in one hand, her fingers scrabbled along the corridor wall for the light switch. When they found the toggle, the room was flooded with light, and Cerita breathed a sigh of relief. Seated in a rocking chair in the corner was the wizened figure of her grandmother.

Like her daughter, Willie Mae, Bertha Brown had once been a large woman. As the years advanced, however, her bulk had diminished until the flesh hung on her frame like a deflated balloon on a stick. Now, looking like an apparition, she rocked back and forth, eyes focused inward on a landscape to which only she was privy.

With shaking hands, Cerita replaced the photograph on the wall, before turning to confront the old woman. "Granny, what are you doing sitting here in the dark? You nearly frightened me to death." Cerita crossed to the ghost-like figure. "Did you hear me, Gran?" She hunkered down, coming eye level with the silent woman. "Why aren't you in bed?"

Gently, Cerita took the woman's claw-like hands in hers. "Let's get you back to your room."

Bertha mumbled an incomprehensible reply.

Cerita was fast losing patience. "Get up, Granny," she implored. It was past one in the morning, and her alcohol-induced good humor had been replaced with an aching weariness and a throbbing head.

After much coaxing, Cerita managed to help her grandmother up and out of the chair. As she closed the door to Bertha's room, the old woman, in a moment of near lucidity, called out to her. "You're a good daughter, Willie Mae."

"Thanks, Granny," Cerita said. "Sweet dreams."

In the morning, Cerita awoke to sticky dampness between her legs. "Damn," she groaned. She felt like hell, and here she'd gotten the curse again. It wasn't fair. Hadn't her last period been just two weeks ago? When she pulled the covers aside and saw the amount of blood that had leaked from her body, she felt lightheaded. Gathering up the sheets, she pressed the bedclothes between her thighs, preparing to make a dash for the bathroom. Woozily, she swung her legs over the edge of the bed and placed her feet on the floor. Before she could take a step, her knees buckled, and she collapsed back onto the mattress. Sweet Jesus. She was weak as a baby. She lay there for a moment waiting for the blood to rush back to her head. Gosh, she really must have tied one on last night.

CHAPTER ELEVEN

FOUR GENERATIONS

Scottly locked the front door and backtracked through the showroom, switching off the overhead lights as he went. He left a few strategically placed table lamps lit. It was season, and he hoped to attract the attention of pedestrians strolling by on their way to dinner at one of the many fine establishments along Ocean Drive. Perhaps they'd pause in front of his shop, lingering to gaze through the plate-glass windows at the artfully arranged vignettes he'd created. He'd landed more than one lucrative design project from just such serendipity.

As Scottly performed these small tasks, his mind was racing with myriad details involved in preparing for one of Vero's biggest bashes of the season, the Beaux-Arts Ball. Dulcie Woodard was the cause of his current distraction. Not more than ten minutes ago, she'd called to deliver the good news in her typical, rapid-fire fashion. She and Nathan were co-chairing the ball, and wouldn't it be divine if Scottly would agree to plan and coordinate the entire event?

Would he? You betcha! Scottly was thrilled at the prospect of strutting his stuff for a select group of potential clients, and he couldn't be more delighted with the theme for this year's gala: Mardi Gras. What fun he'd have designing garish costumes, glitzy invitations, and party favors, to say nothing of glittering table settings for the Treasure Coast glitterati. He couldn't wait to get home and share the good news with Kev.

Scottly made his way toward the back exit, pausing to admire a group of porcelain figurines he'd recently acquired. The miniature collectibles were of Italian origin, a menagerie of life-like replicas cunningly rendered. He'd displayed them atop an ornately carved credenza, certain they'd be quickly snatched up by both collectors and animal lovers alike. His instincts had been spot-on. Of the original dozen, only five remained. Struck by an idea, Scottly palmed the teeny Yorkshire terrier and crossed to the front desk. This little fellow would make a perfect housewarming token for a certain someone. He wrapped the figurine in tissue and deposited it in a small gift satchel embossed with his own Island Home Interiors logo, a chambered nautilus shell, nature's perfect home.

Scottly's face fell when the garage door hitched up, and he found the bay empty. Only then did he remember it was Thursday, the one night of the week when Scandals Salon stayed open late to accommodate the working girls, those not fortunate enough to have booked a much sought-after Saturday appointment.

"Darn it!" he cursed softly.

Kevin wouldn't be back until late, and here he was fairly bursting with news. The thought of knocking around alone all evening held no appeal. Why not drop in on his new neighbor and present her with his gift? He was dying for company, and it seemed the neighborly thing to do.

"What a nice surprise." Tara motioned for him to enter, all the while struggling to contain the wriggling bundle who was demanding to be released. "Chanel, stop it."

"Are you sure I'm not intruding?" Scottly hesitated in the doorway.

"Absolutely. Please come in." Tara led the way to the living room.

As he followed her into the large, airy space, Scottly gazed about with a practiced eye, taking in the bungalow's inherent good features as well as its flaws. Then his gaze fell on the baby grand. "Ah, you play." He nodded toward the piano.

"I do. I also teach. Would you like to take a quick peek at the rest of the house?"

"Love to."

When they returned to the living room, Tara gestured toward the sofa. "Have a seat."

"I can only stay a minute." He perched on the edge of a seat cushion.

"May I get you something to drink? Iced tea? A glass of wine?"

"No, thanks." Scottly's eyes returned to the piano. "I always wanted to play," he confided a wistful note to his voice.

"It's never too late. I could give you some lessons. Mastering piano simply requires lots of practice."

The squirming terrier in Tara's arms whined pathetically." All right," she said, giving Chanel a squeeze. "I'll let you down if you'll be good."

Tara smiled an apology. "Do you mind? He'll be all over you as soon as I release him. Not that he'd bite. He just wants to get to know you."

"Of course. I love animals," Scottly dissembled, for nothing could have been farther from the truth. He'd been terrified of dogs since childhood. Ironically, dogs, cats—all animals for that matter—adored him. The little canine proved no exception. He shot out of Tara's arms like a torpedo, making a beeline toward him. Rubbing against Scottly's chinos, he alternately licked his pant cuffs and the soft leather of his loafers.

"I believe he remembers his rescuer."

In spite of his aversion to animals, this little furball was not without his charms. Scottly couldn't help but chuckle at the Yorkie's persistence.

Clutching the gift bag in one hand, he tentatively patted the dog's head with the other. "I've brought you a little housewarming present," he said, rising to his feet.

"You shouldn't have." Tara accepted the bag and withdrew the small object within. "I can't believe it," she exclaimed, holding the trinket in her hand. "It looks just like Chanel, floppy ear and all. Thank you so much, Scottly. Where on earth did you ever find it? It's absolutely perfect."

"I could tell a little white lie and say I'd spent hours searching for just the right thing," he admitted. "The truth is it's from my shop."

"You own a shop? Really?"

"Yes, Island Home Interiors. Just a small studio on Ocean Drive."

"I *am* impressed. You're an interior designer?"

"Madam, I confess." Scottly bowed, theatrically, before resuming his seat.

Tara placed the miniature figurine on an end table, stood away and beamed at it. Then she turned to her guest. "Thank you, Jesus," she exclaimed. "Please say you'll help me with this place." Waving her arms about, she encompassed the room. "I certainly wouldn't be one of your wealthier clients, but I'm willing to pay whatever it takes."

Scottly paused for a beat before saying, "I'd be delighted to help, and don't worry about the money. As long as you've got a bit of it, we can resurrect this old lady."

"Do you really think so?"

"She has good bones. Just needs a little lift."

"Don't we all?"

"I have an idea. Why don't we discuss this over cocktails at my place?"

Tara tucked a strand of hair behind her ear "Lovely. When?"

"No time like the present. How does this evening suit you? Seven o'clock?"

"Will there be other guests?"

"Just us...and my partner, Kevin. If he turns up. But I must warn you, it's to be a celebration of sorts." Scottly gained his legs. "Please, you must come to mark the occasion."

"You don't have to twist my arm. Beats hanging around here all by myself. What are we celebrating?"

"Not to worry, no birthday or anything like that. Just good news." Scottly crossed to the door. "You'll have to wait to find out."

Chanel trotted behind his newfound friend, and Tara gathered the dog in her arms before he could escape with her guest.

"Ta-ta." Scottly opened the door and was about to depart when a thought occurred. Turning back to Tara, he said, "I think you'll get a kick out of my house. It wasn't all that different from this one before I renovated it."

"I'm dying to see it. Thanks again. I'll be there at seven."

While washing her face at the cracked porcelain sink in her dreary bathroom, Tara marveled at her sudden good fortune. Her head was awhirl with ideas for a renovation. Scottly had concurred with each of Earl's suggestions. In the words of the designer, the kitchen and baths were destined for a "complete gut." He'd deemed the back porch unsalvageable, recommending the enclosure be torn down and rebuilt, and he'd urged her to have a new wing constructed for a larger master suite. It was all very exciting. Having only just gotten settled, she'd now have to pack her things back up again, but that seemed inconsequential. She could hardly wait to get started.

The biggest surprise of the evening had been when the darkly handsome hairdresser made his entrance. Kevin was not at all what she'd imagined. He was charming, she begrudged, in a prickly sort of way, and, although his smile belied the fact, Tara suspected he'd been none too pleased to find her sharing a glass of bubbly with his housemate. Perhaps he'd been jealous? In the next moment, she dismissed that thought. Scottly was so obviously smitten with Kevin, she couldn't imagine anyone coming between the two, lest it be Kevin himself. The man was entirely too slick for her taste.

Slippery as an eel, her father would have said.

Tara gazed at her reflection in the mirror and chided herself for her unfounded suspicions. Her neighbor's relationship was none of her business. Yet, in the short time she'd known Scottly, she'd grown fond of him. Never mind the fact that he towered over her, outweighing her two to one. He was a gentle giant and, she feared, a vulnerable one. The man brought out her maternal instincts, and she felt oddly protective of him. He was so openly candid, neither compromising nor making excuses for himself, a thoroughly elegant and extraordinary man.

She smiled as she recalled Scottly's words, "*One must be sensitive to the integrity of the individual structure.*"

After switching off the overhead light, Tara climbed into bed and, for the first time in many weeks, was asleep almost instantly.

Chanel lay curled beside her, his little legs twitching. In his dreams, he was running toward his new best friend.

He was a dog with a mission.

~

FULTON COUNTY NEWS
WINNING LOTTO TICKET UNCLAIMED

Someone won twelve million bucks. Unfortunately, the person has not claimed the prize from the October 15th Mega Millions drawing. The Georgia Lottery sent out a reminder that the person with the winning ticket has 262 days from the day of the drawing to claim the prize. The winning ticket, which matched the five numbers but missed the mega ball, was purchased at the 7-Eleven Convenience Store located at 400 W. Pike Street in Lawrenceville. The five numbers on the winning ticket were 4, 11, 37, 51, and 69. The mega ball was 18. Gina Harris, special games and promotions drawings manager for the Georgia Lottery and Gaming, said that in her 20 years, it's been "very, very rare for a prize this size to go unclaimed."

~

It had been years since he'd dreamt of Nam, but the nightmares had returned. Rick was finding himself back in that hellhole with alarming regularity, a phenomenon attributed to his recent activities. Eric's murder was one thing, but that business with the kid's old lady, donning the gear—the black clothing, ski mask, and gloves —*that* had reawakened the blood lust. Then he'd gotten pumped up for a repeat performance at the house in Laurel Oaks. It had been a trip, sneaking past the security guard, approaching the house under the cover of darkness. His heart had pounded, and not only in anticipation but from exertion as well.

He'd checked out all the other possible candidates—every model and color in the service center that night—in case his memory didn't serve him. Only one white sedan was being serviced at the time he'd come upon Eric making love to a lottery ticket, and he was certain that was the car he'd seen him in. The broad had it, all right. He'd phoned her a few days before the break-in, and it had been a crushing disappointment to find the garage empty, the house unoccupied. He'd torn the place apart, to no avail, and now he'd have to follow her to Florida.

There was no real urgency to his mission. He was pretty damn sure she was none the wiser. Still, the sooner Connor had the surgery, the better. Rick wanted to be done with this business, to reclaim his life, one that included Sally and the boy. He turned to his PC, keyed in *www.travelocity.com*, and began checking out flights to Orlando.

CHAPTER TWELVE

LEMON DROPS

This Saturday morning was like a thousand others at the Lemon Tree. At least that's what Charlene McKenzie thought before all hell broke loose. She hefted a huge tray piled high with orders of Belgian waffles, pancakes, and eggs of every complexion. In one small palm, she balanced six breakfasts high over her head and sailed out into the dining room. There, she spied her daughter, Grace, nimbly flitting about filling water glasses.

As she hiked back to the kitchen, Charlene passed a pair of teenaged girls seated at Linda's station. She pegged them for St. Ted's students and was happy to think that Grace would have a chance to interact with fellow classmates. Grace was a good girl, and, given her clear skin and mass of red hair, she'd grown into quite a beauty. She was also highly motivated—active in both the Student Council and the National Honor Society, and a star athlete as well. There wasn't anything the girl put her mind to that she didn't make a success of.

Charlene hoped this position at the restaurant might work into something more permanent for her daughter. It would be a load off her mind just knowing Grace had a bit of security with a good-paying job, one that she could step into over semester breaks and summer vacations. Charlene didn't doubt Grace would score full rides at any state institution to which she applied. She'd received scholarships to several summer sports camps in the Northeast and become intoxicated by the rarified atmosphere permeating tree-lined walkways and hallowed halls of learning. Wouldn't you know? In short order, she'd decided state university was not for her. No. The kid wanted Ivy League.

When Charlene grumbled about it, her co-worker, Linda, joked that things could be worse. At least her kids weren't hoodlums or drug addicts, she'd said. Which was true, Charlene granted, but intelligence and ambition demanded their own price. She'd filled out the endless forms applying for financial aid packages, ferreted out scholarships and grants, spent hours behind the wheel driving her children to lacrosse and soccer practices, theater groups, and music lessons, gladly doing whatever it took to ensure her humble circumstances never precluded the advancement of her offspring.

As if that weren't enough of a challenge, the diner demanded something extra of its staff. She'd had to keep up her hours or risk losing her job. Anybody who'd lasted at the Lemon Tree attributed their tenure to an uncanny, almost prescient, ability to anticipate the customer's desires. No matter what went on behind the scenes, they were *always* to be polite and attentive to the patrons.

~

Jennifer and Hillary had their heads together when Grace strode toward them. "Hey, guys. What's up?" Grace asked.

"Grace, I didn't know you worked here," Jennifer said. "Cool."

"Mostly weekends. At least I don't have to work nights."

"Right." Hillary said. "Wouldn't want to cut into your social life."

"Ha!" Grace exclaimed. "What social life? Sports and homework, that's all there's time for. You know that." She turned to go.

"Yeah, we know." Jennifer answered. "Somehow you managed to save a little time on the side for Coach Brandon. Isn't that right, Grace?"

"Gee, I thought Mr. Brandon was engaged," Hillary piped in. "Don't tell me you and Coach?" Hillary's hand flew to her mouth.

The fact that she wasn't much of an actress was not lost on Grace.

"He's a little old, don't you think?" Jennifer asked. "Goodness me, Saint Grace. Who would have believed?"

Blindsided, Grace was momentarily speechless, but her red-hot temper flared as she pivoted back to face her tormentors.

≈

Horrified, Charlene watched as her daughter lifted a carafe of ice water over the heads of the two girls seated in the booth. So completely unexpected, so out of the range of normal, it took her a minute to process. "Jesus, Mary, and Joseph," she prayed. "Don't let her do it."

Time lagged, and Grace seemed to move in slow motion. Heads turned and conversation ceased, as all eyes fastened on the little redhead who was, to the amazement and secret delight of the Lemon Tree's patrons, holding a pitcher of water suspended over those darling St. Ted's girls.

"Holy Mother of God," Charlene pleaded silently, "please stop her."

Like a dog chasing its tail, time sped up, and the water flowed. The two girls shrieked as they were summarily drenched. Grace offered not a word of apology. Rather, with a face rapidly becoming as crimson as her hair, she turned on her heel and fled to the kitchen.

Charlene was aghast. What the heck had brought that on? She wouldn't be surprised if Jon fired the girl on the spot.

Jennifer and Hillary, now dripping and incensed, created quite a spectacle. They bounded from their seats and, looking like native dancers, hopped first on one foot, then the other, while plucking ice chips from their hair and flinging them to the floor.

Jason, the busboy—his hormones flagging him on to new and exhilarating heights—was more than eager to assist. He rushed over with a handful of napkins to sop up the spill, stealing sidelong glances at nubile breasts suddenly visible through clinging clothing. At one point, the kid made an attempt to blot one of the girl's blouses, but he was fixed with such a withering glare, he hastily gave up the effort.

There was nothing for Jennifer and Hillary to do but snatch up their handbags and flee the premises. Which was exactly what they did, leaving a damp, telltale trail of footprints behind them. The wealthy brats hadn't paid for their meals, but no one followed after them or much cared for that matter.

⁓

Throughout the commotion, the kitchen staff hadn't missed a beat.

Grace sobbed loudly into a towel, the delicate skin of her face mottled, trails of mascara running down her cheeks.

Linda, who'd always had a soft spot for Charlene's youngest, patted the heaving shoulders of the disconsolate teen. She raised an eyebrow, silently mouthing to her cohort, "What gives?"

Mystified, Charlene shook her head. "Grace, for heaven's sake, what's gotten into you? You should be ashamed of yourself!"

"Leave me alone." Grace sniffed and swiped at her eyes. "You don't know anything about anything."

"Come on, honey, don't talk to your old ma like that," Linda coaxed. "Tell Auntie Lin what happened."

"Those two girls are the biggest bitches at St. Ted's. They're awful, and I hate them."

"Grace McKenzie, you hold your tongue, or I swear, I'll wash your mouth out. Those little girls looked sweet."

"At least they did until you baptized them, Gracie," Linda said. "Then the sugar-coating melted, and the bitches hiding underneath were plain to see, all right."

Grace's sobs turned into tentative, hiccupping giggles.

"Whose side are you on, Linda?" Charlene hissed.

"Okeydokey, ladies," Jonathon interrupted. "This riveting episode of *Days of Our Lives* will have to be continued at a later date. Food's stacking up, getting cold."

The two women immediately stepped up to the line and filled trays.

"Grace," Charlene called over her shoulder. "Wipe your face, and then get back out there. We'll talk about this later, missy."

"Let's not pitch anything more today, okay, Grace?" Jonathon added. "We're here to feed people, not to christen them."

Charlene glanced up, meeting Jonathon's eyes. He grinned at

her, and, although his voice had been stern, she figured he was teasing. Charlene's faith in humanity chalked up a notch. Relieved, she rolled her eyes. Kids. They'd be the death of her.

"Sorry, for the trouble, Jon. It won't happen again."

Traipsing into the dining room with her heavily laden tray, Charlene came to stop before a table where three elderly ladies were seated. "Here you go, dears." She sat a plate of scrambled eggs and sausage before Ms. Elizabeth Terry, the more formidable looking of the trio.

Terry and her two companions were regulars, and Charlene had been waiting on them for a decade or more. She was well aware of Terry's civic involvement. A longstanding Trustee of the Beach Bank, she'd also served two distinguished terms as mayor of Vero Beach and was now the current chair of the Cultural Arts Council. There'd even been talk of naming a main thoroughfare after her. Except for her stern demeanor she and her two companions looked so alike they could have been siblings—each of them with their tightly permed, gray hair, wearing mannish clothing and sensible, rubber-soled shoes. Terry was a crusty character, but Charlene was fond of her. She admired the old bird's mover-shaker drive and no-nonsense attitude.

"Tell me, Charlene," Ms. Terry said, generously salting her eggs, "has Grace decided on a university?"

Charlene set plates of fried eggs and sides in front of Ms. Terry's lady friends. "She has her heart set on attending some fancy private school up north, which, as you know, we couldn't possibly afford."

"I'm aware of that fact," Ms. Terry replied. "That's why I've decided she must apply to Wellesley. Has she done that?"

"We've talked about Wellesley." Charlene pivoted, snagged a bottle of ketchup from an adjoining table, and placed it in front of Ms. Terry. "Grace attended lacrosse camp there last summer. She fell in love with the campus, but, no, she hasn't applied there. Why do you ask?"

"I believe it would be in your daughter's best interest to do so. The girl has brains and pluck, and I think she might well land a scholarship to Wellesley."

Was the woman toying with her? If that were the case, she was much too busy to waste another precious moment. Charlene eyed the table, making sure the three ladies had everything they needed. "Do you really think so?"

"I do indeed." Ms. Terry smiled smugly. "You might say I heard it from the horse's mouth, from my good friend. Alfredia Abbott, that is."

The woman on Ms. Terry's right stirred sweetener into her coffee. "Don't imagine Frieda would much like being compared to a horse," she chortled. "Although she is a bit horsy-looking."

Ignoring the interruption, Ms. Terry speared a sausage link. "Abbott Laboratories," she said, cryptically. "You've heard of them?"

All three women looked up at Charlene, and the waitress suddenly felt giddy. It was as if they'd been planning this, for they hung on her response with rapt attention. Charlene was dumbfounded. Surely, they'd witnessed Grace's inexplicable treatment of the two St. Theodore's girls, and yet they were dangling this offer.

"You see, dear, the Abbott family funds an endowment at Wellesley. I believe your daughter would make an excellent candidate, and I made some inquiries. I, myself, am an alumnus of Wellesley, class of '51," she said. "Over the years, I've made many a contribution to my alma mater, which, I reckon, entitles me to pull some weight. I'm delighted to recommend Grace be awarded the J.P. Abbot Foundation Merit Scholarship. For that matter, any scholarship for which she is eligible."

"I don't know what to say," Charlene said, and it was true. She was flabbergasted.

"Make sure the child indicates she wants to be considered for all available scholarships and grants. If Grace does that, I'd be willing to bet her future is secured."

Charlene could hardly believe her good fortune. She'd been on an emotional rollercoaster, riding the highs and lows of this interminable morning. Just as she was flying off the final incline and coasting home, her youngest girl chose to reenter the dining room. Composed and angelic-looking, Grace appeared as though she had not a care in the world.

Charlene couldn't help but notice the effect her daughter's presence had on the breakfast crowd, for all eyes fixed upon her. Seemingly oblivious to the attention, Grace resumed filling water glasses as though nothing untoward had occurred. Gradually, conversations resumed, and the diners turned back to their meals. Jason seemed to stand a little straighter as he went about his duties, surreptitiously stealing looks at Grace.

The girl led a charmed existence, Charlene thought, marveling at the amazing person she'd conceived and reared. Which didn't mean she wasn't eager for an empty nest. She was just about at the end of her rope. Her palms were moist, and she was sliding. Magically, a net had appeared below her. Dear Lord, she prayed, get my Grace to Wellesley.

CHAPTER THIRTEEN

THE INTERVIEW

This was a strange interview, Tara thought, as she ticked off her credentials to the handsome Black woman seated across from her. It was impossible not to let her eyes wander about the study while expounding on her musical training and teaching experience. Although it was a large room, the intricate moldings and paneled walls with their book-matched veneers, made it feel almost cozy. Tara imagined the better part of a small forest having been razed in order for this one room to be constructed.

"May I ask a question, Mrs. Brown?" When the housekeeper nodded, she continued. "Where are the boy's parents?"

"Mr. McCourt, he works all the time." The interviewer shook her head in disapproval. "That man is going to kill himself."

"The mother?"

She pivoted in her chair and peered up at the large oil painting behind her. "Passed," she said, turning back to face Tara. "Poor Mrs. McCourt never had much constitution. She died birthing Harry. That child never even knew his own mama."

Tara studied the gilt-framed portrait mounted on the wall. A fragile-looking blonde gazed out at her with eyes the same silvery shade of blue as the diaphanous gown she wore.

Aha! Here was the rightful mistress of this house, the late and very lovely Mrs. McCourt.

"What a tragedy," she murmured.

"I been caring for him ever since. Miss Jenny, too." She indicated a framed photograph on the desk. "That's me with baby Harry."

"Why you…you're so…" Tara stumbled over her words as it all began to make sense. No wonder the housekeeper appeared so at home. She had every right to be. More than a housekeeper, she was a surrogate mother to the McCourt children.

"Skinny, you mean."

"Younger." Tara brought the conversation back to the business at hand. "What do you say? Have I got the job?"

"I'm sure you'd do fine by Harry," the housekeeper said. "There's just one thing that bothers me."

"What do you mean?" Tara's voice was tremulous. She'd thought it was all going so well—that the position was in the bag. She couldn't bear the thought of one more rejection.

"Why haven't you been teaching these last years?"

"Oh, that!" Tara exhaled a sigh of relief. "My ex-husband became quite successful. He didn't want me to work any longer. We didn't need the money." Tara laced her fingers together, unconsciously feeling for the wedding ring that was no longer there.

"You still play? You haven't forgotten?"

"Oh, no. I mean yes, I play. It's a part of me. Who I am." A note of desperation crept into her voice. "I really need this job. I'm not poverty-stricken or anything, but I could use the income for a number of reasons. Why not give me a try? My students adored me, and their parents did, too. I'm sure you'll be very satisfied."

Mrs. Brown paused to reflect for a moment and then rose from behind the desk. She crossed to the doorway, beckoning for Tara to follow.

As they traversed the palatial great room, the temperature seemed to plummet, and the sound of their footfalls echoed hollowly off the gleaming marble flooring and travertine columns. They entered a corridor leading to a set of double doors. The housekeeper produced a key and unlocked them. Tara peered in, but the room was much too dark to make out anything until Mrs. Brown found the light switch, and the chamber was flooded with light.

Momentarily taken aback, Tara gasped at the sight that greeted her eyes, that of a grand, but intimate, concert hall. The soaring

Palladian windows were covered in heavy damask. The floor was wood plank and polished to a shine. The walls and high ceilings were painted off-white, and except for more extravagant millwork, unadorned. On one end of the room were several rows of gilded, Louis XVI salon-style chairs.

Were they authentic?

Tara's excitement mounted. Two ebony Steinways faced off at the room's center, and they were surrounded by a variety of collector-quality musical instruments. Realization dawned, and Tara's eyes roved about the room. With the exception of the pianos, all of the musical instruments—from the four violins in their cracked leather cases, brittle and crumbling with age, to the solitary golden harp—were antique.

Unaffected by the accustomed grandeur, the housekeeper crossed to the nearer Steinway. "Here you go," she said, lifting the lid of the bench to reveal a storehouse of sheet music. "Take your pick."

Tara thumbed through the collections, eventually settling on the Bach Concerto No.1, D Minor, one of her favorites. She'd performed it many times in the past. Nonetheless, she was as nervous as if she were playing Carnegie Hall.

The Black woman retreated to the back wall and took a seat while Tara arranged the sheet music and mentally prepared for the task at hand. She glanced at the key and time signatures, her fingers moving almost imperceptibly as her eyes raced across the pages of the composition. Tara visualized herself playing the piece perfectly in triple time, and her body pulsed with an internal rhythm of its own. When her fingers attacked the Steinway's yellowed, ivory keys, Mrs. Brown sat up with a start.

Tara's slender body curled over the instrument, and she swayed forward then back again, almost as if she were riding waves of music. Her powerful fingers were all over the keyboard, fashioning lush broken chords that provided a framework for the trilling melody. The theme was introduced, diverged from, and repeated, weaving together the melody, countermelody and chords.

Although there wasn't one, Tara had always imagined a lyric in the cadence. *Stand up straight, now, and don't be late,* it seemed to say. *Life is waiting. You're expected. Be on time.*

~

Willie settled back into her chair and closed her eyes, losing herself in the music. Like a film unreeling, the events of that morning replayed in her mind. Her two grandbabies had bickered nonstop while dawdling over breakfast.

"Bet you're scared, Tyrone," Yvonne taunted.

"Am not!"

"Hush now, Yvonne," Willie said. "You're jealous. Maybe you'll get to perform in the concert next year." Willie placed her hands on the boy's shoulders. "I'm real proud of you, Tyrone. It's an honor to be selected to sing with the chorus. Now finish your—"

"Mama!" Cerita wailed, and Willie's hackles rose. Until that moment it hadn't occurred to her that something had been off with this morning's routine, that Cerita had slept late. The girl had been burning the midnight oil. Who could blame her if she tried to squeeze in a few extra winks?

The two children quieted momentarily. Then Yvonne stuck out her tongue, and the boy nearly choked as he suppressed a giggle. He had a mouthful of grits, and rivulets of cornmeal oozed down his chin.

"Ooo, gross!" Yvonne squealed. "You're a pig!"

Tyrone grunted, Yvonne dissolved in laughter, and they were at it again.

"Enough! Finish your cereal." Willie rose from her chair. "I'll go tend to your mother."

Willie's exasperation turned to horror when she found her daughter, her face ashen, swaying with the effort to remain upright while clutching bloodstained sheets. Willie rushed to Cerita's side and wrapped her arms around her.

"Honey, what's the matter with you?"

"I don't know, Mama. I think I'm hemorrhaging."

"Well, I guess." Willie took the bedclothes from her daughter. "Leave that."

"Don't worry. I'll feel better after I bathe."

Willie put a palm to Cerita's forehead. "Girl, you're on fire. Let me help you to the bath and then I'll call an ambulance."

"Too expensive. Just give me ten minutes to freshen up, and you can drive me."

Willie deposited the soiled bed linens in the laundry tub to soak and then phoned Nathan. "It's Cerita, Mr. McCourt. There's something the matter with her. I have to drive her to the hospital, and I don't think I can be at your place before the kids leave for school."

Over the course of the phone call, Tyrone and Yvonne fell silent. By the time she'd disconnected, the children's eyes were wide with fear.

"Your Mom will be fine," Willie assured them. "Just needs a rest is all."

After presenting them with lunchboxes, she shooed them out the door. Willie lingered in the doorway, watching as the two sprinted off down the street to the bus stop. No need to worry them now, she thought. If Cerita truly were ill, there'd be time enough to break it to them.

The woman at the piano continued her performance, but Willie was focused on the scene that had played out earlier.

It hadn't seemed right leaving Cerita alone at the hospital. She'd felt as though she were abandoning her child. Cerita had insisted she go. From that point on, a feeling of impending doom had wrapped its cold fingers around her heart. She'd been a wreck all afternoon, her stomach in knots while awaiting word of her daughter. When the call finally came, she'd lunged for the phone.

"Hey, Mama." There was a reassuringly sassy note to her daughter's voice. "Just checking in."

Willie plopped into a lounge chair. "Baby, how are you?" Willie fanned herself with a cleaning rag, and dust motes sparkled in the air like miniature stars.

"I've had a barrage of tests, and every OBG man within a five-mile radius and between the ages of twenty-five and sixty, dropped by to take a gander up my snatch. Sure am glad I took a shower and shaved my legs. They all seemed quite taken with the view."

Willie responded with a harrumph.

"Then, they hooked me up to an IV and pumped me full of fluids. There must have been meds in the drip because I fell asleep and didn't wake up until just now. I'm starving, and thirsty, and weak as a baby, but I feel human again."

∼

Tara ended the concerto with a flourish. She'd relished this opportunity to play on such a glorious instrument, and she was certain her playing had been more than satisfactory. With her back to the housekeeper, Tara waited for a response of some sort, but the completion of her performance was met with silence. Bewildered, Tara stole a glance over her shoulder only to find the housekeeper slumped in her chair, head thrown back, mouth agape. She'd fallen asleep.

So much for thunderous applause.

What was the protocol for such a situation? Should she get up and rouse the woman or tiptoe out of the room, let herself out, and call back in the morning? It took only a moment for her to decide. She was too pumped to do anything other than turn back to the keyboard and resume playing.

～

Nathan glanced at the clock on the dashboard. It was early, not yet three, but he'd be flying out on the Gulfstream at the crack of dawn. He had to pack, and he wanted to make an early evening of it. After parking the Porsche in the drive court, he grabbed his briefcase and scrambled up the steps to the front entrance.

He opened the door, only to smack into a wall of sound that stopped him dead in his tracks. Strains of music, emanating from somewhere within the house, enveloped him—captivating him.

What was this?

It was obviously not an NPR broadcast, nor was it one of his own recordings. The piece was familiar, a Bach concerto, and it sounded like a live performance. Nathan was puzzled. How intriguing to be confronted with such mystery. He gave himself over to the music, and the heavy door closed behind him with a muffled thud.

The bass reverberated in his gut with dark, smoky chords, over the top of which skated a crisp melody played in the treble clef. The music drew him to its source, and he found himself standing in the hallway outside the open door to the music room. Strangely, he had no desire to enter or to venture a look within. Instead, he leaned against the corridor wall and let the music wash over him.

Unbidden, thoughts of his wife surfaced, and Nathan thought how ironic it was that this salon—Elisa's dream fulfilled—had never been used for its intended purpose. His young bride had coaxed him to incorporate the grandiose chamber with its excellent acoustics, into the plans for their Palacio del Mar estate. Seeing no need for such excess, Nathan had resisted, but, in an uncharacteristic display of stubbornness, Elisa had insisted. Ultimately, her arguments won him over. She had hoped to host intimate musical gatherings at which they might entertain Nathan's clients and their friends. Now Elisa was gone, and the music room that she had envisioned flooded with light and filled with music, remained, for the most part, shuttered and silent.

Accustomed to scuttling past the chamber's double doors in a vain effort to ignore the emotions inevitably evoked, Nathan stood rooted to the spot. The only people who ever set foot in that room were Willie, painstakingly dusting the priceless instruments as she'd been instructed, and Harry, dutifully practicing his piano lessons at one of the two Steinways. He felt a momentary pang for his son, a lonely little boy making music in a great, empty space. Now the chamber seemed to have come alive with the sort of music for which it had been intended.

~

Tara segued into Rachmaninoff's Third Piano Concerto, and her hands were all over the keys. When at last, she played the final, haunting notes, the housekeeper stood and applauded, crying, "Bravo."

Pivoting on the piano bench, Tara bowed her head in silent acknowledgment.

"Lawd, Ms. Cahill, you sure can play."

"Why, thank you, Mrs. Brown," Tara replied. "Does that mean I get the job?

"Oh, oh." The woman's eyes rolled back in her head and then bugged out, round and white as china saucers. "I've seen it," she moaned. "I prophesized."

Tara stared, uncomprehending. "You did?"

"I've seen it clear." Her body went rigid, and she squeezed her eyes shut. "Some pretty lady come play this piano like it should be played, make this a happy house again."

Then the trance was broken. Mrs. Brown opened her eyes and smiled at Tara, as though nothing out of the ordinary had transpired. "Yes, ma'am, you do." She lumbered to her feet. "Let me just show you what Harry's been working on. That way, you know where he's at with his lessons."

~

Nathan listened attentively to this discourse. Mystery solved. The gifted musician was applying for the position of Harry's piano teacher. One thing was for sure, whoever she was, whatever her credentials, she was overqualified.

Feeling like an intruder in his own home, Nathan was loath to confront the two, the talented applicant and his housekeeper, the prophetess. It was as though unforeseen circumstances had thrust him into the role of reluctant voyeur. The pianist had played with such unbridled passion that, although he had not yet set eyes on her, he felt as though she'd partially disrobed, that somehow she'd revealed herself to him. Making as little noise as possible, Nathan crept down the corridor and retreated upstairs to pack. Over dinner, he'd question Willie about finding a replacement for Harry's piano instructor. Just for the hell of it. See where that led.

~

Willie was pleased with herself. She'd found a new piano teacher for Harry. Never mind that she was a petite little thing, that woman could tinkle the ivories. Her cellphone chimed, and Willie dug in her pocket to retrieve it.

"Hi, Mama." Cerita's voice lacked its former vibrancy.

"Hi, sweetheart. Can I come pick you up?" Willie pulled out a barstool and sat heavily.

"Not yet."

Willie struggled to keep the fear from her voice. "You sound tired."

"I am. I've been poked, prodded, and wheeled around from one end of this hospital to the other till I don't know whether I'm coming or going."

"Poor thing. When are they going to let you out?"

"I don't know. I'm scheduled for surgery tomorrow."

"What?"

"Don't go getting all worked up. It's just an exploratory procedure. They haven't found anything conclusive. That's the good news."

"I suppose that *is* good news." Willie said, somewhat mollified. "What time is the operation?"

"Early. Seven, I think."

"Baby, I've got to get dinner, and I promised to stay the night. Mr. McCourt flies to Texas in the morning, but I'll come by to see you later this evening."

"You don't have to," Cerita said. "I'll probably be asleep. I feel like I could sleep for a hundred years."

"That's just the problem, isn't it? You're run down. Get some rest."

Willie swiped her cell to disconnect. This was a fine kettle. She never should have agreed to stay the night. Who was going to look after the grandbabies and her mother? She snatched the phone back up.

"Siri, call Lakisha Jackson," she said.

Lakisha was an alto in the Antioch Primitive Baptist Church choir, and she'd come to Willie's rescue on more than one occasion. Willie prayed that kindly woman would open her heart once again. "Lawd, Lawd," she mumbled, waiting for her friend to accept the call. Couldn't she just about sleep for a hundred years herself?

CHAPTER FOURTEEN

DECONSTRUCTING TARA

It was March. The holidays had come and gone and not a lot of work had been accomplished during that time. It'd had taken Brett, her general contractor, a month to secure the building permit and hire the subs. Now, finally, real progress was being made.

Tara ambled through the utility room to the kitchen, both of which were reduced to skeletal shells. Brett had explained that, at some point in the process, she'd be forced to move out. Scottly had generously offered her his guest bedroom for the duration, but she didn't relish the thought of living under the same roof as the offputting Kevin. If conditions got too unbearable, she'd move in with Earl. It was out of her hands, and she'd decided to cross that bridge when she came to it.

This was a new attitude for her, one she found immensely freeing. Throughout her life, Tara had striven for control over her circumstances. Never one for spontaneity, she'd been a careful planner, plotting her course as carefully as a ship's navigator. Look where it had gotten her. All her well-laid plans had come to naught. Now, strait-laced, uptight Tara was looking like nothing so much as a late-blooming flower child.

She stepped through an opening between two studs of the newly framed lanai, a glass of iced tea in hand. Carefully, she trod across planks of the, as yet, unfinished terrace, and from there hopped down to the lawn. When not teaching, this was where she spent the better part of her days—out of the way of the workmen. The sun was warm on her bare shoulders, and the ice cubes in her tea had nearly melted away. She lowered herself into a chaise lounge, drank deeply, and let her mind wander over the events of the last few months.

Although her current living conditions were unsettled, her life had fallen into a pleasant routine. The online ad she'd placed had elicited a response far in excess of her expectations, and that had enabled her to be selective. All of her students were gifted beyond their years, and many of the residences in which she taught were beautifully appointed estates. She'd enjoyed meeting the families of her students, enlarging her rapidly expanding circle of friends and acquaintants. Given her present circumstances, it was an ideal arrangement.

The only thing missing from this new life was a man, but Tara's mind shied away from the one truly disheartening aspect of her current situation. Instead, she picked up her phone and searched for Josh's latest text message. With a twinge of regret Tara realized that, at this particular juncture, when she'd had to let go of her old life, she must now begin the process of letting Josh go as well. With a sigh, she turned to his text.

> *A couple friends and I are planning to fly down for the semester break. Could you book us a hotel? Somewhere nearby, within walking distance of a public beach?*
>
> *Can't wait to see you.*
>
> *XOXO.*

Tara stared off into space. Where to house Josh and his friends? Ideally, the place should be reasonably priced yet centrally located, a destination that would appeal to a younger crowd.

A shadow fell over her, and Tara looked up into Scottly's cheerful countenance. He had Chanel on leash, and the Yorkie lunged at her.

"The little monster somehow sensed you were here," Scottly said. "He was yapping up a storm, so I brought him by to see how you were faring.

A hard-hat area was no place for a little dog, and Chanel had not adjusted to the strident pop-pop-pop of nail-guns, the high-pitched whine of table saws, or the daily influx of strange men.

Once again, Scottly had come to her rescue, offering his screened pool enclosure as a home-away-from-home for the little canine. He'd given Tara a key, and they'd made an opening in the oleander hedge so that she could pass freely from her backyard to his.

The designer held out the leash, and Tara looped it around a leg of her chaise. She scooped Chanel up into her arms, giving him a cuddle, and was rewarded with doggie kisses.

"I didn't hear a thing," Tara said.

"Little wonder." Scottly motioned toward the house. "It's a noisy go, but they're making good progress."

"That's encouraging. What's next?"

"They're almost done with the framing. The electrician's got to finish up the rough-in, and then they'll lay in the insulation. That'll only take a day or two. After that, the sheetrock goes on, and things will really start to fly." Scottly pulled up a chair and sat. "In another couple of months, everything will be all white and tidy."

"How lovely."

"Change of subject, what are you doing next Sunday?"

"I'll have to consult my social calendar, but I'm quite certain I'm free. Why do you ask?"

Chanel snuggled contentedly in Tara's lap, and she stroked his silvery-gray fur.

"I thought I might get a party together, take in a polo match. The weather's perfect. Pretty soon it'll be too hot, and that's no fun. I was hoping you'd join us."

"Polo? I'm not sure I'd know how to act, rubbing elbows with the upper crust and all."

"You'll do fine," Scottly chuckled. "Besides, we must continue your education—hobnobbing 101."

"Best offer I've had in a long time." Tara fanned herself with an open palm. "Pray tell. What does one wear to a polo match?"

"I'll be dashing in my navy blazer, but since I sweat like a little piggy, it'll be quickly tossed aside to reveal a polo shirt, of course. You'd best get dolled up in something lightweight and gauzy, a linen sheath or a sundress, so long as it's not too revealing. One mustn't expose too much flesh at a polo match. Never mind if it's ninety degrees in the shade. Proper dress and decorum, don't you know? A hat is required to protect that flawless complexion of yours. Besides, hats are fun, don't you think? Oh, and flats. Heels are a no-no. We'll be in the grass, and you'd get stuck, like a dagger to the heart. I've seen it many times, and it's not pretty." He tapped a foot on the ground. "Besides, you'll want to stamp divots, as that's tradition."

"I'm mad for divot stamping." Tara clasped her hands. "Who else is going?"

"Kevin simply refuses. Says polo's like watching paint dry, but Ernestine Hart and Dulcie Woodard are always game. Have you met them?"

Tara shook her head. "Don't ring no bells."

Scottly sat back in his chair and lightly smacked a fist on his forehead. "I fear I've been remiss in your schooling. You must keep up with the social doings of Vero Beach, dearie. Read the *Beachside News* and the *32963 Vero Beach* rag. Look at the photographs, study the captions. Ernestine and Dulcie are two powerful, old scions of society, and I do mean *old*. They've each got five or six years on me, and that's saying a lot."

Tara rolled her eyes. "You're a pup."

"I do adore you. You're so good for my poor, battered ego." Scottly pressed a palm to his heart. "Darling, won't you marry me?"

"Perhaps next Tuesday. We'll see."

"I suppose it's the best I can hope for." Scottly sighed, theatrically. "Anyway, I think you gals will hit it off. Ernestine and Dulcie know everything about everything that matters in this godforsaken backwater. They've both got their fingers in so many pies, Little Jack Horner could only aspire to be an apprentice."

"Scary."

"You'll like them. I promise. Besides, Ernestine's is in possession of a simply incredible vintage Rolls Royce, 1960-something, which shall be our most agreeable transport. We'll be tailgating, you see, and in style, I might add. What a hoot."

"Tailgating, hmm..." Tara thought for a moment. "You mean like a picnic?"

"Exactly so, only black-tie elegant."

"We'll have to plan a menu." Tara placed the terrier on the ground, and he immediately began sniffing, nose pressed to earth.

"Right-o. Shall we cook or purchase prepared?"

"Both." Tara unfolded herself from the chaise and stood. "I'm a really good cook, Scottly, and I'd love to contribute. Would that be okay?"

"Of course."

"All right then. Cucumber sandwiches, curried chicken salad, vichyssoise..." She looked to Scottly. "Have I got it right?"

"Exactly!"

"A lemon pound cake for dessert with fresh strawberries and champagne."

"Perfect."

"Darn it." Tara stopped pacing. "This isn't going to work."

"Why?"

"I don't have a kitchen."

"Good grief." The designer rose from his chair. "For a moment I thought we really had a problem." Placing his paws on Tara's shoulders, he shook her in mock disgust. "Don't scare me like that, woman." He released her and put hands to hips. "Use my kitchen. You have a key, for God's sake. Just walk the hell in. Keep the dog company while you're at it."

Scottly bent to pat Chanel's head. "I never knew a creature could pee so much. His output is greater than his intake." Chanel rolled onto his back, shamelessly demanding a tummy rub. "Where does it all come from?" He hunkered down to tickle the dog's spotted belly. "You sprinkled every bush and flower on the way over here, didn't you, buddy?"

Tara smiled. She remembered Scottly's initial reaction to Chanel. His attitude toward the little canine had changed. Before, he'd merely tolerated him. Now, he seemed enamored. "Thank you so much. You've been a lifesaver."

My pleasure, dear girl." He came to his full height. "Let's take a gander at the house, shall we? I want to discuss an idea that's been knocking around my cranium."

～

Standing in the center of the family room, they were gazing up at the newly expanded, open-beamed ceiling, when Earl poked his head around the corner. "There you are."

"Dad." Tara crossed to her father.

"Hello, sweetie. Scott."

"What a surprise." Tara said, beaming.

"Spur of the moment," Earl explained. It's such a nice day, I thought I'd take a little drive. See my girl."

"What do you think? Like my new digs?"

"It's going to be dandy." Earl turned to Scottly. "You're doing a great job."

"I figure five or six months till completion," Scottly said. "Probably finish up in August or September."

The three walked back through the kitchen to the foyer, where two young men were perched on ladders constructing a tray in the ceiling.

"Guess what, Dad?" Cautiously, the threesome threaded their way between the ladders, stepping over tools and two-by-fours, and out onto the front porch. "Scottly invited me to a polo match."

"That so?" Earl's voice evinced a notable lack of enthusiasm.

"You're welcome to join us." Scottly said. "This Sunday, Windsor at noon."

"Oh, no. Thank you kindly. Polo's not my cup of tea." Earl grimaced. "Getting all gussied up, rubbing elbows with the social gadflies. No offense, but I can think of better ways to spend my time, although I do appreciate the invite. Sunday afternoon, you'll find me at Dodgertown eating peanuts and taking in a game.

"Daddy, you should come. We're going with two rich, old widows."

"All the more reason..." Earl lit up a cigarillo.

"Spring training games are fun, I have to admit," Scottly said. "I try to catch at least one game during season."

"Yes, sirree," Earl agreed. "The Tigers are playing, so I'll be rooting for Detroit."

"Offer stands, just in case you reconsider."

"Duly noted, but I best be getting on my way."

"Can't you at least stay for dinner?" Tara asked. "We could go to the Ocean Grill. My treat."

"No can do, Tara. Don't want to miss *Dancing with the Stars*. I'm hooked on that show. You remember how your mom and I loved to dance?"

"You two were a couple of Fred Astaire prodigies."

"Those were the days." Earl gave Tara a quick hug and turned to go. "Bye, sweetie. See you, Scott."

Tara and Scottly watched as Earl backed his battered van out of the driveway and pulled away from the curb. "He's a funny guy, isn't he?" Tara asked.

"He's a character, all right," Scottly admitted, "but you can't help but admire him. No pretense."

"That's for sure."

The sun was in the west, and the workmen were packing up their tools for the day.

"I'll be going, too," Scottly said. "I'd invite you for dinner, but I signed up for a Zumba class at the gym."

"Good for you."

"Yep. Trying to get this flabby old bod in shape." He strode down the driveway.

"Bye. Thanks again for minding Chanel," Tara called after him.

Scottly acknowledged her words with an upstretched arm and an exaggerated nod of his head.

The heat was bleeding out of the day, and a few of the subcontractors were climbing into trucks or utility vans. Eager for a diversion, Tara cried, "Let's go for a walk, Chanel," and the two set off down the street. Although she would have preferred a brisk pace, Chanel's continual stops to sniff and mark made it a slow go.

They hadn't covered much ground when the sputter of a single-engine airplane drew her eyes skyward. Tara gaped in amazement as she witnessed tiny human forms, their bodies spread-eagled, plummeting toward earth. She counted six of them. In a matter of seconds their parachutes, like miniature rainbows, unfurled above first one, then the other. Each, in turn, hiked up like fish on a line, their direction temporarily reversed. Soon the pull of gravity caused them all to resume a slower, dream-like descent. Mesmerized by the unusual spectacle, Tara watched as the last of the parachutes disappeared behind the tree line on the horizon.

It was a moment to be savored. The unusual sighting was a gift,

Tara decided, an affirmation. How she'd grown to love this place. There was a sensuous quality about air perfumed with gardenia and citrus. South Florida was seeping into her bones, melting in her veins like orange blossom honey in green tea, and, deep in her soul, Tara felt the stirrings of contentment.

CHAPTER FIFTEEN

SO TIRED

Willie's sandals made a slapping sound, marking her passage. She shuffled past a reception desk manned by two senior women and made her way to the elevator. On the third floor, she wended through a confusing rabbit's warren of hallways in search of Cerita's room. All the doors were identical—except for the room numbers, of course—hollow, laminate-finished, masquerading as hardwood.

By the time Willie located Cerita's room, her breath was coming in shallow gasps. The door was ajar, and she peeked in. There were two beds, but the curtain dividing them was open, and only one was occupied.

"Cerita," she whispered. "It's Mama."

The form in the bed stirred. "Hi, Ma." Cerita switched on the bedside lamp. "What time is it?"

Willie was shocked at her daughter's appearance. Eyes red-rimmed, face haggard, the young woman looked far worse than she'd expected. She managed to mask her fears and put a bright note in her voice. "About nine-thirty, I guess. Why do you ask? Have a hot date?"

"Yeah, Jarod and I are going out dancing. Got a problem with that?"

"Don't you sass me, missy."

Cerita yawned. "It's so late, Mom. You shouldn't have come."

"Had to see my girl."

"You have so much to contend with—the kids, Granny, work. Now, this on top of everything. I'm sorry."

"Don't you worry," Willie soothed. "I'm fine. The kids are fine, and Gran, too. You concentrate on getting better." Willie dragged a chair over to Cerita's bedside and lowered herself into it. "Tell me, honey, how are you?"

"I really don't know. We'll have a better idea tomorrow, after the procedure."

"I should hope so."

"Dr. Merrill is one of the best OBGY physicians on staff. What did you tell Tyrone and Yvonne?" Cerita asked, changing the subject. "Who's taking care of them and Gran?"

"Lakisha Jackson. It's under control, and what isn't, that's in the Lawd's hands." Willie rose from her chair and bent over her daughter. She brushed damp tendrils from Cerita's face. "You go to sleep now, baby. I'll see you in the morning." After planting a kiss on her daughter's forehead, Willie turned and crossed the room.

"Night, Mama," Cerita said. "Love you."

"Love you more."

Willie drew the door shut behind her and retraced her steps. Wearily, she wove through the labyrinth of silent hallways until she came to the elevator. Standing open before her, it looked like a giant mouth ready to swallow her up. The sole occupant, she punched the lobby button, and the doors closed with a sibilant hiss. In the next instant, a sense of such isolation came over her, she felt as though she were completely alone on the planet.

The two elderly women at the reception desk smiled sweetly at her, and she nodded a polite reply.

How wonderful it would be to have the luxury of time, to be able to volunteer one's services.

She could only imagine.

The automatic glass doors swished open, and Willie was expelled into the night's warm embrace. Moths flitted high overhead, creating halos around the mercury vapor lamps while frogs burped and shrilled in the retaining ponds. Willie sighed as she headed toward the parking lot. How would she ever get through this?

≈

She'd slept fitfully. By the next morning, Willie was a nervous wreck. She was scrubbing vegetables in the McCourt's kitchen, couldn't keep her eyes off the clock over the range. It was 11:30—two minutes since she'd last checked—and she had yet to hear the outcome of Cerita's procedure. Harry was practicing in the music room, and his playing provided a bit of comfort. So focused had she become on the boy's music-making, it took a moment before the ring of the house phone penetrated her consciousness. Snatching up a dishtowel in one hand, she grabbed the receiver in the other.

"McCourt residence." Willie side-stepped back to the sink to turn off the tap.

"Mrs. Brown?"

"Yes."

"This is Doctor Merrill, Cerita's gynecologist."

"Dr. Merrill?"

"I hope I'm not disturbing you."

"Not at all. How's Cerita?"

"That's why I'm calling. I want to talk with you about your daughter's condition."

∽

"Very nice, Harry. I can tell you've been practicing," Tara said. "Keep working on your fingering. You've almost got it."

"Thanks, Ms. Cahill." The boy slid off the piano bench and made a beeline for the little Yorkie who'd been curled in a ball at Tara's feet. Chanel had waited patiently throughout Harry's lesson, but now he bounded into the boy's arms.

"Good, boy," Harry said, as the dog washed his chin with doggie kisses.

"Yes," Tara agreed. "His checkup at the vet's office was scheduled for two-thirty, and there wasn't time to take him back home before your lesson. I was afraid he'd be a distraction, but he's been very good."

"Can I take him out to play?"

"That would be great." Tara found Chanel's leash in her bag and handed it to him. "He's probably ready for a walk. I'll just go let Willie know we've finished for the day."

After gathering up music and theory books, Tara hiked to the kitchen, but stopped up short at the sight that greeted her there: Willie slumped on a barstool, head-in-hands and awash in tears.

Alarmed, Tara crossed to her. "Goodness, what is it?" She dropped her satchel and rested a palm on Willie's shoulder. The woman moaned softly before turning a tear-streaked face to her. "There, there," Tara consoled. "It can't be as bad as all that. Sit tight. I'll be right back."

Tara scooted around the kitchen, frantically searching for Kleenex. Eventually, she located a roll of paper towels under the kitchen sink. She tore several sheets from off the roll and offered them to the disconsolate woman.

Willie blew her nose with a loud honk. Under normal circumstances, that would have brought a smile to Tara's face. Not today.

"Thank you, Ms. Cahill," she said and sniffed. "I'm ashamed for you to see me like this."

"Oh, for heaven's sake." Tara dismissed the apology with a wave of her hand. "And call me Tara. Come on, now. I don't mean to pry." Tara climbed up on the barstool beside her. "I've cried my own share of tears. What woman hasn't? I've got wide shoulders if you need a pair to unload on."

Willie snorted and ventured a watery grin. "Girl, you barely got shoulders at all."

"Oh, yeah? Try me,"

"It's my daughter, Cerita." Her voice caught in her throat. "She's only twenty-two."

"Yes?"

"She's got the cancer." A fresh course of tears coursed down her cheeks.

Tara gasped. This was far more serious than she'd imagined. Tentatively, she placed her hand over Willie's. Words failed her, and she was uncertain how to proceed. "I'm so sorry," she said at last, the pat phrase seeming woefully inadequate. "But let's think positively. She's young. Great strides have been made in the treatment of cancer. People *do* get cured."

"I know. It's just that..." Willie's voice trailed off, and she pressed her lips tightly together in an attempt to prevent the waterworks from gushing anew.

Tara reached for more paper towels. "What kind of cancer?"

"Ovarian. I believe that's what the doctor said."

"Oh," Tara answered in a small voice, recalling dismal statistics regarding the survival rate of that fearsome malady. It wouldn't do to focus on that. "Well, she's little more than a child, isn't she?"

"My baby girl."

"I imagine, she's strong like her mother?"

"Yes, ma'am...Tara...and stubborn."

"She'll have to fight, won't she? She'll just have to be strong and fight for all she's worth."

Sighing, Willie straightened and dried her eyes. "Yes. I guess she will. We'll fight it together."

"That's the spirit." Tara hopped off the stool and made her way to a glass-fronted upper cabinet from which she withdrew two mugs. She crossed to the coffee maker. "How do you take yours?"

"I'll do that." Willie retrieved a carton of half & half from the refrigerator. "Would you like a cookie?"

"No, no. Come sit down."

The two women sat in silence, each mulling over the day's sudden turn of events. Tara was first to speak. "Tell me, how can I help?"

"Don't need no help, Ms. Tara."

"Maybe you don't need it, but I need to give it."

Willie furrowed her brow, studying the piano teacher. "Don't rightly know what you mean."

"May I speak frankly? You see, I'm alone. Except for my dog, that is. I'm newly divorced, and my son's all grown up and away at college. I have plenty of time on my hands. Too much time, really." Tara paused for a minute, and then, as the idea fully took shape, her words tumbled out in a rush. "The fact is I spend entirely too much time dwelling on my own problems. I'm sure you know that's not good for a person."

Willie stirred her coffee. "Never enough time in the day," she murmured.

"Exactly," Tara exclaimed. "I think I can provide you some. I mean it when I say I want to help. Won't you let me? It might just do us both a world of good."

With a little prodding, Willie opened up to her, explaining how her mother's dementia was becoming more and more problematic, that the two grandbabies needed supervision when Cerita was in school or working.

"Now, that she's sick," Willie confided, "I don't know how I'll manage."

"You must let me lend a hand," Tara said. "I can fill in for you whenever you need me to. My schedule is nothing but flexible."

At first, Willie resisted, but Tara was persistent. Eventually, the housekeeper agreed to her offer, and a course of action was decided upon.

"I might as well start tonight," Tara said. "I'll just have to run home later this evening and collect my things. I can see you've already prepared the meal. All I have to do is heat it up and serve it. That way you can get supper for your grandkids, see to your mother, and then visit Cerita in the hospital.

Sally had prepared a special dinner, beef stroganoff over noodles, a tossed salad, Parker House Rolls, and a strawberry shortcake for dessert. Rick didn't think he'd ever enjoyed a more delicious meal. Sally was so like her mother, outgoing and bubbly, utterly impossible to resist. a home health care aide, she was a natural nurturer. Throughout dinner, she'd regaled him with funny stories about her clients, all of whom, he imagined, adored her. It was ironic, he thought. Because of an accident, Connor, her son—his grandson, required the lion's share of her time, yet she'd had to make a living helping others in order to support the two of them.

Connor did his best to appear outgoing, but Rick detected a deep vein of reservation. This young man wasn't about to unload to a stranger. Interestingly, he shared his granddad's predilection with instruments of destruction.

"I was forever harping on him to get rid of all those chemicals, but he was fascinated, couldn't seem to stop fooling with them."

"Aw, Mom," Connor interrupted, "don't start on that again."

"He might as well know, Connor. The man's family, after all."

Sally went on to explain that her son had spent his free time tinkering with chemicals in the shed out back—the kind of stuff that could be used to assemble an incendiary device. When the shed exploded, not only had he sustained third-degree burns over forty percent of his body, he made the front pages of the local newspaper.

Like grandpa, like grandson, Rick thought, secretly wondering if the boy had been cooking meth. He decided it didn't matter one way or another. Things were going to be different now. He intended to be a positive influence in the kid's life and wasn't about to condone destructive behaviors.

"It was pretty horrific," Sally explained. "Third-degree burns destroy the epidermis, the dermis, and the hypodermis, causing charring of the skin, which he had plenty of. And, although those burned areas are, typically, numb, he still experiences plenty of pain due to the second-and first-degree burns, but Connor's a trooper." Sally poured them all a second glass of Pinot Noir. "He doesn't complain." She turned to her son. "Isn't that right, honey?"

"That would be an affirmative," Connor agreed. "No complaints."

"Connor's doing remarkably well."

Connor smiled. Half his face was animated and handsome, but the other half was frozen in a perpetual grimace.

The old vet's heart went out to his grandson. He was determined to do everything in his power to assure the kid had a future, one that included a reconstructed face. Cochran felt as though he was somehow responsible for this sorry state of affairs. Perhaps he was. In any case, a series of events had been set in motion, and he wasn't about to back down at this juncture. He'd get the money, pay for doctors and the surgeries, or he'd die trying.

CHAPTER SIXTEEN

DROWNING

Chanel rose to the occasion with characteristic spunk, and the kids were in hysterics at his antics. He'd yip loudly then circle the table, pink tongue curled up over his snout in a grin, demanding to be slipped a morsel of food.

"You little beggar," Tara cried. "Go lie down." Her words had no effect. Instead, Chanel sat with his head cocked to one side as if struggling to understand her.

"See that, Jennifer," Harry exclaimed. "He's smiling."

Chanel barked, delighted to be the center of attention and scrambled to all fours to trot around the table again.

Tara had been apprehensive about taking on this chore, knowing full well this first meal might prove a test. Willie had filled her in on Jennifer, explaining how the willful teen had driven off more than one nanny. So, Tara was grateful for Chanel's presence. He'd broken the ice. Thus far, there'd been no challenge to her authority.

"May I be excused?" Harry asked.

"Why don't you take Chanel for a walk?" Tara gestured toward the laundry room. "His leash is in on the hook by the door."

"Come on, boy." Harry scampered away, and the Yorkie chased after him.

"Willie's a good cook." Tara pushed away from the table. "That was a delicious meal."

Jennifer eyed her speculatively. "Cute dog," she said.

"He's been a wonderful companion." Tara gathered up several dishes.

"Dad won't let us have a dog." Jennifer followed Tara into the kitchen. She leaned against the kitchen counter, her eyes fastened on Tara, making no move to help.

"Why not?" Tara loaded the dishwasher.

"He doesn't want to be bothered, says a dog's too much of a responsibility. Dad works all hours. He doesn't have time to care for an animal, and Willie's got too much to do as it is."

"Surely you're old enough to care for a pet."

Jennifer shrugged. "You'd think."

"Have you told your father that you and Harry would be responsible for a dog if he let you have one?"

"Um-hmm."

"Maybe if you showed him you meant it, he'd change his mind."

"Yeah, right. Dad doesn't change his mind about things. Besides, how would I show him I'm responsible? He's never here."

"You could start by giving me a hand with these dishes."

"I don't do dishes," Jennifer sneered. "That's what the help is paid for."

"My point exactly."

"Huh?"

"Look," Tara said, "I'm serious. You should take on some responsibilities around here."

"Like what?" Jennifer eyed her suspiciously.

"Like, for instance, helping me with these dishes. Seems to me it would give you some leverage. You know, prove to him how adult you are, that you're not a kid."

"Ha. What a joke." Jennifer scoffed. "Obviously, you haven't met my father. He wouldn't even notice."

"He would if I told him what a great help you've been to me, what a mature and responsible young woman I thought you are."

"As if you'd do that."

"I certainly would. Hey, we girls have to stick together," Tara said. "Come on, wrap up that leftover chicken and put the gravy in a plastic container. Then, if you like, we'll take a spin down to the boardwalk and get ice cream. Chanel loves vanilla."

~

Tara pulled into her driveway, groaning inwardly at the relatively insignificant amount of progress that had been made, but there was no time to worry about that. Stepping gingerly over the piles of sawdust and wood scraps, she made her way to the one area of the house that still maintained some semblance of order, the master bedroom. Soon, it, too, would be reduced to its bones before being expanded and renovated.

Quickly, Tara packed a few essentials in a small overnight bag and gathered up Chanel's bowls, food, and toys. Once all necessary provisions had been stowed in the trunk of her car, she made her way to Scottly's house to inform him of her plans.

The sun had slipped below the horizon, and the shadows were lengthening when Tara hastened up the newly cleared pathway, brushing against fragrant gardenia and sticky hibiscus blossoms as she went. A pair of stone, temple lanterns spilled puddles of light on the pool deck, but they provided meager sources of illumination. No light emanated from the interior, and the water's surface was murky. There was something sinister about the watery pit, and Tara turned away, thinking to abandon this mission.

This is spooky.

Her retreat was forestalled when movement caught the corner of her eye, and she whirled back about, only to note a churning on the water. Tara's instincts told her to bolt, but her legs refused to move. She stared in horrified fascination at the rippling pool. Then, a hand emerged from the black depths and slapped the deck, and she cried out. It was Kevin! Rivulets of water cascaded from dark coils of chest hair on his sculptured torso, as he hoisted himself halfway up out of the pool. In the hazy glow of the lantern light, Tara was unable to make out the lower half of Kevin's body, but in the next instant, the wily fellow proceeded to haul himself up and over the edge of the tiled curb.

He was naked!

Tara took a step backward, and then pivoted, covering her eyes as she did so. It was too late. Certain intimate details were permanently etched in her brain.

"Why, if it isn't my newest and most attractive neighbor," Kevin said. "Howdy do, Ms. Cahill?"

Feeling as though she'd been made the brunt of some cruel joke, Tara felt her face flush. "You scared the hell out of me," she exclaimed, her voice a strangled squeak. "For God's sake, put some clothes on."

"Didn't mean to frighten you," Kevin said. "Wasn't expecting visitors. It was you who crept up on me after all. Are you spying on me?"

"Of course not," Tara sputtered, her eyes averted. She could hear him rustling about, his wet feet making sloshy sounds as he padded across the deck.

"There now, Polly Pure Heart. I'm decent," Keven laughed. "Well, perhaps not in the truest sense of the word," he amended, "but all offending parts have been tucked away out of sight."

"I'm sorry I barged in on you." Tara knew she was acting prim and school-girlish, but the man had such an effect on her. Why did she always feel clumsy and tongue-tied in his presence?

"No apologies necessary." Kevin flopped down into a chaise lounge. "You're more than welcome to drop by anytime I'm in the all-together."

"I'll pass."

Tara mustered a tight-lipped smile. In spite of his smooth good looks, there was something menacing about the slender hairdresser. Whenever in his presence, she felt as though he were contemplating some mean-spirited prank to embarrass her, and this encounter proved no exception.

"Is Scottly here?" she asked, her voice settling into its natural register.

"He had to run out to pick up a jar of capers. Scott's preparing a feast, veal piccata." Kevin's tongue circled his lips. "Why don't you join us?" he asked, a seductive breathiness to his voice.

"I couldn't impose." Tara wanted nothing more than to make a quick escape.

You'd be doing us a favor," Kevin said. "Scott never gets his proportions right. We'll have food for an army."

"I really can't."

"Sure, you can." Kevin flipped onto his side, propping his head on one hand and grinning.

"Actually, I've eaten. Besides, I have plans."

"Oh?"

"I'm visiting a friend."

Kevin raised his eyebrows. "A friend. I see."

Damn the man. He could think what he liked. She had no desire to explain herself further to this manipulative scoundrel. Tara turned and retreated. "Sorry for the intrusion," she called over her shoulder.

~

It was pitch black when she stumbled down the path toward the welcoming shambles of her home. As her composure returned, Tara's discomfit segued to anger. Could it be that Kevin had been expecting her? He must have heard the rumble of her car's engine as she'd pulled into the driveway. She knew it was insane, but she wouldn't put it past him to have planned the entire episode. What impetus would drive a person to do such a thing?

On the drive back to the McCourt enclave, Tara's mind was filled with thoughts of Nathan and his clan. Theirs was the epitome of a dysfunctional family. Jennifer was bitter and fit the role of the rebellious teenager to a T. Sweet and bright, Harry was gifted, yet terribly withdrawn. Then there was the mysterious patriarch. What kind of man would willingly isolate himself from his family and leave their upbringing to the housekeeper? Didn't he realize how desperately they needed him? To think he wouldn't even let them have a dog.

Tara fumed. She could hardly wait to meet this guy. She'd deliver a scathing lecture that would make him see the error of his ways. *These kids are yours, and they're two potentially great human beings. For all the wealth and privilege you've afforded them, they're emotionally bankrupt.* In Tara's imagination, her words hit their mark, and an impassive McCourt softened.

She let herself in the side door and toted her bag up the grand staircase. When she came to Harry's door, Tara rapped and then opened it a crack. "Hey, Harry," she whispered.

As expected, he was in bed with a book in his hands, and the dog was snuggled next to him. Tara opened the door wide, and the terrier leaped off the bed and raced to her.

"Hi, Tara," Harry said. "Chanel, come." Letting his book fall, Harry held out his arms. "Can he stay?" he implored. "Please?"

Tara hadn't the heart to deny him. "Okay." She placed Chanel in the boy's arms. "Good night," she said. "Lights out?"

"Sure. Thanks, Tara."

Her next stop was at Jennifer's door. She knocked, waited for a response, and then waited some more. Finally, she opened the door. "Hello, Jennifer," she said, her voice pitched low.

The girl lay sprawled across her bed. Earbuds connected her to an iPad, and her thumbs tapped the screen of her cell, as she texted. Cautiously, Tara entered the room. She didn't want to startle Jennifer, but the girl was so engrossed that didn't appear likely. Tara crossed to the bed and plunked down on the edge. Still, the teen failed to acknowledge her.

Tara had had enough. Plucking an earbud from a perfect shell of an ear, she said, "I'm back. Need anything?"

The beautiful teen fixed Tara with a withering glare. "Privacy?" She widened her eyes.

Tara managed a smile and nodded. She was simply not up for confrontation. "I'll see you in the morning," she said. "Good night."

Jennifer replaced the earbud and turned back to her smartphone, dismissing her without a word.

~

Except for the fact that there was nothing to detract from the divinely comfortable bed upon which she reclined, Tara felt like the protagonist in *The Princess and the Pea*. Someone—Willie most likely—had thoughtfully left a few current titles on the antique secretary. Tara helped herself to Carl Hiaasen's latest stranger-than-fiction fable. With her head propped on a stack of luscious pillows encased in Egyptian cotton, she opened the book and attempted to read. She couldn't get past page one. Simply couldn't concentrate.

She missed Chanel's warm little body, and she worried about

what challenges tomorrow might bring. Tara tossed the book aside and replayed the events of the day. How improbable it was that she'd come to be here with these children in this grand home. Yet, somehow, she knew she'd chosen the right course of action. In the weeks and months leading up to this juncture, she'd been entirely too preoccupied with her own little drama. Willie's family needed her just now, and the opportunity to be of some use had presented itself. Tara gazed about the luxuriously appointed room, thinking the gig didn't require much sacrifice. Besides, it felt good to be tending to someone other than herself.

With ears full of the sea suckling at the shoreline, she switched off the bedside lamp, and right on cue, her childhood fear of drowning surfaced. For as long as she could remember, she'd been terrified at the prospect of a watery grave. Her eyelids grew heavy, and at last, Tara gave herself over to the exhaustion she'd held at bay. *Denial was not a river in Africa*, was her last thought as she succumbed to sleep.

River. Ocean.

Water. Death.

In her dream, she was a girl again—five, maybe six years old. She could see herself tearing around the wooded back lot with her brothers, Mikey and Paul. Their German shepherd, Fritzie, gamboling along beside them. It was a Saturday in early spring, and the ground was a muddy quagmire from all the rain. That didn't deter the young Cahill's. They'd been cooped up inside for far too long.

The children raced about, reacquainting themselves with Pembroke Woods, a spit of undeveloped land that abutted their family's parcel. Paul, Mikey, and Tara, intent on their game of cowboys and Indians, occasionally abandoned the chase in order to examine some wonder of nature, a perfect feather, a rock glittering with mica, a fossilized trilobite. Eventually, feeling the exhilaration of explorers come upon an exotic trade route, they pushed through the underbrush and entered the recently cleared lot.

A pile of two-by-fours had been off-loaded, stacked to one side, and shrouded in a protective tarp. The newly scraped lot was raw and punctuated by gray-white tubers that looked like so many bony fingers, poking up out of the soil. Other than a pile of rubbish containing some smaller scraps of wood and chips of cement block, there was little to distinguish this patch of earth. Except, that is, for the backhoe parked on the far side of the parcel near. With its peeling red paint, the dirt-digger looked like a prehistoric lobster, its single mammoth pincer clawing the earth.

When his eyes fell on the piece of heavy equipment, Mikey flew across the lot, and Paul and Tara followed him. With a whoop of delight, Mikey scaled a large tire and scrambled up to the driver's seat, and Paul scrambled up and stood behind his brother. Tara tried to mount the monstrous machine, finding the rungs that would aid her assent, but her legs simply weren't long enough. Her brothers would have to pull her up, and they weren't about to. Instead, they reveled in the opportunity to lord it over their baby sister.

"You'd better get down from there, you boys." Tara shouted.

"Come and get me," Mikey challenged.

"I'm gonna tell Dad."

"Better not." Paul mugged at her.

"I will, and he'll spank your butts for sure."

"Do it, and I'll make you eat worms," Mikey said. "Big, fat slimy worms. Yum, yum."

The boys laughed as they pretended to drive the backhoe, their hands running over the enormous, frozen steering wheel. "Bvoom, bvoom!" They puffed out their cheeks, pushing air through their teeth, and making engine sounds, safe in the knowledge that Tara wouldn't tattle.

When it became apparent that no amount of pleading was going to make her brothers relent, Tara wandered back to the large hole in the ground. Retaining walls of concrete block rose from the excavation to a height of approximately eight feet, forming a four-sided structure. The spring thaw, combined with a solid week of rain, had transformed the half-completed basement into a small, man-made lake.

Tara could hear her father's voice admonishing her and her brothers. "Stay away from the site," he'd warned. "The basement's flooded, and it's dangerous. I don't want you kids anywhere near there. You hear me?"

They hadn't deliberately set out to disobey their father's orders, but there they were, exactly where he'd told them not to be. The allure of the deep pool was irresistible. Tara pulled several small scraps of two-by-fours from the rubbish heap. Standing at the edge of the pit, she launched them. Meanwhile, having lost their audience, the boys soon became bored with the backhoe. They scrambled down from the earth digger and came to stand beside Tara.

"Hey," Mikey cried, "I got an idea. We could make a raft."

"Yeah," Paul said. "Come on."

The boys tugged several lengths of lumber from beneath the tarp.

"What'll we use to tie them together?" Paul asked.

"Take off your belt," Mikey said.

"Oh, right."

The boys struggled to lash the boards together, but their little belts were far too small to gird more than a few widths of lumber. They couldn't get the boards to lie flat, either. When the belts were cinched, the planks had a tendency to scrunch one atop the other, but the boys continued to work on their make-shift raft until a sliver pierced the tip of Paul's pudgy index finger.

"Shit!" he cried. popping the wounded digit into his mouth. "Dang, it hurts!"

"What?" Mikey jumped up, fearfully surveying the ground around their feet, thinking perhaps a snake had struck.

"I got a damn sliver. That's what."

"Jeez. Is that all?" Mikey scoffed. "Don't be a baby." He thrust out a palm. "Here, let me see it."

"Nah, it's okay." Paul said. "I think I got it out."

"Heck," Mikey said. "It's getting dark. We gotta go home soon."

"Yeah," Paul agreed. He unfastened the belts and bent to pick up the makings of their pitiful raft. "Help me, you moron. We've got to put these back, or Dad will tan our hides."

"Look at me!" Tara teetered, balancing herself like a tightrope walker, on a few stacked planks.

The boys were intent on restacking the lumber and ignored her cries. They turned and headed back toward the pile of two-by-fours, never noticing when Tara lost her footing. Struggling to keep her balance, she slipped and stamped on one end of a plank. In the next instant, another board rose up and whacked her on the forehead with such force it sent her flying. One minute she was standing by the side of the water-filled cavity. In the next, she was submerged in a frigid, murky bog.

Tara's first instinct was to open her mouth and scream, but she had sense enough not to. Instead, she held her breath, keeping her lips firmly pressed together. Her eyes were wide open, and she saw, with perfect clarity, the cinderblocks before her. The shock of the icy water drained the strength from her limbs, and she felt as dense and incapable of motion as one of those blocks. Summoning all that she had left, she flailed her arms, her fingers scrabbling over the rough face of the masonry, but there was nothing to grab hold of. Helplessly, she watched as a line of bubbles escaped from between her lips and rose to the surface. Her lungs were screaming for air, but she fought the instinct to inhale and willed her leaden legs to move.

Tara had taken only a few lessons at the YMCA last summer, and that was ages ago. As she felt her lungs bursting with the overwhelming desire to breathe, a familiar mantra resounded in her brain. *Kick, kick! Big arms. Push. Stroke, stroke, kick.*

Fritzie was pacing at the edge of the pool when Tara's head broke the surface. At the sound of his frenzied barking, Paul and Mikey turned in unison. With looks of horror on their faces, they dropped the lumber they'd been wrestling and dashed to the pit. Just as Tara slipped beneath the surface, Fritzie leapt into the water.

Again, Tara held her breath. Weighted down by water-logged leggings and galoshes, it was impossible for her to kick. Slowly, she descended, and a sense of peace washed over her as she felt herself detaching. Then Fritzie was under her, like some furry trident, lifting her up and supporting her as he paddled to the surface.

The boys hauled her out and immediately began mouth-to-mouth. Tara gagged and pushed them away, water spewing from her mouth and nose. They heaved Fritzie out, and he shook, showering them with icy droplets.

"Dad's gonna kill us," Paul complained, sizing up the girl, who, though nearly lifeless, was shivering uncontrollably

"Crap," Mikey said. "She's freezing to death. Look at her. She's blue."

"Take off your jacket," Mikey commanded, as he unzipped his own.

The boys covered Tara with their woolen overcoats, but their sister's quaking did not subside.

"Lie on her," Mikey said, recalling his Boy Scout wilderness training. The boys covered her body with their own small frames, as the sun slipped lower behind the line of trees. They continued to hold her, rubbing Tara's arms with their small hands, blowing their warm breath on her face until Tara's tremors subsided, and her eyes began to focus.

~

By the time they arrived home, the older girls had set the table, and dinner was nearly ready. The house was warm and welcoming, the radiated heat wafting up from grills Earl had installed along the perimeter of the wood flooring. A fire crackled in the big hearth that opened onto the kitchen on one side and family room on the other.

In the laundry room, the boys shucked off Tara's wet clothing and their own, depositing the soiled garments in the laundry tub. They dragged Tara along with them into the adjoining bath and showered under a scalding stream. Finally, Tara began to thaw out. After changing into warm dry clothes, the three miscreants arrived at the kitchen table just as supper was being served.

Lucy had prepared goulash, one of Tara's favorites, but the girl barely touched her plate.

"What's the matter, honey?" Lucy asked her youngest.

The boys shot Tara warning looks, but she didn't notice. Her eyes were glazed and her cheeks, flushed.

"What's gotten into her?" Lucy rose from the table to stand behind Tara's chair. She placed a cool palm on Tara's forehead. "I think you've got a little fever." She cut her eyes to Earl. "Best get her into bed."

"Come on then, Tara." Earl swept his baby girl up in his muscled arms as effortlessly as if she were a rag doll. He carried her up the stairs to her bed, and she was asleep the moment her head touched the pillow.

"You boys, what devilment have you been up to?" Lucy asked.

"Nothing," Mikey and Paul chimed in unison."

"We were just playing, that's all." Paul added. "Got wet in the mud."

"Humph!" Lucy sniffed. "Well then, clean your plates. There's a rhubarb pie for dessert."

CHAPTER SEVENTEEN

LINES DRAWN

Gloria had donned black spandex so that she might blend into her surroundings. Should anyone remark upon her appearance, an early morning run would be her explanation. She coasted into the empty parking garage, slid into the reserved slot nearest the stairwell, and killed the headlights. A glance at the dashboard clock told her it was after 4 a.m.

As she raced up the dark shaft of the stairwell, her heartbeat quickened, and she felt a wanton exhilaration. Senses heightened, she depressed a series of numbers on the alarm pad, disarming the system. It was time to get to work.

She made a beeline to the copy machine and pressed the on button. While it warmed up, she padded to Nathan's private office. Here, yet another key gained her entrance. Gloria rounded Nathan's desk and opened the file drawer where folders of his active accounts were stored. Her eyes raced greedily over Nathan's hand-written notes. One account was that of a well-known recording artist who'd invested in several luxury hotels. Another was the grandson of the founder of a huge food and beverage chain. More detailed information was stored on Nathan's PC, but lacking his password, these files would have to do for now.

Documents in hand, she raced back to the copier and immediately began making copies. With a little luck, she'd be back out on the street in half an hour. Gloria couldn't suppress a satisfied grin. Oh, yes, Nathan dear, she thought, your little Gloria is more than a pretty face. She's a player. She's in the game now, and the stakes are mighty high.

～

The pounding of the surf just beyond her balcony had subsided, and Tara awoke to a muted rumble. It took a moment for her to orient herself, and then it all came flooding back. She had obligations. Springing out of bed, she quickly dressed in a pair of slacks and a loosely-woven cotton sweater. After running a comb through her hair and splashing some water on her face, she hurried down to the kitchen, only to be greeted by the sound of Harry's laughter and Chanel's answering bark.

"Good morning, Harry," she said, pleased to note that he was up and dressed in his school uniform. Such a darling boy. Tara prayed that Jennifer would appear, appropriately dressed, and soon.

"Hey, Ms. Tara." Harry sat cross-legged on the floor, face to snout with the dog. "Chanel slept next to me and didn't budge all night." He kneaded the Yorkie's head. "Isn't that right, pal?"

"Little turncoat," Tara muttered under her breath. "He's going to have to go out. Would you mind taking him?"

"Okay." The boy scrambled to his feet. "Come on, buddy. You want to go outside?" He clipped Chanel's leash to his collar and headed out the door.

"Wait a minute," Tara cried. "What would you like for breakfast?" She glanced at the clock on the range. "I'm afraid there's not enough time for eggs or pancakes."

"I don't care," Harry answered. "I'll just grab a breakfast bar."

"Not on my watch, you won't," Tara shot back. "Just take him out for a quick pee, while I scrounge up something."

The freezer yielded frozen waffles, and she unearthed a carton of fresh orange juice in the fridge. Tara located the toaster, popped in a couple waffles, and then headed toward the stairs to see if she could elicit a response from the resident teenager.

When Jennifer finally flounced into the room, she was wearing jeans and a tee, with a slice of exposed midriff showing between the two. Harry eyed her quizzically but offered no comment.

"Whoa!" Tara cried, taking in the teen's outfit. "What gives, Jennifer? You're not dressed for school."

"Yes, I am." Jennifer countered. "It's a dress-down day."

Perplexed, Tara turned to Harry. "Is that right, Harry? Is it a dress-down day?"

Harry scrunched up his face and gave an exaggerated shrug. No help there. God bless him. He wouldn't rat on his sister. Given Jenn's casual attire, Tara was pretty certain she'd planned to skip school. Perhaps Jennifer was attempting to wrest control from her, mounting the first salvo in a show of defiance. If that were the case, the girl would have to be thwarted, the power struggle nipped in the bud.

"We're going to miss the bus," Jennifer cried. "Come on, Harry."

"Hold on a minute," Tara commanded. "I'm not buying it, Jennifer."

"We'll be late," Jennifer screeched, heading for the door.

Tara was struck by inspiration. "I'll drive. You won't be late, but when we get there, if it's not a dress-down day, you'll feel pretty stupid in that get-up. Won't you?"

"She'd have to do detention." Harry muttered under his breath.

"Shut up!" Jennifer's face boiled with rage. "I hope you're happy," she spat at Tara. "Now you *will* have to drive me." Jennifer crossed to the hallway. "I hate you both." She pounded up the stairway and then slammed her door shut with a resounding bang.

Tara figured that would be the next bone of contention. No more door-slamming. For now, she was willing to let it pass. One hurdle at a time. "Harry, do you want me to drive you, or will you take the bus?"

Harry shook his head and forked a bit of waffle into his mouth. "Bus," he said, cryptically. Tara didn't blame him. At this point, she wouldn't mind taking the bus herself.

The ride to St. Theodore's was tense. Tara's attempts at conversation eliciting not a word from the passenger fuming beside her. It wasn't until they arrived on campus, that Jennifer spoke.

"Get in that lane over there." She indicated a line of cars. "You should have driven one of *our* cars, instead of this clunker. I'll have to tell everyone you're the maid."

"Look, Jennifer," Tara struggled to keep her cool. "I don't want to get off to the wrong start. I was hoping we could be friends."

"As if." Jennifer sneered at the thought. In an instant, the teen had levered the door open and was sprinting toward a group of girls, all of whom were sporting modest skirts topped by cotton tanks and matching sweaters.

Tara figured she'd won this round with Jennifer, but the price of victory had been dear. She felt emotionally drained, and it was only 8:45 in the morning. What had she gotten herself into?

She drove the short distance back to the McCourt compound. There, she poured herself a mug of coffee, which she drank while performing a cursory clean-up of the kitchen. Once the dishwasher was loaded and the counters wiped clean, she sat at the kitchen table with the Vero Beach Press Journal spread out before her, but she was too restless to read. Instead, she felt the urge to explore. Except for Chanel, she was completely alone in the mansion. Ignoring a twinge of conscience, she set out.

On the several occasions she'd been to the house, she'd become familiar with the main rooms and their furnishings, but the residence was enormous, and she'd never been given a proper tour.

Tara made her way down the hall beneath the sweeping stairway that lead to the south wing. Here, the walls had been hung with a variety of framed masterpieces. It was a miniature gallery—a feast for the eyes—every work of art lit from above by a tiny halogen fixture. Tara paused before each canvas. She was no art expert, but she identified a miniature Picasso ink-and-pastel sketch of an infant that stopped her in her tracks, and a Dali charcoal drawing, which she couldn't help but identify, as it was of the artist himself, pop-eyed, with the thinnest of flying mustaches. So far, so very good.

At the end of the hall, she came to a pair of doors. Detailed casing distinguished this portal from the others. Feeling a bit like Pandora, Tara drew them open and flicked on a wall switch. Instantly, the room was awash in light, and her eyes grew wide. She'd seen photographs in magazines, but nothing prepared her this lavishly appointed home theater, one entire wall of which was devoted to video and sound systems.

Surely, with all this high-tech equipment, she could manage to locate a music source. Pouring over the confusing panel of buttons and switches, she searched for the stereo, but it was beyond her.

Craving sound, Tara crossed to the Planar 3 Turntable and immediately began sifting through stacks of vinyl for a suitable album. It didn't take long before her efforts were rewarded. She slid the record from its cardboard sleeve, gently positioned it on the turntable, and lowered the tonearm into place. In the next moment, Lionel Ritchie's mellow voice warmed the space. After adjusting the volume, Tara turned on some speakers, and the house was suddenly alive with music.

Tara glanced at her watch. It was late. She was scheduled to play for a funeral at St. Sebastian at eleven, and she wanted to get there early to rehearse. She found her way back to the great room and charged up the stairs. There'd been enough drama and adventure for one morning.

Or so she thought.

CHAPTER EIGHTEEN

HIJINKS

It was ten-thirty on a Thursday morning, the one day of the week that Scandals stayed open late in order to accommodate its high-powered working clientele. In a lull between customers, Kevin stared idly out the window at the canal that snaked behind the building. As usual, his gaze fell on the handsome Donzi Classic moored there. Across her stern, black lettering outlined in gold spelled *Island Girl*.

Kevin thought about what he'd do with that sweet little hole in the water if only she were his. He'd be making runs to the islands, all right, and it wouldn't be to fish or dive. No. The bounty he desired was not harvested from the sea. Sure, it was dumped there from time to time, white powder formed into bricks and wrapped in plastic. Occasionally, those packages washed up on shore, and the next morning's headlines screamed the street value of the salvage in the hundreds of thousands. More often, the opiate reached its intended destination. Kevin did his own small part to ensure that outcome. The speedboat was fast and, given a few minor modifications, could outrun any Coast Guard cutter.

Kevin's addiction history was not unique. He'd progressed from smoking weed to snorting cocaine, to injecting crack, to shooting heroin, to fentanyl. He was done with fentanyl, though. He thought back to where that road had taken him. At some juncture, he'd found himself leaning precariously over an abyss. He'd lost days, entire weeks that couldn't be accounted for, in his drug-induced delirium, but the oblivion opioids delivered had been seductive. He'd kept it up until awakening one morning in a derelict rooming house in downtown Fort Pierce with no recollection of how he'd gotten there. The terrifying reality of that awakening had jolted him out of his complacency. He was naked as a jaybird and in bed with a corpse.

His party partner of the evening, whoever he was, had overdosed, and the first thought that had penetrated Kevin's reeling conscious was that he'd been spared. For once in his miserable life, he'd been lucky. But then, with mounting dread, Kevin's memory returned. The two had shared the same needle. Shaking, both from fear and withdrawal, he'd dressed and attempted to erase any evidence of his presence. In a frenzy, he'd wiped down door handles and switch-plates, just as he'd seen crooks do in the movies. Then, he'd cut out of that wretched room and never looked back.

He'd followed the investigation, a long, drawn-out affair, probably because the poor unfortunate's uncle was a cop. In the end, it'd fizzled, but he still wasn't off the hook. Months afterward, Kevin agonized over the possibility of having contracted hepatitis C or, worse yet, AIDS. Eventually, he'd mustered the courage to be tested, and the results had come back negative. He'd been lucky after all, and that finally sobered him.

These days, he was sticking with the white lady for the rush he craved, trafficking in whatever he could get his hands on in order to support his little habit. It was back to running lines. A nice, manageable high was all he needed—a little staycation. It was a rich man's vice. Weren't they all?

He made good money at Scandals, and he supplemented that income by selling a little weed, a little blow, and prescription pain meds when he could get them. It was never enough. Kevin pinched his nose. He could do with a snort, just a little something to take the edge off. He glanced at his cell phone display. His eleven o'clock appointment would be here any minute. Nervously, he slid a hand into his hip pocket. His fingers found and caressed Scottly's vintage onyx and diamond ring. This little baby would buy a whole lot of nose candy.

~

Before deplaning, Nathan shook hands with both the pilot and copilot. He clambered down the jet's stairs and out onto the baking tarmac, only to be enveloped in what felt like a steaming, sauna towel.

As he slid behind the wheel of his Porsche, the scorching seat cushion nearly blistered his butt. Fastening his seatbelt, he carefully avoided the metal catch—past experience had taught him it would be hot enough to cauterize. As the air conditioner gradually cooled the interior, Nathan spun out onto Aviation Boulevard and was soon at the southeast corner of an intersection distinguished by a ramshackle bait and tackle shop. Its crude, hand-painted sign proclaimed *Live Shrimp, Clams, and Ballyhoo*. Nathan loved it, a holdout from the inevitable encroachment of national chain stores, pharmacies, and supermarkets that rendered nearly every major intersection across the country homogenous and bland.

Turning right on the causeway, Nathan took in the spectacular view afforded from the first of the two bridges, and his heart expanded. A movement on the water caught his eye, and he concentrated on that spot. In the next instant, he was rewarded when a pair of bottlenose dolphins broke the surface. Nathan took the sighting as an omen, an affirmation of his good fortune.

Although he'd traveled the world, it was always a delight to return to the barrier island, that lush spit of land running from ocean to the palm-fringed Indian River Lagoon. Traversing the second, high-arched span, he admired the sparkling Atlantic directly ahead.

"Ah," he breathed.

Paradise.

Heading south on A1A, Nathan drove past Wabasso Beach, where sun-bleached surfers mingled with tourists and retirees. He eased up on the gas pedal, keenly aware of young families on rental bicycles, venturing out onto the highway from the rambling Disney Resort.

Suddenly, Nathan was seized by an overwhelming urge to kick back. Why not have a quick lunch at the Quail Valley Country

Club, he wondered, and then head over to the marina? Maybe take the Grady White out for a spin?

Yes!

But first, he'd have to get out of this stifling business suit and into a golf shirt and some khaki shorts.

As he pulled into the gated entrance to Palacia del Mar, Nathan eyes were immediately drawn to the white Lexus parked in the circular drive. Who could possibly be here at this hour, and where was Willie's Honda?

Nathan parked the car in the garage and ambled to the side door leading to the laundry room and kitchen beyond. He opened the door only to be assailed by loud music booming from an overhead speaker. What was going on here? Nathan recognized the album. It was one of his favorites, vintage Lionel Ritchie, but who the hell had the nerve to fiddle with his sound system? Then, he spied a dog leash on the counter. A dog? More mystery.

"Anybody home?"

Except for Lionel's smoky voice, there was no answer. On the off-chance Harry might be having a lesson, he made his way to the music room. When he reached the double doors, he heard no arpeggios, no music whatsoever, except for that blasted recording.

Determined to get to the bottom of this, Nathan bounded up the curved stairway, taking the steps two at a time. The door to the guest suite was slightly ajar, and he hiked to it. Flinging the door wide, he peered inside, but nothing seemed to be out of place.

Hello," he called out, entirely unprepared for the series of events he set in motion.

With no warning, a furry little creature exploded from beneath the bed, lunging at him and barking ferociously.

Nathan gasped and backed away. In the next instant, he realized the diminutive canine snapping at his pant legs presented more annoyance than real threat. Nathan had an urge to laugh at the absurdity of his situation. He was, being *terrorized* by a terrier, who couldn't possibly tip the scales at more than seven pounds. Then, his eyes cut to the guest bath on the north side of the room, and his smirk vanished. Too late, he noticed a cloud of steam wafting from the bath.

Before he had time to make a quick exit, a female voice called out. "Chanel? What is it?"

Nathan's first thought was perhaps the apparition appearing before him had been conjured from mist and vapor. The steam dissipated, and he saw that this nude woman was only too corporal and a rather attractive package at that.

Toweling her hair as she stepped from the bathroom, she bent at the waist, damp tresses tumbling over her forehead. When she straightened, her face took on a look of dismay. "Oh, my God!" she shrieked, clutching the towel to her body, while at the same time attempting to back-pedal into the bathroom.

Nathan noted the look of recognition in her eyes before she cried out.

"It's you!" Her voice was full of incredulity. "Oh, oh," she sputtered, as she tried in vain to cover herself. "What are you doing here?"

Stunned, Nathan could only stare at the irate female. How bizarre to find the woman, who'd mown him down on rollerblades, showering in his guest bath.

"Excuse me?" He was the offended party, after all. Where did the hussy get off? "What the hell are *you* doing here?"

The two locked eyes, and for a brief moment, all rancor vanished. Nathan offered a tentative smile, and Tara's stony expression softened. Then, she seemed to remember she was naked before a strange man. "Get out," she wailed, as she retreated into the bath, slamming the door in his face.

Nathan decided to do just that, but the woman's emotional tirade, combined with the slamming of the bathroom door, had further incensed the little dog. He redoubled his efforts, nipping at Nathan's ankles in earnest. Nathan snorted. He had to hand it to the little fellow. He was fearless. Skirting the determined creature, he backed out of the room and closed the door behind him.

What a madhouse.

Nathan had no desire to stick around and sort things out. He certainly didn't feel up to another confrontation, be it with woman or beast. Let Willie handle them. That's what he paid her for, wasn't it? To deal with all the crazy stuff he didn't have time for? You betcha.

"We're gonna party, forever. Fiesta all night long." Nathan sang over the recorded track, all the while thinking that old Lionel had gotten it absolutely right. It occurred to him that perhaps he should feel grateful rather than annoyed by the peculiar events of the last few days. How many guys had the good fortune to encounter not one, but two gorgeous, buck-naked women in the course of a week? First the cool and elegant Gloria, and now this fiery, dark-haired harpy. From the sublime to the ridiculous.

"Oh, yeah. Come on and sing my song."

~

Willie was back, bigger than life, yet somehow, diminished. Seated on her favorite kitchen stool, her face propped in her hands, she listened attentively while Tara recounted her most recent encounter with the man of the house.

"It was horrible," Tara moaned. "How can I ever face him again? I am thoroughly humiliated."

"It's my fault," Willie said. "Mr. McCourt, he seldom comes home early. I should have anticipated something like this. Man's probably fit to be tied."

"Why on earth would he be angry? Tara asked. "He can't expect you to be at his beck and call every minute."

"Umm," Willie muttered, seemingly unconvinced.

"Besides, I had things covered here." Tara's face split in a self-deprecating grin. "Well, not entirely covered," she amended.

Willie raised her eyebrows.

"In fact," Tara added, "certain *things* could definitely have been more concealed." Tara's merriment was contagious, and soon the housekeeper was laughing along with her.

"I guess you showed him a thing or two, Ms. Tara."

"I guarantee it was more than he'd come looking for."

They both dissolved in giggles.

With a glance toward the clock on the gas range, Tara hastily gathered up her things. "I'm sorry to rush off, but I've got to rehearse for Sunday Mass. I promised Harry that the dog would be here when he got home from school. If it's okay with you, I'll leave Chanel. I should be back by five-thirty."

"Dog's no trouble. Tend to what you must. I'm obliged for your help."

With a backward wave of her hand, Tara made light of the housekeeper's thanks and sailed out the door. She hoped Willie would feel the same once the mysterious McCourt returned, but she had her doubts.

CHAPTER NINETEEN

SECOND CHANCES

The line zinged out in an arc, cutting the dense, beating heart of the night with the precision of a scalpel. There was a soft plunk as the lure pierced the water's surface, and from the initial point of contact, an ever-widening ring of concentric circles emanated outward. Earl took a deep drag of his cigarillo and blew out his own series of rings. Those quickly dissipated, like little spirits in the gentle breeze, leaving only malodorous traces of smoke clinging to warm, moist air.

Although Earl's hearing wasn't what it once was, a mad chorus of sound assailed his ears. Insects whirred and thrummed in the bushes, and a colony of tree frogs lustily chirruped an eerie madrigal. An occasional crashing in the treetops overhead heralded a newly awakened coon rustling out of his nest on a quest for his dinner. Over it all, cicadas laid down an incessant, atonal accompaniment.

Earl coughed a ragged cough and hawked a wad of spittle.

Damn things.

He ground the glowing nub of the cigarette butt in the sand. Doc said he had to quit. Hadn't they all been telling him that for twenty years or more? Earl jiggled his pole causing the lure to dance just below the water's surface.

In the next moment, the river spit up a fish. Briefly, it soared and then fell back into the depths.

"Come on, fish. Bite," Earl muttered.

Was he any wiser than that wily old mangrove snapper for whom he'd been angling? One trades his life for a bit of shiny metal, the other for a smoke. Maybe not, Earl conceded, but what of it? He did a quick calculation. Hell, he'd been smoking for fifty years or more, ever since he was a boy. It was one of the few pleasures he'd treated himself to. Besides, he didn't want to live forever. He was too damn lonely. Not that he hadn't had his share of women chasing after him.

The Casserole Brigade, he'd dubbed them—empty-headed, flighty women who couldn't survive lest they had a man to cling to. Nothing like his Lucy, who'd been so capable and sure of herself. He'd ignored them all, their offers of a home-cooked meal, their less than subtle suggestions regarding promised favors. Eventually, they'd stopped calling on him. Off beleaguering some other poor sucker, he figured, and good riddance.

How he missed Lucy. Now, there was a woman. He'd spent the best years of his life with her. Earl thought back to when the kids were little, when he and Lucy were young and fearless, carving out a legacy. There'd been plenty of hardships, but he'd never been happier. They'd had a houseful of babies and a mountain of bills, but those had been grand times.

A single tear worked its way down the creviced landscape of Earl's face. He dashed it away with the back of his gnarled hand and shook himself out of his reverie. He was a sentimental old coot feeling sorry for himself.

Here he was, living high on the hog, right smack dab in the middle of Paradise, and now that Tara was here, he'd be seeing more of her, and the boy, too. Earl patted his chest pocket and reached for a smoke.

Then he hesitated. Maybe he *should* quit or at least cut back. Truth be told, he wasn't quite ready to throw in the towel just yet.

A tug on his line and Earl forgot all about craving a smoke. Instinctively, he jerked the pole, his face cracked with a sly grin. Hot diggity dog. He'd sure as hell hooked something.

"Come on, baby," Earl breathed, while slowly reeling in his catch. Wasn't he one lucky son-of-a-gun, after all?

~

Tara climbed out of the car just as the automatic sprinkler activated, raining arcs of spray down on the lawn and flowerbeds with a sibilant hiss. She raced up the back steps, dodging the shower and called out a hello as she let herself in through the side door. No sooner had she reached the kitchen, than she heard the click of Chanel's nails as he tore down the stairway. In the next moment, he flew in, yipping a hello, and Harry was right behind him.

"He must have heard your car," Harry panted, his face rosy from his exertion. "He started barking, jumped off the bed, and took off." Harry hunkered down by Chanel. "You knew she was here, didn't you?" The boy massaged the little dog's head. "You couldn't wait to see her."

"Hey, baby." Tara hunkered down and gave Chanel a cuddle before she turned to Willie. "That smells wonderful. What is it?"

Willie stood before the range, her hands encased in oven mitts. "Nothing fancy, just pot roast." She opened the oven door a crack and peered in.

"May I help?" Tara dropped her keys on the kitchen counter.

"No need."

Tara eyed the cooktop. "How about the potatoes? I'm a great potato masher."

"If' you like. The hand mixer is in that cupboard." Willie nodded toward a base cabinet.

Tara went to fetch the mixer. "Harry, would you take Chanel for a quick walk before dinner?"

"Sure. Come on, boy."

"How is she?" Tara asked when the two were alone.

"Not sure yet." Willie transferred the roast and root vegetables to a porcelain platter. "We'll know more when the test results come back."

Tara plugged in the hand mixer and drained the potatoes.

"She says it's like a family at Indian River Memorial. They look out for their own."

"That's encouraging. Just remember. I'll stay here whenever you need me, especially over the next few months. Honestly," Tara scooped the potatoes into a serving bowl, "if you saw my house, you'd realize you were doing me a favor."

"That's very kind of you."

149

Tara glanced at the kitchen table. "Shall I set the table?"

"I already set it." Willie stirred a slurry of cornstarch and water into the roasting pan. Mr. McCourt is home for the night, and he takes his dinner in the dining room. As soon as I get this meal on the table, I'll be on my way."

McCourt!

Tara's heart sank. She hadn't expected him to be home. After this morning's debacle, she had no desire to confront that annoying man yet again. "Oh, dear," she said. "I'd better get going, too."

"Nonsense," a male voice boomed from the hallway. "Of course, you'll join us."

Tara pivoted, coming face to face with her nemesis. Upon catching sight of him, a strange thing happened. She gazed into his eyes, and her heart skipped a beat. Surely, this wasn't the same person, the angry jogger she'd steamrolled over, the crass and blundering fellow who'd come upon her in an embarrassing state of dishabille? It couldn't be. This man was impossibly good-looking, and he was smiling at her so openly. Not at all as she remembered him. Tara found it impossible not to return his smile.

Nathan thrust a hand toward her. "How do you do?" he asked, "I don't believe we've been *properly* introduced."

The man's hand was in front of her.

Move, move, Tara's inner voice commanded, but her body failed to respond.

"I'm Nathan McCourt," he said, hand extended.

Duh, no kidding.

Finally, Tara's brain kicked in, and she took his hand. "Hello," she said, her words tumbling out in a rush. "I'm Tara Purcell. I mean Cahill. Harry's piano teacher."

"Which is it, Purcell or Cahill?" Nathan's eyes twinkled.

"I'm not quite sure myself. Born a Cahill. Married a Purcell, but that didn't work out, so it's back to Cahill," Tara stammered, still holding his hand. Now that she'd taken the thing, she seemed incapable of releasing it, which left Nathan no alternative other than to just go on holding hers.

~

Thinking back on it, Tara was mortified. The two of them had stood like that, awkwardly, until Harry burst upon the scene with Chanel on his heels. That had broken the spell. As she drove down the A1A corridor, Tara consoled herself with the fact that she'd managed to get through dinner without spilling anything or making any overt gaffes. The dinner conversation had been stilted, interspersed with long periods of silence, broken only by the clink of cutlery on china.

Tara, who remembered family dinners as boisterous affairs, had to bite her tongue, repressing an urge to fill the void with mindless chatter. It wasn't her place, and they weren't her people. She'd sympathized with Nathan as he attempted to draw Jennifer out, questioning her about her day. The teen had given him no ground, evading his queries and offering only monosyllabic replies. When Nathan wasn't looking, she'd glared at Tara, baiting her with narrowed eyes, as if daring her to mention the morning's rocky beginning.

In the end, it was Chanel who'd kept the meal from being a complete disaster. For the better part of it, he'd lain quietly, curled beneath the table. Apparently, deciding he'd been patient long enough, he finally broke his silence and whined for a handout.

They'd all ignored his pitiful cries, until Nathan said, "Good heavens. Who released the hounds of Baskerville?"

At that, Jennifer's pout transformed into a grin, and Harry slid beneath the table, where he was met by an exuberant battery of doggie kisses.

The biggest surprise came when Jennifer offered to help clear the table. As they scraped plates and wrapped up leftovers, Tara related the details of Willie's predicament.

"I had no idea," Jennifer said. "I always thought she was happy."

"Willie has a naturally sunny disposition. That doesn't mean she doesn't have problems."

Jennifer frowned, and, seeing that her words had hit their mark, Tara went on to explain her own situation. "You see, Jennifer, there are a number of reasons why I volunteered to fill in for Willie." She turned toward the girl and looked her square in the eyes. "I hope that you'll accept me, that we can try to be friends. If not for me, then for Willie's sake."

Jennifer paused to consider, then gave a grudging nod of assent.

"All right," she said, "but don't go getting any ideas. You're not my mother, and I don't have to do what you say." Jennifer dried her hands on the dishtowel. "Can I go now?" Not waiting for an answer, the teen tossed the towel on the granite countertop and strode away.

Tara realized that a fragile truce had been established. She didn't want to say anything that might jeopardize it, but she had to maintain a certain level of authority over the girl. Otherwise, Jennifer would walk all over her. "Wait, Jenn," she said. "Here's the deal."

The teen turned a sullen face to Tara.

"I'm going to be absolutely straight with you. I won't treat you like a little kid unless you act like one. I expect you to be totally honest with me from now on. If you act responsibly, you'll be treated like the young adult you are. If I think you're trying to pull a fast one on me, like you did this morning, or engaging in an activity which could prove harmful to yourself or others, there will be consequences."

"Ooo!" Jennifer rolled her eyes in mock terror, turned, and continued on her way. "I'd love to stay and chat," she called over her shoulder, "but I've got to finish my homework."

In the next minute, Harry, Chanel, and Nathan burst through the door. Harry dropped to the floor to deliver a quick tummy rub to Chanel's belly, then jumped to his feet. "I'm going upstairs to read," he said. "See you, Ms. Tara."

Tara wanted nothing more than to make a quick exit. "Night, Harry," she said. As soon as the boy had gone, she glanced in Nathan's direction, unwilling to meet his eyes. "I guess I'll be going now."

"Don't rush off."

Tara considered. It had been a stressful day, and she'd had quite enough of the McCourt family, but Nathan needed to be told of Willie's situation, and she was the one to bring him up to speed.

"Please," Nathan coaxed. "Stay awhile."

Tara allowed herself to be led out to the lanai, where French doors opened out onto the pool beyond and the air was fragrant with the scent of tropical blooms. Nathan indicated she should sit in a lounge chair, then went to the bar and proceeded to fill two crystal glasses with ice.

"What's your pleasure?" he asked. "I'm having a gin and tonic."

"Fine."

Drinks in hand, they sat for a moment, staring out over the pool with its splashing waterfall. Then, both spoke at once.

"I wanted to—"

"You know, I..." Nathan furrowed his brow. "Sorry."

"No, no." Tara shook her head. "You go first."

"It seems we didn't get off on the right foot. No pun intended." Nathan made a wry face and chuckled.

"Right. My feet ran over your feet. I am *so* sorry. I'm a terrible klutz."

"And then this morning..."

"Ugh, could we just forget this morning?"

Nathan cupped his chin in hand. "I'd say yes," he finally said, "but I'd be lying. You, madam, were a vision, one which is indelibly imprinted on my disgustingly masculine brain."

"Ah." Tara's cheeks burned. "I guess I'll have to live with that."

"Me, too. It's an onerous a burden, I admit."

Tara chuckled. She was being teased, but a compliment was implicit. Feeling more composed, she dared meet his deep-set eyes, and, once again, got lost in them. "I'm afraid I owe you an apology," she ventured.

"Oh?" Nathan raised his brows.

"I was completely off base. There I was, in your guest suite, screeching at you to leave. Poor man, you must have thought I was insane."

"No, I thought you were naked, flustered, and rightly so. Had the tables been turned, I'd have..." Nathan paused, as he searched for the right words. "Let's just say things might have turned out differently."

Tara could picture Nathan naked, vainly trying to cover his large frame with a towel while backtracking into the bath, and she burst out laughing. "Yeah, right. Probably not."

The air seemed to clear, and for the second time that evening, Tara recounted Willie's sad state of affairs and went on to explain her own offer of assistance.

"That's incredibly generous of you, Tara." Nathan leaned forward and pinched the bridge of his nose, while he mulled over this new development. "I have to say," he resumed, "I'm ashamed not to have been more aware of Willie's situation. Of course, I'll pay you—"

Tara bridled, cutting him off. "You will do no such thing. I might just as well pay you room and board since I'm practically homeless. Don't you see? My offer has nothing to do with compensation. Willie is in over her head, and I'm in the perfect position to help her. It's a win-win all the way around. Besides, I get to rehearse on your magnificent Steinways."

Nathan seemed taken aback by her outburst, and Tara had run out of patience. It had been an emotionally draining day, and, as attractive as she found this enigmatic man, she was at her wit's end and eager to be on her way.

Nathan concentrated on his glass, twirling the small bits of ice remaining. "How about another?" He unfolded himself from the chair.

"It's late. I really must be going."

"If you insist."

They made their way back through the great room, coming to stop at the base of the stairway. Tara called softly for Chanel, but the dog failed to appear.

"We'll go find him." Nathan gestured for her to lead the way. Tara climbed the stairs, supremely conscious of her undulating hips.

She imagined Nathan was getting an eyeful of her ass, but there was nothing to be done about it. They tiptoed into Harry's room, where they found the little dog nestled contentedly beside the sleeping child. The two paused for a moment, gazing at the sweet tableau.

"He's a wonderful kid," Tara whispered. "So talented. You must be very proud of him."

"Yes."

Tara could feel Nathan behind her. It was as though gamma rays were shooting from his body to hers. She'd been so lonely. How long had it been since she'd felt a man's arms around her? In a weak moment, she turned to him, and he was so close she could feel his warm breath. Did she imagine the look of desire in his eyes? Tara wanted nothing more than to fall into Nathan's arms, to be kissed deeply and passionately.

Harry cried out in his sleep, and Tara whirled back around to face him. The boy sighed, but did not awaken, and, in that instant, Tara reined in her foolish longings. It would be another two weeks before her divorce was finalized. Technically, she was still married. Never mind that she couldn't remember the last time she and Jack had been intimate or that she felt completely betrayed by him. He was the father of her child. This attraction to Nathan? She was his son's piano teacher, nothing more, and she wasn't about to make a fool of herself and act like a schoolgirl with a crush.

And yet...

~

Before the first light of dawn, a mockingbird began practicing his considerable repertoire, loudly and gustily, outside her bedroom window. Tara pulled the blanket over her head, but that did nothing to muffle the bird's raucous chorus. She threw off the coverlet and dragged herself to the bathroom, brushed her teeth, ran a comb through her hair, and did all those things one does to appear fit for public consumption.

By eight o'clock, the pickup trucks and vans began arriving. Coffee cup in hand, Tara watched as workmen spilled out onto the front yard and began unloading tools while exchanging good-natured greetings. After parking his Dodge Ram on the curb, her GC strode across the lawn toward her.

"How are you doing, Tara?"

"Just fine, Brett, and you?"

He went on to explain that he planned to push through to the master bedroom and bath in the next couple of days. "I'm afraid you're going to have to find somewhere else to nest. I know we talked about the possibility of you moving into the spare bedroom while the new master suite is completed. But, honestly, that would just delay the process and put off the completion date by another couple of months. If the drywall and trim guys can go to town in one fell swoop, rather than work piecemeal, it'll go a whole lot faster."

Tara had been dreading this day. Now, all she felt was relief. It had been so difficult living amid all this chaos. She couldn't wait to reestablish some semblance of order around here and get on with her life. "I'll be out of here today."

~

Tara called Pat. "I know it's the height of season, Patty, but could I possibly stay at your place while they finish up my renovation?"

"No problem," Pat said. "Cliff and I were planning to spend a month down there in April, but now he's begging off. Says he'll be lucky if he can spare a long weekend. Go make yourself at home. You know where the key is."

"You are a lifesaver."

"Just remember. You owe me big time, girlfriend."

After stripping the bed, Tara directed the sub-contractors to haul her bedroom furniture to the garage. Then, she cleaned out her closet, which took no time at all, as she'd never completely unpacked her clothing. Finally, she emptied the vanity cabinet, boxing up all but the essentials. She was ready to vacate by eleven-thirty, and that's when she called Scottly.

"Tara, darling," he said, "It's been ages. Where've you been, kitten?"

"It would take a month of Sundays for me to tell you what's been going on in my heretofore mundane existence."

"How about condensing it? You can relay the gory details over lunch," Scottly said. "On me."

"Wonderful. Where shall I meet you?"

"How about Bobby's? I'm dying for a burger, and theirs are the best in town."

"See you there at noon."

By the time Tara arrived at the sports bar and grill, Scottly had secured a booth by a window fronting Ocean Drive. He waved her over, and Tara motioned for him to remain seated rather than risk him tumbling from the elevated banquet. She slid in across from him, a wide grin on her face. As always, the designer was immaculately groomed, elegantly attired, and boasting his signature gems.

"You look fabulous," Tara said, suddenly struck by the fact that she'd grown accustomed to Scottly's spectacular jewelry. What, at first, she'd deemed an ostentatious display, now seemed an integral part of the man. He didn't need to draw attention to himself, for that occurred naturally. With his imposing figure and disarming smile, his presence filled any room he entered.

They ordered cheeseburgers, rare, accompanied by sweet potato fries and slaw.

"And two Absolute Bloody Marys," Scottly said to the waitress. "Yummy."

While waiting for their orders, the designer entertained Tara with juicy tidbits about his clients, and she laughed at her friend's droll humor. "You're incorrigible."

"I can't persuade you to bunk with me?" Scottly polished off the last of his burger. "You realize that Chanel and I have become best buds."

"You're a dear, but I'm staying at Pat's condo. If she and Cliff decide to fly down, I can move in with Dad. That is when I'm not filling in for Willie at the McCourt compound."

"What a vagabond you've become."

"I know. Who would have believed it?"

Scotty motioned for the waitress to replenish their drinks. Tara protested, but there was no stopping him. "Ah, yes," Scottly ruminated, "Nathan McCourt." The designer waggled his eyebrows. "Now there's a catch for you, darling. It's absolutely brilliant of you to have finagled your way into his household."

"For heaven's sake, Scottly. That's not the way it is. I just met him. Officially, anyway."

"Oh," Scottly's eyes grew round. "Running him over doesn't count? Did I strike a nerve?"

"No!" Tara exclaimed. "Well, maybe," she admitted. "Surely you, of all people, understand my motives. Which, by the way, are completely honorable."

"Of course," Scottly soothed.

"I imagine people are bound to think that, aren't they? Honestly, I never considered how it might look. Yikes."

"Screw what people think." Scottly threw a hand in the air. "Who's to know, anyway? I mean, duh. You're the piano teacher. Hell, I'd trade places with you in a heartbeat if I thought it'd do any good. McCourt's gorgeous and loaded to boot. Straight as an arrow, unfortunately for moi."

"How do you know this?" Tara asked, her interest piqued.

"He's a man about town, our Nathan is. It's rumored his weakness runs to leggy, young blondes."

"There you go." Tara laughed, mirthlessly. "That lets me off the hook."

"Don't give up so easily," Scottly scolded. "I'd say you had a fighting chance."

"The house is amazing, but it's sad in a way. For all the material things they have, not one of the McCourt clan seems happy."

"You'll change that, darling." Scottly wrinkled his nose. "Just like...What's her name?" He snapped his fingers. "Maria, the governess in *The Sound of Music*."

"You haven't met Jennifer." Tara's brow stitched up. "Suffice it to say, I've got my work cut out for me." Not wanting to spoil the mood, she quickly steered the conversation in another direction. "You're finally going to meet my son."

"Can't wait."

"I took your advice and booked the Driftwood Inn."

"Trust me. The kids will love it." Their waitress brought the check, and Scottly signed his name with a flourish. "And now," he said, tucking his credit card into his wallet, "about that polo match."

CHAPTER TWENTY

SURRENDER

They arrived in high spirits, a handsome trio of youths on holiday, eager to cut loose and have some fun in the sun. Aaron was a striking African American, and the tiny diamond stud glittering at his ear couldn't hold a candle to his radiant smile. Alexander, an international student hailing from Germany, towered over the other two. Thin as a rail, with an improbable mop-top of auburn curls, he spoke unaccented English perfectly seasoned with au courante American slang.

Tara met them at the terminal and herded them the short distance to the Hertz rental counter. There, they took possession of the keys to a late model Mustang.

When they emerged out onto the pavement, the heat hit them like a furnace blast. "Whew!" Josh cried. "Guess we're in Florida, guys."

"Awesome!" Alexander exclaimed, at the sight of the sporty convertible parked beneath a towering Washingtonian Palm.

"Whoo-hoo!" Aaron crowed, slapping Josh on the back. "Your mom rocks."

Behind the wheel of her Lexus, Tara led the way—from Nasa Drive to U.S. Highway 1. They snaked along the Indian River Lagoon, where fishing boats plied the briny waters. Forty-five minutes later, they turned in between the two stone columns topped by weathered lanterns leading to the Driftwood Inn compound.

"Super cool!" Alexander whooped, taking in the quaint seaside lodge constructed of ocean-washed timbers and festooned with tarnished art objects and Spanish antiques.

"Wow. Totally rad," Aaron agreed.

After a cursory inspection of their suite, the boys made a beeline to the French doors and the balcony beyond. They gazed out over the Atlantic, but it was more than the panoramic scenery that held them rapt. A boardwalk ran directly beneath their room, and, as luck would have it, a couple of pretty girls, scantily clad in bikinis, were leaning out over the railing gazing seaward. The young men hooted and laughed, overjoyed at their good fortune. At last, they'd arrived at their destination, and a week of lazy, sun-drenched days stretched before them.

They could have eaten there, at Waldo's, sat on the deck, and enjoyed a casual repast while being caressed by soft sea breezes, but Tara figured the boys would be doing a lot of that. Instead, they walked two short blocks north to the more upscale Ocean Grill, world renown not only for its fresh seafood but for the many unique artifacts embellishing every nook and cranny.

"This place is amazing," Aaron said, as they took their seats at a table overlooking the ocean. "I gotta say, I think I'm in love with Vero Beach."

"I told you." Josh grinned.

"It's like being on a ship surrounded by water." Alexander tore his gaze from the high tide lapping at the Grill's pilings, to encompass the interior. He took in the unusual ornamentation, the reclaimed treasures adorning the walls. "And a kitschy museum at the same time."

"Yes," Tara said. "It was Waldo Sexton who purchased the land and oversaw the building of both this and the Driftwood Inn, where you're staying, as well as a number of other similarly constructed buildings in the area. He was an eccentric entrepreneur, traveled the world collecting all sorts of things, like church bells, wrought iron pieces, ships' lanterns, Spanish tiles, mahogany, and other exotic woods, which he incorporated as decorative elements in his projects. He had the land cleared from here to A1A with a team of mules. Can you imagine? Originally, the Grill was designed as an open-air restaurant, way back in the early forties, but the no-see-ums—"

"The what?" Aaron interrupted.

"The gnats. They're so tiny as to be almost invisible, but their bite can drive you crazy," Josh explained.

"Which is exactly what happened, so they put a roof on it and enclosed it."

"I can't believe we're this close to the water's edge," Aaron said.

"Scottly told me if this place were ever destroyed, it could never be rebuilt, at least not in this location. Over time, there's been a great deal of erosion with each Nor'easter and tropical depression that blows this way. In the short time I've been here, I've heard a lot of objection. You know, making that kind of investiture on landfill, sand that is inevitably washed away."

"Money well spent, if you ask me," Josh said.

They ordered the house specials, freshly caught red snapper, and Jake's steak. The boys ate with gusto, plowing through their meals as though they might be their last, unabashedly requesting multiple refills of both bread and sodas. Once sated, the young men excused themselves, eager to be on their way. The night was young, and the thrill of possible conquests beckoned enticingly from the many saloons and nightclubs that dotted the strip. With their stomachs full, they had an appetite for something else entirely. Girls.

For Josh, there was only one girl that would do, and that was the flaming-haired hottie, Grace McKenzie.

On those rare occasions when Grace was free, Josh ducked out on his buddies to see her. Her spring break didn't coincide with his, and Grace felt like a puppet whose strings were being pulled in every direction. She was nearing the end of her senior year, and her days were crammed full of activities. What with lacrosse practice after school and homework assignments to complete in the evenings, a prom to organize, and college applications to complete, she barely had time to squeeze in a few hours on weekends waiting tables at the Lemon Tree.

"Unlike some people we know," she complained, "I have to work."

Maddeningly, when Grace was available, there was simply no

place where the two could be alone together. Josh had extended repeated invitations, but she'd steadfastly refused to come to his room at the Driftwood. Although he was disappointed by her refusal, he accepted her decision with equanimity. Who could blame her? The place was a hovel. With wet towels draping the furniture, empty pizza boxes, malodorous sneakers and discarded clothing strewn about, it was hardly a romantic setting. Instead, they returned to the scene of their first tryst, the isolated stretch of beach north of town.

Grace packed a picnic lunch, throwing in a few beers she'd lifted from the fridge at home. As before, the beach was nearly empty. They raced into the water, throwing themselves at the cresting breakers, and, before long, they were clinging to one another in the roiling surf. Waves crashed over them and then retreated, sucking the sand from beneath their toes. When Grace lost her footing, Josh hoisted her up, and she squealed when he carried her ashore.

After depositing her on a beach towel, he plopped down beside her. They lathered suntan oil on each other, taking pleasure in the sensuous kneading of flesh. Josh slipped his fingers beneath her suit, and Grace protested, laughing as she wriggled away. Desultorily, they'd nibbled at the sandwiches she'd packed, neither of them hungry, but they made fast work of the beer. The blue-green radiance of the sea dazzled them, and the effects of the alcohol and the warmth of the sun against their skin, made them drowsy. Sun-stunned, they lay beside one another, fingers interlaced, feeling momentarily happy and carefree, as white gulls swooped and soared overhead.

Grace awoke to the pressure of Josh's body against hers. He kissed her lips, and she could feel his manhood swell, poking at her through the damp fabric of his swim trunks. She closed her eyes running her fingers through his hair. When she opened them again, she spied a couple at a distance, walking toward them along the shoreline.

"Josh," she cried, squirming out from beneath him. "Someone's coming." Grace dug her cell phone from her bag. "Oh, my God," she wailed. "It's nearly three. I have to be at work at four-thirty."

Once again, Josh wrapped his arms around her, and they kissed.

Grace extricated herself from his embrace. "I'm sorry. I just can't be late again. You don't want me to lose my job. Do you?"

They gathered up their things, shook the sand from their beach towels, and trudged up the wooden steps to the dune crossover where the wild vegetation provided a protective wall around them. With Grace leading the way, they padded down the path in silence.

The hammock was an enchanted grotto. Cicadas bowed in the underbrush, filling the air with a shrill melody. Josh reached out and spun Grace around, drawing her to him. He pressed his lips against hers and kissed her deeply. Willingly, she succumbed to Josh's kisses, until they both surfaced for air. Josh took Grace's hand and picked his way off the trail and into the thicket. Here, trees and vines crowded in so that there was hardly room to turn around. When they came to a small clearing that afforded them a modicum of space. Josh drew the towel from around Grace's neck and spread it over the uneven ground.

Falling to his knees, he reached for Grace and pulled her down with him. They knelt before one another, exploring each other's mouths with fervent kisses until Grace's breath came in little gasps. Josh slid the straps from her shoulders, and like a child, Grace allowed herself to be undressed. Josh bent his head to breasts that were perfectly formed, suckling at pink nipples that had become engorged under his ministrations. Grace moaned with pleasure as a delicious pulling sensation streaked from her breasts to her loins.

Gently, Josh lowered her to the ground, and the two clung to one another, bodies aflame with sweet desire. "Is this okay?" Josh breathed.

"Yes," Grace gasped, pulling him to her. "Oh, yes."

Josh mounted her, staring deeply into her eyes, as he did so, and Grace arched at the waist, rising to meet him. At his first thrust, Grace cried out. Their bodies were slick with suntan oil and sweat, and, after a momentary resistance, he entered her.

Josh plunged into her moist welcoming center, and Grace opened herself to him. She pressed her heels into the firm flesh of his pumping buttocks, and Josh responded in kind, driving at her with the force of a battering ram. He raised himself above her, supporting his weight with the palms of his hands. Holding her gaze with his, he lunged at her, probing that deep secret chamber again and again.

Grace met him thrust for thrust in that primal dance, dizzily riding wave after wave of pleasure until, at last, all sensation seemed to concentrate in one pulsating rhythm. She was at the edge and ready to fall, whimpering, and, at the same time, screaming silently for release. Then she was tumbling out over a precipice she'd never imagined. There was an imploding, and something burst within her in one glorious, shuddering explosion.

Josh dove into her once more, his body taut, all sound and sensation reduced to this rushing, joyful climax. Groaning with pleasure, he collapsed heavily, his body blanketing hers. He could smell the salt in her damp tresses, feel her warm breath against his cheek. Sated, they lay together, partially conjoined, Grace's slender white legs intertwined with his, until the stickiness between their thighs became annoying. Then, suddenly self-conscious, they drew apart.

Grace arose, turned away, and shimmied into her bathing suit, while Josh hauled on his clammy swim trunks. They didn't speak, merely retraced their steps until they were seated in the Mustang and heading back to town.

Silence loomed between them.

Josh was the first to speak. "Grace." Briefly, he took his eyes off the road and searched the girl's face, desperate to know what was going on behind those sunglasses.

Grace returned his gaze, tilting her head slightly, as she waited for him to continue.

"I want you to know I never intended to..." Josh fumbled for the appropriate words. "I mean, I'm sorry for what happened back there."

Grace eyed him coolly. "You are?" So, this was how it was going to play out. Moments before, her heart had soared, but now it plummeted with a sickening thud. What a fool she'd been. Silently, she castigated herself. This is what she'd been saving herself for? "Hmm," she muttered, giving him no ground.

Josh stole another glance at Grace. She appeared maddeningly unruffled and perfectly self-possessed. "Damn," he cursed softly. "Hell, no. I'm glad. It was awesome. You're awesome. What I meant to say is I'm sorry...that is...if you're sorry. I never intended to hurt you or make you mad at me. I care for you, Grace."

Grace took a moment to process this information while her heart settled back in her chest. Josh seemed genuinely concerned for her well-being, and that made her very happy, but she wasn't about to let her defenses down just yet.

"I'm not sorry." Grace drew her sunglasses away from her eyes and gave him a pointed look before replacing them. "I'm not mad at you, Josh," she said, a small smile playing about her lips. "And you didn't hurt me one little bit."

"Great." Josh breathed a sigh of relief. "And, furthermore, I don't ever intend to." He hoped the implications of his statement were not lost on Grace. The future beckoned enticingly, one that suddenly included this beautiful young woman.

"You'd better not, you big dope." Grace threw a playful punch in his direction. "My guy friends would kill you."

Josh caught her fist in his right hand. "Like that's going to happen," he scoffed. Prying her fingers apart, he threaded his between hers. Then, he squeezed her small hand in his large one, and he didn't let go until he dropped her at her house so that she might shower and change for work.

While driving back to the Driftwood Inn, Josh pondered this new development. Of course, it's what he wanted. God knows, he adored Grace. She was...she was incredible, and he knew he needed to grab hold of her before someone else did, but he wasn't stupid. The future was uncertain. They were young and naïve, and the chances of their staying together throughout college and beyond were slim. Yet, he was bound and determined to hold her fast and keep her.

There was no denying it. He was in love with that girl.

CHAPTER TWENTY-ONE

MARCO

A car horn beeped, and Tara gathered up her picnic basket. "Coming, Dad," she hollered, before hunkering down to address Chanel. "You stay here and be a good boy while I'm gone." She then made her way to the front door, opened it, and came face to face with a very tall, very handsome stranger.

"Well, hello," Tara said, taken aback. She'd been expecting her father, but she quickly realized this fellow was her date.

"Hello, yourself. I'm Skip Valiant." He relieved her of the basket, pretending to stagger under its weight. "Ugh! What have you got in here, woman? Gold bullion? And you must be—"

"Tara. Sorry. It *is* heavy, isn't it?"

"Is there anything else you'd like me to tote?" He glanced at the baby grand swathed in its plastic shroud. "The piano, perhaps?"

Tara chuckled. "We'll need to get the cooler, too."

Skip grimaced. "Good God."

"Never mind," Tara said. "Scotty can handle it."

The two made their way down the drive where a Rolls Royce, sporting a tan convertible top, was parked.

After much cajoling, Earl had reluctantly agreed to accompany them, and Tara could see that he'd already been assigned his seat. She giggled at the sight of him, wedged in the backseat between two very well-preserved women, vainly attempting to steer clear of their wide-brimmed hats.

"Wow! Great car." Tara scooted in next to Scottly, while Skip stowed her basket in the trunk.

"I'll say," Scottly agreed. "Reminds me of—"

"It's a 1963 Silver Cloud," the more zaftig of the two women interrupted. "My late husband collected antique automobiles. This model was always my favorite, and I simply didn't have the heart to part with it."

"I, for one, am glad you didn't."

"Would you mind running inside to get the cooler, Scottly?" Tara asked. "I'm afraid Dad can't. He's packed in rather tightly."

"In very good company, might I add," the plump one said, wrinkling her nose at Earl.

Scottly turned to the ladies. "Sure thing, but first, allow me to introduce Dulcie Woodard and Ernestine Hart."

Ernestine smiled a greeting, but Dulcie, the more severe of the two, merely nodded. At that moment, Tara silently vowed to charm them both. If Scottly loved them, then she most certainly would, too.

Once the picnic things had been stowed in the enormous trunk —sharing space with a faux rattan, collapsible table, and matching folding chairs—they set off. Earl asked if they could put the top down, but the women promptly nixed that idea, not wanting to risk mussed coifs or windblown bonnets.

The balmy spring afternoon stretched before them enticingly, and it wasn't long before the beautiful day, in combination with Scottly's good humor, loosened them all up.

Even Dulcie warmed to the occasion." I haven't been to a polo match at Windsor in ages," she confided.

"That's right," Ernestine agreed. "I can't think why they stopped having those wonderful affairs. I remember when Prince Charles was the guest of honor. Such a dashing fellow."

"Yes," Dulcie said. That was back in the '90s. He visited Vero twice, actually, a few years apart. I sat with him under the tent at the Kent's table the first year."

Ernestine tapped Tara on the shoulder. "That would be Kent of Abercrombie and Kent, my dear. Safaris and all that, you know."

Tara turned to Earl, and he shot her a quizzical look. Tara smiled reassuringly but wondered what she'd gotten them into.

Scottly motored north on A1A, past the posh John's Island community.

"I used to live there," Ernestine pointed toward the west gate.

Tara glanced to her left. Except for the gatehouse, there was little to see. The lush landscaping created a barrier that shielded the private residences from prying eyes.

"I loved it. When my husband was alive, that is. We positively lived at the clubs."

Tara's head was spinning. So much information to process. She turned and cut her eyes to her father, but he was gazing at Ernestine and took no notice of her. Ten minutes later, Scottly was braking to join the parade of vehicles in the center turn lane. Tara took in the white painted fences on either side of the highway and was immediately reminded of Kentucky horse farms. Unlike Kentucky, however, this property abutted the Atlantic Ocean to the east and the Indian River to the west. They inched along, part of a well-heeled queue, and eventually gained the entrance. Scottly pulled up to the gatehouse and waved a ticket toward the guard. "Tailgating," he said.

"Keep to the left," the uniformed guard instructed.

Skip's hand had found its way to Tara's shoulder, but she shrugged it off. She straightened in her seat and craned her neck, eager to take it all in. Her first impression was of concentrated development amid spacious, well-tended copses. The grassy polo fields abutting A1A separated the residences from the traffic corridor, the gracious old-world-style homes having been platted further west near the lagoon. Nearly identical in outward appearance, they were, for the most part, two-story edifices with a charming, minimalist quality about them. Most boasted peaked roofs and narrow windows so unlike the typical Florida mansions, sprawling and pretentious with their acres of thirsty lawn and soaring Palladian windows. Instead, there was a European feel to the layout and a sense of community. Many of the residences were partially concealed behind stucco walls, and surprisingly, many had minimal lot-lines with only the tiniest of private yards. Yet the common areas were vast. It was as though an insular, color-coordinated village had sprung up in a pastoral countryside.

Scottly acted the tour guide. "There's the tent. See, Tara? That's where Dulcie and I met Prince Charles. Not in that exact tent, of course. Ah, it was an amazing experience." He paused to reminisce. "Honestly, you're going to have more fun today, slumming it, mixing it up with the hoi polloi."

"Ha!" Tara exclaimed, as her eyes encompassed the enormous tent with pennants flying. "Some kind of slumming." Sensing her excitement, Skip clasped her hand, and she turned to him, smiling hugely. "This is fabulous."

"You're in for a real treat." Ernestine reached over the seat and patted Tara's shoulder.

"Yes," Dulcie agreed. "What's not to like about good-looking, wealthy playboys dashing about on horseback? I mean, could they have invented a better sport?"

"Dulcie," Scottly chided. "Let her form her own conclusions. Lighten up."

"You're right. I am *so* jaded. Forgive me."

"Love you, too," Scottly said, waggling the fingers of his right hand as if to dispel any negativity.

"What's that about playboys?" Earl asked.

"It takes enormous amounts of cash to participate in this sport," Dulcie explained.

"Each of the players must have several strings of ponies. Polo is such a taxing workout for the mounts, the players require several ponies in the course of a game. Which translates to trainers, and vets, and, well, lots of money."

Scottly interjected, "These fellows must have the wherewithal to spend a great deal of time in the saddle, which means they're not punching a clock anywhere."

"To say nothing of the travel involved," Ernestine added. "A good number of the players you'll see today globetrot to compete. It's another world."

"The home team is usually made up of well-to-do, A-type personalities, locals who get a thrill out of pitting themselves against the true athletes," Skip added.

"I beg to differ. They're *all* athletes," Dulcie corrected. "You have to give them that."

By this time, Scottly had driven completely around the polo field. A security guard motioned for him to pull to the perimeter, and Scottly eased in next to a big black Range Rover from which a young family was emerging.

"True on all accounts," Scottly agreed. "The sport you're about to witness is much more difficult than it appears." He shifted into park and turned to address the passengers in the rear seat. "Chickens, we've arrived," he said. "Let's party."

They piled out of the grand old automobile, laughing and chattering. The men hoisted the coolers out of the trunk and set up the table and chairs, while the women brought out the first course, Tara's cucumber sandwiches, a small silver bowl of glistening black caviar, and a round of brie baked in puff pastry. While Scottly uncorked a bottle of champagne, Skip placed a single, long-stemmed red rose in a crystal vase on the tabletop. Then he bowed in the direction of the females, and they applauded enthusiastically.

Tara sized up her date. He was a charmer, all right. With his full head of silver and his trim, athletic frame, he was an extremely attractive man. Of course, he was much older than she, but what did that matter? This was a casual date, nothing more. When he offered her a champagne flute, she smiled her thanks.

Skip not only met her gaze, he leered at her. "Bottoms up," he said.

Tara struggled to swallow before she burst out laughing. What was the harm in flirting? It was fun to be the object of a man's attention after what had been a long dry spell.

Across the field, the bleachers were filling up with spectators. Having purchased tickets for the formal meal, the local elite were gathering. Meanwhile, Scottly's party nibbled their way through Dulcie's snapper ceviche and Ernestine's cocktail shrimp, all freshly plucked from the sea. They'd polished off a dozen of Willie's miniature cheese biscuits and were starting in on Tara's dilled chicken salad when a bugle blast sounded the beginning of the match.

The mounted steeds thundered onto the field distinguishable only by their colors, and the crowd greeted the players with boisterous applause. If there were fierce rivalries between the teams, it wasn't apparent. The finely choreographed play between rider and mount, the swoop and crack of the mallet, the ball careening across the green, and the charge of the racing horseflesh all combined in an exhilarating spectacle. An announcer, replete with a British accent, not only called the game but also provided a witty, running commentary interspersed with amusing anecdotes about the individual players, keeping the crowd engaged. The polo players, seemingly glued to their saddles, magically maintained their mounts and swung their mallets with such force Tara cringed at the resounding *smack* as the ball was sent flying.

After the second chukker, the announcer invited the spectators onto the field to tamp down the divots and pulverize the grassy clods unearthed by the horses' hooves. Dulcie and Ernestine rose from their chairs. "Come on, Tara," Ernestine said. "Let's go do our bit."

The three women joined those assembling on the field, while the men hung back, refilling glasses.

"This seems silly," Tara said, dutifully stamping the upturned soil.

"It *is* silly," Dulcie said, "but it's tradition."

"We don't take it seriously, Tara," Ernestine added, her eyes encompassing the enormous playing field. "How much good do you think we're really doing?"

"Probably not a lot," Tara admitted.

Skip's long legs cut across the field. "Say, Tara, how'd you like to take a stroll around to the other side? See what's cooking in the bleachers?"

Tara looked to the women, and both smiled their approval.

"Go ahead," Ernestine encouraged. "I'm going to find the facilities and freshen up."

"I'll join you," Dulcie added, and the two faded beauties set off in the direction of the upscale construction trailers that had been tastefully appointed and were serving as temporary restroom facilities.

Skip linked arms with Tara, an awkward development being as he was so tall, and the two tottered across the field.

Tara said, "You're an old friend of Scottly's?"

"I'm old," Skip said, "but still randy."

Tara chuckled. "What do you do?"

"As little as possible these days. I'm currently in reduced circumstances, shall we say. I've had a number of professions."

"By that you mean?"

Skip went on to tell her of the fortune he'd inherited and lost, explaining how his father had made millions, manufacturing automobile parts that he'd sold to Ford and Chevy during the auto industry's heyday, in the '70s.

"When my parents died, I came into a great deal of money. I decided to take early retirement rather than continue operating the family business. Instead, I sold it and made more money. I was twenty-five years old, at the time and decided to chuck it all and live the high life. You have to understand, Tara, my father was..." Skip paused to consider. "He was a disciplined man, very reserved. I don't believe I ever saw him at the breakfast table without a bowtie. Can you imagine?"

Tara shook her head.

"He ran a tight ship. I was made to toe the line, to follow in his footsteps. I didn't balk, never gave it much thought, to tell the truth. Then, one day, he and Mother were gone. I lost both of them in an automobile accident. It was traumatic. When the shock wore off, I realized another world had opened up for me. I was a free man and very wealthy. After mourning their passing, I decided to travel the world." Skip screwed his face up at the memory. "I did lots of foolish things. Played volleyball with Tom Sellick in Hawaii—"

"When he was filming the Magnum PI series?" Tara asked, her eyes shining.

"Exactly," Skip said. "It was the '80s. I was in Hawaii for a year or so. Had the time of my life."

"I was just a kid, but I loved that show."

"It was something. I was even cast as a bad guy in a few episodes, which involved a lot of waiting around for the sun to be at the proper angle and re-shooting scene after scene. Not nearly as exciting as one would think." Skip paused, lost in another time.

"After Hawaii?" Tara brought him back to the present.

"I returned to Detroit. I'm a big Lions fan. I chummed around with the team, partied, chased women with them. Like an overgrown mascot, I guess you could say, not exactly part of the team, but attached to it like an appendage. I keep in touch with some of the players." Skip sniggered at the absurdity of it. "I had many adventures until, one day, I realized the gravy train—that is to say the money supply—was not inexhaustible. I needed to do something about it."

"And?"

"I went to Washington and became a Secret Service agent."

Tara stopped mid-stride. "You're kidding."

Skip raised his right hand, palm forward. "Scout's honor. I served in the Carter administration. He was pretty cool, by the way, despite the bum rap he's been given."

"You packed a gun?"

"Of course. Still do."

"What?" Tara squeaked.

"I have a permit and happen to like firearms." Skip turned to Tara. "Would you like to see my pistol?"

Tara squeezed his wrist and giggled. You mean right here?" she asked, egging him on.

"We'd best go behind those bushes." Skip motioned vaguely toward the river.

"Maybe another time."

"I'll gladly take you up on that."

"Now what?" Tara asked. "What're you doing these days?"

"Alas," Skip admitted, wryly, "I'm forced to toil to keep myself in the style to which I had become accustomed."

"You and the rest of the world," Tara said, not pitying him in the least.

"My current profession isn't held in high esteem."

"Oh?"

"I'm a traveling salesman."

"You certainly broke that mold."

"I sell computer software to school systems, and I find it very rewarding. In my own small way, I help kids get a better education. I'm just a working stiff, your average Joe."

"Hardly average and most all of us have to work for a living."

Skip cut his eyes across the field, extending an arm toward the tented pavilion. Then he turned, singling out the Silver Cloud and the scattering of tailgaters. He pointed a finger toward Dulcie and Ernestine. "Not those two," he said and flung his arm wide as if to encompass the polo field, the tent, and the bleachers. "Or a good many of that crowd, either."

"Oh well," Tara said. "It's better to have loved and lost than never to have loved at all."

"Perhaps," Skip said. "The same isn't true of money. Losing it is far worse than never having had any.

"I wouldn't know," Tara said. "But isn't this a glorious day, and aren't we lucky to be here?"

"You're absolutely right. Forgive me for grousing. I'm getting crabby in my old age." Skip took Tara's elbow and led her to a booth where souvenirs and gift items were available for purchase.

Tara gravitated to a display of Pashmina shawls woven of threads in rainbow hues. "These are fabulous," she said.

"Would you like one?"

"When would I wear it? I'm always so hot."

"I noticed that right away."

"You are so bad." Tara chided. But she realized Skip's suggestive banter was merely his way of teasing while throwing her a backhanded compliment at the same time.

"We have the odd cold day," Skip continued, unabashed. "Last winter was positively frigid."

"I'd just have to store it, as I'm presently between houses. Surely you noticed mine is being renovated. Where do you hang your hat?"

"I've been visiting Vero for as long as I can remember," Skip said. "Now that I'm here permanently, I'm not sure where I want to be— south beach, north beach, east, west. I'm currently renting a little hovel on the river."

"I'm sure it's charming."

"Not really. It's across from that unsightly power plant everyone is so keen on tearing down." Skip drew a hand from his chest to his hips. "Can you see the peculiar green light emanating from my otherwise perfect body?"

"You're a nut." Tara pivoted back to the shawls.

"Surely you'd like a memento?" Skip turned up the charm. "You know, a token of our first date?"

Tara snorted. The man was such a wit. She couldn't help but respond to his silliness.

"Actually, I do love this one." She held up a scarf woven in threads of scarlet, copper, and black. "It's so dramatic."

"As befits your personality." Skip approached the vendor. "We'll take that one, ma'am." He nodded toward the shawl Tara was holding, withdrawing a few bills from his wallet."

"Are you calling me a drama queen?"

"Absolutely. I think you may be the genuine article." Skip took the shawl from Tara's hands and draped it about her neck. Then he pulled the ends of the wrap toward him, drawing her face to his, and planted a tiny kiss on her mouth.

"Let's hope you're not thinking Lady Macbeth or Juliette," Tara admonished, lifting the shawl from her shoulders and folding it loosely.

"No. I was thinking more on the lines of Maggie in *Cat on a Hot Tin Roof*."

"I'll take that as a compliment."

"As it was intended." Just then a trumpet sounded. "Let's go." Skip took her hand. "They're about to start the third chukker." He led her back, this time circumventing the field, just as the mounted chargers galloped onto it.

The ponies drummed across the green, kicking up clods of earth and raising a cloud of fine dust. The excitement was palpable, and Tara's heart beat an accompanying staccato. When she and Skip rejoined their little party, Tara turned a concerned eye to her father. Although delighted that he'd finally agreed to join them, she'd had her reservations. Always a bit of an eccentric, Earl's solitary lifestyle had only made him more so. She couldn't help but wonder how he'd comport himself, rubbing elbows with the likes of Dulcie and Ernestine. Happily, her qualms seemed to have been unfounded.

Having declined Scottly's offer of the bubbly, Earl had produced a small cooler of beer on ice. In defiance of the order of the day, he drank directly from the bottle. Tara was relieved to note that, other than this small transgression, he seemed to be behaving himself. Nonetheless, she vowed to keep a watchful eye on him, dreading the moment when he would light up one of those odious cigars.

The real surprise of the day was that Ernestine seemed genuinely attracted to him. The refined widow fluttered over the tan and trim gent, offering up one tasty morsel after another. Whether from the heat or excitement, the dowager's face was flushed. She chatted up Earl nonstop, at one point even drawing him from his chair to demonstrate the art of divot stamping.

"What in hell's a divot?" he'd asked, and Ernestine laughed gaily.

Watching the two, Scottly chuckled. "If ever there was a more unlikely pair... I believe Mrs. Hart is smitten with Tara's father. "

Dulcie followed his gaze and paused to collect her thoughts, finally saying, "Ernestine is the most kind-hearted soul I've ever known. She is completely non-judgmental, and there's not a mean bone in her body. Although he's certainly unpolished, Earl is not without his charms."

Scottly appeared astonished by this revelation. "Dulcie, not you, too?" he asked.

"What do you mean?" Dulcie countered, her Botoxed brow refusing to furrow.

"I mean, dear heart, I can't for the life of me see what the attraction is."

"I'll tell you, then, if you must know. He's just so ruggedly masculine. Straight forward, take-me-as-I-am, and no apologies. I find it refreshing. You have to admit, Scottly, many of the people with whom we surround ourselves are self-serving. Not an open book among them, except for you, of course. Sure, he may not provide her with the intellectual stimulation to which she's accustomed, but then..." Again, Dulcie's voice trailed off. "Who's to say? He might be just the thing for her."

The hours flew by in a flurry of flying hooves. The home team made a fine showing, but, in the end, the Argentines were victorious. The team captain held a golden trophy aloft, amid a great deal of backslapping and handshaking between the winners and the Vero equestrians.

The sun crept toward the lagoon while Scottly and his guests packed up their picnic trappings and climbed back into the vintage automobile. Sun-dazzled and replete with food and spirits, they were in no hurry to call an end to this splendid day. A new dynamic had formed between them, the shared histories and personal anecdotes having formed a bond that not only strengthened old friendships but provided a framework for new alliances, as well.

Dulcie was the first to be dropped off. "Ta-ta," she said, stepping away from the automobile and blowing Scottly a kiss. "It's been absolutely delightful." Then she looked pointedly at her best friend.

"Ernestine, darling, let's plan another outing with this crazy cast of characters, soon. I swear I haven't had this much fun in ages."

When they pulled up to Ernestine's estate, Earl accompanied the sweet-faced widow to her door. "Well," he said, making as if to shake her hand. "I really enjoyed it…and…" His voice trailed off.

"Yes. I did, too." Ernestine grabbed his hand giving it a squeeze as she ducked in for a quick kiss to Earl's whiskered cheek. "Call me," she said, before letting herself in the front door.

When Scottly wheeled onto Pelican, Tara cringed at the sight of her house. It stuck out like a sore thumb among the well-tended properties lining the street. A hulking green dumpster, overflowing with old flooring, sheetrock, and other discarded building materials, squatted like a monstrous toad on her front lawn. Next to it stood an unsightly, brilliant blue Port-O-Potty.

"Here we are," Tara said, putting her best face forward. "I cannot wait to move back in and set the place to rights."

Skip unfolded his long legs from the front seat and rounded the car. He held the door for Tara, while Earl hung back, chatting with Scottly.

Skip lifted Tara's cooler from the boot. "I'm so glad Scottly included me."

"Yes. I had a wonderful time," Tara agreed. "Just set those things down over there. I'll stash them in the garage along with everything else."

"Renovation is no fun." Skip toted Tara's picnic basket to her front door. "I'm sure the final product will be well worth your inconvenience."

"I'll have you over when it's completed, and you can be the judge."

"I'd enjoy that very much." Skip turned to face her. "I'd like to see you again."

"Me, too."

"How about joining me for dinner one day next week?" Skip asked, as though the thought had just occurred to him.

"I'd love to."

"Great. I'll be in touch."

Before Tara could answer, Skip was striding back down the driveway. Tara watched as the tall, gray-haired fellow first shook hands with her father, then slid into the passenger seat beside Scotty. Her neighbor lightly tapped the horn, and Tara and Earl waved their good-byes.

"Well, what did you think of that?" Tara asked when she and her father were alone.

"A very nice day. Good people," Earl said.

"I think Ernestine's sweet on you," Tara teased.

"Aw," Earl waved a hand in the air. "I'm dying for a smoke." He crossed the short distance to the minivan parked in front of the garage, opened the driver's door, and withdrew a pack of cigarillos from the glove box.

"Oh, my gosh," Tara exclaimed. "You didn't smoke all day."

"Trying to quit. It's not easy." Earl lit up a cigarillo and took a deep drag.

"I'm proud of you."

"Yeah, I'm a prince."

Tara waved the smoke away and brushed her lips against Earl's bristly muzzle. "Then I'm a princess," she said. "After this glorious day, I almost feel like one."

Earl snorted. "Does that mean old Skippy is your knight in shining armor?"

"Don't laugh, Dad. You never know."

CHAPTER TWENTY-TWO

CAN YOU IMAGINE THAT?

It was Monday morning of the following week, and Grace was not off to a good start. Sequestered in a narrow stall in a St. Ted's restroom, she held her wiry locks away from her face and retched into the toilet bowl. There wasn't much in her stomach, but what little there was, she managed to bring up.

"I must be coming down with something," she told herself, thinking how it had rained during last Friday's game, and now half her teammates were complaining of colds or sore throats.

Eventually, the stomach spasms subsided. Grace tore a wad of toilet paper from the dispenser, wiped her eyes, and blew her nose. She couldn't afford to linger. Shakily, she stood before a sink, collected water in her cupped hands, and rinsed her mouth. She pressed a dampened paper towel to her red-rimmed eyes, was rummaging through her purse for a lip-gloss when the door flew open, and Jennifer McCourt stumbled in.

Startled by the intrusion, Grace kept her face impassive while furtively surveying the girl's reflection in the mirror. Here she was, the brat whom she'd drenched at the Lemon Tree, insufferably arrogant in her Juicy Couture skirt, with her David Yurman jewelry, Fendi bag, and three hundred dollar-highlights. And yet, Grace mused, for all the pricey bling, the girl looked miserably forlorn.

Karma is a bitch, Gracie thought with a smug sense of satisfaction.

It took a moment for Jennifer to realize she'd come face to face with her former adversary. When she did, she struggled to regain her composure, dashing tears from her eyes with the back of her hand. "Well, look who's here," she sneered, her eyes narrowing to slits. "Shouldn't you be in class? Or are you off to a secret tryst with Coach?"

"What the fuck, Jennifer," Grace snarled. "Why don't you give it up? Isn't it difficult carrying around that monumental chip on your shoulder?" Grace turned to the mirror, feigned a nonchalance she did not feel and applied a coat of pink gloss to her lips. "Speaking of class," she added, scathingly, "I'm sure you must have one this period, or does daddy's money buy you extra school privileges, as well?"

"Go to hell!" Jennifer pulled a paper towel from the wall-mounted dispenser and dabbed her eyes. "Everyone thinks you're so perfect, but I know better. I've got the dirt on you and don't you forget it."

Grace spun around and put her face in that of the younger girl's. "You don't know jack shit about anything. I've got a boyfriend," she hissed. "He's a college freshman and he's gorgeous. I am totally not interested in Coach. Maybe the guy's got a problem, but I don't. Let it go."

"Well, good for you," Jennifer shot back, but then her face crumpled. "As usual, you have all the answers."

"Come off it, Jennifer. What's up with you?"

"Nothing. Forget it," Jennifer mumbled.

"I mean it, Jenn. Spill."

"As if you care," Jennifer sniveled.

"Look, girlfriend, you'd better tell me what gives." The beautiful teen was a spoiled brat. That was a given. Still, she couldn't help but feel sorry for her. Besides, she was eager to get to the bottom of this little melodrama.

Jennifer exhaled a ragged sigh. "Okay, if you must know, I *had* a boyfriend. At least I thought I did. Now he's blabbing to everyone that we hooked up, which is *so* not true. As if that's not bad enough, my best friend can't keep her mouth shut about it. My freakin' reputation's in the toilet," she wailed. "I hate this school. The guys are jerks, and the girls are two-faced bitches."

"*Did* you hook up with him?"

"Not really," Jennifer said. "We didn't go all the way if that's what you mean. He wanted to, but I wouldn't let him. Then he got angry. Real angry."

"There you go," Grace said. "Obviously, he wanted one thing only, and when he saw he wasn't going to get it, he figured he might as well trash you." Grace turned back to the mirror. "Chalk it up to experience. Believe me, Jennifer, you're better off without the bastard."

"I really liked him," Jennifer sniffed.

"Forget about him," Grace advised. "There're lots of fish in the sea. That one was a barracuda, and you don't need him."

"Can I use your lipstick?" Rather than wait for a response, Jennifer thrust an arm into Grace's handbag and withdrew the tube. "I feel like a total loser."

Grace ventured a sidelong look at the girl. Some chicks have all the luck, she thought. Even the effects of crying did nothing to mar the perfection of Jennifer's creamy complexion, and unlike her own wild curls, Jenn's white-blonde mane fell from her head in glossy strands with not a hair out of place.

"You know, Jennifer," she said. "You really don't have to try so hard."

"What do you mean?" Jennifer tossed the lipstick into Grace's open bag and turned to her newfound champion.

"I'll let you in on a secret." Grace leaned in and eyeballed the girl. "I learned my lesson a long time ago about playing the one-ups-man game. As you know, it's the most popular game around here, what with everybody trying to outdo one another, whether it's the car they drive, the designer clothing, the ski vacation, the yacht in the Caribbean, or even the boyfriend. It's a game I can't afford to play, and it's one you can't win. Not ever. No matter how hard you try, somebody's always going to do you one better. Who gives a shit? None of it's really important, anyway." Grace collected her purse and headed toward the door. Before exiting, she turned back to Jennifer. "A word to the wise," she added. "If your best friend turned on you, then she's not really your friend."

Jennifer's eyes welled up again. "I have to have friends," she cried. "What am I supposed to do, hang out with the geeks?"

"I'm a geek, Jenn, or have you forgotten? If you really get desperate, you might think about hanging with me." Grace winked and with a toss of her red tresses was out the door, leaving Jennifer staring after her in bewilderment.

~

Later that day, seated in a cozy restaurant in a suburb of Atlanta, Rick signed his name on the printout and tucked his credit card back in his wallet. "Thanks, Dad," Sally said, skewing Connor with a pointed look.

"Yeah, thanks," Connor chimed in. "Great ribs."

"Thank *you* for taking the trouble to make the trip."

"You paid for it," Connor said.

"It was the least I could do. I'll fly into Fayetteville next time," Rick said. "Wouldn't mind seeing how things have changed."

He eyed the two of them sitting across from him in the booth. Connor had positioned himself by the window so the scars on the right side of his face would be less noticeable. Rick felt a wave of compassion wash over him. Connor was a good-looking young man and so bright. It was heartbreaking to think that his disfigurement kept him from fully realizing his potential. Then there was resilient Sally, a force of nature. How he'd like to unburden her, offer her a little comfort and security. "The boys and I like this place for lunch. Food's always good."

"Say, Dad," Sally interjected, "while I'm thinking of it, Connor has a birthday coming up. May tenth. Do you think you could come for the weekend, maybe celebrate with us?"

Cochran thought of the unsavory bit of unfinished business he had yet to attend to. "Gee, honey, I'd love to," he finally said, "but I've got to fly out on business at the end of the month. Already purchased my plane tickets."

"That's too bad." Sally couldn't keep the disappointment from her voice.

"It's okay," Connor said. "It's just a silly birthday."

"Why don't we celebrate when I get back?" Rick suggested. "Maybe do something special. Fly somewhere. How about it?"

"That'd be great," the young man exclaimed.

"That's what we'll do, then." Rick warmed to the idea. "I have a great idea for a birthday gift for Connor, too."

~

Coach Brandon squeezed her shoulder. "Go get 'em, Grace," he said, and she burst out of the huddle with the rest of the girls.

Though mildly disturbed at the feel of Brandon's hand on her, she was pumped. As she took the field, Grace thought about the events leading up to this defining moment. Coach had cautioned that St. Andrews would be their toughest adversary of the season. St. Theodore's had been undefeated seven years running, winning districts five of those years. Grace was determined to continue that winning streak.

Weeks before, he had taken Grace aside, told her they'd be having some one-on-ones after the regular sessions. He wanted to drill her on a new line of mark-ups, practice her sprints and dodges. Grace had readily agreed. She appreciated the individual instruction —anything that would help make her a better player.

Lately, though, she'd been uneasy around him, harboring vague suspicions regarding his motives. That kiss under the bleachers... God knows, Jennifer and Hillary had thought there was something to it. It gave her the creeps when he stood behind her, holding her arm and manipulating it in what he said was the proper rotation. Yuck!

There was no time to think of those things now. She needed to concentrate on the task at hand. There were recruiters in the stands, one of whom was from Wellesley, and she wasn't about to blow it.

Tied five to five, the game had gone into overtime. It was time for the draw, time for Grace to save the day. Scarlet curls flying, she trotted out onto the field to face-off, taking her position opposite the St. Andrews' center-attack. Molly Condon was a pretty, little blonde with a button nose and enormous blue eyes. Looks were deceiving, and Grace had no illusions regarding her adversary. Molly was a powerhouse, lithe and quick as a gazelle, yet tough and wily as an old goat. The referee hefted the ball, and Grace felt an adrenaline rush. Her heart was beating so wildly, she could feel it in her throat.

"Ladies, are you ready?" the referee asked. Grace and Molly

nodded. "Draw," the ref commanded, and the girls crouched down and took their stances.

Grace focused on Molly's stick. The referee blew the whistle, and Grace's stick shot up into the air as though it had a life of its own. Elated, she could feel the weight of the ball in her stick's net. Condon, her own stick flailing at Grace's, struggled to wrest the ball away, but Grace lunged to the left, and then dove right, leaving Condon in her wake. She worked her stick, rocking it back and forth, centrifugal force keeping the ball in the net as she sped down the field.

Jennifer was screaming behind her, "Go, Grace!" The St. Andrews middies challenged, but Grace breezed by them. From the stands, her name was being chanted, like some frenzied incantation, "MaaacKeeeenzieee!" Before her, the right defense appeared, and Grace dodged left. Jennifer was there, covering her, and Grace feinted, first left then right, sprinting toward the net.

Grace knew that her teammates were working with the precision of a well-oiled machine, for the way ahead was clear. Unbelievable! Oh, this was so sweet. She prepared to shoot. The rounder was there for backup, but Grace needed no help. There was no way she wasn't going to score. For one brief moment, Grace chanced a look at the stands, searching for the recruiter. When she spied her, Grace knew the night was hers. She charged toward the net, and with all the force she could muster, snapped her stick, and sent the ball hurtling.

Unfortunately, Grace committed an error that would ultimately prove her undoing. Venturing that look at the stands, she hadn't noticed the St. Andrews defense, Marisa Sherry, hot on her heels until it was too late. Sherry body-checked her, and Grace staggered, struggling to remain on her feet. She might have recovered, had it not been for her own teammates, who were running, full tilt behind her. Despite their best efforts to avoid the inevitable collision, forward motion propelled them, and they bowled headlong into her. As Grace toppled, her stick caught in a soft depression on the field, the mark of some player's cleat, and she fell upon her unyielding lance. It didn't impale her, but with the weight of the girls heaped on top of her, it inflicted considerable damage.

On an adrenaline high, Grace didn't realize the extent of her injuries. As the world started to dim, she felt as though she were rushing down a tunnel. She could hear the scree of the ref's whistle. In the stands, they were calling her name. MaaacKeeenzieee, MaaacKeeenzieee. The voices grew fainter and fainter, the whistle became a buzz, and then there were stars, just like everybody said there were supposed to be.

Can you imagine that?

～

A small coterie huddled together in the waiting room outside the surgical unit. Noticeably shaken, Charlene sat between Linda and Jon, both of whom offered silent support. She had no family nearby, no one to call except the Lemon Tree staffers, who were as close to her as anyone.

Coach Brandon paced the hallway, his brow in a frozen furrow.

The surgeon, a weary-looking woman in blue scrubs, approached Charlene. Linda and Jon scrambled to their feet. "How is she?" Charlene asked.

"She's resting," the surgeon said. "She's going to be fine."

"Thank God," Charlene cried, putting a fist to her mouth.

"She's a lucky girl," the physician stated. "We had to remove her gallbladder, but she'll recover."

"I can't thank you enough," Charlene said, tears coursing down her cheeks.

"May we see her?" Linda asked.

"Only family." The surgeon gestured for Charlene to follow. "It'll be a while before the anesthesia wears off." She led the way to the recovery room. "Don't be alarmed if she seems out of it." Once they were alone in the recovery area, the physician turned to Charlene. "Did you know your daughter was pregnant?"

Stunned, Charlene shook her head.

The doctor registered the shock in Charlene's face, and her expression softened. "My condolences," she said. "She lost the baby. It was a boy."

～

Tara brought the cell to her ear, instantly recognizing Willie's distinctive drawl. "I'm sorry to bother you, Tara, but could you come spend the night? Mr. McCourt has a function. Won't be home till late, if at all, and I have to pick Cerita up from the hospital."

"I'll be there," Tara said. "It's absolutely no problem; I'm giving Harry a lesson this afternoon, anyway."

Jennifer's head was full of Toby Mitchell. Not only was he totally hot, but he was also the sort of person you could talk to and not feel like it was a contest or something. She'd thought it a happy coincidence that their paths had crossed more often of late, almost daring to believe he was seeking her out. That couldn't be, she'd reasoned. What senior boy would be interested in a lowly freshman? Today, however, when he'd asked if he could give her a ride home, she figured he was.

"My baseball practice ends at six," he'd said. "You're finished with lacrosse then, too. I pass right by your place on my way home, so it'd be no trouble."

Jennifer was thrilled. She'd had a crush on Toby ever since middle school. Unable to concentrate, the rest of the school day had passed in a blur, and then she'd stumbling through the drills at lacrosse practice. It hadn't mattered. Nearly everyone was in shock over the events of last night's game and Grace's horrific accident. Annoyingly, Hillary proved the exception.

"Well, at least that bitch finally got her comeuppance," Hillary said as they ducked into the locker room.

"She's not a bitch, Hill. We had it all wrong." Jennifer sat on a bench and unlaced her cleats.

Hillary slid her feet into a pair of flats. "But she and Coach—"

"Nothing to it." Jennifer went to stand before a mirror and brushed her hair. "At least as far as Grace is concerned. She has a boyfriend, and he's in college."

"Oh, so now you like her?"

"Yeah, and you should give her a break. She's cool."

"If you say so." Hillary sounded unconvinced.

"I do, and I'm not taking the bus tonight. Toby's driving me home. I'll see you tomorrow."

"What?" Hillary's jaw dropped.

Jennifer had thought Hillary would take the hint and leave. Instead, she'd tagged along behind her all the way to the parking lot.

Toby had been easy to spot lounging against his silver Beemer, looking like a page from GQ. Jennifer's irritation with her so-called friend only intensified when Hillary didn't peel off to catch a ride on the late bus. Instead, the little witch had called out to Toby, asking if he could drop her, too. Without waiting for an answer, Hillary had deposited herself in the front passenger seat, leaving Jenn to climb into the back like some poor relation.

On the ride home, Hillary had flirted shamelessly while Jennifer seethed, her hair whipping about wildly in the wind. But Toby had thwarted the scheming wench. He sailed past Palacia del Mar, driving the distance to Hillary's home on Coral Way, where he'd divested himself of the interfering girl.

By that time, Jennifer was fuming. She castigated herself for not having taken Grace's advice and dumping Hillary. The girl was nothing but trouble. Thank goodness, Toby had it under control. As soon as they dropped Hillary, he jumped out of the car and held the front passenger door open for her. She laughed at his exaggerated gallantry, and all thoughts of the meddlesome Hillary vanished.

Casually, Toby draped his right arm over the back of her seat. "It's just the two of us, at last," he chuckled.

By the time they pulled into the Palacia del Mar drive, his hand was on her shoulder, and she felt as if it were burning a hole in her blouse. During the ride, she'd inched closer to him. When he'd killed the ignition, they just sat there, both unwilling to move and break the spell.

Then he turned to her and said, "Come here." Just like in the movies, he tilted her chin toward his and kissed her lightly on the lips—an incredibly delicious kiss.

"How about being my date for the Senior prom," he asked, and Jennifer's heartbeat quickened.

He really liked her.

"Chanel could use a walk. Would you take him?" Tara asked at the conclusion of Harry's lesson.

"You bet!" The boy scampered off the piano bench and dashed out of the music room.

Earlier, Jennifer had charged into the house and stormed up the stairs with her usual drama. Tara was determined to get to the cause of this latest fit of pique. Preparing herself for a skirmish, she knocked on Jenn's door, but there was no answer. Cautiously, she turned the knob, drawing the door open a crack.

"Jennifer, may I come in?" she asked. Not surprisingly, there was no response. Tara opened the door further, only to find Jennifer sprawled across her bed, sobbing into her pillow.

"Sweetheart," Tara cried, crossing the distance to her, "what's the matter?"

"Go away," Jennifer growled, her voice thick with tears.

Tara perched on the edge of the bed, feeling woefully inadequate. Jennifer's shoulders heaved as she wept. "Jenn," Tara said, "you can tell me. Maybe I can help."

"You can't. No one can," the girl wailed. "I wish I'd never been born."

"It can't be as bad as all that." Tara stroked Jennifer's hair.

"How would you know?"

"You're right," Tara admitted. "I don't have a clue. Please. What is it?" In the next moment, the teen flung herself into Tara's arms. Startled by this unexpected intimacy, Tara attempted to comfort the distraught girl. "Come on, sweetie," she coaxed. "I don't care what it is. Anything you say will stay between us. I promise."

What followed was an outpouring of teenaged angst that alternately shocked and amused. Once started, Jennifer seemed eager to recount her tale of woe. She spoke of a girl who'd been injured in last night's lacrosse game.

"I used to hate her," she confided. "Grace was always sucking up to the teachers, flirting with Coach, but then I got to know her, and she's totally awesome. To think she could have died. It was really scary. I mean, she was out cold, and the girls were all screaming. Then, today, I got asked to the prom."

Aha, Tara thought. They were getting to the crux of the matter. "That's wonderful," Tara said. "So why the tears?"

"Because I can't go. Freshmen aren't allowed at the senior prom."

"I see."

"Except that Grace, you know, the girl who was hurt?" Jennifer gazed up at Tara, trying to fathom if she were following.

Tara nodded, indicating that she was.

"She invited me. She said I could help out, serve refreshments, that kind of thing. Her boyfriend's away at school, so she doesn't have a date, but she's on the prom committee. She asked me to go with her," Jennifer explained. "Not like a date or anything. Just to help her."

Tara raised her eyebrows and shrugged. "What's the problem?"

"Now, it's all screwed up," Jennifer complained, her face crumpling. "Grace is in the hospital, which means I won't be going after all. It doesn't matter, anyway." Her voice conveyed otherwise.

"Because?"

"I don't have a dress."

"Oh." Here it was at last. Tara pressed her lips together, to keep from smiling.

"All the girls go shopping at the Garden's Mall. Like at Bloomie's or BCBG, you know? Their mothers take them. They have lunch, make a big deal of it. I suppose I could go find a dress by myself, but honestly, I don't even want to go to prom unless my dress is perfect."

Before Tara could fully digest this news, Jennifer was off on another tangent. "And my birthday's next week."

"It is? No one told me."

"Everybody gets their learner's permit when they turn sixteen. Not me, though. My stupid father refuses to take me to the DMV. It's so unfair." Jennifer collapsed back onto her pillow. "My life is a joke."

Before wading into this quagmire, Tara took a moment to collect her thoughts. "Okay, Jenn, let's tackle one issue at a time. First up is prom. I'll speak to the headmaster. You'll go to work in Grace's place. Since she invited you, I'm sure that's what she'd want."

"But the dress..."

Tara placed her palms on Jennifer's narrow shoulders, and Jennifer eyed her hopefully. "Would you like me to help you find shoes and a gown? We could go on Saturday, have lunch at PJ Chang's or Brio?"

"Really?" Jennifer asked, seemingly thrilled at this unexpected turn of events.

"We'll leave early. That way we'll have all day to shop," Tara said, warming to the idea. "As for your learner's permit, I believe I can get your father to come around."

"He thinks I'm still a baby."

"He's just being overprotective. That's what dads do, especially with daughters."

"I'm really sorry I've been so bitchy," Jennifer confessed. "I'll try to be better. I promise."

Once again, she threw herself into Tara's arms.

The poor thing needs a mother, Tara thought, her mind reeling at the hurdles that lay before her. She'd manage the headmaster, and she doubted she'd have much trouble getting Nathan to finance their shopping expedition. Persuading him to allow Jennifer to drive, on the other hand, might prove a more daunting task.

CHAPTER TWENTY-THREE

THE PROMISE

"Grace?" Josh paced the floor of his small dorm room while speaking into his cell.

"Yes?"

Her voice was raspy, lacking its usual effervescence, and Josh frowned. "I heard you're in the hospital. How are you?"

"I'm okay."

Josh's brow furrowed. "Do you want me to fly down? I'm worried sick about you."

"I'll be all right, but Josh…"

"What is it?"

"I was pregnant." Grace's voice wavered. "I didn't know. And now…" She choked back a sob.

Josh could feel her anguish, and his heart went out to her. "Oh, God, Grace. I am so sorry."

"They say I might not be able to have children."

"Don't you worry about that. After we graduate from college, we'll have a passel of kids. That is if you want them, Grace. Or one. Or twins. Whatever. Trust me on this. Okay?"

"I want to believe that."

"Believe it. I'm here for you, Grace. I always will be. You'll be fine. You'll see. We'll get through this. You just remember that. I love you."

"Okay. Love you, too."

CHAPTER TWENTY-FOUR

GLORY BE

Tara was nearly asleep, but she hadn't fully entered her dream when a commotion outside roused her. Drowsily, she climbed out of bed, padded across the darkened room, and came to stand before the French doors. Separating the drapery panels a crack, she peered out. At first glance, nothing seemed amiss. The nearly full moon, a white hole in the black sky, shed its cool reflection upon the blue-black water of the pool.

In the next instant, a blonde head broke the surface. Transfixed, Tara watched as the female propelled herself to the pool's edge. Then Nathan strode into view. Having removed his dinner jacket and bowtie, he was clad in tuxedo trousers, the sleeves of his dress shirt rolled up to his forearms. Toting a bottle of champagne in one hand and two crystal flutes in the other, he crossed to the woman and spoke.

Tara couldn't make out his words, but the female tilted her head back and laughed a reply, splashing water in his direction. Nathan filled a champagne flute and offered it to her. Like a sea goddess, the sprite ascended the stone steps, making no attempt to cover her nakedness. As she wrung the excess water from her slick helmet of hair, her long-limbed body glowed effervescently.

Tara knew that she should draw the drape and return to bed, but she was unable to tear her eyes from the intimate scene playing out below.

The woman accepted the glass, drank, and placed the flute on a side table. Leaning into Nathan, she pressed her wet body against him. He responded by drawing her closer, his fingers groping her buttocks, his mouth on her neck. She undid the buttons of his shirt while he half-carried her to a lounge chair. Nathan lowered himself into the chaise, and the nymph fell upon him. Nathan reclined, and the woman straddled him.

Suddenly, Nathan shot a look directly at Tara's window. It was as though his eyes were boring into hers. Tara recoiled, letting the drape fall. She told herself she was imagining it, but she could have sworn he'd been staring up at her.

Mortified, Tara crept back to her bed and drew the covers to her chin. She'd been fooling herself all along. She wasn't here for altruistic reasons. She'd fallen for the handsome tycoon from the very start, and this stint provided her an opportunity to insinuate herself into his presence. It was pathetic. Now, more than ever, she longed to feel his arms about her, his mouth and hands upon her, but there was absolutely no likelihood of that happening. She was nothing more to him than a strait-laced, music teacher.

In Jennifer's words, it was just so totally unfair.

∾

The next morning, when she crossed paths with him in the hallway, she was unable to meet his eyes. Her discomfiture didn't seem to register with Nathan, however. If he'd spied her at the French door last night, he gave no indication. He'd only needed to have searched her face, and any such suspicions would have been confirmed, but he hadn't.

"I'm off," he said, breezily. "I've arranged for breakfast on the plane, so I'll get out of your hair."

"Um," Tara mumbled, thinking he looked awfully chipper, and no wonder considering his activities of the previous evening.

"Thanks for your help, Tara," he cried, letting himself out the side door.

"You're welcome," Tara said darkly, but he'd already gone.

In the kitchen, she found incriminating evidence of Nathan's nocturnal tryst, a pair of long-stemmed glasses, one bearing a telltale lipstick imprint. After carefully washing the glasses, Tara returned them to the cupboard.

What a fool she'd been. Acting the part of a nanny to some self-absorbed eccentric's screwed up kids and getting ever more deeply involved in the life of a man who viewed her as nothing more than a domestic. From now on, she would comport herself with cool dispassion. She'd pitch Jennifer's prom and learner's permit, and as soon as Willie no longer needed her, she'd move on with her life. That would be infinitely better than living in close quarters with the most attractive, desirable man she'd ever set eyes upon. Wouldn't it?

Right!

∿

Her cell phone rang, and Willie lunged for it. The voice that came to her was an unfamiliar one, and she nearly disconnected, thinking it was a solicitor hawking life insurance or some paid volunteer shilling for a charitable cause to which she could ill afford to contribute. Willie's suspicions were soon allayed, however, and, by the time she swiped to end the call, she could hardly contain her delight.

"Cerita!" she cried, hastening toward her daughter's room. "Baby, you'll never guess."

CHAPTER TWENTY-FIVE

A GRAND NIGHT FOR SINGING

The Treasure Coast Chorale Spring Concert was an annual event that drew crowds from communities all up and down the coast. Even retired snowbirds, with no family members in either the public or private school systems, clamored for tickets. It was an event not to be missed. Only the very best singers from the local school choruses were selected to participate in the songfest. Rehearsals began in January and were arduous, and every number was choreographed and finessed to perfection.

The upper school boys wore rented tuxedos, and the girls were attired in long black gowns. The children from the lower schools were dressed in white shirts and black trousers or skirts. Just the sight of all these young people, so earnest and full of promise, brought a tear to many an eye, never mind the fact that they could sing.

Backstage was sheer pandemonium. For the first time in a very long time, Jennifer was more concerned about the wellbeing of someone other than herself. She was keeping a close eye on Grace. The redhead had only returned to school a week ago, and now her face was ashen beneath her vibrant curls. Then there was Willie's grandson, Tyrone, to contend with. That child was like a perpetual motion machine.

"It's so hot," Grace complained, her legs suddenly wobbly.

"Get me a chair!" Jennifer yelled, supporting Grace and swaying under her sudden weight. "Please, somebody help me."

One of the assistant directors appeared with a folding chair and helped her slide it under Grace. Tiny beads of perspiration dotted the pale girl's brow, and her skin was clammy to the touch. Jennifer placed a palm on the back of her friend's head, gently applying pressure. "Put your head between your knees, Grace," she instructed. "That-a girl. You're going to be fine. Deep breaths."

Gradually, Grace began to revive.

"God help us," Jennifer muttered.

Things weren't much better in front of the curtain. It was ten minutes past seven, and the audience was growing restive. Finally, the lights dimmed, and a lone figure appeared on stage. An audible sigh arose from the audience, when the emcee made his introductions, thanking the patrons, teachers, and parents for their support. The curtain parted, and the entire combined choruses were revealed. They opened with a rousing medley of patriotic songs, immediately captivating the assembly.

The program was varied and fast-paced, alternating between small ensembles, individual choirs, solo performers, and the combined choruses.

Getting all the kids on and offstage was a logistical nightmare, but the production seemed to flow seamlessly. If there were any snafus, the audience was none the wiser. Cerita and Willie were amazed at Tyrone's composure while on stage, and Grace performed her solo, *I Believe I Can Fly*, in a voice as sweet and pure as a mountain stream. When the last note of the final song resonated throughout the auditorium, the audience rose to its feet and lustily voiced its approval.

Afterward, people remarked how professional the older students had been, so mature and composed, and weren't the little ones adorable? There wasn't a parent or teacher among the lot who didn't come away with a renewed sense of hope for the future.

∼

Willie gripped Yvonne's hand, and Tara and Cerita followed them, joining the flow of people surging down the aisles toward the exits.

"Over there," Cerita cried, waving a hand over her head. "Look, Mom." She tapped her mother's shoulder. "Tara, see?" She pointed toward the uniform across the room. "It's Jarod."

Tara scanned the crowd, her eyes coming to rest on the striking, young Black man at the back of the auditorium. The paramedic was every bit as handsome as Cerita had claimed. She hoped, for Cerita's sake, that he was the genuine article. Willie's daughter was especially vulnerable now, and she surely didn't need her heart broken. As they inched toward the exit, Tara plastered a smile on her face. She didn't want any of her concerns to sound a discord on the high note of the evening.

"Hi, baby," Jarod called out.

"Hi, yourself," Cerita said. "I didn't know you'd be here."

"Thought I'd surprise you." Jarod extended a hand toward Willie. "How do, ma'am? Pleased to meet you."

"Nice to meet you, Jarod." The two shook hands. "And you must be Tara."

"One and the same." Tara took his hand. "So, you're the fearless fellow Cerita rattles on about."

Jarod looked taken aback. "What you been telling these folks, girl?" Although his voice was stern, Jarod's eyes gleamed, and he flashed Cerita a conspiratorial smile, as he turned to Yvonne. "Let me guess," Jarod teased. "Harry?" He stared at the girl, and she erupted in giggles. "Sooorrry. I beg your pardon, miss." He snapped his fingers. "Yvonne."

They exited the building, and the humidity hit them like a steam iron, but after the confines of the auditorium, it felt good to be outside and to move about freely.

Eyeballing Harry, Jarod inclined his head. "You, sir, must be the inimitable maestro."

"Harold McCourt," the boy said. "You can call me Harry."

"You're not that hairy," Yvonne laughed.

"Girl, you hush," Willie remonstrated.

"I'll go around back and collect Tyrone and Jennifer," Tara said, darting off.

"Are you on official or unofficial business?" Cerita asked.

"A bit of both," Jarod explained. "I volunteered to cover this event, knowing I'd stand a good chance of running into *you*. I'm off the clock now. My partner left with the van, so I'm at your mercy. Would you give a poor public servant a lift?"

"Where you are going, son?" Willie asked as they drifted toward the parking lot.

Jarod shot Cerita a silent question, and she shrugged. He asked Willie, "Could you drop us at the hospital? My car's parked there. I'd like to take Cerita out for a bite to eat."

"I already ate," Cerita quipped.

Willie raised a brow but said nothing.

"By the look of you, darlin', another meal wouldn't hurt," Jarod gave her the once-over. "Besides, I was thinking of dessert rather than dinner."

When they reached the Mercedes SUV—a vehicle Willie had requisitioned from Palacia del Mar—Jarod opened the rear passenger door and waved Cerita in.

"Won't you please be seated, Madame," he said.

Yvonne hooted, and Jarod tugged on one of her braids as she scrambled in. "What are you laughing at, midget? You'd better believe I know a place where they make a great Bombon Cubano."

At that, Willie looked mystified, and Cerita burst out laughing.

In the Green Room, Jennifer had Tyrone by the hand, which was a bit like trying to hold on to a tornado. All the suppressed energy was rolling off him, and he was high from the aftereffects of jitter juice.

"Tyrone," she implored, dragging him away from another hooligan who could have been his twin except for the fact that he was white and tow-headed. "We've got to go."

Her eyes searched the room for Toby. He was taller than most, and it took her but a moment to spot him. He was off in a corner, and he and Grace had their heads together. Then the redhead glanced her way and grinned, and Jennifer gestured for the two to come join her.

Toby linked arms with Grace, and they crossed the crowded room together. As they neared, Grace— looking every bit as giddy as Tyrone—broke away from him and rushed to Jennifer,.

"Thanks, Jenn." Grace wrapped her arms around the blonde. "I almost lost it there."

At the same time, Tyrone bent Jenn's arm, nearly causing her to lose her balance. Toby stepped in and pried Tyrone's fingers from Jennifer's.

"Hey, Jenny," he whispered in her ear. "You were terrific."

When Tara found them backstage, they were all laughing over Tyrone's hilarious mimicry of the various performances.

"I believe I can fly," he sang, flapping his arms about and batting his eyelashes, his pristine falsetto a near-perfect imitation of Grace.

"I believe I'm gonna smack you." Grace clapped a hand over the boy's mouth. "Put a lid on it!"

~

"Hi, kids." Tara broke in on the group. "Great concert."

"Guys, this is Ms. Cahill," Jennifer said. Tara nodded to Toby and turned to Grace. "Wonderful solo," she exclaimed. "Do you plan on majoring in music?"

"I'm not sure," Grace admitted. "I was hoping for a lacrosse scholarship."

Tara looked surprised. "You should consider music," she said. "You've obviously got talent."

A moment of awkward silence ensued until Jennifer jumped in to fill the void. "Ms. Cahill is Harry's piano teacher," she explained. "You should hear her play. She's terrific."

"So I've been told." Grace turned to Tara. "I'm acquainted with your son."

Tara gave a flick of her wrist, as if to brush away the compliment, but, in the next instant, the girl's words registered. "You do?" She eyed the redhead, curiously.

"We've hung out from time to time," Grace admitted.

Tara did a double-take. "You're the girl." Tara studied the young woman with heightened interest. "Well," she said, recovering, "he has good taste." Silently, Tara vowed to have words with her secretive son.

Yes," Toby piped in, "Grace is our shining star."

"No." Tyrone interjected. "I be the star."

"You're more like a meteorite," Jennifer admonished.

"And your light's beginning to fade, mister," Tara said. "It's time you were in bed." She smiled at the teens, took Tyrone by the hand, and led him off. "It was nice to meet you," she called over her shoulder, as she headed toward the exit. "Come on, Jenn. Time to go."

"Say, would it be all right if I drove Jennifer home?" Toby asked.

Tara turned back, and the silent plea in Jennifer's eyes was impossible to miss. Jennifer and Toby were good kids, and they'd worked hard to make tonight's production a success. "Okay," she said. "Just don't be late. Remember, Jenn, we're shopping in the morning."

The little boy babbled on about the concert, but Tara was lost in her own head. Everywhere she looked, people seemed to be pairing up, starry-eyed and in love. Everyone but her, that is. It was ironic. Now that she was finally feeling as though she'd begun to heal, that she was ready for another man in her life, there were no likely candidates. She was fond of Skip, but he was far too old for her, and although she was sharing digs with the most eligible bachelor in town, she was not on his radar.

Tara thought back to what Scottly had intimated, that she shouldn't write herself out of the equation. He'd thought she had a fighting chance at McCourt. Could it be that he was right?

Yeah, she'd been wounded, she told herself, gotten the stuffing knocked out of her. On the flip side, she was an attractive woman, and she had a lot to offer. Besides, she was gaga over the guy. Maybe she *shouldn't* give up quite so easily.

Then and there Tara decided to make the most of this once-in-a-lifetime opportunity. She'd pull out all the stops and make a last-ditch play for McCourt.

What did she have to lose?

∼

The two women sat at the breakfast table, mugs of coffee before them, while the children entertained themselves upstairs.

"How's it going, Willie?" Tara selected a packet of sweetener from a small china bowl.

"Last week, I would have told you another story." Willie poured cream into her coffee. "But now, things are looking up."

Tara angled her head. "How so?"

"Mr. McCourt arranged for someone to care for my mother so that I can be here."

"How noble of him," Tara sniped, immediately regretting her uncharitable comment.

Willie seemed not to notice. "Yes," she said. "Now, Cerita and I come and go as we please. Mr. McCourt, he sees to it Mama has a nurse to look after her. It's a blessing."

"That is such good news, but tell me about Cerita. How is she responding to the treatment?"

"Mr. McCourt has been helping her, too." Willie shook her head, as though she could not believe her good fortune." Cerita gets the chemo twice a week, and it makes her so tired and sick. She's supposed to take it easy, but that girl…she doesn't know how to do that. She's so afraid she'll fall behind. I like to tie her down."

"She's determined, "Tara said. "Just like her mother."

"Humph," Willie muttered, deflecting the compliment. "Mr. McCourt arranged for a tutor for Cerita, to help her pass her exams."

"How wonderful. I know she wants to finish as soon as possible and get her degree."

"That's not the best part," Willie confided, drawing out this last bit for dramatic impact.

"Yes?"

"He's flying her to Shands Medical Center, where she'll receive state-of-the-art therapies."

"No kidding? Shands is a teaching hospital, right?"

Willie nodded. "One of the best. Mr. McCourt says there's nothing too good for Cerita."

"I guess not." Tara was truly delighted over this unexpected turn of events. It appeared as though Nathan had a heart, after all. If only there were room in it for her.

Tara's musings were cut short when Chanel came bounding down the stairs, barking excitedly. Seconds later, the garage door could be heard hitching up. "Speak of the devil, the Laird returns,"

Tara muttered, putting a smile on her face just as Nathan walked through the door.

"Hello, ladies." Nathan nodded first to one, then to the other. "How was the concert?"

"Fabulous," Tara said. "You should have been there."

Now there's the way to a man's heart.

Her words seemed to go over Nathan's head, and he appeared even more preoccupied than usual. "I'm really sorry I couldn't make it, especially for Jenn's sake." He unknotted his tie and loosened his collar. "There were some, ah…irregularities at the office I had to attend to."

For a moment, Nathan seemed lost in thought, but in the next instant he was back in the present scrubbing his five o'clock shadow as though trying to erase an unsightly stain.

Tara had never seen him look so haggard. What was the matter with him? Tonight, this supremely confident man seemed alarmingly defenseless, and she had all she could do to keep from brushing back the lock of hair that had fallen across his temple.

"Oh, Mr. McCourt," Willie said, "you'd have been proud of your girl. And Tyrone was a wonder. They did real good."

"It was video-taped," Tara added. "I'm sure I can get you a copy."

"That would be great. Yes, please do that, Tara. Maybe you and Willie could join us for a family night screening."

"I'm on it."

The housekeeper came to her feet. "May I get you some coffee?"

"No thanks, Willie." Nathan crossed to the bar cabinet and drew out a bottle of Scotch. "I prefer something stronger. Anyone care to join me?"

"I will," Tara said, thinking she might as well begin laying her trap.

Careful, her inner voice cautioned. *Beguile the guy. Don't come on gangbusters.*

"Great." Nathan opened an upper cabinet and pulled out three Waterford crystal glasses. "How about it, Willie? Don't be an old stick in the mud."

Tara glanced at the housekeeper, noting the emotions playing across her face. Surely, this was unfamiliar territory. She smiled when

Willie finally said, "Pour me a little one, Mr. McCourt. I feel like celebrating."

"No time like the present," Nathan said, and Tara couldn't have agreed with him more. He filled their glasses with ice and then poured a generous slug of Dewar's into each one.

"There you go, ladies." Holding his glass in the air, Nathan jiggled it, making the ice tinkle. "What are we toasting?" He seated himself between the two women.

"Better days," Willie said.

"Talented children." Tara raised her glass.

"To the children," Nathan agreed.

"God bless them," Willie added.

Tara stifled an urge to choke when the fiery liquid burned a path down her throat, but Willie wasn't as successful. Tears sprang to her eyes, and she patted her chest. "That's a strong drink, Mr. McCourt."

Nathan took a long pull from his glass. Then he glanced from one to the other. "Listen, you two," he said. "I don't want you calling me Mr. McCourt any longer." Willie opened her mouth to protest, but Nathan shot her a warning look. "Call me Nathan. Hell, call me dumbass, but don't call me Mr. McCourt. Okay?"

Willie's eyes grew round, and Tara feared she might be on the brink of a prophecy.

"Okay, Mr. Mc..." Willie cleared her throat. "Nathan," she said, rising and taking her nearly full glass to the sink. "I do thank you for the drink and all, but I best be going. I'll just fetch Yvonne and Tyrone."

Tara leapt to her feet. "I'll go with you." She trotted out of the kitchen and followed the housekeeper up the sweeping staircase.

When they returned, Willie was bearing Yvonne in her arms, and Tara had a sleepy Tyrone in tow. The little tyke was barely able to keep his eyes open. Nathan swooped in and scooped him up, indicating that Willie should lead the way. After having safely deposited the children in Willie's Honda, Nathan and Tara stepped away from the vehicle.

"Goodnight, children," Nathan said. "Thank you, Willie, so very much."

"Thank *you*, sir...Nathan...for everything."

Once back inside, Nathan refilled his glass, and without asking her approval, did the same for Tara.

Tara, who wanted nothing more than to stay with this man forever, felt compelled to say, "I should be on my way, too."

"Keep me company for a little bit, won't you?" Nathan gestured toward the living room. "Wouldn't you prefer to sit there? It's such an attractive room, yet no one ever uses it."

"I don't know," Tara said, thinking that room, with its vaulted ceilings, was far too imposing for this late-night tête-à-tête. "It's a lovely evening," she blurted. "Why don't we sit outside?" That little voice inside her head nagged. *This is your chance. Don't make a fool of yourself. Go slowly.*

The alcohol was having its effect, and she threw caution to the wind. Hadn't she decided to grow a backbone and be more aggressive?

No time like the present.

She'd been lusting after Nathan since that night of their first awkward dinner together, when she couldn't let go of his hand.

But you're not a blonde goddess.

Shut up!

The two wandered out to the lanai and then the patio beyond. Tara eyed the chaise lounge, and the image of Nathan being ministered to by the lithesome mermaid burned in her brain. She veered away from the chaise, selecting a chair instead. "I have to talk to you about Jennifer," she said, suddenly all business.

"Oh? What about?" An aggrieved expression briefly crossed Nathan's face.

Watch it, watch it.

"She says you won't let her get a learner's permit."

"She's a child," Nathan scoffed. "What's the rush?"

Tara realized she could really make a mess of things if she didn't handle this delicately. She had two objectives. To fulfill them, she needed to have her wits and feminine wiles about her. Turning toward Nathan, she ran a hand through her hair and gazed into his eyes. "She's a young woman," she said, "and it's time. She's been a help to me around the house, and I think you should reconsider." Then she placed her glass on the end table and crossed her legs, bringing every ounce of sexuality she could muster into her next words. "You won't be sorry," she said, wetting her lips with the tip of her tongue.

A spark of interest gleamed in Nathan's eyes, and Tara figured he was taking the bait.

"You know," he said, his eyes lingering on her trim figure, "you are a very attractive woman."

If your taste runs to dark-haired munchkins.

"Why, thank you," Tara said, trying to remember how to flirt. "You, sir, are a very handsome fellow, but then I'm sure you're fully aware of that fact, what with the women hanging all over you."

Oops.

"Yeah." Nathan chuckled and sat back in his chair. "If that were the case, I wouldn't be in this quandary."

"Quandary. What?" Tara shook her head, not following.

Nathan's face took on a rueful expression. "I need a date," he said, and Tara widened her eyes. This was going better than she'd hoped.

"The Beaux-Arts Ball is in two weeks, and I'm co-chair. Of course, I have to make an appearance."

"I should say." Tara suddenly made the connection. "Scottly's handling the decorations. I'm sure it'll be lovely."

"It'll be one of those boring affairs with everyone dressed up to the nines and oodles of vapid conversation. On the plus side, the band's supposed to be really good, and the caterer is very highly regarded. The food will be divine."

"Doesn't sound so onerous."

"I was wondering if you'd go with me."

Struggling to maintain her composure, Tara turned to face Nate. "You're kidding." She couldn't believe her ears. Nathan was asking her to the Beaux-Arts Ball.

"Not kidding. Help me out here, won't you?"

Tara paused, pretending to consider, but it was all an act. "I'd be delighted."

"Don't go getting all worked up about it. It's just one of those functions I'm required to attend, but you'd be doing me a great favor."

Tara got his message loud and clear. This was no romantic date, and she needn't think it meant anything more than Nathan having to fulfill an obligation. Yet her heart soared at the thought of having him to herself for an evening. This was her chance. She'd take full of advantage of this opportunity and do everything in her power to win him.

Before she could say another word, Chanel's barking brought an end to that conversation. There was a mechanical click of the security lock being automatically deactivated and Jennifer let herself in the front door.

"Hi," she called out, her eyes immediately drawn to the patio where her father and Tara were seated. "Hey, Dad." Jennifer hiked across the great room. "Hello, Tara."

Tara registered the surprise in Jennifer's eyes. The girl hadn't expected to find her dad and the piano teacher together at such a late hour.

"Come here, sweetheart," Nathan said. "Tara's been telling me that you're all grown up and ready to get your learner's permit." Jennifer shot Tara a grin before crossing to her father and wrapping her arms around his neck.

"Yes Dad," she said. "I really am."

Tara tamped down her disappointment. One of her objectives had been met. As for the other, all was not lost. She had a date with Mr. Dreamy.

"I'd better be going." She came to her feet. "No, no. Don't get up," she remonstrated when Nathen made as if to rise. "I'll let myself out."

"Thanks, Tara." Jenn's eyes gleamed with happiness.

"You bet, kiddo." Tara winked at her. "Don't forget about tomorrow. I'll pick you up at ten."

"What's going on?" Nathan asked. "I am always the last to know."

Tara pivoted back to him. "I'm afraid you're going to have to hand over your credit card. We girls have some shopping to do."

Nathan waved a hand in the air by way of agreement. "Bye, Tara, and thanks."

"My pleasure. Come on, Chanel," Tara cried. "Time to go home."

CHAPTER TWENTY-SIX

TOO CLOSE FOR COMFORT

Tara had nearly reached Pat's condo when her iPhone chimed. She glanced at the center media display, saw Scottly's name, and tapped the accept prompt. "Hi. Why are you calling so late?"

"You'd better get over here." Scottly's voice was uncharacteristically grave, and a chill ran up Tara's spine.

"Is it Josh?"

"Not Josh. Your house."

"Oh, no."

She arrived at a surreal scene. Two police cars were parked in her driveway, their bubble lights casting tracers that bounced off the surrounding trees and shrubs in an eerie, strobe-like display. Her garage door was open, and the chaos within gave her a macabre sense of déjà vu. It was as though a maniac had attacked her packing boxes. The floor was littered with shards of broken pottery, papers, books, and tangled clothing.

Tara climbed out of the Lexus, and two uniformed deputies materialized out of thin air. One was middle-aged and heavyset, his fat face ballooning out over his starched collar. The other was younger, of medium build.

"Ms. Cahill?" the stout one asked, his bulky frame, blocking her way.

"Yes?" Tara assumed he was in charge

"I'm Lieutenant Wilcox. We need to talk to you."

"Of course," Tara said, suddenly weak-kneed.

Scottly was beside her, placing an arm around her shoulder. "Come on, kitten," he said, reaching into the car for Chanel. "Let's all go over to my place. I'll make us some coffee."

He speared Wilcox with a pointed look, and with an almost imperceptible nod of his head, the Lieutenant signaled his approval. Scottly led them over to his house, through his kitchen, and to the cheery alcove beyond. Once there, he pulled out a chair for Tara, indicating that she should sit at the breakfast table. Tara collapsed into the chair, and Scottly deposited the dog in her lap while the two officers eased themselves down as well.

"Coffee?" Scottly said.

"That won't be necessary," Wilcox said. "Ms. Cahill, first let me say I'm very sorry. We don't get too much of this kind of thing on the barrier island. I know you must be upset."

Feeling numb, Tara merely nodded.

"It's not as bad as it looks." Scottly soothed. "Only a few boxes were broken into."

"Really?" Tara clung to that shred of hope like a lifeline.

"That's right," the younger cop said. "You can thank your neighbor for that."

"What happened?" Only then did Tara note Scottly's formal attire.

"That's what we'd like to know," the heavy-set deputy replied. "Perhaps you could go over it with us one more time, Mr. Preston?"

"Sure. I'd just returned from a wedding reception at John's Island. It was late. After eleven, I guess. When I drove on to Pelican, I noticed a mid-sized Toyota parked a little way from the intersection, and then when I pulled into my driveway, I saw a light on in Tara's garage. I thought I'd best investigate to be on the safe side. You see, Tara had entrusted me with both her housekeys and the garage door remote."

"My God, Scottly. You didn't!" Tara cried.

"Thought nothing of it. I stood there, powering the remote. Next thing I know, some guy comes charging out at me like a bull at Pamplona. I was there you know…" Scottly paused, reflecting, "… back in the '90s."

"Mr. Preston," Wilcox interrupted.

"He was dressed all in black," Scottly resumed. "Not a young man, but a powerful-looking fellow. What really struck me as odd was the that he was wearing surgical gloves."

The two deputies exchanged meaningful looks.

"Who would do such a thing?" Tara asked.

"Go on," Wilcox encouraged.

"Like I said, he charged. Rammed right into me. It was like being run over by a Mack truck. Reminds me of the time——"

"What were you thinking?" Tara interrupted. "You could have been killed."

"Nah." He waggled a hand in the air. "I spooked him. I think he was more scared than I."

Wilcox and the younger deputy raised their brows.

"Right." An indulgent smile played about Tara's lips.

"Yeah, probably not," Scottly recanted. "I really didn't have time to think, let alone worry about the consequences. When he socked into me, I tried to get my hands around his neck, which was like wrapping my arms around a Prius. He probably could have overpowered me, if he'd wanted to. Okay, I'm sure he could have, but the guy was in a hurry to get out of there. That's just what he did. He walloped me on the jaw, which put me down for a couple of seconds. By the time I'd regained my legs, he'd disappeared."

"He punched you?" Tara rose from her chair to examine Scottly's face more closely.

"It's nothing." Scottly fended her off. "Did I ever tell you about the time I went a few rounds with Mike Tyson?"

The young cop guffawed, and in spite of the gravity of the situation, Tara chuckled.

"I'm serious. Remind me to tell you about that, sometime."

"Did you get a good look at him, Mr. Preston?" Wilcox asked. "Could you pick him out in a line-up?"

Scottly grimaced, shook his head. "I'm afraid not. It all happened so fast. The door rolled up. I caught sight of him. In the next instant, he was on me. Then, just as quickly, he'd vanished."

"Ms. Cahill, do you have any idea what this intruder might be looking for? Why he was searching your garage?"

"No, but this is not the first time something like this has happened."

"It's not?" Wilcox pushed away from the table.

Scottly stared hard at Tara. "What are you saying? You never mentioned that."

The lieutenant's eyes bored into Tara's. "Will you kindly fill me in?"

"Just before I moved here, my house in Atlanta was ransacked."

Wilcox placed both of his hands on the table and leaned in toward Tara. "That's rather pertinent."

"Why did you never tell me?" Scottly asked, a look of incredulity on his face.

"I thought it was a random act," Tara said. "There was no rhyme or reason to it. I have nothing that anyone would want. Only some sterling and a few pieces of jewelry. Which, by the way, were untouched. Nothing was missing."

The deputies sat back in their chairs, seeming to digest this information.

Scottly swiped a palm across his face. "I'm sorry," he said, "I've had too many champagne toasts and then fended off a burglar. I'm afraid my mind's turning to mush."

"To say nothing of having taken a blow to the chin in the process," Tara added.

A beam of light caromed around the breakfast alcove when a car pulled up in the driveway. Wilcox peered out the window. "It's the guys from forensics. They'll take up where we left off. As for us, we can pick this up again in the morning."

"Officers, I'll show you out." Scottly came to his feet.

The two policemen nodded at one another as they, too, gained their legs. Wilcox pressed a business card into Scottly's palm. "Get her to headquarters tomorrow," he said, and then the two policemen were out the door and hiking down the drive to brief the forensic team.

"Will do," Scottly called after them.

Tara crept up beside Scottly. "I must be going," she said, "and you need to call it a day."

"Stay here," he commanded.

"I can't. I'll be fine. Trust me on this."

"Against my better judgment," Scottly said. "Let's get you two to your car, and don't even think of tidying up the garage. I've got this, okay?"

Tara nodded, realizing at this moment she needed all the help she could get. Scottly took her arm and led her to her car. Once there, he stood before her, blocking her view of the garage so that she had no time to dwell on the disarray within. "Call me as soon as you get home.

Tara met his gaze, and the implication behind his words hit home. She was in danger.

"Lock all the doors and—"

"Don't worry, I will, and I have Chanel." She gave the dog a squeeze. "You're a great watchdog, aren't you buddy?"

"Tara, sweetie, I adore Chanel, but right now, I wish he were a junkyard cur, so mean and ugly only his mama could love him."

CHAPTER TWENTY-SEVEN

RIDING THE GATOR

The Jeep bucked and swayed on the uneven surface, tires kicking up plumes of dust that rose, like smoke, from the loosely packed track. The windows were tightly sealed, yet a mist of fine grit insinuated itself inside the vehicle. It was a shitty road, not more than a rutted trail that snaked its way through the lowlands. Keeping his right hand on the steering wheel, Kevin pinched his nose with his left, thinking he could use a hit right about now, but that would have to wait. He gazed about at the forbidding landscape. The swamp spread out before him as far as the eye could see in a wavering sea of green occasionally punctuated by a scrubby cabbage palm. Although there were no signs of life, he knew the marsh was teeming with wild critters.

After two hours of this desolate and monotonous scenery, Kevin was drowsy. He was just beginning to nod off at the wheel when he saw a flash of red ahead. Not a cardinal or a creeping scarlet blossom, but a bandanna, hanging like a flag from a tree branch alongside the road. Had he not known to keep an eye out for the marker, he surely would have missed it.

Steering off the main road and onto a weed-choked path, he expected to see another vehicle and was surprised to find none there. The only structure on site, a ramshackle cabin, appeared empty. A quick look about the place told Kevin it was deserted.

"Damn," he cursed under his breath. The prospect of cooling his jets in this hellhole was far from appealing. He climbed out of the Jeep and approached the shack. "Hello," he called out.

Except for the indignant cries of a pair of crows lifting off the roof, there was no answer. Kevin peered into a fly-specked window but could make out little detail. Cautiously, he mounted the steps to the porch, the weathered boards protesting under his weight. With little hope of success, he tried the door, but it was locked. A check of his cell phone told him that it was half-past twelve. Where the hell was Combs?

He hunkered down and withdrew a cigarette pack from his breast pocket. Inside the package, half a dozen neatly rolled joints shared space with a few Chesterfields. Kevin lowered himself to a sitting position, feet resting on the rotting wood of the crudely constructed steps. Beads of sweat popped out on his brow as he smoked the reefer.

Half an hour had passed, and Kevin was getting antsy, his mind playing out one catastrophic scenario after another. Maybe Combs had been found out, a routine traffic stop or, worse yet, a double-cross. Perhaps the Coast Guard had intercepted the shipment. All sorts of possibilities occurred to him, any one of which might have queered the deal. One thing was for certain, he didn't trust Combs. That slimy cracker was nothing but trouble, living like some feral creature in this hidey-hole out in the swamp. He vowed that this would be the last time. After today, he wasn't going to have anything to do with Melvin Combs and his sordid little operation.

Kevin made a conscious effort to rein in his runaway imagination, reassuring himself that Combs was simply late. He told himself he was paranoid, that he shouldn't have smoked that joint.

With each passing minute, Kevin's unease grew. Was the entire drop-thing an elaborate trap? Was he being set up? If that were the case, then he'd played right into their hands. Whoever *they* were. Kevin felt vulnerable, out in the middle of nowhere, like a sitting duck. He slid off the porch thinking to stretch his legs and decided to take a walk down to the lake. Maybe it'd be cooler there. If in twenty minutes Combs didn't show, he'd hightail it out of here and never look back.

The saltwater bayou was surrounded by an untidy thatch of vegetation, wildflowers, and weeds interlaced with a snarl of twisting vines and exposed roots. Kevin picked his way carefully over the rough terrain, thinking how easy it would be for a man to trip and be sent sprawling, never to be seen again.

Saw palmetto and gumbo limbo grew right to the shoreline where a thorny crown of reeds ringed the hammered bronze surface. At the water's edge, dozens of dragonflies, transparent except for their red stick bodies and the faint rosy smudges on their wingtips, hovered and swooped. An excess of nature that did nothing to improve Kevin's black mood.

Off to his right, a twig snapped, and Kevin tensed. Instinctively, he crouched down, fixing his sights in the direction from where the sound had come.

"That you, Kev?" Dense underbrush crunched underfoot as the lanky Melvin Combs appeared.

Kevin relaxed, unfolding himself. It was about time to get this show on the road. "Not too smart sneaking up on a fellow like that," he said, patting the bulging right pocket of his cargo shorts. "Could get a guy wasted."

"Whoo-ee." Combs cackled, seemingly unimpressed by Kevin's bravado. He spat out a wet rag of chewing tobacco. "Ain't you one, ornery sonofabitch."

Melvin's skin was leathery as a tanned hide. Kevin couldn't venture a guess as to the age of the old drug-dealing geezer. He only knew that Comb's hair, once brown, was graying, unwashed and unkempt like the rest of him. Melvin eschewed sunglasses, and his brow was furrowed in a perpetual squint, his eyes permanently slit like those of a snake. An unsavory fellow altogether, Kevin thought, taking in the man's filthy jeans, sweat-stained shirt, and boots caked with dried mud. There was only one way to deal with lowlifes like Melvin, and that was to cut them no slack and maintain the upper hand.

"Fuck that!" Kevin said. "Have you got the shit or not?"

The sun was at its apex, pressing down like a giant hand and squeezing the living breath out of the day. Not a trace of wind blew to cool the perspiration that glued skin to clothing. A mosquito buzzed annoyingly in Kevin's ear, and he swatted at it. At that moment, there was nothing he wanted more than to grab what he'd come for and get the hell out of this godforsaken quagmire and back to civilization.

"Hell yes, I got it," Melvin said. He scooped a fresh wad of tobacco from a small cylindrical tin and packed the leaves between his gum and lip, obviously in no hurry to proceed with the transaction.

"Where the hell is it then?"

"Back at the house."

The house?

Kevin envisioned the miserable shack. His skin was beginning to crawl. "I was there," he said. "The door was locked."

Combs sucked on tobacco-stained teeth. "I'm here now, ain't I?"

Melvin stepped toward Kevin. His shirttails flapped as he moved, and Kevin detected a glint of steel at his belt. "Hold it right there!" Kevin held up a palm.

"You sissy," Melvin taunted. "What's your problem?"

"Let's go back and get this over with," Kevin said. "You get your money, and I'm on my way."

"About the dough, five big ones," Melvin said. "You got the cash on you?"

"I'm heading back," Kevin said, taking a step up the path. He didn't like the way this was going down. A loud plop, like something smacking the water, startled Kevin. He turned toward the lake just in time to see a monstrous gator, ten or twelve feet long, slithering from the bank into the bayou. Transfixed, he watched as the prehistoric-looking creature slowly sank into the cool depths until only reptilian eyes and a snout—two hillocks and a spiny protuberance— glided above the surface. Quickly recovering, Kevin pivoted. Too late. In a flash of silver, sunlight bounced off the shiny barrel of Comb's pistol. He'd drawn on him! Kevin struggled to make sense of a situation playing out like a ghastly nightmare.

"Fuck!" He went for the pistol in his pocket, but Melvin fired a shot into the air, and he thought better of it.

"I wouldn't if I were you," Combs threatened. "Could get a guy wasted." He pitched his voice high, in a poor imitation of Kevin, but Kevin was too intent on finding a way out of this horror show to take offense.

"Come on, Combs." He struggled to keep the tremor from his voice. "You're not going to shoot me. For a lousy five thousand dollars?"

"I've killed for less." Combs jerked his head up, motioning for Kevin to put his hands in the air. "You shouldn't have offed that cop's nephew."

"What?" Kevin raised his arms as a sick realization came to him. *This can't be happening.* "I don't know what you're talking about."

"Don't be a wimp." Combs snorted. "I'm just messing with you. Shit happens. Right?"

"It was an accident," Kevin said, thinking maybe he'd get out of this after all and feeling somewhat relieved. "I didn't even know the guy." He cast about for a distraction of some sort. There was nothing.

"Keep your hands up, pretty boy," Combs cried.

Kevin glanced in the direction of the cabin. "Your money's in the ca—" Before he could finish his sentence, something slammed into his chest with such force he was hurled backward, and his feet flew out from under him. Kevin's mind reeled while he attempted to process the unthinkable. He'd been shot! Strangely, there was no pain, just an enormous pressure, as though he'd been whacked with a wrecking ball. Then Combs was on him, rifling through his pockets.

Crazily, Kevin's mind veered. He should have heeded his instincts. Now it was too late. With a Herculean effort, he tried to muster his waning strength, to make his hands move and throw Combs off. It was no use. He could smell the sour breath of his assailant, could make out Comb's crab-like hands as they skittered over his blood-soaked shirt. Even that seemed unimportant. Kevin's eyes filled with the blue sky. Such a color. Overhead, a lone gull soared, light reflecting off its breast with the radiance of a star.

Then, as unbelievable as it seems, he was standing outside his body, watching, dispassionately as the scene played out. *This was bizarre.* At the same time, he felt a deep sense of comforting peace— to disconnect mind from body. The melodrama, his life bleeding away before him, seemed of little consequence. It came to him that he couldn't actually feel anything anymore, no sensation whatsoever, except for that of floating, like the gull.

A voice came to him from a distance, or was it inside his head? "Everything's going to be all right," it seemed to say.

Perhaps he only imagined it. In any case, he figured it was probably true, that everything would work out for the best. Still, it wasn't supposed to end like this, he thought, as darkness descended.

Not like this.

In the next moment, he was riding the gator. So exhilarating. Or maybe he was the gator? Slipping below the surface into the cool, cool depths. He looked up, only to see the dragonflies darting, like fairies, in the pellucid air, their wings nearly transparent, as though they were creatures merely imagined and not real.

It was all so beautiful.

Funny, he'd never noticed before.

CHAPTER TWENTY-EIGHT

THE LONELY HEARTS BALL

Tonight, was the Beaux-Arts Ball. He'd put so much hard work into planning it, but now, it was just another dinner dance, another thousand dollar ticket. For once, Scottly wasn't up for a night of festivities. All he wanted was to slip into some sweats and pig out on junk food in front of the TV. Kevin was working late, so he'd be going stag, and he couldn't bear the thought of tripping around a dance floor with a succession of old biddies, none of whom interested him in the least.

Well, that wasn't altogether true, he silently admitted, while fastening his silk bowtie. Dulcie and Ernestine would be there. Tara, too, and he adored them. In typical Scottly fashion, he regaled himself. Of course, he had to go. It was *his* party, and he was darn well going to enjoy it.

He rummaged through the contents of his jewelry case. This was one of those occasions when he could go all out, load up on the jewelry, and no one would bat an eye.

Where was that onyx and diamond ring?

Exasperated, Scottly dumped the contents onto the marble countertop and sifted through his baubles. A creature of habit, Scottly was never careless with his treasures. Unless the ring adorned his finger, it was in the case. A terrifying thought occurred to him.

Surely, Kevin wouldn't have taken it.

Panicked, he ripped open drawer after drawer, rifled through his toiletries and peered into corners, but to no avail. Falling to his knees, his fingers scrabbled along the baseboard. Then, he craned his neck, checking to see if the bauble had fallen behind the commode. He even went so far as to toss soiled undergarments and damp towels from the laundry hamper and sift through them, but it was useless. The ring was missing!

~

Tara was giddy with excitement as she crossed the short distance to the Vero Beach Museum of Art on Nathan's arm. The entrance, a glass and steel portal, was lit up like a purple, green, and gold Christmas tree, hinting at the splendor that awaited within. She placed her feet carefully, trying not to teeter on the six-inch stilettos she'd purchased with the thought of growing longer legs while in Nate's company. Fleetingly, she'd considered bleaching her hair blonde, but decided that might come across as too desperate. Instead, she'd had a smattering of highlights applied, and her hair cut and layered.

"This is such a treat," she said, clinging to Nathan's elbow while the two navigated the parking lot. "I can't remember the last time I got dressed up."

Nathan shook his head. "How you women love to dress, while we single-X chromosome-types prefer sneakers and jeans."

Tara took in Nathan's custom-tailored dinner jacket, his impossibly long legs looking even more so in the narrow tuxedo trousers, the pink bow tie that added just the right note of I-don't-take-this-too-seriously, and she sighed happily. Lightning could strike her down at that moment, and she'd die a contented woman.

Well, almost.

Once inside the brightly lit reception area, a babble of voices bounced off the hard surfaces of the museum walls and floors, accosting their ears. Nathan stepped up to the reception table. "Cahill and McCourt," he announced to one of the women seated there.

"Oh, Mr. McCourt," the blousy volunteer gushed. "Thank you so much for making this wonderful event a reality. The proceeds go to *such* a good cause." She detached their name tags from the sheet in front of her. "You're at table number one, of course. Here you go."

Tara thrust out a hand. "I'll take them." She palmed the handwritten, sticky-backed labels, stepped away from the desk, and peeled off one of the backings.

"There you go," she said, affixing Nathan's name tag to his lapel. Then she made as if to do the same for herself, but where to plant the thing?

"Here, let me." Nathan plucked the name tag from Tara's hand and made a show of looking her up and down. "Wherever shall we glue this?" he asked. "To that pretty little upturned nose of yours?" He made a stab in that direction.

Tara giggled, batting his arm away. "No, let me do it." As she gazed down at her dress, with its spaghetti-straps and heart-shaped bodice, she realized there simply was no place to put it.

"I could plaster it to your forehead."

"Please don't."

"How about we put it here?" he grabbed her wrist and pressed it to her black satin clutch. "Just hold it up, like a cue card, when anyone wants to know who you are."

"Good plan."

In the next moment, Dulcie swooped in with eyes only for Nathan. She looked regal in a vintage beaded gown, her lustrous silvery hair swept up in a chignon and held in place with a bejeweled comb. "Nathan," she cried, and then her gaze fell to Tara. "And Tara!" Looking momentarily nonplussed, Dulcie took an involuntary step backward while processing this development, but she recovered quickly. Eyeing Tara, she simpered, "How delightful," and then she concentrated on Nathan. "I see you took my advice."

Nathan smiled, but there was a glint of steel in his eyes. "Yes," he said. "The most talented and beautiful woman in Vero Beach agreed to be my date."

Dulcie smirked. "Well, good then. She'll do." With that, she sailed off to greet another VIP.

"What did she mean by *that*?" Tara asked, bewildered.

"Nothing. She's a nosy old maid. Don't pay her any mind."

"I like Dulcie." Tara frowned, considering. "At least I *did*."

"I do, too," Nathan said. "However, she always has her own itinerary, oftentimes misguided."

Tara's brows knit. "Huh?"

"It's not important." Nathan grabbed her arm. "Come on. Don't let her spoil our fun." He led her down the hall, past the galleries, to the spacious open-air loggia. "See, isn't this lovely?"

Tara had attended plenty of toney affairs in her lifetime, but nothing had prepared her for this. Her breath caught in her throat when she stepped through the opening and out into the magical Mardi Gras world that Scottly had created.

"Oh, my goodness," she breathed. "He's truly a wizard." She chuckled and misted up at the same time. It was all so beautiful.

Thousands of lights twinkled in shades of purple, green, and gold. Strung from the rafters overhead, framing doorways and windows, they coiled around tree trunks and entwined in shrubs on the periphery. An enormous three-tiered fountain, recently installed in the center of the patio, featured a nude Bacchus as the central figure. From the flagon in his hands, a stream of plum-tinted water flowed, and the shell-shaped basins were festooned with garlands embellished with glittering clusters of hand-blown glass grapes. The banquet tables were draped with crisply starched white linens and each one boasted a lavish floral centerpiece framed by a pair of sterling silver candelabra. The folding dining chairs were transformed with slipcovers in white linen and embellished with gold tasseled cords.

Even Nathan, as jaded as he was to this society and its excesses, appeared impressed.

"Oh look, there's Scottly." Tara pointed to the far side of the room.

Nathan quickly spotted the designer, for he was hard to miss in his vermillion-hued tuxedo, "Aha. Let's go say hello."

They set off across the large space thronged with partygoers. Some were in masks and costumes, but the majority were dressed in their comfort-zone, oh-so-safe formal wear. The two had taken only a few steps when a strident voice stopped their progress. "Mr. McCourt."

Tara turned to find a slender young man dressed in shirtsleeves and khakis, hefting a very serious-looking camera.

"Sir, can I get a photo, please?"

Nathan looked to Tara, and she nodded. "Sure," he said. "Where do you want us?"

"This is fine, lots of people in the background. Very festive." He hunkered down and peered through the lens.

Nathan draped an arm around Tara's shoulders. She angled her head and smiled. The shutter *click-click-clicked*, and they relaxed.

"One more, please," the photographer inveigled. "You two get a little closer."

Nathan bent slightly and put his head next to Tara's.

"That's great," the cameraman said. "Don't move." *Click, click.* "There, that should do it."

Embarrassed, Tara laughed and pulled away from Nathan.

"Your name, ma'am?" the photographer asked.

She held up her clutch. "Tara Cahill."

"Ah. Got it." The young man turned to Nathan. "Thanks, Mr. McCourt. Can I get a few more shots—maybe with you and Mrs. Woodward?"

"Perhaps after dinner," Nathan said. He faced Tara. "Just now I have to fetch Ms. Cahill a drink."

"Understood, sir. I'll catch up with you later." The young man disappeared into the crowd. Nathan took Tara's arm and attempted to cut through the mob, which was no small feat. In the few minutes it had taken to be photographed, the place had filled up until there was barely room to navigate.

"Nathan, there you are," A husky voice purred.

Tara pivoted, only to encounter a statuesque blonde, heavily made-up and clad in a sheath that clung to her curves like snakeskin. Tara glanced at Nathan, who was at eye-level with the woman, and she couldn't help but notice the pained expression that crossed his face.

"Alexia," he said. "How are you?"

The willowy creature arched a brow and feigned a pout. "Long time no see."

"Yes, well…" Nathan turned to Tara. "May I introduce Tara Cahill? Tara, Alexia Hargrove."

The woman gave Tara the once-over, saying, "Very pleased to meet you," but her voice lacked enthusiasm, and she quickly pivoted back to Nathan. "Hope to see you soon, Nate. Ta-ta." She waggled her fingers, before diving back into the crowd.

"Who was that?" Tara asked.

"Ugh!" Nathan grimaced. "She's an artist and the local maneater."

"I believe it. How do you know her?"

"It's a small town. I know *everybody*."

Tara nodded, thinking he'd probably known *that* one more than he cared to admit, but she clasped his hand when he said, "Come on," and allowed herself to be steered toward the drinks table. Nathan had made it all too clear: this date was about practicality, not passion. She certainly had no hold over this enigmatic man, but she was here with him now, and she was going to make the most of it.

"Tara!" Scottly's unmistakable tenor resounded.

"Scottly!" Tara broke away from Nathan and rushed to him. "The man of the hour." She nestled against his broad chest for a moment and then broke away and held him at arm's length to better assess his flamboyant costume, and the rhinestone-studded eyeglasses that nearly obscured his face. "Look at you, Elton John wannabee."

"Hello, Scott." Nathan thrust out a hand.

Scottly took Nate's hand in his. "Nathan, welcome to my little party."

"You have outdone yourself, sir." Tara gestured vaguely about. "This is fantastic."

"All part of a day's work," Scottly said, making light of the compliment. "Please, excuse me for a moment, won't you? I have to check up on the caterers. We're seated at the same table, though. I'll join you there in a bit."

Tara nodded, and Nathan said, "Of course," as Scottly hurried off. Nathan turned to Tara. "What can I get you? White wine, champagne?"

They were seated between Scottly on Tara's left and Dulcie and Ernestine, on Nathan's right, and the arrangement had made for interesting conversation.

"Well, hasn't this been nice?" Dulcie said, the sour expression on her face seeming to say otherwise.

Nathan didn't respond. Instead, he held up his empty glass, silently entreating a waiter for a refill.

"It's lovely," Ernestine gushed.

"It truly is," Tara agreed. "I feel as though I've been transported to, I don't know where, another planet, maybe." She turned to Scottly. "I'd say you pulled it off."

Once all traces of the meal had been whisked away, the band segued from low-key dinner music to in-your-face popular tunes that had the guests pushing away from their tables and heading for the dance floor. Nathan and Tara sat out a few numbers, but when the keyboardist played the distinctive chords to the intro to Calvin Lewis's *When a Man Loves a Woman*, Nathan rose to his feet.

"Shall we?"

"Sure," Tara said, eager to dance yet terrified of making a fool of herself.

"Come on then."

Before she could worry it to death, they'd crossed the distance to the dance floor, and she was in Nathan's arms. She'd been so concerned about their difference in height, but it didn't seem to factor in, and she was delighted to find that they fit together quite nicely. Even more surprising, was to learn Nathan was a wonderful dancer. Rather than simply sway side to side, marking the languorous beat, he traveled across the dancefloor, spinning her out and then drawing her close. By the time he dipped her, at the song's conclusion, she was flushed and breathless.

"Wow! You are an amazing dancer," she said, as the band segued into Marvin Gaye's sensual *Let's Get It On*.

"I could say the same of you." He grabbed her hand. "Let's," he said, grinning wolfishly. Tara laughed as he spun her out in a dizzying array of disco moves that literally had her on her toes for the duration of the number.

When the band took a break, Tara and Nathan returned to their table.

"Quite the dancers," Scotty said, raising his glass in a toast. "You two make a handsome couple."

Tara shot him a warning look, but she could barely suppress the giggles that threatened.

"Yes, Nathan's very smooth on his feet," Dulcie simpered, "and off them as well."

Nathan's face clouded as he turned to his tormentor. "By that you mean?"

"Don't mind me." Dulcie met his gaze and smiled tightly. "I'm just an old woman prattling on."

Nathan glowered at her. "Stop," he said, his voice so low as to be nearly inaudible over the strains of music suddenly emanating from the bandstand.

"Oh, it's *I Swear* by All-Four-One," Tara announced, hoping to dispel the negative vibe Dulcie seemed hellbent on generating. "I love this song."

Just then, as if conjured from a bad spell, the towering Alexia appeared. All eyes at the table turned to the woman hovering over Nathan's shoulder. "Dance with me, Nate," she coaxed in her throaty baritone. "They're playing our song."

Nathan grimaced.

"Oh, go ahead," Tara said, not really wanting him to, but what else could she say?

"Yes, do." Scottly encouraged. "It's not fair for you to monopolize this lovely lady the entire evening." He bounded to his feet, saying, "Come on, Tara. Let's show them how it's done."

Nathan shot Tara a bleak smile before allowing Alexia to lead him to the dancefloor.

"They don't call me light on my feet for nothing," Scottly said while helping Tara from her chair

Despite the double entendre, Tara decided it was true. For a big man, Scottly was surprisingly agile. More exuberant than Nathan, he, too, was an accomplished dancer, and, although she longed to be in Nathan's arms, Tara thoroughly enjoyed herself. It was exhilarating to follow his lead as he executed one intricate dance move after another. She had to concentrate to keep up.

When a shriek rent the air, Tara and Scottly halted mid-step, as did the other dancing couples. They craned their necks, searching for the cause of the commotion while the live music raggedly petered out. The dancers gradually cleared a space on the floor around where Alexia now sprawled in a pretty heap.

"My ankle," she mewled, propping herself up on her elbows.

"What happened?" Nathan crouched on his haunches next to her. "Are you all right?"

"No, I'm not all right." Alexia's face was twisted in pain. "I think it's broken."

"Here, take my hand." Nathan made as if to lift her to her feet, but a slightly built, dark-skinned fellow pushed through the crowd crying, "Vait! Don't move her." Nathan backed away giving the man clearance. "I'm a doctor," the man explained. "Let me take a look."

He knelt beside Alexia. "Vere does it hurt?" he asked.

Alexia raised her right foot slightly. "My ankle. I don't think I can walk."

Gently, the man manipulated her ankle. "No svelling or bruising," he said, "That often manivests later." He rose to his feet. "No more duancing for you tonight. Best get you to hospital vor an Xray."

"Shall I call an ambulance," Nathan asked.

"No, no," Alexia cried. "That's not necessary. Didn't you drive your Porsche? The one with the reclining seats?"

Scottly bulldozed through the throng, dragging Tara along with him. "I can help," he said, breaking away from Tara and reaching for Alexia's arm. "Now," he said, taking control. "I want you to stand on your good foot."

"Yes," the doctor said. "Don't put any pressure on your vright ankle. Ve'll do the lifting."

Between the three of them, they got Alexia on her good foot and managed to propel her across the dance floor, into the gallery, and to the entrance beyond. Tara followed along behind, and Ernestine and Dulcie met them at the door.

"I've got her," the doctor said, as he stepped in to relieve Nathan of his burden. "You go get your car,"

Nathan turned to Tara and offered her a sardonic smile. "I am *so* sorry."

"Oh, oh," Alexia cried, piteously. "Nathan!"

"On my way," Nathan said, hiking out the door.

"Are you sure it's broken," Dulcie asked, a bemused expression on her face. "It doesn't look swollen."

"Yeah, it looks okay to me," Tara added. "I've had broken bones, and they always swell up right away."

"It hurts something awful." Alexia spat out the words, her face suddenly hard.

"Hmm…" Dulcie muttered. "I'll just bet it does."

"Poor thing," Ernestine said. "What an end to such an enchanting evening."

Dulcie looked as skeptical as Tara felt, but all she did was give a slight shrug of her shoulders. "Ernestine, you have the kindest heart," she said.

In the next moment, Nathan pulled up to the curb and hopped out of the sports coupe. As he sprinted around to the passenger side, Tara and Dulcie held the heavy museum door open, allowing the doctor and Scottly to maneuver Alexia out the opening and down the short flight of steps. The men deposited Alexia in the passenger seat with minimal whimpering on her part.

"Strap yourself in," Nathan commanded, before closing her door and rounding the hood of the automobile.

Dulcie applauded for the three heroes of the day, and Ernestine and Tara quickly joined in. "Bravo!" Dulcie cried, "Our knights have rescued the fair maiden."

"Humph!" Tara muttered as Nathan bowed slightly at the waist before climbing in behind the wheel.

Scottly came to stand at Tara's side, "That was quite the theater."

"She's a drama queen, all right," Dulcie said, as Nathan pulled away from the curb, stomped on the gas, and was soon lost to view. "I'll bet she faked the entire thing."

"I must find my wife. She'll be madder than a vet hen," the doctor said, excusing himself. "I'm always leaving her like this." He sprinted back into the museum to find and placate his wife.

"What say you?" Scottly looked from one woman to the other. "Shall we salvage what's left of the evening?" He quoted Shakespeare, *"entertain a cheerful disposition.* Let's all lift a glass and then take another turn around the dancefloor before calling it a night."

"What the hell," Dulcie said.

"I'm game," Ernestine burbled. "You haven't danced with me once this evening."

"Why not?" Tara said, again ruing her bad luck.

~

Dulcie and Tara, the sole occupants of their table, moped while Scottly whisked Ernestine around the dancefloor. "I have to say," Dulcie said, raising her head from her hand long enough to take a long pull from her drink. "I'm really sorry, Tara."

"For what?" Tara's eyes were at half-mast, but she managed a rueful grin.

"I was in a foul mood, a perfect bitch, and you don't deserve that."

"Oh, please," Tara remonstrated. "No apologies necessary. I sometimes get in the blackest of humors. I think it's hormonal." She raised her champagne flute. "To Scottly and the Beaux-Arts Ball."

"And to you, dear. This evening didn't turn out like any of us expected."

"That's an understatement. Here's to you, Dulcie." The two clinked glasses. "You sure know how to throw a party."

~

He eased his foot off the gas pedal, taking the Coco/Cape Canaveral exit and turning onto the Bee Line Expressway. During the last couple of days, he'd had plenty of time to think about what a muddle he'd made of this mission. Rick admitted to himself he was over the hill. The last debacle only proved it. Hell, that oversized fop had nearly taken him down. Worse, it wasn't just a physical failing of his less-than-perfect hearing, the dulled reflexes, his diminishing strength. Sure, all that factored in. He'd lost the mental edge, that steely resolve that had always seen him through the most difficult and dangerous of circumstances. He'd gotten soft.

As he drove across miles of desolate swampland, Rick toyed with the idea of just walking away from the whole damned tangle. That's what he wanted to do, tender his resignation at the dealership, begin collecting his pension, and enjoy his newfound family for the few good years he had left. As tempting as that rosy picture was, he knew he couldn't do it. He was in way over his head, and there were too many loose ends that would, should they be knit up, form an arrow pointing directly to him.

He needed to cash in that ticket, collect his millions, and play the part of the magnanimous savior to Sally and Connor. He'd fund the pricy skin grafts, the rounds of plastic surgery that were not covered by Medicaid. He'd shower them with gifts and set up trust funds so that neither would have to work another day in their lives. First, he had to get his hands on the winning ticket.

Rick followed the directions to B Terminal Parking at Orlando International. He was flying out to Greensboro, where he'd meet up with Sally and Connor. They'd lease a car at the airport and drive up to Cashiers. He'd rented a luxury three-bedroom cabin in the mountains, and he couldn't wait to spend some quality time with them. His plan included treating them all to some golf lessons, maybe do some fishing. Rick smiled at the thought of Connor and him tooling around on a golf course in one of those little carts. Never, in a million years, would he have imagined such a thing. The burly vet relegated Cahill and her foppish neighbor to the back of his mind and switched to vacation mode. He'd be back at it soon enough, and then there'd be an end to the whole sorry debacle.

~

Nine o'clock in the evening, a day after the Beaux-Arts Ball, and Tara had never seen Scottly so distraught. He was pacing back and forth in his living room, his black velvet slippers fast wearing a path in his Aubusson carpet.

"When was the last time you saw him?" she asked.

"Not since yesterday morning. He was in a rush." Scottly's face was florid, and Tara was certain his blood pressure was spiking.

"Did you call his cell?"

"Of course, I called. All I got was the recorded message."

"What do they say at the salon?"

"I spoke to the receptionist. No one's heard from him. He was a no-show today. I had her pull up the schedule. Kevin's next appointment isn't until tomorrow morning at ten."

"Wait till then. He'll turn up, like a bad penny. You'll see." Tara reached out and patted the seat cushion of the chair across from her. "Come sit down. You're going to give yourself a heart attack."

Scottly continued pacing. "I just have this feeling that Kevin has gotten in over his head."

"Don't you think you're overreacting? He's a grown man. I'm sure he can take care of himself."

Tara didn't mention her own misgivings. It wasn't difficult to imagine the sly Kevin dabbling in illicit activities and falling out with a dangerous crowd.

"You don't know him like I do." Scottly wrung his hands, and, for the first time, Tara noticed he wasn't wearing jewelry. "He's like a child."

Some kid.

"What makes you think he's in trouble?"

"Oh, a few of my things have gone missing." Scottly shrugged, making light of the statement. "I've probably misplaced them. The mind is beginning to go, I'm afraid. Not that you would know anything about that, my dear, but your time will come. I can't remember a thing anymore unless I write it down."

"For heaven's sake, Scottly. You're sharp as a tack. *What* has gone missing?"

He shook his head.

"How can I help you if you won't tell me?"

Scottly stopped pacing and plopped down on the chair. "Just a few pieces of jewelry," he admitted. "A little cash."

Bingo!

"How much jewelry and cash?"

"One of my rings, a few other pieces." Scottly held his head in his hands.

"And?"

"A couple thousand."

"You never questioned him?"

"How could I? Don't you understand? I didn't want to say or do anything that would push him away."

"Well, he's gone now," Tara said, immediately regretting her words.

"I have this terrible feeling he's not coming back…ever." Scottly cradled his head in his hands.

Tara went to sit on the arm of his chair. "You don't know that."

Scottly let his hands fall to his lap and turned to Tara. "I think he may have been into drugs."

"No!" The thought had never crossed her mind.

"Lately, I've had this feeling that he'd somehow gotten mixed up with a bad lot."

"But why…" Tara's voice trailed off. She saw Kevin's face in her mind's eye, his indolent manner and hooded eyes. Maybe, on those occasions when he'd made her feel so uncomfortable, he'd been stoned. Perhaps that's why she'd always thought he was leering at her.

"I guess I should call the police."

"I don't think so. Not yet, anyway. If Kevin *is* mixed up in something, you don't want to involve the authorities. Take my advice and wait until tomorrow. See if he shows up for work."

"How will I ever get through the night?"

Tara's heart went out to her friend. He was so miserable. "I have some Benadryl. Works for me."

"I believe I have a bottle of Ambien stashed away somewhere." Scottly gained his legs. "Come on, sweet," he said. "Time for us chickens to roost."

Tara wrapped her arms about him. "I am so sorry." She buried her face in his silk-dressing gown, for a moment, before releasing him. "Get some sleep. With any luck, he'll be back in the morning."

What she really thought was that they both had poor taste in men.

～

It wasn't until two days later that the news of Kevin's disappearance broke. Having heeded Tara's advice, Scottly postponed alerting the authorities until the following afternoon, by which time ten of Kevin's appointments had to be reassigned to other stylists. The hairdresser was more than merely late for work. He was MIA.

Scottly was beside himself, but there was little he could do except wait and hope for the best. He'd gone through the motions at his shop, filling out purchase orders, conferring with subcontractors, but his heart wasn't in it. Tomorrow was his first meeting with potential new clients. All he wanted to do was cancel, but the thought of a new project, a fresh palette awaiting his artistry, kept him going.

He was sitting before his Mac, working on a CAD drawing, when his poor attempt at concentration utterly failed. A movement on the flat-screen TV mounted to the wall above his desk caught his eye, and he scooted his chair closer to better view the coverage. A television news chopper was hovering over a swamp deep in the Everglades, while a pair of divers in wet suits searched the murky depths. On the shoreline, a team of sharpshooters, their rifles drawn, prepared to fire on any man or beast that threatened. The cameraman panned wide, and Scottly watched, transfixed, as a tow truck fed a length of chain into the lake. Once the winch was engaged, the front end of a vehicle slowly broke the surface, and Scottly's heart plummeted.

He snatched up the remote and increased the volume to better hear the broadcaster's commentary. He didn't have to be told it was Kevin's Jeep that was being hauled up from the bog or that he'd seen the last of his duplicitous lover.

CHAPTER TWENTY-NINE

RIDING THE HOG

Skip stood before the entrance to a modest but well-maintained walk-up and pressed the buzzer. When no one answered, he rapped loudly on the door. That produced immediate results: A frenzied barking ensued. In the next instant, the door opened revealing a smiling Tara with a squirming bundle of fur in her arms.

"Hello."

"Hey. I don't think your bell works," Skip said, with a twinkle in his eye. "But I'd ring your chimes anytime, ma'am."

Tara smiled at his silliness. "Won't you come in?" She led the way through a tiny vestibule and into a small living room where Earl was intent on a televised ball game. "You remember my father."

Skip covered the distance between them, hand extended. "Hello, Earl," he said, shaking the wiry man's hand. "Are the Tigers still leading?"

The men chatted about baseball while Tara went to fetch her handbag. When she returned, she set Chanel down next to Earl, saying, "There's half a meatloaf and a baked potato in the oven."

"Okay, honey," Earl winked at Skip. "I keep telling her not to fuss, but she doesn't listen."

"They *are* difficult to train," Skip said. "Guess you'll just have to grin and bear it."

Tara stooped to plant a kiss on Earl's bald pate. "Night, Dad. Don't wait up."

"Those days are gone," Earl called after her as she and Skip crossed to the front door. "I'll be all tucked in by nine."

"Goodnight," Skip said. "I won't keep her out past her curfew."

Tara swung at him with her handbag, and the two were out the door.

"Lock up the women and children!" Skip exclaimed. He took Tara's arm and helped her up into the passenger seat of his Voyager SUV.

Driving across the causeway, they were treated to a glorious display. The sun melted into the tree line in a molten blaze of crimson and gold while overhead the sky was striated orange and purple. The river reflected fiery colors that seemed to grow more intense with each passing moment.

"Wow!" Skip said. "Am I good or what?"

"It's beautiful," Tara agreed. "Awfully nice of you to arrange it for me."

Skip took his eyes from the road long enough to shoot her a self-satisfied grin. "We aim to please," he quipped, but Tara thought that he meant it.

"Just why is it I'm picking you up at your Dad's place? It's a bit of an inconvenience, you know."

"Sorry about that. My house is such a mess, I simply can't stay there, and I couldn't stay at my friend's condo. She and her husband are flying down unexpectedly. They're making one last ditch attempt at salvaging their marriage, which, by the way, has been a long time coming. I thought I'd best leave them to it."

"Gotcha. I hope you don't mind a little road trip. There's a place I want to take you to, but it's north of Vero."

"The night is young." Tara searched her bag for a lipstick, and her fingers found the lotto printout that she'd discovered while parked at Carmine's in West Palm Beach. "That's strange," she muttered, eyeing it.

"I've been called many things..."

"No, silly." Tara held up the chit. "I found this in my car last fall. Forgot all about it."

"I don't play the lottery."

"I seldom do. How long is a ticket good for? Do you know?"

"A year, I think. Got a winner?"

Tara shrugged. "Who knows?

They drove out of the city onto I-95 North and, in little over an hour, were exiting at the sleepy fishing village of Sebastian. Skip followed the directions to US Highway 1, and they were soon traveling along a corridor as different from Palm Beach as oysters to caviar.

"I love this little town," Skip said. "It's so old Florida. Fishermen ply the sea by day, and their harvest is served up fresh nightly at a number of fine little eateries."

"It sounds terrific," Tara said. "I love seafood."

Skip pulled off the highway onto Indian River Drive and was soon parking in front of a modest, low-slung building. "It' not fancy, but you won't be disappointed."

Their host, a slightly overweight gentleman with a melodic, island voice, led them to a booth overlooking the river. After perusing the enormous menus, Tara ordered the house specialty, shrimp curry.

"I'll have the grouper with ginger and lemongrass," Skip said. "And bring us a bottle of the house Sauvignon Blanc."

Throughout the meal, Skip regaled Tara with a seemingly endless supply of anecdotes regarding his romantic conquests. "When I returned to the mainland, I dated an old friend, Charlotte Ford." He nodded at the waitress, indicating that she should top off their glasses. "Which might give you an idea of how ancient I really am."

Tara figured he was name-dropping, but she stored that information away for future reference. She had no idea how old the Ford heiress was, but she figured Skip was probably in his late sixties, and far too old for her. Yet, there was something undeniably appealing about him. He detailed his escapades in such a self-deprecating tone, poking fun at his own indiscretions, she realized he didn't for one minute take himself too seriously.

Tara hadn't felt so relaxed in ages. The harrowing events of the last many months were forgotten as the two of them laughed their way through the meal. Afterward, they linked arms and strolled outside and down to the docks, where a plethora of sea craft bobbed at their moorings. There were pleasure boats and skiffs, dinghies and yachts, but the majority were working vessels.

A sliver of moon gleamed against the black curtain of night. If not for the few dock lights reflected in the murky water and the slice of moon overhead, they would have been immersed in total darkness. Tara leaned back onto Skip's broad chest sighing contentedly. When he wrapped his arms around her waist, she was unprepared for the wave of desire that washed over her.

To hell with logic.

She was in the arms of an extremely good-looking man, and it felt incredible.

Who cares if he's not Mister Right? I'm always thinking too much. Right now, he's all the man I've got, and that's not half bad.

Skip slid his hands from her waist to her breasts, and reason returned. She pulled away from him, saying, "Hey, slow down, mister."

Instead, Skip spun her around and covered her lips with his, stifling her protests. A moment later, his tongue was in her mouth.

This fellow is a real smooth operator, Tara thought, as her body responded to his kiss.

Whoa!

Alarms sounded in her cranium. She had her objectives, but maybe it was time to rein in this cowboy. Did she really want to become another notch in his belt, another risqué story to add to his anthology? Besides, things were suddenly heating up with Nathan. With that thought, Tara broke away from Skip's embrace. "Come on," she said, taking his hand. "We'd best get back."

Ever the gentleman, Skip allowed himself to be led up the embankment to the street. Distant music and the occasional muffled shout sounded from an open-air pub a few blocks up the road.

"What's that?" Tara asked, thinking any diversion was a good one.

"Earl's Hideaway, of course."

"Earl's? You're kidding. Wonder if my Dad knows about his namesake."

"I'll bet he does. This place has a reputation. Care for a nightcap? Maybe a fistfight, thrown in for good measure?"

"What do you mean?" Tara's curiosity was piqued. Once again, she linked arms with Skip, and the two strolled toward the source of the music.

"Are you telling me you've never heard of Earl's?"

Tara glanced up at him. "I'm the new girl in town. Is it famous or something?"

"More like infamous." Skip gave her the once-over, eyeing her lime green Lilly Pulitzer sweater and coordinating print skirt. "You're a tad overdressed, but I doubt they'll hold that against you. As for me, however," Skip feigned a look of horror, "with my pink polo shirt and aristocratic beak of the same hue...I doubt I'll last ten minutes before some redneck decides to make me his bitch."

They rounded a street corner, and Tara got her first glimpse of Earl's. The parking lot was awash in motorcycles of every size, configuration, and hue. She'd never seen so many bikes. There were hundreds of them. Then, she took in the saloon. Constructed of weathered planks, it was packed, full-to-bursting, with leather-clad roisterers. Ribald laughter and honkytonk music spilled out into the night in equal portions. Although Tara had never been to Daytona, this place was exactly how she'd imagined Bike Week, boisterous, loud, and tipsy. Outside on the sidewalk, they hesitated, listening to the raucous voices and blaring music. Skip raised an eyebrow in a silent question.

"I'm game if you are," Tara said.

Skip muttered apologies as he cut a swath through the crowd, and they were immediately swallowed up in a crush of bodies that gleamed with both sweat and silver-studded piercings. Every seat at the bar was taken, so they stood once removed from it. Skip hollered their order of two drafts to the bartender, and Tara nodded her approval. This was not the place to order a glass of wine or a martini, although, given the array of bottles lining the shelves, either could be had.

As she waited for her beer to arrive, Tara examined the heavyset fellow seated on the barstool directly in front of her. His brawny arms were a road map of crudely executed tattoos.

"How do you like it?" Skip's eyes roved about the place. "Suit you?" He spoke in a deadpan, not wanting to ruffle any feathers.

"Great," Tara said, tightly. "My new favorite place."

"I figured you'd take to it."

Perhaps they'd spoken too loudly, or maybe it was Skip's Brahman accent that caused the giant to slowly turn on his barstool and face Tara. He encompassed her with bleary eyes, his expression purely malevolent.

Tara's breath hitched in her throat, and she stared back at the brute in horror. She longed to skitter away, but she couldn't tear her eyes from that broad face with its oddly flattened nose and cruel-looking mouth. The man's neck was the size of a Volkswagen and deeply creased from over-exposure to the elements. A blue bandana circled his ruddy pate, and what little hair he had was tied in a greasy ponytail that did nothing to disguise the fact that he was balding on top.

Light-headed and shaky, Tara's instinct for self-preservation rose to the occasion. Rather than faint dead away, she turned on the charm. What the hell, she thought, affecting a devil-may-care attitude. It was the one ploy that had always worked for her in the past.

"Hey!" she said, flashing the monster a flirtatious smile. "How you doin'?"

The cretin's eyes narrowed, and Tara struggled to keep the terror from her face.

Skip wasn't taking any chances. "How do, my friend?" he bellowed. "What say I buy you a drink?"

Animated, the fellow pounded a fist on the bar. Glasses rattled as he demanded service. "Joe, you sumabitch, get over here." In the next instant, he'd slid off the barstool and weaved unsteadily before Tara, his face transformed by a sappy grin. "Here you go, li'l lady," he said, patting the recently vacated stool. His voice was guttural, a Hoover with a broken belt.

"Oh, no. I couldn't."

Once again, the man's eyes became hooded, and he swayed from side to side peering at her. Skip shot Tara a meaningful look, silently communicating that she should do as the brute said.

"Thank you." Tara scrambled up onto the barstool.

Skip draped a protective arm around her while giving the biker his full attention. "Name's George," he said. "And this is Tara."

George?

Tara nearly choked. Where did that come from?

"Plez'ta meetcha, George. I'm Ronnie, Ronnie Bliss." The man took Skip's hand in his own meaty mitt, and Skip winced as the bones in his fingers were crushed in a powerful grip.

"Say there, Ronnie," Skip said, when at last he'd recovered from the fierce salutation. "About that drink..."

"Nah," Ronnie said. "You don't have to do that, man."

"I'd like to," Skip said. "Being as you were such a gentleman, offering your seat to my girl."

"Chivalry's not dead," Tara quipped.

Skip looked at her as though she'd suddenly turned as green as her Lilly Ps. Then he pivoted back to the bartender and ordered another round of drinks.

"Ronnie," Skip ventured, "how much time did you do?"

At that, Tara did choke, struggling to keep from spewing a mouthful of brew all over the bar. Was old George trying to get them both killed? She searched Ronnie's face for a reaction, but none was forthcoming. I'll be darned, she thought. Either their new friend was too drunk to take offense, or her date actually knew how to talk to men of Ronnie's ilk. Her estimation of Skip edged up a notch.

"Busted. Did a little over a year. I stay away from that shit now."

"Good for you, buddy." Skip raised his glass.

"Yup. Booze is my drug of choice, my friend." Ronnie and Skip clinked glasses.

Before you know it the two of them will be riding off into the sunset.

"What do you do for a living?" Skip asked.

"Landfill. Got my own rig."

"Gosh," Tara exclaimed. "You mean one of those great big, yellow, shovel thingies?"

"Yes, ma'am."

"Those babies must cost a small fortune." Skip eyed Ronnie with new respect.

"You got that right," Ronnie growled.

Skip leaned in, intrigued. "Where do you do most of your work?"

"All over." Ronnie put an elbow on the bar and fanned the air with thick fingers. "You see how much development there is going on here? It's a freakin' gold mine." He glanced at Tara. "Sorry, miss."

Tara shook her head. "Not at all."

"I hire out by the day, by the week. Whatever. Work from sunup to sunset, five, six days a week." A scantily clad barmaid walked by, a rhinestone bauble glistening at her navel. Ronnie grabbed her, drawing her close in an awkward embrace. "But I play on the weekends. Don't I, Caitlan?"

"You sure do, Ron." The barmaid squirmed out of Ronnie's grasp. "What can I getcha?"

Skip ordered another round, and she was gone as quickly as she'd appeared.

"I bet you make good money moving earth," Skip said.

"It's sweet, all right," Ronnie admitted. "Clear upwards of a grand a day."

Skip whistled.

"No kidding?" Tara said. "So you make five or six thousand dollars a week?"

"On good weeks, yes, miss, I do. If the weather's bad, then I can't work at all."

"I bet that's why you're in Florida," Skip said. "Am I right?"

"There's always work now that the housing bust is over and the economy is chugging along. The weather cooperates most of the time."

"Do you own a housh, Ronnie?" Tara asked, cringing at the slur in her voice.

Oh great! Plastered on your first real date with Skip. Way to make a good impression.

"Nice li'l house on the water, and I send money to my daughter."

"You have a daughter?" Tara said. "Where ish she?"

Stop talking, you fool!

Tara's brain seemed to be hardwired to her mouth.

"In Michigan. That's where I come from."

"Good man," Skip said. "I, myself, hail from Detroit."

Tara giggled. She thought it was funny the way Skip said *DEE*troit, with the accent on the first syllable.

"Good place to be from." Ronnie guffawed at his own joke.

"Grosse Point, actually," Skip muttered. "What else do you do with all that dough, Ronnie?"

"I bought me a sweet li'l hog. You guys wanna see it?"

Skip nodded, tossed some bills on the bar, and helped Tara down from the barstool. Tara was grateful for Skip's support, for the floor of the saloon seemed to pitch and roll beneath her feet. Not waiting for a response, Ronnie muscled his way through the press of bodies, and Tara and Skip followed behind, neither wishing to cross the likes of Ronnie Bliss.

They rounded the side of the building, and there, parked directly under a streetlamp, was Ronnie's pride and joy—a monstrous scarlet and chrome-plated Harley. "She's a li'l smaller than a Humvee," Ronnie proclaimed proudly, "but a whole lot faster."

Tara had to admit the bike seemed to fit Ronnie, unconventional and menacing, but strong and, somehow, dependable looking.

"She's a beaut," Skip agreed.

"You wanna ride, sweetheart?" Ronnie eyed Tara.

"No thanks, Ronnie. I'm a real chicken."

"Aw come on, just a spin around the block. Don't be a scaredy-cat."

"Go ahead, Tara," Skip encouraged. "Chanch of a lifetime."

Chanch? So that's how it was. Good old George wasn't sober as a judge, after all.

Before she knew what was happening, Tara was hoisted up onto the back of a beast sprung to life. Straining to be released, the bike roared even louder than Ronnie Bliss. Someone clamped a helmet on her head, but it was much too big for her and kept sliding down over her eyes, making it difficult to see.

There was no time to struggle. The thrust of forward motion pitched her back with such force all she could do was throw her arms about Ronnie's tree trunk of a waist and pray for deliverance. The wind whipped at her face and arms as they zoomed around the block and out onto the somnolent main street. Halfway around the quadrant, she started screaming at the top of her lungs, partly out of terror and partly in sheer delight. At one point, she opened her eyes and ventured a look skyward. The stars rushed by.

Skyrockets in flight!

Quickly, she clamped them shut again. The sensation was something like being on a rollercoaster, so fast, and terrifying, yet thrilling and fun for the dare of it. In less than five minutes, they had returned to the parking lot, and Skip was lifting her down.

"Good heavens, woman," he said. "You were wailing to wake the dead. Do you want to get Ronnie arrested for kidnapping or something?"

Tara giggled and leaned back into Skip. She was dizzy and didn't trust her legs to support her. "Oh, my gawd, Ronnie, you're so baaad. You're a naughty boy, Rooonnieee. What a trip."

"Thanks, my friend," Skip said, smacking a palm on Ronnie's shoulder. "I doubt she'll ever forget that."

"Yes, sirree," Ronnie said. "You take care now, li'l lady." He nodded in Tara's direction.

"Be safe," Skip said.

Ronnie put a finger to his forehead by way of a salute and disappeared in a cloud of exhaust. A good thing. He got out of there just in time to miss the spectacle of Tara upchucking on the pavement.

So much for the li'l lady.

Skip supported her while she tried to avoid splattering his Italian leather shoes. Still, Tara clung to the thought there might yet be hope for salvaging the remains of the evening—that she could somehow compose herself, laugh off her indiscretions, and get back home with some shred of dignity intact. No sooner did that thought cross her mind than the world spun out of control.

Then the lights went out.

≈

When Tara awoke, it was to a throbbing head and a mouth that tasted like the bottom of a bilge tank. She was dressed in her nightgown, and her clothes were a crumpled heap beside the bed. She couldn't remember changing out of her street clothes, and she only hoped she'd managed by herself. If that weren't the case, she couldn't think what would be worse, if it had been her dad or Skip, who'd done the honors.

She stumbled into the bathroom, tossed two aspirin down her gullet, and scoured her teeth with Colgate. After splashing her face with cold water, she surveyed the damage. Her eyes were red and puffy, and her stringy hair and sallow complexion did little to improve the overall effect.

Standing under the shower, she let the water run as hot as she could stand. When she emerged, she blew her hair dry and applied enough cover-up and eyeliner to conceal the ravages of her intemperance. Beginning to feel halfway human, she padded out into the kitchen and poured herself a glass of Natalie's Orange Juice. That did the trick. Tara could actually feel her cells plump up and rehydrate.

Umm, is there anything better than orange juice?

Earl was nowhere in evidence, but he'd left the morning paper on the table. Tara gave it a cursory glance, but then a headline grabbed her attention. *Junior Securities Adviser Charged in Fraud Case*, it screamed. Staring out at her was the image of an attractive blonde who looked vaguely familiar. Tara racked her brain. Where had she seen that face before? She poured over the article, and her eyes grew wide when the words *Nathan McCourt, of McCourt Enterprises,* jumped off the page.

Then, it came to her. The midnight mermaid of Palacia del Mar was in jail. She reread the article, but the details were sketchy. Apparently, the woman had been doing a little business on the side, engaging McCourt clients in an investment scheme, the sole purpose of which was to fleece the unsuspecting victims. Tara couldn't wait to hear more about this juicy tidbit. She'd head up to Palacia del Mar in the afternoon and have a chat with Willie, but just now, she had to get moving. Kevin's funeral was at eleven, and she'd promised Scottly she'd handle all the details surrounding both the music and the ceremony.

CHAPTER THIRTY

AWAKENING

St. Sebastian's was packed. The Scandal's crew was there, as were a few of Kevin's personal acquaintances. For the most part, it was Scottly's large circle of friends, clients, and associates who'd come out to support him. From the viewing to the graveside service, they were there for him, lifting him up, offering words of comfort.

All week-long, a barrage of casseroles and hams, potato and pasta salads, and an assortment of baked goods had arrived at his door, until his once tidy kitchen resembled a Publix deli. Happily, as the wake was to be at his place, it was all put to good use. Scottly had hired a catering service, which provided waitstaff, skirted tables, china, glassware, and the like, and they'd begun setting up at nine. By the time Kevin's body was lowered into the ground, the buffet was laid out, the tables and bar fully stocked, and the celebration of life just waiting to happen.

At half-past one, the first members of the funeral party started arriving. Two hours later, the bash was in full swing. The day was Florida perfection, which was a blessing, for the house was filled to overflowing. The guests, bearing plates laden with food, spilled out onto the patio to enjoy the fresh air and sunshine. Tara sat under a large market umbrella next to Dulcie and Ernestine.

The silver-haired widow popped a canape into her perfectly painted red mouth, then sucked a lacquered nail. "I, for one, am glad it happened," she said in a stage whisper. "Don't quote me on that, for heaven's sake."

"I know exactly what you mean," Ernestine agreed. "Isn't this tortellini salad delicious?" She savored a forkful. "I mean, he was a wonder with hair. You have to give him that. I can't even imagine who'll take care of me now that he's gone, but, honestly, there was something creepy about him. Don't y'all think?"

"He gave me the willies. That's for sure," Tara agreed. "Here he was, living with our darling Scottly, taking him for all he's worth. It's shameful. I swear, he came on to me. Not that that kind of thing happens to me so often that I'm an expert, but I think I can read the signs."

"Shush. Here he comes," Dulcie breathed. They all turned guileless faces toward Scottly, whose own poor face was haggard. "Hey, baby." Dulcie beckoned to him. "Come to mama."

Scottly did as he was told, folding his large frame into the chair next to hers.

"You look like hell," Dulcie announced.

"Thank you, Dulc." Scottly ran a palm over his fleshly face and then opened his eyes wide.

"Are you getting any sleep?" Ernestine asked.

"I've got a prescription that knocks me out. I believe I've become an addict." For one uncomfortable moment, no one spoke. "Sorry," he said. "Bad joke."

"It was a lovely funeral, dear," Ernestine said. "The flowers were gorgeous."

"Yes, it was nice. Thanks to this angel." Scottly placed a palm on Tara's shoulder. "The music was splendid, sweet pea. Loved the *Pie Jesu*."

"What a difference good music makes," Ernestine said. "It was very moving." She turned to Scottly. "The eulogy was perfect. As always, Scott, you said just the right things."

"I agree," Tara said. "A brief history, a few humorous anecdotes. Not too maudlin. I've played at some funerals where they go on and on, sobbing and breaking down at the pulpit. Absolutely ghastly."

"There's a time and place, isn't there?" Dulcie looked pointedly at Scottly. "It's time you started getting back into the old swing of things and stopped grieving."

"Not quite yet." He shook his head. "It still doesn't seem real. This has been a nightmare. Loss is one thing, but the betrayal? When my worst fears were confirmed, and I learned what he'd been up to…" He looked off into the distance and then turned back. "I honestly thought he was *the one*. That we'd grow old together."

"I am *so* sorry." Dulcie took his hand in hers.

"I guess we see what we want to see," Scottly said. "No fool like an old fool."

"Isn't that the truth," Dulcie soothed.

"There isn't a soul on God's good, green Earth who can't be brought down, completely bamboozled, when it comes to matters of the heart." Ernestine interjected. She reached over and patted the distraught man's knee. "Take, for instance, that fellow over there." She pointed toward the covered porch, and they all peered in that direction.

Tara did a double-take when she spied Nathan. She hadn't seen him at the funeral, and she certainly hadn't expected to find him here. Quickly, she averted her eyes, praying Nathan hadn't spied them all staring at him. After this morning's press, it was a sure bet tongues were wagging. She imagined he was getting a lot of unwanted attention, and she didn't want to add to his troubles.

"I read about it," Ernestine said, her chins quivering in excitement. "What a scandal."

Dulcie shot her a meaningful look, and Ernestine wisely changed her tack.

"He manages my portfolio and yours, too, Dulcie," she said. "I've always been completely satisfied."

Dulcie nodded. "I don't imagine that will change. It's a good thing that little opportunist he was screwing didn't tamper with our investments."

"What are you talking about?" Scottly asked.

"You don't know?" His puzzled expression was all the answer Dulcie needed. "Nathan hired some bimbo straight out of university as an assistant. She was slick, an MBA, and smart as a whip."

"A real con-artist," Ernestine interjected.

"Anyway," Dulcie continued, "while Mr. McCourt was taking liberties with her, she was taking him to the cleaners."

"No!" Tara exclaimed, feigning ignorance.

"Yes!" Dulcie and Ernestine chimed in unison.

Dulcie glanced in Nathan's direction and shook her head. "Men are such fools."

"You can say that again," Scottly agreed.

～

Once the sun slipped below the horizon, the wake took on a new rhythm. The caterers had packaged up and put away all the food, cleaned the kitchen, and moved the bar inside. Only a few young people and some of Scottly's closest friends remained. Someone had found the stereo, and Jimmy Buffet was sailing away to Margaretville.

Tara sat curled in a lounge chair opposite Nathan. Over the course of the evening, she'd polished off the better part of a bottle of wine and her heels had long since been discarded.

"I think it was wonderful of you to arrange for Cerita's treatments," Tara ventured, at long last daring to meet Nathan's eyes.

"It was the least I could do." Nathan brushed off the compliment. "Willie has been a godsend. I couldn't have managed without her all these years."

"Bringing in someone to care for her mother, too. I know that's been a tremendous help."

"Hmm," Nathan muttered, seemingly uncomfortable with the praise being heaped upon him. He veered the conversation in a different direction. "Speaking of which, I hope you'll continue to help us out now and then."

"Anytime you need me. Just let Willie know. She has my numbers."

"Is that privileged information?" Nathan gazed at her.

"What do you mean?"

"I think you know what I mean."

Scottly appeared, a glass of Scotch in hand. He crossed to Tara and settled his large frame on the ottoman at her feet. "Well, ducky," he said, "it's been quite a day."

Tara glanced around the room, suddenly realizing she and Nathan were the last holdouts. Poor Scottly. Surely, he yearned for peace and quiet after all the emotion of this most trying day. She tilted her face to his, and he leaned in for a kiss. "Indeed, it has. You must be exhausted."

Nathan came to his feet. "I've stayed far too long. Forgive me." He extended a hand toward his host.

Scottly folded Nathan's hand in his. "Not at all. When one of us is in trouble, we all must pull together. Isn't that right?"

Nathan screwed up his face and nodded, and Tara silently blessed Scottly for extending the proverbial olive branch. Even at his lowest, he was thinking of others.

Nate turned to Tara, only to find her on the floor groping under the chair for her shoes. "It was good to see you, Tara," he said, eyeing her backside.

She pirouetted around, flopped back down in the chair, and proceeded to slip, first one foot, then the other, into the heels. "You, too." Tara's eyes found Scott's. "Although I wish it'd been under different circumstances."

"Indeed. Oh, and the kids asked me to tell you how much they've missed you this last week."

"It's been an eventful one."

"Yes, well…" Nathan addressed his host. "Scott, again, my sincere condolences."

Scottly escorted them to the entrance, and Tara ducked in for a final kiss to his cheek before they said their good-byes. Then she and Nathan were out the door and strolling down the drive.

When they reached the sidewalk, Nathan turned to her, and held her gaze. "Tara…"

"Yes?"

Nathan's face was unaccustomedly grave. "I want you to know I appreciate all you've done for me and my family."

"You're welc—"

He cut her off, saying, "Please, hear me out."

"Of course."

"Sometimes I'm preoccupied. I realize that. I take things for granted—secure in the knowledge that everything is being cared for, in spite of my absence." Nathan sighed and briefly looked away before turning back to her. "I'm really not a cold-hearted, callous jerk."

Tara's brow knit. "I know that." She searched his eyes. Was there something else he wasn't telling her, or was she merely imagining it?

"Good, because once I sort out this mess, I plan on proving it to you."

"You've nothing to prove."

"I do." Nathan drew her to him and kissed her lightly on the lips. Before Tara knew what had happened, he'd nodded curtly, and strode off, leaving her utterly perplexed.

Yet hopeful.

What a complicated man. Could nothing in my life be easy?

∾

She drove carefully, taking the back roads and keeping well within the posted speed limit. When she arrived at her father's apartment building, she found him puttering in the carport, a collection of disassembled carriage lanterns scattered about on newsprint spread before him. Overhead, insects darted and swooped, beating their little heads into the fluorescents as though they'd found a direct path into bug heaven.

"Hey," Tara called. "What are you doing?"

"Hey yourself," Earl replied. "Bought these babies at a garage sale."

"Umm," Tara mumbled, unimpressed. The fixtures all shared a common trait. Each was frowsy with corrosion.

"A little Rust-oleum and they'll be good as new."

"Say, Dad," Tara said, changing the subject to the one that was burning on her brain, "about last night..."

"What about it?"

"You know what I'm talking about."

"Guess you had a pretty good time, huh?" Earl unscrewed an escutcheon from the body of a lantern. "By the way, your new boyfriend called. Said to ask you if you'd like to go out with him again. Maybe to an AA meeting?"

"Don't have to rub it in." Tara hunkered down beside her father. "I got pretty wasted, huh?"

"I guess."

"What happened?"

"Hell, nothing happened. Hand me that wrench." Tara reached for the nearest tool. "Not that one, the little one," Earl said, palming the implement. "Sir Skippy, your knight in shining armor, delivered you home safely. Between the two of us, we got you into bed."

Tara leaped to her feet. "You're kidding me, right? This isn't funny."

"Don't get your knickers in a snit," Earl placated. "Skip was a perfect gentleman. He carried you up and over the threshold. I guess that means you're hitched. Congratulations." Earl winked at his daughter, seeming to enjoy her discomfort.

"And?"

"I helped you to your bedroom."

"Oh." Tara chewed on this bit of information. Things didn't look as bad as they'd first appeared. Then another thought occurred to her. "Who undressed me and got me into my nightgown?"

"Good grief," Earl grumbled. "I got your nightgown out of the closet and put it on the bed next to you. You were drooling, so I knew you were alive. I said take those damn clothes off and put your nightie on. I guess for once, in your stubborn life, you obeyed me."

Tara exploded in laughter, and once she started, she couldn't stop. Earl gaped at her, thinking perhaps she'd lost her marbles, but then he'd raised a bunch of girls and was accustomed to female hysterics.

~

After scrubbing her face and changing into silk pajamas, Tara had a sudden urge to call Pat. It was a Saturday night, but she figured her best friend would be home, and she was not mistaken. "Hey, Patty. How are you?"

"Super. All's quiet on the Midwestern front. How are *you*, sweetie?"

"Really good. Gosh, it's great to hear your voice. I've missed you."

"Me, too. What's going on down there? How's your love life?"

"Funny you should ask. How's yours?"

"Are you kidding? I wouldn't recognize a penis if it walked up and poked me in the...Say, wait a minute, will you? I need a refill."

Tara giggled. How she loved Pat.

"Ah'm back," Pat announced. "Spill."

"You first. How did it go with the marriage retreat in Vero?"

"Not so good. My apologies for not seeing you. Cliff and I were going at it pretty hot and heavy. I wasn't up for socializing."

"I'm sorry."

"Three days together were three days too many. Enough of that. What's shakin' in the tropics?"

"Patty, my head is spinning."

"How much wine did you drink?"

"There's that, too."

"Tara, Tara...What do you hear from Jack?"

"Jack? Not much. I am *so* over him."

"Reeeally? When did that happen?"

"I don't know." Tara realized that she had, indeed, moved beyond Jack. "Gosh. Months ago."

"Why the sudden angst?"

Tara brought her pal up to speed, her words tumbling out, one over the other. "I think I'm in love with this guy. Then there's this other guy, who's absolutely charming, but there's just no chemistry on my part. I'm definitely in love with my next-door neighbor, but he's gay. Besides which, I'm becoming an alcoholic. Not really, but my life seems to be spinning out of control. I had another break-in, and I think someone is following me. I need a Patty-fix."

"Someone broke into your house again?" Pat's tone was suddenly serious. "What the heck have you gotten yourself into, kiddo?"

"I don't know. It makes no sense. At least this one wasn't nearly as bad as the last time. My darling neighbor, the gay guy, confronted the burglar before he could wreak too much havoc. It's a wonder he wasn't killed. Unfortunately, the creep's still out there, and I'm becoming accustomed to looking over my shoulder."

"And the police? What about your place in Atlanta?"

"They call from time to time, but there are no leads. It's become a cold case."

There was a pause at the end of line. "Okay, I'm seriously worried," Pat finally admitted.

"I know. It's a freakin' mystery," Tara said. "Will you be my Watson?"

"I'd love to, but I'm booked up for the summer. I can fly down in the fall, though. Wasn't planning on getting down there until after Christmas, but it sounds like you need reinforcements."

"I do."

"I'll get back to you with dates. Sometime before Thanksgiving?"

"You're the best."

"Tell the rest of the world, would you?"

"By that you mean?"

"I mean I've given Cliff the old heave-ho, and I'm feeling like a shit."

"What?" Tara sat back in her chair, reeling. "Are you kidding me?"

"Nope. He finally went too far. I kept making excuses and adjustments, telling myself it was okay, that his whoring around didn't bother me...until I realized I'd been fooling myself. It mattered."

"Oh, Pat, I'm so sorry, but I'm glad for you, too. Wish I could be there for you."

"It's okay. It really is. I'm in counseling. I have a wonderful therapist and a terrific support group. I'm doing all right."

"Look at us, huh? Who would have thought it? At our age, starting over. It's crazy."

"It's personal growth, Tara. Moving forward."

"I suppose you're right."

"Now listen, whichever one of these guys you're going to dump, let me have at him, okay?"

"You got it. Love you, girl."

No sooner had Tara disconnected, than a picture of Skip and Pat formed in her mind's eye. The two had so much in common. They were both class acts, tall, sophisticated, smart, and funny. Tara cupped her chin in hand, a new sparkle in her eye.

She had some matchmaking to do.

CHAPTER THIRTY-ONE

STORMY WEATHER

Even by Florida standards, Tara's first summer in Vero was chalking up to be a scorcher. September came and went with not a hint of relief or a glimmer of fall. It had been widely touted that the weather pattern was cyclical, the current trend being one of heightened storm activity. In the last days of October, Floridians collectively breathed a sigh of relief. With so many close calls and near misses Tara, like most residents, had become complacent. She'd stockpiled the requisite batteries, flashlights, and oil lanterns, and her pantry boasted cases of bottled water and canned goods. She'd even gone so far as to purchase a manually operated can opener, but this late in the season, the likelihood of a major hurricane striking south Florida was remote. Just a few more weeks and they'd be out of the woods entirely.

It was late in the day, and she'd been summoned. Which is how Tara found herself savoring a tall glass of iced tea in Dulcie's solarium—a shimmering, white room comprised of latticed walls punctuated by great panes of glass. The veins of the plantation shutters were slanted to minimize the sun's glare. Beyond their angled openings—like so many half-hooded eyes—a glimpse of ocean and sky was afforded. The two elements were barely distinguishable, both a milky haze in the heat of the day. Breakers lapped drowsily at the shore, one wave falling gently upon another, like fluffy towels being folded. A pair of gulls sailed overhead on a phantom current, too lazy to fish.

"It's wicked warm." Ernestine complained, mopping her flushed face with a linen napkin. "Either that or I'm having a hot flash."

"It's simply hot, Ernestine," Dulcie chided. "Your menopause days are history, honey, and you know it."

"Will it ever cool off?" Tara asked, petulantly. She sliced off a thin wedge of sponge cake, transferring it from the sparkling crystal cake stand to a delicate plate of nearly translucent china.

"Soon, darling," Scottly said. "Just another week or two, and we'll be blissfully cool."

"Won't that be lovely?" Tara said. "I'm sick to death of worrying about my house, especially now that it's been renovated."

"I've resided in Vero nearly all my adult life," Dulcie reassured. "In that time, I've lived through only two category four storms, Jeanne and Francis, and I believe they were anomalies. Your house is built to the new building codes. Unless we take a direct hit, it'll be fine. It's being without power that's a bother." She tossed both hands in the air for emphasis. "I finally took Nathan's advice and had a monster generator installed. Kicks on in fifteen seconds and powers the entire house."

"Whew!" Tara fanned her face with an open palm. "In the event of a power outage, I'm bunking here. I simply cannot take this heat."

On Monday, the following excerpt appeared on the lower right-hand corner of the front page of the Vero Beach Press Journal.

New tropical storm forming in the Caribbean *Miami – A tropical depression that developed in the southeast Caribbean Sea is expected to become Tropical Storm Uma today, forecasters at the National Hurricane Center said. Tropical Depression 17 formed late Sunday is expected to be south of Jamaica by the end of the week, over Caribbean waters still warm enough to feed a major hurricane, said hurricane specialist Stacy Jamison. At 10 p.m., its maximum winds were near 55 mph, and it's moving east-northeast near 25 mph.*

∼

Tuesday morning while driving to the McCourt compound, Tara found it hard to believe there was a monster storm brewing out over the Atlantic. The sky was crystalline blue, marred only by a few wispy, feather clouds of white and pink, and the humidity had lifted.

"A Bermuda high is what it is," Willie confided as they sat at the kitchen table over coffee.

Suddenly, the housekeeper's eyes grew round as she stared blindly into the future, and her body rocked back and forth. "That she-devil storm's just a whirling and turning, sucking all the wet out of the air. She's growing bigger and bigger, swelled up like a hussy at a pie-eating contest. Lawd, I see it. She's taking in more and more, till her belly pop. Then watch out. All hell going to break loose."

Willie sighed and returned to the present, acting as though nothing out of the ordinary had occurred.

Tara had become accustomed to Willie's prophecies, and she didn't set much store in them. But this time, Willie's words sent a tingle down her spine. "Where will you go, if we're forced to evacuate?"

"I have a cousin in Kissimmee. We'll stay with her till it's safe. What are your plans?"

"I'll stay with Dad," Tara said. "His place is far enough inland we should be all right."

"Humph!" Willie snorted. "Mister McCourt says he'll fly to Texas. Darned foolishness, if you ask me. Storm can go there, too."

"I suppose." Tara pushed away from the table and carried her coffee cup to the sink. "Let's just hope it blows itself out like the rest of them. I don't even want to think about it anymore. I'm ready for blessed cool and turkey.

∼

Wednesday, Nathan and the children left for Houston on the Gulfstream jet. Scottly, Ernestine, and Dulcie had taken a commercial flight out the day before. With plans for shopping and theater in NYC, the threesome had booked adjoining suites at the Waldorf.

Thursday, the weather began to deteriorate, and Tara awoke to a gray day of clouds and spitting rain. By noon, Melbourne, Orlando, Miami, and Palm Beach International Airports had shut down. No flights were scheduled in or out until Sunday at the earliest. Both Pat and Josh had canceled their flights and were staying put for the time being. Governor Scott called for a mandatory evacuation from the barrier island to Old Dixie Highway—the old dune line, which ran west of Federal Highway and US Highway 1. The exodus was to be completed by no later than four o'clock p.m. Only fire rescue, law enforcement, and certain government employees were exempt.

By mid-afternoon, Tara and her father had hunkered down in his little apartment for the duration. Uma had strengthened to a category three hurricane and was to make landfall sometime in the early morning hours. There was little to do but sit it out and wait for the storm to pass. By dinnertime, the wind had picked up and rain pelted fiercely at the windows. They kept the TV tuned to WPTV in order to track the storm. Tara had thrown together a dinner of stir fry, using up as many of the fresh vegetables from the crisper as possible.

Father and daughter were seated before the television, following updates from the Weather Channel when they lost the TV signal. Miraculously, they still had electricity. Earl found an old Star Wars DVD, and they lost themselves in that familiar sci-fi fantasy world of robots, villains, aliens, and heroes. An hour into the movie, there was a loud *pop,* and the two were plunged into darkness. For a moment, they simply sat there, stunned, while outside the storm raged on.

Then when they came to their senses, Earl jumped up and lit the oil lamps and wax candles while Tara took Chanel out before the full force of the storm struck.

They stood in the garage looking out at a world strangely devoid of light, one that had taken on a new and hectic life. Rain slashed down with the force of a jackhammer and palm trees and shrubs bent and shimmied in the wind. Palm fronds, scraps of wood, leaves, and an occasional shingle flew past the garage door opening. Tara urged Chanel to venture out into the elements. Eventually, her coaxing was rewarded, and he squatted, briefly, beneath the eave, before darting back into the relative safety of the garage.

Once back inside, Tara attempted to read by the light of an oil lantern, but she was too distracted by the storm's fury to concentrate, and exhaustion soon overtook her. By ten o'clock, she and Chanel were in bed sleeping soundly.

Four hours later, Tara was awakened by Chanel's low growling. In the gloom, she could discern nothing, and she strained to hear some sound that would explain the reason for the dog's agitation. Then it came to her. There was *no* sound—no howling wind, or pounding rain, or creak of groaning timbers. Curious, Tara climbed out of bed and crept to the living room. There, two oil lanterns still burned, casting a golden glow over nearby walls, but Earl was nowhere to be seen.

Tara crossed to the front door and opened it, only to spy the solitary figure of her father, standing like a sentinel in the flooded yard. Gingerly navigating small lakes, she made her way to him. A tangle of palm fronds and branches littered the lawn, while, overhead, a nearly full moon shone brightly and a plethora of unusually brilliant stars speckled the sky.

"Is it over?"

"Nah," Earl took a drag from his cigarette. "It's the eye of the storm."

"The eye? Really?" Tara marveled at the calm that had replaced the screeching gale, the serenity of a suddenly tranquil night sky. "Gosh. It's mind-boggling."

"Don't worry. It won't last. Ten, twenty minutes max. Then she'll be coming at us from the other direction."

"Will it be worse?"

"It might be. Probably not, though." Earl flicked the half-smoked cigarillo onto his waterlogged lawn.

"I thought you'd quit."

"I did. Figured I'd treat myself, calm my nerves. Damn thing tastes awful, though."

"How're the apartments holding up?"

"Tight as a drum. Lost a few roof tiles, but that's to be expected." Earl nodded toward the side yard. "I'm just glad that big old Australian pine didn't come crashing down on us."

～

In the morning, they surveyed the damage. As Earl had predicted, the apartment building was in relatively good condition. It had withstood the 120-mile per hour gusts with no water intrusion and only minor roof damage. The yard was another matter. Shrubs and trees were leafless, the flower beds in tatters, and the lawn, a coarsely woven basket of downed twigs and palm fronds. Until the power was restored and the mandatory evacuation lifted, they had nothing but time on their hands. They set to work, and they were in good company. The neighbors were all about the same business.

A cheerful camaraderie descended on them. They'd been spared, and everyone was on their best behavior. Many power lines were down, and there was no electricity. The street lights were inoperable, which meant forays for gas or ice—if they could be had—were a slow go. Radio broadcasts instructed motorists to treat every intersection as a four-way stop, and that's exactly what they did, politely yielding the right of way. It was enough to give even the most jaded among them hope for the species.

Neighbors who hadn't spoken in months opened up to one another. The men shared tools and lent a hand wherever needed. The women tied bandanas around their heads and worked alongside the men. The children played outside from dawn till dusk, for it was too hot inside, and there were no Nintendo or email, no television or YouTube. They were all survivors, and the shared experience united them.

Meals were community affairs as thawing freezers demanded to be emptied and cause for celebration when the day's labor was done. The repasts were hearty and diverse. One night, it was a mixed grill comprised of rack of lamb, sirloin, and pork cutlets, the next evening, shrimp kebobs, and marinated chicken breasts with a variety of salads. All meals were cooked over gas or coal grills and accompanied by copious amounts of beer, wine, and spirits. The kids drank soda and bottled water and ate on the run. They played baseball until the light completely faded and the ball couldn't be seen anymore.

For a time, it was a better world.

~

Nathan let himself in the front door of the sprawling stucco and fieldstone mansion he'd leased for the short term. Tucked inside the Houston beltway, it was convenient to his downtown office, and he felt the kids were safe here. He heard muffled clattering and voices coming from the kitchen, and he hiked through the great room to investigate. At the sound of Harry's voice uttering the word, "Tara," he stopped up short. Pausing just outside the entrance, he peeked in. It was rare for those two to exchange more than a few words these days, and he was both curious and hopeful. Could a truce have been established? Dare he hope that peace might once again reign in his household?

"I've been helping her out, and she's teaching me to cook." Jennifer had her back to him as she pressed a spatula to the grilled cheese sandwiches she was frying in a skillet.

"Cool."

"Yeah. Go get some chips from the pantry."

"Okay." Harry scrambled to his feet. "You like Tara, don't you?"

"Uh-huh." Jennifer transferred the sandwiches to a serving plate. "She's pretty awesome."

"Me, too. I like her dog,"

"Do you want milk or a soda?"

"Milk." Harry put the bag of chips on the table and sat back down. "Why doesn't Dad like her, do you think?"

Jennifer set a plate before her brother, crossed to the refrigerator and snagged a milk carton. "Who knows?" She sighed. "Sometimes I think he does like her, but..."

"Yeah." Harry reached for a sandwich and took a bite. "Wow! This is great, sis."

"Thank you." Jennifer poured them both glasses of milk and then sat opposite Harry. "Next, she's going to show me how to make chocolate chip cookies."

"All right!"

"Maybe we could get the two of them together," Jennifer said between bites.

"Huh?"

"Dad and Tara."

Harry considered his sister's words then shook his head. "Nah, Dad would never go for it."

"You're probably right, but it'd be nice, huh?"

Nathan crept away from the doorway, cleared his throat loudly, and tramped the short distance into the kitchen. "Hey, guys. What's happening?"

"Hi, Dad." Harry swiveled to face him. "Jenn made lunch. You should have some. It's really good."

"Want a sandwich, Dad?" Jennifer asked. "I made plenty."

"Sure." Nathan sat between them. "It smells delicious."

Jennifer jumped to her feet and took another plate from the cupboard. "Here you go." She placed it in front of Nathan, and he wrapped an arm around her narrow waist, giving her a quick hug.

"I see Tara is right. You're all grown up." Harry and Jennifer exchanged pointed looks, and their expressions were not lost on Nathan.

"Well, not *all*."

"I'm real proud of you, sweetheart."

"Thanks, Dad."

"When do you think we can go back home?" Harry asked.

"Oh, boy." Nathan dragged a paw across his chin. "I really don't know. I don't believe they've rescinded the evacuation order yet, and I doubt there's power. From what I hear, our house is in bad shape. So, it'd be pretty miserable. We might be dug in here for a while."

"Oh, no. I hope my closet's still intact," Jennifer said. "All my clothes."

"I hope Tara's okay," Harry said, shooting his sister a meaningful look.

"Clothes can be replaced," Nathan said. "As for Tara, you needn't worry. I'm sure she's fine. Maybe we'll call her tonight and see how she's doing. How would that be?"

Jennifer raised her eyebrows, and Harry choked on a bit of crust.

"Are you all right?" Nathan pounded the boy on the back.

"Yulp." Harry swallowed loudly, and Nathan had all he could do to keep a straight face in front of the pair of scheming conspirators.

~

"Tara, how are you?"

"Nathan." Tara's face split in a grin. "I'm fine." She held her cell before her and plopped down on a lawn chair. "I can't believe I'm hearing your voice. I just now turned my phone on. This is crazy. What a coincidence. I've been trying to save what little charge is left. Dad and I have been powering up, connecting to the car battery, but the towers are down. Service is sporadic. Sorry…I'm babbling. It's just so good to hear someone from the outside world. What about you? How are the kids?"

"We're okay. The kids are getting antsy, want to go back home."

"Tell them to cool their jets. There's no electricity here, and it's beastly hot. No one's allowed back on the island yet, anyway. Schools are closed. They would definitely not like it."

"Ah! Oh, wait." There was a pause as Nate conferred with his children before resuming. "Jenn says to tell you hello. We're all enjoying her cooking 101 skills, by the way. Harry says he misses Chanel, but not piano practice."

Tara laughed. "He's just saying that because he knows that's what kids his age are supposed to say. That child *loves* the piano. Tell them Chanel and I miss all of you."

The line crackled. "Nathan?" Tara struggled to make sense of the garbling, but it was no use. "You're breaking up." She came to her feet, holding her cell above her head then lowering it to speak. "Hello, Nathan?" she cried. "Hello?"

After two scorching days in the merciless sun, a semblance of order had been restored to Earl's lawn. Tara felt a sense of satisfaction at having contributed to the effort, but, as the time neared for her to leave and inspect her own property, her unease grew. On Monday, when it was deemed safe to travel on roadways that had been inspected and cleared of downed power lines and debris, the evacuation order was lifted. A parade of barrier island residents snaked over the causeways eager to return home, yet nervous about what they might find upon their arrival.

Tara pulled off the turnpike and headed east, evidence of the storm's fury stunning her with a surreal landscape she could never have imagined. An industrial complex with its metal roof pried away like a half-open can of soup. A mobile home park in tatters with prefabricated awnings and aluminum struts mangled and strewn alongside the highway. A high-rise condominium, missing its entire west wall, looking like a huge dollhouse, its furnished interior spaces exposed. Everywhere toppled trees and telephone poles, missing traffic lights, and twisted directional signs.

It was eerie.

As she neared her neighborhood, Tara's anxiety heighted. How had her home fared? She turned on to Pelican and was heartened to see that all the houses lining her street had been spared. Breathing a sigh of relief, Tara pulled into her driveway and performed a quick assessment. The newly planted yard was mayhem, and one large uprooted palm straddled the sidewalk, but the house appeared intact.

"Oh, Chanel, we're home!" Tara cried as thoughts of Dorothy and Toto came to mind. After unlocking the front door, she zipped from room to room, opening windows as she went to let out the stale air. She could hardly believe her good fortune. Except for a puddle of water that had collected at the base of the refrigerator, nothing seemed amiss. Tara dashed to the piano, lifted the keyboard cover, and let her fingers dance across the ivories in a celebratory tribute. It was out of tune, which was to be expected, given the pressure change generated by the storm.

Giddy with relief, Tara headed out the side door to survey the backyard. Circling the house, she noted broken roof tiles, now scythed into the lawn, her lovely new windows and screens plastered with a tangle of dried leaves, threads of plant fiber, and bits of grass, but she was thankful. Things could have been so much worse. Feeling blessed, she set to work.

As the daylight faded, so did Tara's resolve. Exhausted, both emotionally and physically, she desired nothing more than a tepid shower and a glass of wine.

~

Life gradually returned to a semblance of normalcy, but it was a new normal, one that included Red Cross relief stations, where food, water, and ice were dispensed to those in need—one in which convoys of electricians in trucks from as far away as Louisiana rumbled down thoroughfares alongside Humvees packed with National Guardsmen dressed in fatigues. All of those heroes were greeted with a joyful honking of horns and thumbs up, so grateful were the storm-weary, power-starved residents for the services they were there to provide.

That first trip back to Publix had been an eye-opener. The meat and produce aisles roped off, vegetables sprouting mold, melons split and oozing, spoiled meat reeking of decay. Waiting in line for ice—sans make-up, hair pulled back with a clip—was humbling. Living through the storm's aftermath was an experience that blurred class lines, and where they existed, broke down racial barriers. Nothing was taken for granted, not electricity or running water, or all that they made possible—warm baths, cool rooms, hot meals. For many, basic necessities such as security, shelter, and communication with the outside world seemed forgotten luxuries.

The storm's survivors were on an equal footing, they'd all lost something, many only complacence, others much more. At the same time, they'd all gained something of immeasurable value. They were stronger than they'd been before, more keenly aware of the precariousness of life, the vagaries of nature, and the elusive quality of material goods. There were times when Tara wished she were in New York with Scottly or in Houston with Nathan and his family, but, for the most part, she was glad she'd stayed on.

~

Dulcie and Ernestine's estates had withstood the storm, but Tara was shocked to learn that Nathan McCourt hadn't fared as well. The Palacia del Mar mansion had been hit by a tornado, a not uncommon phenomenon in a hurricane, and the house was in ruins. Happily, Willie's little bungalow was unharmed, and her electricity had been restored days ago. Which is why Tara and Cerita had gathered there to catch up on the news. The two were seated across from one another at the kitchen table.

"Just as well." Willie placed a glass of iced tea before Tara. "I never much cared for that house. Palacia del Mar...Humph!"

"I thought it was a lovely house, Mom. I feel sorry for Mr.

McCourt and his kids. No one should lose their home," Cerita chided. "And after all he's done for us…"

The young woman's head was swathed in a classically patterned Hermes silk scarf that Dulcie had purchased in New York at Tara's request. Despite the ravages of chemotherapy, she looked stunning. Thinner, her high cheekbones and prominent brow even more pronounced, she could have passed for a runway model.

"I agree with you, Willie." Tara said. "That house was too *done* for my taste. Yes, it was fabulous, but it wasn't homey. Staying there was like spending a night at the Ritz. Thank goodness Nathan had the presence of mind to store his collection of paintings and artwork, but what a travesty, to have lost all those beautiful musical instruments."

"He can afford to buy more if he wants to," Willie said. "Man's got more money than God. Don't need to fret about Mr. McCourt. He doesn't feel sorry for himself. Fact is, he's relieved." Willie set plates of Salad Niçoise before Tara and Cerita. "Place was a mausoleum. Ghost of Elisa was what made it cold if you ask me." She seated herself with a harrumph.

"You shouldn't say such things." Cerita rolled her eyes at Tara.

Tara smiled. Those two would be fine. Since starting on Weight Watchers, Willie had lost twenty pounds. Now, she avidly counted points, determined to drop another fifty. Cerita had completed her second round of chemo and she was committed to beating her disease. Tara figured that was half the battle. As a result of Nathan's intervention, the young woman was receiving cutting-edge therapies, and her cancer was in remission.

"Anyway," Willie continued, "Mr. McCourt and the kids are flying in from Houston in a few weeks. The house they're renting in Old Riomar is real nice, and it's going to be a whole lot easier to keep up. Mr. McCourt is looking for another property to purchase. Says he wants riverfront instead of ocean."

"Can't say as I blame him." Tara raised her glass. "Cheers, my friends. Here's to new beginnings."

"Eat," Willie commanded. "I used low-fat mayonnaise and fresh lemon juice in the dressing. One serving counts for only four points, and there's fresh fruit for dessert."

"I have some news," Tara said between mouthfuls. "This is delicious, by the way."

"Good news, I hope," Cerita said.

"Yes. I'm thinking of throwing a party next month. Hopefully, by then things will have returned to a semblance of normalcy here."

"You want me to help?" Willie's eyebrows hitched up in eager anticipation.

"I do *not* want you to work. I'll have it catered," Tara exclaimed. "I'm dying to entertain in my new digs, and after what we've all been through, I think it would do us good. What do you think?"

"Great idea," Cerita said. "May I bring Jarod?"

"You'd better."

"Can't I help?" Willie asked.

"You can help me plan it."

CHAPTER THIRTY-TWO

DROWNING IN THE CARPOOL

Six days passed before Tara's electricity was restored, and never in her life had she been happier. Many hadn't been as fortunate. In two weeks, the water oaks began to sprout tiny green buds, and everyone breathed a collective sigh of relief. It would all come back. Even the birds.

As she drove north on US 1, Tara's head was filled with thoughts of Nathan and plans for her party. It seemed like ages since her garage had been broken into, and she'd begun to let her defenses down. The burglary was simply another isolated act, she reasoned, another iteration of her lousy luck. There were no leads, not in Gwinnett or Indian River Counties. Wilcox hadn't called in months, which told her the case was cold. She was ready to relegate the entire incident to the ancient history department.

Tara whizzed past McKee Jungle Gardens, vowing, as she always did, to pay a visit one day. She turned onto Indian River Boulevard and headed for the causeway. Taking a left at seventeenth Tara glanced into her rear-view mirror and noted a gray Altima behind her. The car looked familiar. She was quite sure she'd seen it earlier. Wasn't it following a bit too closely?

She told herself she was just being paranoid, but a bubble of fear rose in her throat. On high alert, she tapped the media display, saying, "Hey, Siri, call Scottly." It rang and rang and then went to voice mail.

"Darn it!" she muttered, certain that Altima had whizzed by her when she'd parked at Willie's place.

Tara looked up, only to see the car passing on her right, but not before the older fellow behind the wheel glanced her way. In the next instant, he'd sped ahead, blew through the green light at the intersection, and headed south on A1A. Relieved, Tara steered into the turn lane on the left, heading north in the opposite direction.

~

Rick cursed a blue streak. She'd made him. He was sure of it, stared right at him as he passed her. Could he do nothing right anymore? He'd had a hell of a time keeping tabs on the bitch. Her schedule remained a mystery. When she wasn't off teaching piano at some kid's home, she was either in church practicing with a choir or gallivanting around with those two old bags. The woman was elusive as a popcorn fart.

Cochran pulled into a Seven-Eleven, shifted to park, and hurled himself out of the Altima. He figured since he was there, he might as well grab something to eat. After purchasing a Coke, a large bag of Lay's Chips, and a couple Milky Way bars, he headed back toward the causeway. His plan was to hole up at a discount hotel until after dark. Which, he thought, is what he should have done in the first place. He was going to have to be really careful from here on in. No more mistakes. Tonight, he'd get in and out quick, and be done with the whole sorry business.

~

Two hours later, Tara wheeled into her neighbor's circular drive, shifted into park, and tapped the horn. She and Scottly had made a date for a seven-thirty dinner, and it was her turn to drive. Strange, she thought, when forty-five seconds elapsed, and her neighbor hadn't yet appeared. The designer was nothing but prompt. Seconds ticked into minutes, and Tara cast about for something to occupy her. She raked through her purse, searching for a lipstick. Instead, her fingers closed around a slip of paper. It was that confounded lottery ticket!

From the corner of her eye, she detected movement and Tara's head snapped up. A wisecrack died in her throat when she took in Scottly's ominous expression, the fact that his hands were raised over his head. Only then did she notice the stocky fellow prodding him forward. It was the guy in the Altima! Fleetingly, she wondered if this was in some way connected to her break-ins. When she spied the gun in his hands, she was gripped by terror. Whoever this malcontent was, he was deadly serious.

Rick's eyes fastened on the lottery ticket. "Open up," he commanded. Tara pressed a button, and the window slid down. "Give me that." Cochran nodded, indicating the ticket.

Scottly's eyes implored her, silently mouthing words Tara couldn't make out.

"Now," Rick snarled. Tara thrust an arm out the window, and the gunman snatched the stub from her hand. He glanced at it briefly before tucking it into his breast pocket.

"You," he cried, eyeing Scottly and waving the pistol toward the car. "Around to the other side." Almost imperceptibly, Scottly shook his head no. Tara was confused. What was he trying to tell her?

Don't let him get in the car with you and drive away. Once you do, your chance of survival is diminished by ninety-five percent.

Tara had heard that bit of advice on an Oprah rerun, and she figured it was probably true. What was she to do? She couldn't abandon Scottly. Or could she? He was hitching his head up and rolling his eyes, as he shuffled to the passenger side of the Lexus. If only she could understand what his plan was.

The heavyset guy was in control of the situation. He rammed the firearm into Scottly's kidneys. "Open the door and get inside," he roared, "or I'll blow your fuckin' brains out!"

Scottly climbed in beside Tara and jerked his head in the direction of the back yard. Suddenly, Tara understood. Scottly wanted her to use the car as a weapon. Okay, she thought, but how to do that without killing them both?

Dear Lord, please save us.

In the meantime, the man positioned himself in the back seat. "Buckle up, mates," he growled. "Don't want to get pulled over for a seatbelt violation."

Tara obliged, and Scottly made a show of doing so, pretending to struggle with the seat belt.

"Okay, start 'er up and head south on Pelican Way."

As Tara shifted into drive, Scottly leaned toward her, eyes narrowed, jaw set.

"Don't even think about it," Rick hissed, seeming to sense Scottly's resolve.

In the next instant, Scottly stomped on the accelerator, nearly crushing Tara's foot. The car leapt forward. Tara screamed as her neighbor grabbed the wheel and yanked it to the right. Tires squealed on pavement then cut through the lush green lawn, tossing up clods of earth and grass clippings in their wake.

The assailant was hurled back in his seat, and the gun discharged with a muted pop, tearing a hole in the leather upholstery. As they crashed through the hibiscus bushes, he recovered, coming up behind Scottly. "You sonofabitch," he muttered, putting the cold muzzle of the gun to the back of his head.

Scottly was in the Zen moment. He let go of the wheel, lurched forward, and then rocketed back, crashing his thick skull into his attacker's forehead in a reverse head-butt. The assassin slumped back in his seat, momentarily dazed, while Scottly reeled from the effects of the blow he'd delivered.

All the while, the Lexus was careening across his back yard, making a trajectory for the pool. Tara slammed on the brakes, but her efforts met with disastrous results. The tires skidded over the wet lawn and lurched onto the pool deck, but not before crashing into and annihilating a Chinese lantern.

The automobile went airborne, and Tara was screaming like a banshee when it smacked into the water. For a moment, it appeared as though it might float, but it slowly responded to gravity's pull. The hood tilted forward, and it began to sink. A crushing tidal wave surged through the sunroof, swamping both Scottly and Tara. The water was rising at an alarming rate. Frantically, Tara searched for a way out.

"Unbuckle your seat belt," Scottly shouted. Tara's fingers scrabbled over the locking mechanism, but all she managed was to jam it. The water was to her chin, and she realized she was going to drown. How would Josh reconcile the fact that his mother had drowned in her neighbor's pool? In a car, no less.

Scottly pushed her hands away and worked at the seat belt. In a matter of seconds, it released. The water was over her head, and Tara grabbed for the door handle, trying to lever the door open, but the pressure was too great. She couldn't budge it.

Scottly wrestled her away from the door and nodded toward the sunroof, and Tara spied their means of escape. Kicking for all she was worth, she jettisoned out through the opening.

Afterward, Tara could have sworn she'd felt the presence of Fritzie, the dog of her childhood. Once again, he was rescuing her from a watery pit, propelling her to safety. Tara's head broke the surface and she gasped for breath.

"Scott," she cried when he popped up beside her. "Oh, my God!"

"Come on. Let's get the hell out of here." Scottly cut through the pool with expert strokes, but Tara was too sapped to do anything but tread water. He hoisted himself out and over the edge of the pool, then extended a hand to her. After a few failed attempts, Tara was dragged from the water.

Scottly peered at Tara. "Are you all right?" She nodded, taking in great draughts of air. Satisfied that was the case, he turned and dove back into the pool. Tara watched, incredulous, as his large body shot through the sunroof of the Lexus. A minute passed, then two, and Tara began to panic. A tracery of bubbles rose to the surface, and she knew Scottly was desperate for air.

Just as Tara was about to dive in after him, Scottly emerged, the unconscious carjacker in tow. He kicked to the pool steps, the stout man's head in the crook of his arm. Scottly lugged the unresponsive madman up and onto the deck. Tossing the handgun aside, he immediately fell to his knees and administered CPR.

"You should have left him," Tara muttered darkly.

Scottly ignored her and redoubled his efforts but to no avail. "He's gone," he muttered, his voice devoid of emotion. "We'd better call 911."

He made no move to do so, and Tara crossed to him and placed a palm on his shoulder. Slowly, he rose to his feet, wrapped his arms around Tara, and they clung to one another, all the while firing off inane comments.

"Where the heck did you learn to head-butt like that?"

"Didn't I ever tell you about my father?"

"No."

"He was CIA. Was possessed of all kinds of skills that he passed on to yours truly."

"Well, I guess..."

Scottly brushed damp tendrils away from Tara's face. "What was that business with the lottery ticket?"

"I'm not sure," Tara said. "I found it—"

"You stupid bitch," the attacker's waterlogged voice gurgled. "You never had a clue." He stumbled toward them, the reclaimed firearm in hand.

Scottly shoved Tara aside and faced down the revived specter.

"What are you going to do? Shoot us? Don't you think you'll be found out?"

Tara was paralyzed with terror.

Why hadn't Scottly kept the gun?

"That's exactly what I'm going to do." He aimed the pistol at Scottly's chest. "Then, I'm going to claim my jackpot, and disappear." His index finger curled around the Beretta's trigger. "Adios," he cried, exultantly.

In the next instant, his eyes bulged out, and the gun slipped from his grasp. Toppling forward, his forehead smacked into the pool deck with a sickening thud.

Tara screamed. "Oh, God!" she cried, falling to her knees.

Scottly staggered to her, arms extended. "It's okay, sweetheart," he crooned. "He can't hurt you anymore."

CHAPTER THIRTY-THREE

SMALL WONDER

Overnight, the temperature took a nosedive. Usually a top sleeper, Chanel had burrowed down beneath the blankets for warmth. It was the first week of November, and, up till then, the weather had remained summerlike with temps hovering around eighty degrees. Today's forecast called for highs in the sixties with projected overnight lows in the forties. Tara dressed accordingly—in jeans and a cotton sweater—before venturing out for her morning walk with Chanel.

Later that afternoon, she was polishing a silver chafing dish when the phone rang. Why was it, she wondered, putting down her polishing rag and finding her phone, whenever one was throwing a party, everybody and their brother had to call? Didn't they know the hostess had a million things to do? She could hardly get anything accomplished for having to answer the phone. First the caterers with a question about the menu, then Scottly asking if he should pick up a few more bags of ice, and did she need his large cooler? Josh had called from the airport to let her know he'd gotten in safely and was on his way. The bartender rang, asking if she needed more mixers.

"Hello," she barked.

"Hello, yourself. A little stressed, are we?"

The sound of Pat's voice warmed her like a shot of brandy. "Pat! How are you?"

"I'm here. What's left of me, that is. How I am remains to be seen."

"What do you mean, what's left of you?"

"Just you wait and see. I've got a teensy weensy, and I do mean tiny, surprise for you."

"I've missed you. You're all the surprise I need, girlfriend."

"Exactly. Tell me what I can do to help."

At five-thirty, Tara left the hustle bustle of the kitchen. The final preparations were now in the capable hands of her caterer, and it was time to bathe and dress for the party. Tara allowed herself a five-minute soak in her new Jacuzzi, water scented with her beloved Bulgari. Her hair wasn't much trouble. Just last week, she'd had it cut in a layered bob. She took pains with her make-up, though, adding a bit more shadow to her eyelids than usual, and finishing with a mineral-based powder that lent her skin a flawless glow. She zipped herself into the gown she'd chosen for this evening—a winter white confection with a form-fitting beaded top and a slightly gathered, tea-length skirt. It was elegant and understated, and it made her feel like royalty.

She'd nearly finished dressing when the phone rang again. Tara snatched her cell from the bedside table.

Would the phone ever stop ringing?

"Hello."

"Ms. Cahill?" An unfamiliar man's voice addressed her.

"Yes?"

"Sorry for bothering you on the weekend."

"Not at all."

"My name's Adam Cohen, assistant director at the Riverside Theatre."

"Mr. Cohen, what can I do for you?"

"Actually, that's why I'm calling. I'm hoping you *can* do something for us. Your name came up in our production meeting yesterday, and I was asked to contact you. You see, we're in need of an accompanist for our next musical, *Talisman.* Unfortunately, our accompanist is experiencing some health problems. We wondered if you might be interested in filling in."

Tara sat on the edge of the bed, her mind racing as she considered this unexpected proposal. "Why, yes. I'm very interested," she said.

"Good. How about stopping by my office next Tuesday? Eleven, shall we say? I can go over the rehearsal schedule with you, explain the compensation package."

"Next Tuesday at eleven. I'll be there, Mr. Cohen."

"Call me Adam, madam."

Tara laughed. "Okay, Adam, as long as you call me Tara. I'll see you then."

"Oh, and Tara, just so you know, this may well lead to a permanent position."

"As I said, I'm very interested." Tara swiped to disconnect and bounded off the bed. Unable to contain her elation, she danced about the room. This was a dream job. To be an integral part of a professional production company was exactly the kind of gig she'd been yearning for. Her victory dance was interrupted by a rapping on her bedroom door.

"Hey, Mom." The sound of Josh's voice brought her back to reality.

Tara glanced at her reflection in the mirror over her dresser. "Josh," she cried, "come in." The door opened, and there, standing before her, was her son.

"How's that for timing, huh?" The young man grinned at her, obviously pleased with himself.

The sight of him, dressed in a navy blazer and khakis, took Tara's breath away. He'd grown. Nearly an inch, she estimated, and his hair was longer, curling over his ears and collar. His face had lost its softness. With his newly hollowed cheekbones and chiseled jaw, he was, clearly, no longer a boy, and although, she hadn't thought it possible, even more handsome than she'd remembered. What really socked her in the gut, though, was the resemblance between him and his father. She hadn't been prepared for that. In an instant, she recovered her initial shock and rushed to embrace him.

"You look good enough to eat," she gushed.

"Aw, Mom." Josh extricated himself from her arms. "My girlfriend's here."

"Humph." Tara cuffed him playfully and ruffled his hair.

Josh grabbed her wrists and held her away from him. "You know, you don't look too bad yourself, lady, for an old broad, that is."

"Watch yourself, mister," Tara said. "This old broad's still your mother, and she can take you across her knee if she has to."

"Some guys pay a lot of money for that kind of thing, Mom."

~

Willie was the first to arrive, a huge basket of fragrant cheese biscuits in her arms. Following her were Cerita and Jarod.

"Willie, you shouldn't have," Tara said, motioning for one of the servers to take the basket to the kitchen. "I'm sure they'll be the hit of the party. Thank you and welcome to my home."

Willie gazed about. "It's just beautiful, Tara," she gushed. "And look at you. You're a vision. For the life of me, I can't understand why some man hasn't snatched you up."

Next to arrive was Pat, noticeably slimmer and looking chic in an off-the-shoulder black sheath.

"My God, Pat! You're more fabulous than ever. Divorce seems to agree with you."

"I do feel like a new woman."

"Gosh, how much weight have you lost?"

"Since my divorce? Two hundred and eighty pounds of ugly fat." Pat grinned. "Twenty of which melted off my own svelte frame."

Next to arrive were Sarah and Cal Hazelton, and Ralph and Deena were right behind them. Tara greeted the couples at the entryway, only to be bedazzled by the large square-cut diamond flashing from the plump blonde's ring finger. Tara smiled broadly, assuming wedding bells would once again be ringing to the matrimonial-minded Deena.

It wasn't long before the party was in full swing. For Tara, there was a dreamlike quality to it. Like any good dream, it flew by all too quickly. Surrounded by old friends and family, and new friends who'd become like family, there were so many magical moments she vowed to remember and savor. Like snapshots, those images were now permanently imbedded in her brain. Dulcie and Willie in a corner, the dowager queen of Vero Beach chatting up the housekeeper, inveigling her to reveal the recipe for her cheese biscuits. Cerita and Jarod looking deliriously happy while chattering away with the ethereal Grace, who was hand-feeding her strapping Josh hors d'oeuvres from a plate, while delicately balanced upon his knee. Her father and Ernestine holding hands, the two laughing with Marguerite's husband while his wife banged out a jazzy, *This Joint is Jumpin'* on the baby grand. Cal and Sarah dancing a spirited swing dance around the fountain. Deena and Ralph grilling Scottly about his fees for decorating the new house they were planning. Last, as hoped for, Skip and Pat, though fully aware of the set-up and even though awkward at first, seeming to take a shine to one another. It was, she thought, almost too perfect.

Only one thing was missing.

~

The young people had departed for Riverside Café where, it was rumored, Jake Owen—local country singer who'd hit the bigtime— might stop by and take the stage. Yet now, as the party began to wind down, the decibel level, fueled by alcohol, only increased. It's no wonder no one heard the doorbell.

Tara was seated in a lounge chair, Scottly straddling an ottoman at her feet, when Nathan strode into the living room. At the sight of the dashing fellow bearing a white rectangular box, Tara tensed. The look that came over her face prompted Scottly to swivel around, and he jumped to his feet and thrust out an arm.

"Well, here he is, at last," he said, shaking Nathan's free hand. "Better late than never."

Dulcie and Ernestine, who were seated in opposite corners of the room, shot meaningful looks at one another. Then Dulcie stood, preparing to make a quick exit.

"Hello, Nathan. We thought you weren't going to make it," Tara said, coming to her feet.

"Please, don't get up on my account," Nathan said, holding the carton before him. "These are for you."

Dulcie barged in, brushing her lips against Nathan's cheek while relieving him of the florist's box. "You should have listened to me," she said in a stage-whisper. "All your current troubles could have been avoided." Nathan merely raised his eyebrows. "What have we here, oh tardy one?" she continued, removing the lid from the box. "A dozen red roses for the hostess? How perfectly proper of you."

"Hello, Dulcie," Nathan muttered, glumly.

Dulcie handed the box off to a passing server, "Find a vase and put these in water," she instructed, before turning back to Tara. "Your home is absolutely lovely. Thank you so much for a wonderful evening, but I must be going now."

"I hope you're not leaving on my account," Nathan said.

"No such thing, darling." Dulcie's voice dripped sarcasm. "It's way past my bedtime. You should know that."

Ernestine made as if to follow, but Tara skewered her with a look that spoke volumes, demanding she stay. "Let me see you out," she said, sweeping past Ernestine and taking hold of Dulcie's elbow. She escorted the ornery heiress to the door, while, at the same time, Scottly led the chastened financier out to the patio and the fully stocked bar.

"Come, gentlemen, I hope we shall drink down all unkindness" Scottly regaled, invoking the bard. "What's your pleasure, Nate?"

～

Dulcie's departure seemed to prompt a further exodus. Was this some sort of conspiracy, Tara wondered, as she stood in the doorway saying her good-byes?

"What, have they all gone?" Scottly asked, when he and Nathan entered the living room, drinks in hand.

Tara crossed to them. "Yes, it's just us three," she said. "And the caterers, of course."

"No, it's just you two," Scottly corrected. "The caterers have packed it in, and I must be going as well."

"What?" Tara peered at her friend. "Don't abandon us. Won't you stay for a nightcap?"

"I'm afraid not," Scottly chirruped. He downed the quarter-inch of Scotch in his glass and then set the tumbler on the coffee table. "I'll be up at the crack of dawn to look at that manse your friend, Ralph, is so eager to purchase for his soon-to-be blushing bride."

Scottly's eyes twinkled as he rubbed his hands together in anticipation of a new project. "What an agreeable evening." He bent to kiss Tara's forehead before turning to Nathan. "You're on your own, old man. Think you can handle it?"

"I'm out the door," Nathan answered, making as if to leave.

"Oh no, you don't." Tara placed a restraining hand on his arm. "Stay for a bit. At least have something to eat. I have tons of food."

"Bye, doll," Scottly said. "Great party." Again, he shook Nathan's hand. "As always, it's a pleasure to see you." Then, the elegant man strode out the door, his parting words echoing in the brisk night air. "Good luck," he cajoled, chuckling merrily.

Tara could feel her heart fluttering. Here she was, at long last alone with the man of her dreams, but instead of what she'd imagined—being cool, collected, and in charge of the situation—she was a bundle of nerves. Struggling to conceal her unease, she smiled tentatively.

"I'm so glad you finally made it,"

"I debated whether or not to come at all and risk spoiling your party." Nathan admitted, looking sheepish. Quite a few people are on the outs with me these days. The trial... Let's just say that old axiom about no such thing as bad publicity..."

"Huh?"

"It isn't true." He tossed his head as if to quell any negativity. "In the end, I decided to make an appearance. Face the music, so to speak. Sorry I'm so late."

"No apologies necessary. Shall I make you up a plate?"

"I'm not really hungry."

"Well then," Tara said, "let's sit. I've got to get out of these shoes. They're killing me."

"I'm terribly sorry. My timing stinks. Are you sure you wouldn't rather I go?"

"Absolutely." Tara collapsed into a lounge chair, pried off her heels, and wiggled her toes "Ah...that's better. Scottly nearly broke my foot when he stomped on the gas and sent us plunging into his pool." She sighed, tossing the pumps beside her chair.

"What a nightmare you've been through." Nathan looked her up and down. "I have to say, you appear none the worse for wear."

"Looks can be deceiving."

"Sorry. Damn. I need to stop saying sorry."

"I agree."

"May I get you a drink?"

"A gin and tonic would be wonderful."

Nathan bowed slightly before disappearing out the back door, leaving her in turmoil. She was delighted that Nathan had finally shown, but why had Dulcie acted so offended, giving him the cold shoulder? As far as she knew, Gloria hadn't made off with any of her money. It was all so puzzling.

"Here you go." Nathan strode toward her, bearing her drink. "Cheers." The two clinked glasses. He seated himself on the ottoman, and they gazed at one another as an uneasy silence loomed between them.

"I'm really glad you decided to come," Tara finally said.

Nathan drank deeply and then held his glass before him, gazing into its depths rather than meeting her eyes. "It's more than that nasty business at the firm," he said, looking uncomfortable. "I'm embarrassed to admit the real reason." He raised his eyes and peered at her over the rim of his glass.

"Embarrassed? Good heavens. Why?"

"To be honest, I've been afraid to see you." Nathan set his drink on an end table and met Tara's gaze."

"Because?"

"Because I...I've made a muddle of it. How could I have been so blind? During these last difficult months, I've had lots of time to think about all the things I've done wrong—how I'd closed myself off emotionally, not just from women but from my children as well. And it hit me with the force of a sledgehammer."

"What?"

"It's been right in front of my face all this time. I hope it isn't too late."

"For?"

Nathan offered her a rueful smile. "The woman I love." He pried Tara's glass from her hand and placed it on the coffee table. "The perfect woman."

"Ha! Hardly perfect."

"A woman my children adore. Beautiful, talented, strong, kind…" He took her hands in his. "For the longest time, I wouldn't let you in. That was wrong of me. I realize that now. I knew if I did so, I'd be saying good-bye to Elisa. You have to believe me. I was just marking time with those other women. They didn't mean a thing to me. I'm crazy in love again. The past is past, and I can't get you out of my mind." He drew her to him. "What do you think about that? Would you be willing to spend the rest of your life with me?"

The scent of Nathan was intoxicating—lemons and leather. "I…" Words failed Tara, which was all right, for in the next moment his mouth was on hers, and the sweetness of his kiss was indescribable, like that first kiss of passion one never forgets. She pressed her body against his, yearning to be even closer—to transcend human form, bones and flesh to dissolve—spirits to unite.

For the present, the kiss would have to do. It went on and on until, at last, Tara drew away, breathless.

"Sir, you are a very good kisser," she said, remembering how she couldn't seem to let go of his hand, all that long time ago, when she'd first fallen in love with him.

"Practice, practice, practice, isn't that what you tell Harry?"

"Yes." Tara reached up and draped her arms around Nathan's neck. "Please, sir," she entreated, "may I have more?"

Nathan responded by kissing first her mouth, then her neck. Then, he reached around and very slowly unzipped the back of her dress. "You are so beautiful," he said, lowering the straps of her chemise, and putting his lips to her breast.

With an effort of will, Nathan untangled himself from Tara's arms. "If we don't stop now, I'll have to ravage you on the spot," he said. "Although the thought is tempting, that's not how I want to go about this."

"I suppose you're right," Tara conceded. She wanted nothing more than for him to go on kissing her and for that to lead to the inevitable conclusion, but she knew he was right, that they shouldn't rush this.

Nathan ran a hand through his hair, and that wayward lock fell down upon his forehead. For the first time, of all the many times she'd wanted to, Tara brushed it away, smiling happily.

"What do you say?" Nathan asked. "Will you go out with me?"

"Out?" Tara slipped the satin straps of her camisole back up her shoulders and shrugged into the bodice of her dress.

"You know. Like on a real date."

"You want to date me?"

"Dear God, woman, what do you think this has been about? I want much more than to date you."

"I'm not your type."

"Type? I don't have a type. If I did, it'd be your type." Nathan angled his long frame down, fingers scrambling to retrieve one of Tara's high heeled shoes. He sat up, a wry grin on his face, and held a pointy-toed pump before her. "Here you go, darlin'. It's after midnight, and you haven't turned into a pumpkin. Why not take a chance?"

"Does this mean you're my Prince Charming?"

"The story's not over. We'll just have to wait and see, won't we?"

Chanel tugged on his leash, the scent of a rabbit luring him onward. The houses flanking the street were dark and silent, her neighbors having long since retired. Tara gazed heavenward where a pearly crescent moon held sway over a black sky littered with a zillion glittering stars. She pondered the events of the past year, marveling at how dramatically her life had changed in so short a time and how far she'd come.

She would continue to maintain ties to her past. Old friends would forever be constants in her life, but now, she owned a newly remodeled home in a charming seaside community, and her circle of friends had expanded to include a whole cast of characters, all of whom she cherished. She had a number of promising students, and she was about to embark on a new and exciting career at the Riverside Theatre. More importantly, the madman who'd been stalking her had been permanently decommissioned.

As for the lottery ticket that had caused so much devastation and anguish, had it been a winner? Cochran had certainly thought it was worth killing for. But, by the time she'd had a chance to examine it, the thing was sodden and disintegrating, the ink running and illegible.

Never had Tara felt so empowered, secure in the knowledge she could stand on her own and not merely survive, but thrive. She ran her tongue across lips that were swollen and bruised—a token of Nathan's ardor. Would that mysterious man be her Prince Charming, or would he merely break her heart? She realized it didn't matter, that none of the negative possibilities were worth worrying about. Tonight, she was the luckiest woman alive, and an irrepressible joy welled up within her.

Only Chanel, and the moon, and the nocturnal creatures of the night heard her laughter.

THE END

~

**Don't miss out on your next favorite book!
Join the Melange Books mailing list at**
www.melange-books.com/mail.html

THANK YOU FOR READING

∼

Did you enjoy this book?

We invite you to leave a review at your favorite book site, such as Goodreads, Amazon, Barnes & Noble, etc.

DID YOU KNOW THAT LEAVING A REVIEW...

- Helps other readers find books they may enjoy.
- Gives you a chance to let your voice be heard.
- Gives authors recognition for their hard work.
- Doesn't have to be long. A sentence or two about why you liked the book will do.

ABOUT THE AUTHOR

Award winning author of the gripping memoir, "Dancing with the Devil," and the children's book, "Dune Dragons." Gretchen Rose spent most of her adult life operating a high-end interior design firm in Vero Beach, FL. A classically trained soprano, she has performed in countless professional musical and theatrical venues and penned four musical comedies. Gretchen's love of music and theater colors all her writing. She is currently at work on an audiobook of her "Dune Dragons" series. Look for the second in her "Very Vero" series, "A Little Vice in Vero," in 2022.

www.gretchenroseauthor.com
www.gretchenroseauthor.com/blog

facebook.com/Gretchen-Rose-Author-2163047320474640

instagram.com/rose_gretchen

ABOUT THE AUTHOR

Award winning author of the gripping memoir, "Dancing with the Devil," and the children's book, "Dune Dragons." Gretchen Rose spent most of her adult life operating a high-end interior design firm in Vero Beach, FL. A classically trained soprano, she has performed in countless professional musical and theatrical venues and penned four musical comedies. Gretchen's love of music and theater colors all her writing. She is currently at work on an audiobook of her "Dune Dragons" series. Look for the second in her "Very Vero" series, "A Little Vice in Vero," in 2022.

www.gretchenroseauthor.com
www.gretchenroseauthor.com/blog

facebook.com/Gretchen-Rose-Author-2163047320474640
instagram.com/rose_gretchen

Made in United States
Orlando, FL
10 March 2022

15632419R00178